IVORY'S RUIN

ALSO BY SIBERIA JOHNSON

Lovesick (Contemporary Romance)

Nia's Resolve

Ivory's Ruin

Serena's Grace

Riley's Inferno

The Monster's Mate (Paranormal Erotica)

Sin, Secrets, and Summoning

Alpha Affinity

Crimson Vow

Embers of Eternity

Omnibus - 2027

& more TBA

IVORY'S RUIN

A BAD BOY MALADY

SIBERIA JOHNSON

LOVEsick

This book contains topics that may be sensitive to some readers, including explicit sexual content, profanity, and violence.

To find out more about Siberia's books, visit her website (https://beacons.ai/siberia) and join her exclusive reader group (www.facebook.com/groups/sweetsinners).

Editing by Shawsome Reads Editing Services
Proofreading by Lindsey Clarke

ISBN: 978-1-963206-09-8

Dedicated to the ones who see bite marks as love notes and scars as a testament to survival—pain is our privilege.

CONTENTS

ONE

AN ENIGMA—THE BLACK KNIGHT. THE KIND OF MAN WHO SEES everyone while obscured in shadow.

But she saw him.

At first, he'd been just another face at the inaugural college parties. Someone new and nameless like all the rest. Night after night, she began to notice how he stood in the background rather than drawing attention his way. He'd flirt with girls but didn't lead them onto the dance floor. Didn't make a move to take them upstairs. Only scanned the crowd as if danger lurked within the frat houses' dirty, patched walls.

Maybe it did. Whatever he'd been watching for, whatever he searched out, it must've meant something—because he hadn't seemed to care about anything else.

A certain melancholy hung about him like a cloak. It emanated from his grim expression, etched itself into the faint trace of honey-brown stubble at his jaw and the long hair he tied in a bun. Darkness clung to the leather jacket on his shoulders and the ripped jeans snug around his hips.

The shadows he possessed didn't oppress, rather

accentuated his presence with a low, menacing snarl. A warning to those who might get too close.

She'd never been good at making the first move and certainly didn't know how to explain what she felt from his presence. An emotion that tugged at her from deep within. Empathy, perhaps.

Or something darker.

As much as he captivated her, and as willing as she might be to let him lead her down a path of passion, she knew that wasn't what he needed. Had anyone else noticed the look in his eyes? That emptiness?

Despite her hesitation, Ivory watched him as vigilantly as he did their surroundings. The gaze from his eyes, molten and warm to their core, wound around her like fine threads of gold —then passed over her every time.

He hadn't seen her. Not then, nor any time after.

A disappointed sigh fell from her lips as the strobe of a blacklight flashed across yet another disheveled living room. She'd wasted enough energy on searching for the man in the shadows, her only discovery being new piles of plastic cups on the floor and more discarded costumes sprouting from the couch cushions.

He wasn't at this party, either.

Macabre skeletons swathed in fake webbing hung from the ceiling and bloody masks on the walls stared into the throng with empty eye sockets, indifferent to the raucous laughter and cheers for another round of shots. Maybe he'd only been a visitor for those first few weeks of the semester, the kind that hops from one party to the next and disappears as soon as students remember their noses are better off in textbooks than looking down cups of beer.

Maybe he found whatever he'd been looking for or had simply given up.

Still, the subtle lack of his presence bothered her almost as much as her inability to do anything about it. He'd become familiar, like a landmark on the horizon or the detail that set one dorm apart from another. Something about him enraptured her. He gave off the impression that he wasn't like the other guys here whose aim landed no further than the nearest available girl.

She also kept an eye out for Jace, the only one who still cared about their unfortunate fall from grace a few weeks ago. Probably because out of the two of them, he had been far less inebriated than she thought, and even though he wouldn't outright mention the details of their drunken fling, the cold, degrading look in his eyes said enough.

So far, he'd been too busy dancing with her friends Avril and Serena—people who actually wanted his attention. They could keep him busy for the rest of the night. Being president of Beta Rho, the fraternity hosting the Halloween party, meant Jace should have plenty to do. Not to mention he'd been surrounded by a crowd of admirers ever since he got a dragon shaved into his newly buzzed hair.

If he liked being the cool guy so much, he could soak up the spotlight all he wanted and forget about her.

Ivory turned and caught sight of a petite redhead—or one who was usually a redhead, but tonight donned the persona of Aphrodite the Greek goddess, complete with a wig of dark tumbling curls. A smile quirked the corners of Ivory's mouth, and pride overtook her dismay at seeing Nia let off some steam.

"Oh heyyy," Ivory called, waving over the top of nearby halos and horns. In a show of theatrics, she tipped her witch's hat to the side. The attempt at a cackle slurred as it left her lips, transforming into a giggle.

Darn it. The whole badass-dark witch look just wasn't working. Didn't mean she would stop trying.

"Whatchu been up to?" she asked as Nia came close enough to hear over the vibrating bass. Her friend swayed, a little tipsier than expected since it was the first party Nia had come to. She looked gorgeous nonetheless, with smoky cat eyes and a golden rope cinched around her tan hourglass waist.

"Nothin impourtant." Nia's words strung together as a jumbled mix of syllables, and her face faltered.

Ivory frowned. That wasn't the goal, not at all. "Awww that makes me saaad. How can I cheer you up?"

During their first week, Nia set a new record of introversion, but Ivory slowly got her to open up, and now watched her friend in full bloom. She wanted nothing more than to share the same shy, genuine bookworm she'd gotten to know with the rest of the world. And if she had anything to do about it, that good-for-nothing college playboy who broke Nia's heart had something headed his way.

"Already better," Nia mumbled, leaning on Ivory and humming along with the music. "And I think I'm getting a hang of navergating when the room does song—somersaults."

"Oh dear," Ivory giggled. That would be an issue. This room —like most after a few drinks—had a nasty habit of turning and flipping when it shouldn't. "You sound like you need a glass of water."

Grabbing Nia's hand, she led them through the horde of grinding ghouls and ghoulettes. Strips of her purple, hand-crafted witch's robe sashayed around her back and legs and dispersed some of the stifling body heat, but not nearly enough. "I know just the thing. Or—" She giggled again. "Maybe it's more for me than you."

It was about time she had some fun at this party, too. Tonight was supposed to be her break. One evening when she didn't have to worry about acing tests and finding her place at college as a quiet freshman.

Another cup of the house special—tropical margarita mix with a heavy dose of tequila—was just what she needed to take her mind off the disappearance of her shadow man.

He wasn't coming back any—

Oh. No.

She froze mid-step. Scratch that. He was here.

Right here, in fact.

One glimpse of the long auburn hair and black leather jacket on the man rummaging through the fridge brought her to a screeching halt.

Nia smashed into her back with a groan. Stammering out an apology, Ivory dragged them both into a corner before he could look in their direction.

"Oh my gosh, I didn't mean to shove you." Ivory fumbled with the brim of her witch's hat as it contended with the wall in a losing battle. "I wasn't expecting...he hasn't been..." Words rushed out as she pressed a hand over her chest, attempting to contain the panic coursing through her system.

He hadn't been around in an entire month. He wasn't *supposed* to come back. At this point, it would've been better if he'd simply been a figment of her imagination.

Now he stood mere feet away, and with the main light on in the kitchen, there was no way he wouldn't see her if they went in there.

"What?" Nia asked, lost to the extent of their predicament. "Who?"

"The guy..." Ivory mumbled, eyes darting behind them to the open doorway, where white light filtered through the haze that had settled throughout the rest of the house.

Nia grabbed her shoulders and gave a light shake. "Who?"

The question shocked Ivory back into focus. "From before."

Nia had been the only person who knew she'd even noticed

him, and even though her friend was too good of a student to go to any other parties, Nia had listened to her secret confession of developing a *slight* crush.

Okay, maybe more than slight. Didn't help that he was stupidly handsome. Stunningly beautiful. Spectacularly out of her league.

"*The* guy?" Nia asked to confirm.

She nodded vigorously. "*The* guy."

"Are you scared of him?" Nia asked, looking concerned. "Or just nervous?"

Multiple answers came to mind—he might look intimidating, but she'd never gotten the impression he'd hurt someone for no reason—and yes, she was nervous. Sinking into a pit of quicksand would be better than attempting to be nonchalant with the man she'd spent entirely too much time watching months ago and still remembered every detail.

"Maybe both?" She giggled to cover her nerves. "I'm scared I'll sound like an idiot." She glanced over Nia's shoulder again. "Has he left yet?"

Nia sighed and pursed her lips.

Please say yes. There was still time to try and forget with the power of margarita mix.

But at this critical moment, what did Miss *I-Didn't-Come-To-College-To-Fall-In-Love* do? Her loyal friend, not to mention the introvert of the century, decided this was the opportune time to throw the world's most wicked curveball.

Still reeling from shock, Ivory found herself being dragged *into* the kitchen as Nia declared resolutely, "Come on."

TWO

GOLDEN EYES.

Dark, angled eyebrows and the shadow of rough stubble framing the hard line of his jaw.

Long auburn hair that faded to a pastel pink at the ends—tonight it wasn't in a bun, but fell past his shoulders like that of a medieval king. He didn't have a costume on, nor did he need one. The black leather jacket hanging off his shoulders opened on either side, and a graphic t-shirt stretched across his chest.

His gaze finally landed on her.

He saw her. This time, he definitely saw her.

"It's *you*?" Nia's exclamation should have added a layer of intrigue to the situation, but Ivory still couldn't figure out which way her feet wanted to move.

She became rooted to the spot, capable only of watching as the scene played out. The kitchen felt unbearably hot, yet she wished her costume consisted of more than a tank top and spandex shorts veiled in nearly transparent chiffon.

The man's face twisted in confusion, and he closed the fridge door with a beer in hand. "Yes?"

"You're the guy from the hair salon," Nia clarified.

He straightened and leaned back into the counter, which only made his muscles all the more apparent, only emphasized every time his gaze shifted to her.

Such a shame he was a masterpiece. Breathing would be a lot easier if she weren't on the verge of cardiac arrest.

"Ah, yes," he said, recognition flashing across his face. "Can I help you?"

"My friend Ivory wants to dye her hair," Nia blurted, then added after a pause, "Purple. She wants purple hair."

All things considered, it was sound enough reasoning. Anyone who knew anything about her knew she loved purple. It wasn't just her favorite color—it might as well be the shade of her aura. Everything from the sheets on her bed to her palettes of makeup to the background on her phone was some shade of purple.

And she really wouldn't mind switching from dusty brown to purple, but perhaps under different circumstances.

"Do you need it done...right now?" he asked, raising his eyebrows.

Thoughts momentarily disrupted, her tongue loosened, and she managed to come up with a reply. "N-no! I came in for a refill, that's all."

She took two quick steps to the counter, where several large drink coolers sat next to a diminishing stack of red cups. Pouring a cup of water for Nia, she tried to explain the odd request. "I've been talking about my hair for weeks now, you see, so when Nia saw you, she had to say something."

She ended with a nervous laugh.

"I saw an opera—opportunity and took it." Nia smiled, accepting the cup of water Ivory handed over.

This was going great. Between the two of them, they looked like a plastered mess. At least Nia might get better after hydrating, but she had a feeling her pulse would still be racing if this guy took the wise option and decided not to stick around.

"If it's that important, I'd be glad to do it for you," he said, taking her by surprise. "We can dye it in my apartment. That way I can waive the salon fee, providing you buy the dye." Wrapping a palm over the beer bottle, he used one of the gold rings on his fingers and popped off the lid. It fell to the ground with a metallic clang.

She nodded, not trusting herself to speak. How nice of him to offer, but she'd rather risk botching the job herself. Being alone together at his place sounded like a disaster waiting to happen.

Turning to the drink coolers, she became *very* preoccupied with filling two cups of liquid courage. Nia's water had disappeared, so she handed one cup to her friend and downed the other herself.

He extended the same offer to Nia, and as they conversed *like regular people*, she prayed to the tequila gods for an opportunity to slip away.

But Nia had other plans. Winking, she announced, "I'm gonna find Avril. You can get Adrian's contact info, and I'll catch ya later."

Then she left.

Avril was their designated driver tonight, meaning Nia intended to return to the dorms. Which also left her alone, with the only other person in the kitchen—Adrian. Her mouth went dry, and they both fell silent.

"I didn't mean to bother you," she said after an awkward pause, voice much quieter than before.

"It's no bother," he hummed. "I'm going out back for a smoke. Join if you want." He didn't wait for her response and pushed off the counter, turning to go out onto the deck.

This was her chance to walk away. But the thought of losing his presence again made her feet follow behind his, shuffling out of the stuffy frat house and into the autumn air. The cool breeze came as a welcome change. It tickled her skin and whisked around her ankles, making the hair rise on her arms.

Beta Rho boasted a large backyard, equipped with a volleyball net and hot tub around the opposite corner of the deck, where red lights and conversation trickled over. Over on this side, however, long shadows stretched across a vacated space, and it fell quiet enough to hear the trees whisper with dying leaves. The faint cast of street lights from the side street dispelled some of the dark, but not the shadow around him.

There was always a shadow around him.

Several chairs lay scattered at the edge of the deck, and as Adrian sat, she found a spot a few paces away. This place suited him. His black clothes both blended into the night and stood out—metal accents glinting small reflections of light from the party behind them. Adrian inspected his beer without taking another sip.

Unlike inside, relative silence hung around them. Neither spoke, and the music faded into nothing more than a heartbeat.

She didn't mind.

Even anticipating rejection, she found comfort in finally being alone together. The rough exterior he carried wasn't imposing like Jace's, and it didn't make her feel small. In fact, just sitting here felt more enjoyable than being around everyone else.

Working up the courage to speak, she sipped more house margarita and tried not to let her eyes wander too much.

After a minute, he dropped the beer bottle between his parted knees and held the neck with ringed fingers, hair falling in front of his face. The movement caught her attention, and heat reignited in her cheeks. If only he didn't have such an embarrassing effect on her. Everything he did caused a reaction in her body, his every breath practically triggering her heart to skip. The tequila certainly wasn't helping. Chewing her lip, she tore her eyes away and took a sharp inhale of cold air.

The moon had been out earlier, but now clouds covered its silver light. The yard had grown so dark that anything more than fifteen feet out looked pitch black.

What would it be like if they went further into the trees, where the branches blocked out the party and the cloak of darkness concealed them—would he teach her why he liked being in the shadows? Would she like it if he did?

Adrian set his beer on the ground, and she clutched her cup tighter, then cringed as the plastic crinkled. She should've refilled it before coming out. At this rate, more would be better than less.

And she needed to look somewhere other than the yard. Somewhere safe, so her drunken mind wouldn't get away with those kinds of thoughts. His eyes drew her in, their golden glow swirling as warmth spread through her chest and saturated her veins. Her breathing slowed to an even pace. Perhaps it'd be better to let him make the first move. Mostly because she still didn't know what to say.

He met her gaze, and something stirred in their depths as his lips parted. "I won't bite unless you ask."

He spoke in a subdued tone, a whispered confession in a smooth baritone that bridged the distance between them. She finally mustered up enough courage to reply, "Do you get asked often?"

"Not by you." His undivided attention held her captive far too thoroughly.

She averted her eyes. Surely, it had been a harmless joke, but a part of her hoped he might be serious. She lifted her cup, only to find it empty.

Unbothered by her reaction, he pulled a pack of cigarettes from his jacket pocket and, balancing one pale stick between long fingers, flicked the lighter. The cherry flared orange, and her nose scrunched as the sharp, smoky smell of toxin released into the air. She let her gaze follow the cigarette to the place where his lips met, dark and red. Probably soft and warm, too.

A puff of white smoke swirled out of his nostrils, lazily drifting into nothing before he opened his mouth and blew out the rest.

She coughed, batting at the air.

"I don't do relationships," he said, back to using the blunt, emotionless tone.

She gave a polite smile to hide the pang of disappointment. "I wasn't looking for one."

That's not what this was supposed to be about. If she'd been given the chance, or rather forced, into finally talking to him, then she wanted to find out why he seemed so haunted—try to get a hint at his burden and offer what she could to help. Not indulge in her personal fantasies without caring about the other person involved.

"Then are you looking for a game?" he asked. "To let me play with you until I've had my fill? Because that's what I offer."

The words stung like a slap to the face, thrown out to unsettle—but coming from him in that calm, controlled voice, she almost wanted to say yes. Almost.

She shook her head. "No."

This wasn't the time for her hidden desires to intervene or for her to remember all the times he appeared behind her closed eyelids—this was about him. Not her. Not the part of her she wished didn't exist in the first place.

"Such a sweet girl," he mused, taking another long drag of the burning cancer stick, and met her gaze. "You don't want me."

She held her breath, unable to confirm or deny his declaration even to herself. Her gaze traced along the subtle movements of the tendons in his hand as he tapped the end of his cigarette.

"And yet..." he continued, "Somehow, I believe you'd still let me bring you to my place tonight. Ever since you first saw me, you've been working up the courage to say something. Your eyes haven't lingered on another guy for more than half a second, but you followed me out here alone and haven't broken eye contact once."

Smoke seeped out from between his lips, and she let her eyes wander down just to prove him wrong—that she could look away—but immediately felt the pull to look up again.

"I wouldn't go home with you," she insisted. Struggling to keep up the smile as her nose wrinkled at the bitter smell of smoke, she forced herself to believe her words. "Because you don't take girls home, do you?"

"Ah. Should've realized you picked up on that," he hummed. "I don't take girls home until they're aware of the rules, what they're getting into. That doesn't happen on the first night."

He tapped the end of his cigarette, then frowned. "If you don't like the smoke, say something."

"I don't like it," she admitted softly, torn between examining the outline of his slender fingers and fighting the urge to look back into his eyes. Her thoughts were hazy, tongue leaden.

He turned and blew the rest of the smoke downwind, a white stream curling into the night and spreading out in a ghostly wisp. She took a deep breath of clean air, mourning how obvious it made the difference between them.

Maybe their worlds couldn't intersect, but that didn't mean she couldn't try to see into his.

"Wasn't so bad, asking for what you want, was it?" he asked.

She met his eyes. "I want to know why you look empty. Like something took your soul, and you're still searching for it."

He stared back at her, brow furrowing. Then he looked away and smiled—a sad, forlorn curve of velvet lips. "Don't waste your time on me, sweetheart. All you'd be is something to fuck."

The force of a hammer hit her hard in the chest, and she slowly cracked from the inside out.

Dropping the cigarette on the wood, he smothered it with his boot and handed her a business card from the salon with a handwritten number on the back. "I can be professional, though. Call if you actually want your hair dyed."

Then he stood and left, but she knew he wouldn't come back.

This time, he really would disappear into the shadows.

THREE

Adrian

There are certain things we shouldn't want. She was one of those things.

The only reason he came to the Halloween party was to give Caspian, his ex-roommate turned friend-and-neighbor, a good kick in the ass to get over a broken heart. Stepping away from the playboy life was one thing, but sulking over a girl who took him for granted was another.

Caspian had become so pathetic that getting him outside had been worth going to Jace's frat house—the pretentious prick whose family controlled one of the most violent biker gangs in town, Red Dragon. Jace was their spoiled heir, and he acted like it. Best to avoid the kid.

But like clockwork, *she* found him—cloaked in dark fabric that brought out her porcelain skin like a Halloween apparition, complete with vibrant, glittering green eyes and lips that begged to be kissed and bitten. Her witch costume had easily become his favorite of the night.

The first time he'd seen her, the brunette blended in like any average college student, albeit a cute one with a sweet laugh, but she did nothing to stand out. In fact, he wouldn't have singled her out at all if she hadn't locked onto him, almost as if a target had been placed on the center of his forehead.

Ever since he'd been a teenager sneaking into the club, he learned when a woman wanted to hook up. They each had their own way of preening their feathers, of highlighting the assets they thought would be most desirable. He found it amusing to see what they thought he liked, even though his interest had always been drawn to their eyes.

Most importantly, he learned to feel out their desire. Whether they sought immediate gratification or wanted to satisfy a deeper need. He made a point of picking up on what *they* wanted, what turned them on, and what they fantasized about. Things other men had obviously missed.

Yet when this girl studied him, he got the impression she'd want more than to be alone together in a dark room. As if she actually wanted to figure out who he was instead of sharing a quick moment of mutual indulgence.

She looked at him like she saw something more, and that's why he wouldn't return her gaze.

Whoever she thought he was—whoever she assumed he might be—he wasn't.

They all found out one way or another.

But stubbornly, her eyes returned every time. Every night, when they ended up in the same place, she'd spot him. He wondered if she recognized him from somewhere or remembered his face from the news five years ago. The latter was unlikely since he long outgrew his boyish features.

Still, her attention unnerved him. So he started keeping tabs on her, developed the habit of sensing her before she noticed him, and picked up little details along the way. Like how she wasn't keen on flaunting herself, the kind of girl who didn't notice all the attention she got because she was too focused on everyone else, and how she liked to spend more time listening than talking.

Between glances at him, she would search out her friends. She hardly drank, whether out of preference or forbearance, he didn't know, but she had an uncanny ability to be where she was needed the moment others needed her. More often than not, he'd catch her tending to a drunken friend and staying sober enough to drive them safely back home.

Above all else, she was kind. She deserved to be cared for as much as she cared for others.

So he handed her a business card and left. His heart wasn't soft like hers; it was hard and jagged and would only cut into those who touched it. A fair relationship wouldn't be something he could offer. Better that she moved on because he wanted nothing to do with her. Or that's what he told himself.

He wanted everything to do with her.

Another trait stood out about her nature, written all over those round doe eyes and that sweet smile, even when she painted her lips in sinful plum. No, especially then. It came out in the way she migrated to dominant energies without shying away, yet remained reserved. The way she responded to his every movement out on the porch, as if she'd been waiting for him to take control.

In the bedroom, she'd be a natural submissive.

She'd want to be tied up and put on display for her master, praised for being such a good girl. Her pleasure lay in serving someone else as they drew out her hidden desires. She'd crave a little bitterness to balance out all that sweetness inside her.

And he bet she tasted as sweet as she looked.

But that wasn't for him to find out. He wasn't just a dose of bitter medicine—he was poison. The kind that took all the sweetness away from girls like her. There were more ways to lose innocence than kinky sex, and she didn't need to learn about the dark corners of the world.

He needed to put an end to it, this growing curiosity that continued to draw them together.

Her look of dejection as he walked away clawed his heart, but only a little. A small scratch would be nothing next to the older scars that marred his ability to care the way she could—the way she cared about him without even knowing.

Certainly, it was nothing compared to how he'd feel if he hadn't taken this step now, if he waited until the sadness in her eyes spilled out in clear streams because he tried to be someone he wasn't. Her tears would've hurt ten times more. So he made sure he'd never make her cry. Not even once.

His words may have stung, but they proved his point that she had to protect her heart from the beginning. Tonight, she could still have a good time, go back to her friends to call him a jerk, then write him off for good. Ironic how the one time he made an exception to give out his number, he hoped it wouldn't be used.

He watched from just inside as she refused to move from their spot on the deck. Her hands circled the red cup, strangling it much like the dark night that had slowly begun to swallow her. Goosebumps pebbled her skin as her costume swayed in the breeze. He frowned. She'd catch a cold like that.

Finally, her gaze dislodged from where he'd last been, and a faint glow from her phone lit her features. He pretended to sip his beer and kept her in his peripheral vision. The first drink had already worn off, but the party might as well be over.

A group of three loud Beta Rho boys interrupted the scene and sauntered into the kitchen. His scowl deepened as Jace walked by, strutting around in a supposed 'costume' of a red robe and flashy jewelry. Jace's father must be so proud to have *that* as heir to the Red Dragon empire. Good thing Jun, the older brother, acted as a more adequate representative.

The boys jostled past without acknowledging him and went out onto the porch. Looked like they just wanted to pass around a joint, but he didn't trust them. Not by themselves, and certainly not with her.

Yet Ivory still didn't get up to leave, too caught up typing on her phone.

He cracked his knuckles, trying to feign an air of indifference as they started up a conversation. Maybe he should let it go. Turn and walk away.

Two of the boys stepped over to smoke by the hot tub, but Jace couldn't keep his damn eyes off her.

He set the beer down, no longer concerned with whether it was his place to supervise or not. Call it overbearing, but he'd spent too many years watching over his mother and sister to ignore a predator when he saw one.

The way Jace looked at Ivory disgusted him, as if she was some kind of trivial possession whose purpose was to feed his entitlement. Worse, the moment her lips tipped down, Jace's curled into a smile. Like he'd won some sort of twisted, one-man competition.

Ivory stood and crossed her arms. Her eyes flashed, and despite gnawing irritation at the scene, a glow of admiration pricked his thoughts. A little flare in her did wonders.

She kept inching toward the house, but Jace met her step for step. Then he leaned in close—too fucking close—and reached over to fiddle with the edge of her purple cloak. The fire in her eyes blazed, and she swatted away his hand, but it only seemed to egg him on as he brought it back to caress her face with a laugh.

Adrian took a step toward them, hand hovering by the handle of the glass door. She'd done a decent job of standing up for herself, but it was time for her to leave. If Jace and his friends dared try and follow, they had another thing coming.

He almost wanted them to. A broken nose and a black eye would be a start if he were feeling nice.

He wasn't feeling nice.

Waiting for her to come inside, he watched Jace's smile grow into a smirk, and he murmured something low to Ivory.

She crippled. That sweet, delicate face fell even further than before, and her flames diminished to smoky defeat.

That was the last straw.

Ripping the door open, Adrian clenched his hand into a fist and squared his shoulders, coming up to stand beside her as an emissary of destructive karma. Her eyes flicked over him and widened.

"What happened to that smile of yours, sweetheart?" he asked, locking eyes with Jace. "Did he steal it?"

A small sound left her lips, a hint of a low laugh and a little gasp of surprise. "Didn't think you cared."

"I care much less about his smile than yours."

"Come on, bro," Jace interjected, lips curved in that irritating shit-eating grin of his. "I didn't do anything. We were just catching up. Besides" —Jace shifted his attention back to Ivory, twirling a wayward strand of her hair— "we're friends. I can get Ivory to smile for me anytime."

She stiffened, and the tension in her muscles sliced through him like the edge of a knife. An exaggerated version of how she reacted when he blew smoke in her face. He'd done it to test if she'd call him out, but she hadn't. Now, when confronted with someone far worse, she wouldn't call this bastard out, either.

"Is that true?" he asked, directing the question to her.

She shook her head, the brim of her witch hat hiding her expression as her hair fell from Jace's hand. "I'm just waiting for a ride."

Of course it wasn't fucking true. This pathetic waste of particles couldn't make anyone smile, but the rejection meant more coming from her mouth.

Then she added in a whisper, "We aren't friends, either."

Jace laughed. "Come on. Are you really about to do this? Call me a mistake after—"

"You weren't a mistake," she said, flames rekindling as she turned to face him. Her head lifted, eyes locked onto Jace's with the same perseverance he'd seen in her night after night. "You're a *joke*."

Jace sneered, and anger flashed behind his eyes. He took a step closer, positioning his body over hers like a threat—as if he'd really be able to get away with hurting her more. Adrian stepped between them.

"That's how it is?" Jace hissed, glaring at Ivory. "I think it's much more hilarious that this good-girl thing you've got going on is a fucking lie." He stretched his fingers, balling them into fists, and turned to Adrian. "I'll tell you the truth. She's a whor—"

Yeah, no way was he about to finish that sentence.

FOUR

The tequila gods had spoken.

Not only had the deck started spinning in every direction, Jace had morphed into two Jaces, and her pink-haired leather-clad black knight had learned how to fly. No, not exactly—his *fists* could fly.

Little twinkles of light reflected off Adrian's gold rings as they soared toward both of Jace's faces, colliding squarely into both their noses and merging them into one. Jace stumbled backward and clenched his jaw, then grit his teeth and stalked over to Adrian before throwing his own fist.

Her heart pounded, both in horror at the scene unfolding and—although it was certainly not the time—in admiration, along with a hint of confusion. He'd just told her she meant nothing to him.

He'd left.

Now he came back, and in her defense, at that. Or maybe one of the Jaces had managed to piss him off. Wouldn't surprise her. Either way, this couldn't be good.

Before she could say anything to stop them, the men began

to exchange blows. Blood smeared across Jace's face and left a dark stain over one cheek. She really hoped none of it belonged to Adrian. Then she'd feel bad. But Jace could suffer an injury or two, as long as it wasn't serious. Maybe then his face would match his personality.

Hearing the ruckus, Jace's two friends stumbled over from the hot tub, bringing the heavy sour scent of weed and several girls complaining about the noise. "Shit," one cursed, too high and drunk to be of much use. "What the hell's happening?"

"Where the fuck were you?" Jace hissed, spitting out blood onto the deck as he and Adrian finally separated.

Attempting to refocus her splitting vision, something slipped from her fingers and clattered to the ground. Oh no, that something had been her phone. She groaned and tore her eyes away from her black knight. This better not end in a cracked screen.

Bending to retrieve it, her witch hat tumbled off and rolled away as the deck lurched to the side. Great, now gravity had it in for her, too. A steady hand gripped her arm as she swayed. The cool metal of her phone slid into her hand.

"Watch yourself, sweetheart."

The now familiar tone of Adrian's voice and his pair of leather boots made her flush as she clutched the phone, which had been handed to her from bloody fingers. She mumbled a thank you as Jace started up again.

"This motherf—"

Adrian cut him off with a boot to the knee. She gasped as Jace crumpled, then that same black boot connected with Jace's stomach. He groaned, rolling over on his side.

"Don't let me hear you disrespect a woman again," Adrian threatened. "Unless you're referring to yourself." The scowl on his face did not look pleasant. If she thought he cloaked himself in shadow before, now he'd evolved into something straight out of the underworld. Adrian glared down at Jace. "But I'd say from this angle, you look more like a bitch than anyone else here."

"I think he got the point," she stammered, tentatively taking a step closer. Starting a scene, or more than they already had, would be a bad idea. If anyone else came, they'd assume Adrian had started it, and she didn't want him to take the blame.

"Get the fuck off our property," Jace's friend hissed, turning to them while doing a poor job at being intimidating. Despite being taller than her knight, Jace couldn't stand straight, nor walk in a straight line. However, reaching into his pocket, he pulled out a slender silver blade and brandished it.

Even in her present state, she knew that was very, very not good.

"I-I'm sorry," she started, but then a pair of gold eyes shifted to hers, and her voice died.

"We're leaving anyway," Adrian muttered. Then he turned and walked off towards the street.

Without her.

But hadn't he said...

Stunned for the umpteenth time, she rushed after him, abandoning her witch hat and a still-moaning Jace.

Sticking around for more of Jace's threats would be much worse than stumbling over patches of grass and facing further heart-wrenching rejection. She felt bad enough about her muddled night with Jace without his constant reminders. But clearly he wasn't ashamed, trying to blackmail her into a threesome she wanted no part in.

"Wait," she called, tripping over an exposed root and trying to figure out which moving sidewalk was the real one. She couldn't give up now, not after Adrian defended her like that.

"I'll be fine," he replied.

He didn't sound fine. Even though she was sure this wasn't

his first brawl, that didn't mean he was okay. She may not be built for throwing punches, but she wasn't weak.

"I don't believe you," she answered, catching up as her feet finally found flat ground. Swaying back and forth, she anchored her gaze on his jacket, and he slowed to a halt.

"Don't you have a ride coming?" he asked.

Oh, yeah. She should check her messages to see if Avril had replied.

"Wait, don't go." She grabbed his arm but dropped her hand as soon as his muscles tensed. "In case Jace comes back," she whispered.

He turned away, his features far less intimidating without the red party lights. "Trust me, that piece of shit won't be chasing anyone down for a while. Stay out here, and you'll be safe."

"I'm...I'm scared of the dark," she said in a rush. More like she was scared of the dark leaving—of *him* leaving.

She stopped herself from reaching for his arm again and stepped to the side to read his expression. He frowned but didn't move.

Taking out her phone, she tapped the screen to see a message pop up from Caspian, Nia's ex. What could he want?

CASPIAN

Nia's going home with me, she's drunk. Don't worry. I'm just keeping an eye on her.

Well, then...that meant Avril hadn't taken Nia home after all. Hopefully, Nia and Caspian were patching things up, though. She'd been rooting for them from the start, even if they had some big hurdles to overcome.

The small puff of joy vanished as she realized Avril wouldn't already be in her car after giving Nia a ride back to the dorms. Now it felt more like Avril had been ignoring her text the whole time. She sunk her teeth into her bottom lip, trying not to worry. The message had been delivered fifteen minutes ago. Maybe Avril was busy giving Serena a ride.

Something rough and warm tugged her lip free, and she looked up as Adrian's hand withdrew, two golden rings winking under the light of a distant streetlamp.

Her breath caught. The touch was too brief to relish, but her heart raced, nonetheless.

Too drunk to keep her thoughts in check, she wondered if those rings would be cold or hot when pressed to her neck. If he'd keep them on when he found out she'd take as many or as little fingers as he saw fit to give her.

She shook off the deviant thoughts and noticed a stain across one ring that marred its shine. "You're bleeding."

No response.

She flicked her eyes up to his, dark and glittering in the pale light. He'd pulled his hair into a bun, the pink ends hiding under natural brown.

"I knew you weren't okay."

What an awful first impression—the one time they actually got to talk ended with a set of bloody knuckles. Maybe he'd been right to want nothing to do with her. He'd already rejected her, so there was no point in feeling bad. Still, she couldn't push down the small rise of guilt.

"Where's your ride?" he asked, breaking eye contact to pull out his pack of cigarettes.

"Oh, I—um..." She glanced toward the house, where the faint pulse lights blurred into streaks through the trees.

The dorms weren't that far. Even if Serena had gone home, Avril would've seen her message by now. Maybe she hadn't heard her phone. The music was really loud.

"I might have to go back and find her," she said at last.

"You're not going back in there."

Her brows furrowed. She didn't really want to, but she challenged him anyway. "Why not, Sir?"

His jaw ticked, and he exhaled, shoving the pack of cigarettes into his jacket with a sigh. "Don't call me that."

Something about his irritation lifted her spirits—maybe because *he'd* done a good job at irritating *her*, or maybe because this was the most reaction he'd given her all night.

Jace got a handful of bruises, and all she got was an exhale. Hardly seemed fair.

"What, don't like your nickname, Sir Knight?" she continued. If he didn't, that was really too bad because the name had already grown on her.

He scowled.

She pouted.

"Fine," she conceded. The air outside did feel a bit chilly, but she'd already been dealing with it, and to be honest, she didn't want to go near anyone associated with Jace. "I can walk to the dorms." Even if it would take her the rest of the night.

"You can hardly stand." This time, his tone was dry rather than demanding, but the point couldn't be denied either.

"I'll be fine." She arched a brow, satisfied that the words seemed to have the same effect on him as they did on her earlier.

"I don't believe you," he replied with a twitch of his lips, repeating her previous response.

He wanted to play this game, did he?

Before she could think of something witty, he offered, "I'll take you."

"I promise I'll be—what?" She must've misheard. Winning wasn't supposed to be easy.

"I'll give you a ride," he repeated.

She stared back, questioning whether to believe him or not. "Why?"

He smiled, not a full grin, but enough to make her breath

catch. It might as well have been a shot of adrenaline straight to her heart. "Because I want to." He paused. "And to apologize for being rude earlier. I meant what I said, but maybe I shouldn't have said it like that."

She managed to remember how lungs worked in time to reply. "I think I knew how to respond better when you were being rude." Her eyes met his. "But that doesn't mean you should go around beating people up."

He turned away, and the smile vanished. "Probably not. Although Jace is less of a person and more of an asshole."

She stifled a laugh, looking around. "So...where's your car?"

"At my apartment, and it's not a car."

She frowned. Usually, people weren't so picky about distinguishing cars from trucks. "Oh. Do you live around here?"

"It's not that far, but it might take a while to get there in your state."

She pouted. "You're being rude again. I'll have you know my current state is an exception."

He snorted. "I'm being realistic, not rude—and I know. What made you decide to drink so much tonight?"

Checking her phone in case Avril replied, disappointment crashed over her again at the blank screen. Her shoulders slumped. "I volunteer to be the designated driver most of the time," she replied. "And I won't drink if I go somewhere new. Or if I'm behind in my studies." She sighed. "There's always something to worry about, but this was my last chance to get out before midterms spank my ass."

"Lucky midterms," he scoffed.

She giggled, blushing as she tried to wrangle in her wayward imagination. "Unlucky me."

"Come on." He offered his arm. She swallowed, staring at him. He might as well have died and been reincarnated with the shift in moods. "Unless you'd rather wait here."

"I'll go," she said, hurrying to take his offer.

The tilting sidewalk was no match now, with the help of her black knight's sturdy arm.

He sighed once more, then looked over at her as his lips tipped up, fighting a smirk. "I knew you'd let me bring you to my place tonight."

FIVE

Adrian

A SCAR OR TWO ON HIS KNUCKLES WOULDN'T HAVE BEEN HALF bad, but the brunette clinging to his arm proved to have a much greater impact on his health. And he had a feeling her effects would linger far longer than any pain in his hand.

This girl really knew how to get under his skin. Not just under it—if he was being honest, Ivory had been wedging herself deeper and deeper into his psyche for a while now. She'd watched him ceaselessly, and now that he'd proven he wasn't worth her effort, she went and chased after him. What made her go out of her way to make sure he was okay?

He had to keep reminding himself that she was restricted. Forbidden. Yet every drunken slip of her body into his felt much more apparent than it should've.

She could never be his. He didn't—shouldn't—mix with the kind of person who led a decent life. If he got too close, he'd likely burst into flames. By that logic, however, his eyes should've been charred to a crisp because they kept wandering over her ass. The short spandex shorts under the sheer fabric of her costume left too little to the imagination and too much at the same time.

That, and her infectious voice, which relaxed the further they got from the frat house.

"If you don't want to be my knight, what should I call you, sir?"

He exhaled slowly, trying not to notice how that word sounded from her lips. Or how it conjured images of her bound at the wrists, legs spread as he taught her how good of a girl she'd be for him.

If anyone was due for a punishment tonight, it was him.

"My name," he replied in a flat, disinterested tone.

"Adrian, right?" she asked with that happy lilt to her voice, words less slurred than before. Her breath smelled of fruity margaritas, and a faint floral perfume wafted from her hair and clothes. The witch costume blended almost too well with the night. Flashes of purple teased glimpses of her pale skin every time they walked under a streetlamp, only to fade to black like a mystery he could never unveil.

"Yeah," he answered, forcing himself to look straight ahead.

She giggled. "I like it, but you do look like a black knight."

His gaze shifted, and he took in the drunken glee on her face, which was ten times as potent as the rest of her. That gorgeous smile had recovered from Jace's transgression, and her dark lipstick wore off at the crease to reveal her lips' natural strawberry color.

"You look sweet," he stated.

"That's no good—" She stepped in front of him and pouted, pushing out those sweet berry lips. "I'm supposed to look like an evil witch."

He stopped. "Then you're a sweet, evil witch. The most dangerous ones appear innocent, after all."

That made her laugh, and his heart skipped a beat. The ring of her voice faded as she stared into his eyes. The silence grew still and heavy. She seemed at a loss for words, but he couldn't trust himself to speak, either. Under the moonlit shadows, it wasn't far-fetched to imagine her weaving a secret spell.

Then her body tipped forward, and he reached out to catch her before she hit the cement—but she wasn't falling. He froze as the velvet of her lips brushed his jaw. The warmth of her body pressed against his. Fuck, she felt so soft, but for some reason his chest tightened and he couldn't find the strength to breathe.

His hand stiffened on her hip, and he gently pushed her back. "Ivory," he whispered. "You're drunk."

A pause, punctuated by the low roll of tires and the crunch of dead leaves as a car drove past.

"Right," she mumbled and took a step back.

"I won't hold it against you," he replied. "Don't worry."

"No, I shouldn't have—" She turned awkwardly and started walking again. "I already imposed too much on you tonight."

"Don't blame yourself," he said, matching her pace. An attempted kiss, and not an unwanted one by any means, was one thing, but he didn't like how she made it seem like everything had been her fault. Last time he checked, she hadn't beaten anyone up or gotten them kicked out of the party. He also doubted she realized even half of the thoughts that had run through his brain, which didn't make him better than the next guy, but he wasn't about to make her the wiser. "You haven't imposed."

"Yeah, kinda," she replied. "You punched Jace for me, and now you have to take me home."

"I punched Jace to teach him a lesson," he replied. "Guess it's muscle memory from looking after my mom and sister. Let's call it even." His fingers flexed, and he furrowed his brows. Why was he saying all this?

"If you say so," she hummed. After a while, she asked, "Are you a student?"

Small talk wasn't his thing, but it was better than walking in silence and dealing with his pestering thoughts. "A sophomore, psychology major. You?"

"Freshman, education major with a minor in astronomy." Her face lit up, and he could tell she'd be a great teacher someday. With her perception, no student would be left out. She had a bright future—one more reason he couldn't be in it.

He tilted his head back, searching the sky. "Too cloudy for stars tonight."

She followed his gaze, leaning into him when her feet couldn't depend on her line of sight. He held his breath, her proximity chasing away the chill of night, but this time, he didn't push her away.

"Do you want to know why I picked astronomy?"

"Why?" he asked, gathering up every detail, every crumb of information she offered like some sort of depraved beggar.

Maybe Jace hit him harder than he realized.

"Because sometimes it feels like there's no one else but the heavens," she answered. Her eyes gleamed, almost as if they could reflect the stars through the layer of clouds. Smoky, purple eyeshadow made the green of her irises pop, like symbols of life and growth, despite it being the season of harvest and death.

"I'm not talking about God," she continued. "Just whatever's up there, floating in space as we spin around and around. I'll end up teaching kids the basics of math and science, but I know they're going to have struggles that those things won't fix. I want to teach them something they can always find, something they can see when the world goes dark."

He didn't have a reply to that. Not a good one. Not one that came anywhere close to the beauty of her answer.

"Why'd you pick psychology?" she asked, recreating some semblance of distance between them as she looked back down at the sidewalk.

He cleared his throat. "I've had to be extra aware of the

people around me for a while, and I don't think I could sit through four years of anything else. School wasn't—isn't—really my thing, but my sister hates it worse than I do, and my mom wanted one of us to get a degree. Be the first in the family and all."

His father would have wanted him to graduate, too. They'd planned to do it at the same time, after saving enough money at the mechanic shop. But fate had other plans.

Ivory smiled, though her eyes didn't sparkle like before. "Gotta give credit to parents and their high expectations."

He frowned. Something about that sounded off. "Well, I'm sure I've let my mom down more than I've lived up to her hopes and dreams," he said. "But she's always been supportive."

Ivory fell silent, then whispered, "I think I've let people down more times than I can count."

"Can't imagine how you'd be a disappointment," he murmured. She was obviously a good enough student and, from what he'd observed, didn't fool around with drugs. He'd be the last person to judge, but this girl looked like the epitome of a parent's dream. Everything about her appeared conservative, from the lack of piercings or tattoos to how she spoke.

She scoffed. "We all have our weaknesses."

He hummed in agreement. It wasn't his place to know hers. Wasn't his place to even ask, but he wanted to. He wanted to know why she didn't feel strong, especially after getting a small glimpse of her potential.

His apartment complex loomed in front of them, a slab of brick and cement with stacked rows of darkened windows—including Caspian's. He wondered if his friend was back at the party or if he'd decided to call it a night. Hopefully, he hadn't gotten any messages because he'd been too preoccupied with Ivory to check his phone. It wasn't like Caspian needed a wingman anyway.

Squashing the urge to draw out their conversation, he took in a deep breath of cold air and led them through the parking lot, where a mountain of weatherproof canvas covered his bike.

The time he got to spend with his sweet witch had come to an end, and it was time to get her out of his head.

"Well, we managed to get you here in one piece," he said, unhooking her hand from his arm so he could kneel and unlock the chain connecting the front wheel to the light post.

"All thanks to you, good sir." She giggled, and again, he had to ignore the irregularities in his heartbeat.

"This is a very small vehicle," she noted. "Can't be a truck. Is it like one of those tiny electric cars? Will I even fit inside?"

A smirk stretched across his face. At least he'd get to leave her with a better impression than being a heartless jerk or a bully. This beauty here was a joy to ride on—a fucking privilege. The only woman who had ever been on it before was his sister, and that's because she'd threatened to castrate him if she didn't get to take it for a spin.

"Don't doubt my ability to fit things in tight spaces, sweetheart." He dropped the chain and unhooked the cover. "But no, you won't be *inside*."

SIX

A SURGE OF PRIDE SWELLED AS HE TOSSED OVER THE CANVAS AND revealed his one and only beauty, a Harley Davidson V-Rod that cost almost as much as his tuition. Sleek and black, the motorcycle's chrome and gold accents showed off their coat of polish under the bright streetlamps.

The leather seat would be just large enough to fit them both, but she'd have zero wiggle room between her and the rear tire.

He looked up from his prize possession and back to Ivory—whose expression was less than impressed. More like terrified.

Her wide eyes finally tore away from the bike and locked onto his. "This...is your car?"

"Like I said, not a car."

She stared at him, speechless.

"She's all I got, though," he added. "As reliable as any other, and a hell of a lot more fun."

"I can't ride this," Ivory whispered, rubbing off the goosebumps on her arms.

He plucked his helmet from the seat and brought it over. What had made her so afraid? She'd trusted him enough to walk all the way here in the dark, so this shouldn't be too much of a leap of faith. At least, he hoped so.

"I swear on my life you'll be okay." He meant it. He never would have intervened if he didn't trust himself to keep her safe.

She shook her head as if to emphasize the point. "These things are dangerous. I'm—I'm not built for that. I'm the kind of girl who watches from the sidelines, from the safety of her sofa. What if I lean the wrong way and it tips over?"

Her eyebrows pinched together as she groaned. "I'm too drunk for this."

"Ivory."

She looked up, relaxing slightly as her eyes met his, but worry lines returned the second they flicked over to the bike.

"I've driven this bike for years. Don't let go, and you'll be fine."

She leaned on the streetlight, fighting a battle he already knew she'd give into. Her hands pulled at the ankle strap of one shoe and exposed a painful-looking red line on her skin, while a dark purple tone had crept into the tips of her toes, blending with her sparkly purple nail polish.

His frown deepened. No way would she have made it to the dorms on foot without regretting it in the morning. Her feet deserved better treatment than being strapped into those torture chambers.

She sighed and nibbled on her lip. "I guess I don't have any other option." Setting her foot down on what he noticed were tired ankles, she peered at him. "You promise? On the Knight's code of honor?"

He shook his head. Of all things, she had to ask him to swear on that. Reaching out, he pulled her lip out from her teeth and carefully moved her hair out of the way. "I promise on every code of honor."

"All right," she hummed.

"Close your eyes if you want to. It'll only be a ten-minute ride." He slipped the helmet over her head and double-checked to make sure it fit. She fiddled with the helmet straps, shifting nervously on her feet. "I haven't put you in danger yet, have I?" he asked.

She shook her head and took a deep breath, rolling her shoulders as she stepped towards the bike.

Damn, she looked good. Sexier than he'd been prepared for, with his black helmet framing that gorgeous face. The streetlamp cast a warm glow over her pale skin, where little shadows formed in the pout of her bottom lip, and traveled down the curve of her neck, dipping even lower to pronounce the gentle swell of her breasts. Remnants of her costume clung to her petite waist and fell from hips that could destroy any man.

Visibly calmer, she looked at him through the clear plastic visor. "Are you sure you're not a secret agent or something?"

He scoffed. "I'm just a guy who rides a bike."

A smile lit up her face, and shit, it almost transferred to his face, too. She shouldn't have this much of an effect on him.

"You could be," she said. "First you come to my rescue, then take me away on a badass bike? It doesn't get better than that."

His smile broke loose, and he attempted to hide it by swinging one leg over the bike. "What if I'm a spy for the wrong side?"

She started to laugh, but it got cut off by a sharp inhale as she got on behind him and felt just how much freedom two wheels gave. No doors, no roof, and no seat belt.

Her hands gripped the sides of his jacket like she was trying to preserve distance between them. While he would've appreciated her earlier, she'd have to hold on a lot tighter than that.

"I always fall for the bad guys, anyway," she whispered.

Before he could read into that—whether she was talking

about Jace, or him, or what each might imply—he started the engine, and it let out a roar into the night. Her arms flew around his waist in a grip tight enough to put a strain on his next inhale.

"I got you, sweetheart," he murmured over his shoulder. "Relax and enjoy the ride."

He felt her nod, but her grip didn't loosen in the slightest.

He sighed, knowing which words would do the trick and hoping no one else was near enough to hear them come out of his mouth. "If you trust the knight, then you have to trust his steed, right?"

He could *hear* her smile in response—a little hum followed by a breathless laugh as her head dipped into his shoulder. She squeezed tighter, and for a second, he wondered if she really was trying to break his ribs, but then he got what he'd been aiming for. She relaxed, arms circling him in a comfortable grip.

Then they took off.

Some people thought airplanes had wings, but they were only chunks of metal with tiny windows showing the same scene ninety percent of the time. Bikes had wings, round ones that felt like they hovered over the ground and let you bend with the wind as it whipped past. Bikes had the power to travel anywhere, to leave worries behind in a trail of dust and smoke.

Bikes were awesome.

Riding was the pure essence of freedom. Nothing could compare.

This time, though, the ride felt different. Usually, he'd focus on nothing other than the road ahead and feel nothing but a slight chill or the kiss of the sun on his skin, but tonight, the sky was dark, and all he could feel was Ivory.

Her head lifted from his shoulder, and he envisioned her jade eyes bravely opening to take in the thrill of a night ride— when cars didn't cram the street and the asphalt unfurled under their wheels like it'd been paved just for them. Streetlights blinked past, and he imagined their twinkle reflected in her gaze, experiencing it all for the first time.

His stomach tensed as her fingers curled between the folds of his jacket and under the open zipper, seeking out his body heat against the near-icy wind. Then there was the heat she didn't even know she had, her warm softness permeating through the leather on his back as if their clothes were as thin as paper. The way her thighs hugged his, the rise of her chest as she took in deep gulps of air.

All too soon, they slowed to a stop in front of the university dorm building. It looked almost as quiet as his apartment, save for a few students walking on the other side of the road who paid them no mind.

Ivory slipped off the bike, and his one-man-mount felt emptier than ever.

"Thanks for the ride," she offered quietly as she found her footing on the curb.

"Stay safe," he cautioned. His voice came out with more grit than anticipated, but he ignored it and hoped she would, too.

Ivory fumbled with the helmet, searching for the clasp with what must have been numb fingers. He leaned closer and helped her take it off. "Good luck on those midterms." He offered a faint smile, and the next words spilled out before he could think. "I'm sure you can handle a little spanking."

Dammit. Probably shouldn't have said it like that.

Her smile softened in that sweet way of hers. "Adrian—" Then her expression faltered, struggling with a sadness hidden behind her eyes. "Thank you for being nice to me tonight. I know it was a one-time thing, so I'll do my best to try to forget. From now on, I won't bother you."

She turned and left him with his heart in his mouth. Their ride had tangled her costume around her waist, showing every curve of her perfect form as she retreated into the dorms. Light from inside glowed around her face and outlined his last glimpse of her in ethereal beauty.

It wouldn't take much to walk her inside, make sure she got into her room and locked the door, but he'd already played it too close to the line. Especially with that last comment.

No, it'd be better for both of them if he didn't go in.

He swallowed the lump in his throat and looked down at scarred, bloody hands. His sweet witch knew exactly what he wanted, remembered what he'd told her and what *had* to be said—but the words still stung like hell.

SEVEN

Ivory

Gahhh you're too freakin cute. I can't handle it—give me more!

Ivory added a few, or rather an entire line and a half, of purple heart emojis and posted the comment under the photo of Nia and her boyfriend-recently-turned-fiancé, Caspian. If it weren't for the pile of blankets that had become one with her and the couch, she'd be floating in mid-air out of excitement.

Caspian had gotten a hold of Nia's phone and used it to document their first Christmas together. In most of the photos, Nia tried to hide—behind her hand, under a large bow, or even around Caspian himself, but he snuck in a kiss at the end and caught the moment his fiancée's lips tipped up in a grin. The last photo showed Caspian's smile, half-blurred by Nia's fingers as she reached for the phone. Those two proved true love still existed, and she couldn't be happier for them.

Even so, a sharp pang cracked through her heart. Aside from the good news for her favorite couple, everything had returned to normal after the Halloween party. Her one night of magic came to an end, and she went back to being the girl people didn't notice.

She'd always been average. Never a class president, or athletic, or creative, or funny, and she couldn't pull off anything but basic fashion. Despite that, Adrian had made her feel like there might be more to her. That maybe she could be a magical witch if she wanted to.

But not only had her black knight deliberately left her glass slipper on the ground, it had been crushed under the wheel of the metaphorical carriage—into tiny bits of unrecognizable dust. She was certain she wouldn't be seeing him again. At least Jace had nursed a black eye for days and stayed off her back ever since.

The staccato ding of a timer shot through the silence in their living room, and before she could even set her phone down, her younger brother shouted, "The cookies are ready!"

"I heard," she called back.

Blankets and pillows tumbled along with her as she slid off the sofa. Her mom had made sure their holiday decorations were put away by New Year, including the tree, and only small scraps of tinsel and pine needles remained wedged into hard-to-reach places or hiding behind family photos on the fireplace mantle. But nothing felt more like the season of joy than a batch of home-baked goods.

"Bring me two—no three," Brey yelled, even though he was just in the next room with the door open and would've heard without raising his voice. "Thanks in advance, bestest big sister!"

She rolled her eyes and bounced into the kitchen, reaching for her purple oven mitts. "You know they have to cool off first, dork. Being nice won't change my mind."

"You're so annoying," he groaned, tone transformed into the whiny one she knew so well.

"I *know*," she groaned back in mock agony.

The kitchen filled with the rich smell of butter and brown sugar as she opened the oven. She was glad she'd made three sheets of cookies because a dozen would be enough just for herself. Setting the first batch onto a hot mat to protect the table, she checked the bottom of a cookie and made sure it was done, not burnt or flimsy, and that the chocolate melted into gooey but fluffy perfection.

As if summoned by the confectionary gods, her dad walked out of the office into the kitchen and swiped a cookie off the counter. His work attire consisted of a button-up top and sweatpants, with a ballpoint pen stuck behind his ear. She shot him an accusatory glance but broke into a laugh as he took a huge bite. His jaw immediately fell open as he panted, "Hot!"

"Duh, I just took them out of the oven." She set down another sheet for emphasis, heat from the stove fanning over them.

"Doesn't change the fact they taste amazing." Her dad gave her the proud father grin and took another mouthful of cookie. So easily pleased.

She finished taking out the rest of the cookies and separated a small plate for herself, which she'd hide until they cooled properly, then took out another plate and piled on five cookies for Brey.

Venturing down the hallway and to the left, his room wasn't as much of a disaster as it used to be—meaning she might catch a glimpse of the floor if she got lucky, and dropping off a plate of cookies wouldn't leave her running for the shower.

Endless volumes of anime and video games lined the walls, but when she entered, only his face was visible, lit by the blue hue of a computer screen. He didn't even look up from whatever game held his attention as she set the plate next to the hand not smashing the keyboard.

"Don't burn your tongue like Dad did," she warned.

"Oh, hey." He glanced over, then grabbed a cookie and shoved it in his mouth without a second thought.

She shook her head. "Still playing the same game? Or have

you branched out from your middle school crush?" She peered over his shoulder in time to watch his character slice through a mob of monsters, an array of confusing numbers flashing on the screen.

"Switching is pointless when I've put so much eff—damn, Ivory," he interrupted himself as he devoured a second cookie. "These are good. I've missed your cooking—I mean you—so much."

"Uh-huh," she hummed. Whatever he was playing, he was really good at it. "I missed you too, little bro."

"Yeah, yeah, whatever."

She looked over and caught his little smirk. Such a brat. "You should start streaming your games online. People get really into that."

"You know Mom would kill me if I spent any more time on this," Brey replied, searching around the plate to locate another cookie while his eyes stayed locked on the screen. "I'd have to be active to maintain a channel."

She sighed...he was right. "I'm still going to force you to watch a movie with me later," she said as his avatar made it to what looked like a final boss.

Brey grumbled an imitation of a reply, lost to the digital world. Taking her leave, she got her own plate of cooling cookies and returned to the couch, then nestled into a makeshift fortress of pillows.

Spending Christmas with her family had given her a few weeks of much-needed respite, but spring semester was gearing up to be gloomier than ever. Her GPA took a nosedive after finals, and the pressure to make Dean's list sucked out any chance at a social life.

She wouldn't have minded if that only meant missing out on a few lackluster house parties, but a huge rift had formed between Nia and almost everyone else in their friend group thanks to Jewelle—the woman who framed Caspian as a cheater *and* who happened to be Jace's charming cousin. Ivory didn't know why Serena chose to defend someone like that, but she had a sneaking suspicion it had something to do with staying on good terms with Jace.

She took out her phone and saw that Nia had liked her comment and sent a text.

NIA

How has your break been?

Warmth replaced her pessimistic thoughts as she responded.

Break's been good! Nice to be home, see family and all. Have you and Caspian decided on a date for the wedding?

Nia had told her they didn't have any solid plans for the big day, but Ivory couldn't help making Pinterest boards with ideas for them. Not that she was their official wedding planner or anything, just very well prepared. She had also made a secret board filled with motorcycles, leather, and golden rings. But no one needed to know that.

I see what you're doing, and trust me, you'll be the first to know.

It's still a lot for me to process. Lining up schedules for both sides is more difficult than it looks, not to mention the stress of everyone watching me.

Of course, she'd be stressed about the idea of being the center of attention. Still, weddings weren't supposed to be about being under a spotlight. They were about the joy of companionship. Of remembering what was important.

I'm not rushing you, I swear!

> You should celebrate, though. What about an engagement party—it doesn't have to be big.

The app showed Nia typing a reply, but then she stopped. Ivory played with the tuft on a decorative pillow to keep herself busy until the response came in, two at once.

> After all the drama last semester, I think the only one who would come is you.

> We'd love to have you over, though. Like you said, as long as it's nothing big.

Ivory scrunched her face, fiddling with the plate on her lap. She knew Nia's family didn't come around much, and now it looked like she didn't have anyone at college to support her either, aside from Caspian. That had to be remedied.

> What about Caspian's friends? I'm sure he knows people.

The screen went blank for a few minutes before Nia's reply came in.

> ...I'm not so sure about that.

> Come on, I don't believe you.

Ivory huffed—excuses, excuses. The next reply came almost instantly, but it took a while before her brain processed the three simple words.

Well, she really only stumbled over one of them.

> He'd invite Adrian.

Adrian.

That name she was supposed to have forgotten.

The man who didn't do relationships, especially not with her. Nia knew about his rejection at the Halloween party, but she hadn't told Nia about Jace or what happened after, and certainly didn't mention the last promise she'd made to him.

While she couldn't erase him, she hadn't failed at forgetting, either. She'd done her very best to disregard the memory of golden eyes warming her soul and ignore how she'd felt atop his scary motorcycle. Not once had she looked for him again in a crowd or conjured up a fantasy about her name on his lips. That was, except for a few nights when she couldn't help but think of calling out *his* name.

And sometimes, when she looked up at the stars, she wondered if he'd found what he'd been looking for.

That didn't matter, though, because he made it clear she had no place in his life. She knew he'd only been nice because of what happened with Jace.

Before she could reply to Nia, the front door opened, and a burst of January air sent a chill through the room. Her mom stepped in looking like a snowman, shivering as she quickly shut the door. "It's freezing outside! Oh, are those cookies I smell?"

"Yep, chocolate chip." Speaking of which, the plate on her lap should be perfectly cooled now. She'd timed them to be done when her mom returned from her luncheon, the one with all the other moms who still got together from the time she'd started kindergarten. "How did your meeting go?"

"Oh, it's lovely to get together again." Her mom hung her coat in their front closet and shed her winter heels as she shook snowflakes from her hair. "Tanya's going on vacation to the Caribbean, and Diana has a grandbaby on the way. We got carried away reminiscing about the good days. You know, the ones when you all were small and chubby." She made a face and pinched Ivory's cheeks. "Even if you're all grown, at least I still get to see some of your baby fat."

"—Mom!" Ivory groaned.

Her mom laughed in response and carried the plate of cookies into the kitchen. "These look great, honey, but you shouldn't be filling up on this stuff before dinner. You know how bad carbs are without eating real food first."

Ivory pouted, remembering to fix her expression before she got caught. Arguing would only make things worse. Maybe carbs weren't the best, but she was pretty sure they had to be consumed to have any kind of effect.

"Amy says to tell you hi, by the way," her mom added, rummaging around in the kitchen.

Ivory stiffened.

"Um, that's good to hear," she lied.

Amy, meaning the person she once thought would become her mother-in-law. Not that she'd defended the relationship when her ex told her a long distance wouldn't work. Going to Harvard was a big deal, after all.

Too big of a deal for her to get in the way. Too big of a deal for him to send a "how are you" text, and if she were being honest, that was just fine. Hearing from him now would only feel like rubbing salt in the wound. At least Jace had been cold from the beginning, like a therapeutic wake-up slap.

Maybe she'd had more practice at forgetting than she thought.

Looking down, she picked up her phone and forced herself to believe the words she sent in reply.

That's okay.

Nia and Caspian's party had nothing to do with Adrian. He'd probably forgotten her by now, anyway. She wanted to be there for her friends, and if this would show them someone cared, then nothing else mattered. Sucking up a bit of wounded, school-girl pride for a silly one-sided crush would be worth it.

Are you sure? We could have a girl's night instead.

Movie nights had always been their favorite pastime—neither she nor Nia could naturally hold a conversation for long—and it'd be nice to share that dynamic again, despite not living two doors apart. But did that mean Caspian would end up being kicked out of his own apartment? Ivory frowned. None of those options sounded like what she'd envisioned.

And then, there was something else. She must be more of a masochist than she thought—because she wanted to see Adrian again.

Even if he didn't want her.

Even if he felt absolutely nothing from their night together.

Even if she had to work to forget him all over again because, despite his demeanor, he'd never been cold. He'd been honest. Real—even when it hurt. Something she couldn't help but want to experience again.

No, it's fine. We're all adults, and I want to celebrate with both of you together. I'll bake a special cake if you let me borrow your oven ;)

She allowed herself a moment of excitement. Friends, cake, and her black knight? Finally, something to look forward to.

Okay. I'll talk to Caspian about it.

Ivory clutched a pillow to her chest. Next semester might not start off so bad, after all. And she knew exactly which movie to watch tonight—one where the lead rode a motorcycle.

EIGHT

THE SOFT TONES OF A CHIME RANG THROUGH THE SALON AS THE customer walked out, and the glass door swung closed. On the other side, small white flakes drifted lazily down to the pavement, dusting the empty parking lot in pale monotone. At least the roads were still dry enough to ride on, and he wouldn't have a problem getting home.

"Was that your last one?" his boss, Vera, asked. They'd been the only workers today. Not many people ventured out in the cold unless they already had an appointment.

"Yep, think so." He refocused on sweeping up the scraps of hair from around his station.

Faint background music dispersed the silence as Vera clicked through the computer at the reception desk. Her natural silver hair fell around her heart-shaped face, bangs swept to the side.

"Been a slow day, not the best for business, I suppose, but I'm not complaining."

Neither was he, with a fixed paycheck. A slow day also meant he might get to leave before the evening traffic and squeeze in some dinner before Caspian's engagement party.

Turns out all that pining had done his friend some good, after all.

"I meant to ask before we got busy," Adrian said as he took out an alcohol wipe to sterilize his sheers. "Why didn't you take today off? You'd have every right to."

Vera smiled at the screen, occupied with spreadsheets, as she replied, "Still got to live life, you know? Even when your world stops turning, you have to force yourself to move forward. I'd rather be here than sitting on my couch staring at old photos."

He hummed in response. Today would've been her daughter's twenty-third birthday—if not for what happened five and a half years ago.

The world looked so different back then. Heat waves had distorted the patchy grass he and his best friend called a field. Sweat ran down his spine, and loose gravel relentlessly wedged its way into his shoe. But that didn't stop them from passing the ball around for hours. Didn't detract from the sheer joy of counting how many times it swished through the air. It had felt as if the last days of summer could last forever.

It didn't.

That was the last day he'd hear his best friend laugh. The last time he'd see a spark of joy in his father's eyes—memories overshadowed by a black Corolla with rusted wheel wells and the passenger window rolled down, blending into the shadows of dusk. Its slow roll down the road past the park.

The three shots in quick succession.

Three bodies.

All dead before the police arrived.

The first bullet hit its mark, dove right into the center of his best friend's heart. The second had been aimed at him, should have stopped his heart, too, but all he got was a pair of skinned knees when his father pushed him aside.

Seconds later, the blood spilling onto the dirt, pooling

between his fingers and staining his clothes, didn't belong to him.

The last bullet was the reason the story made the news—it wedged into the skull of a young woman who happened to be passing by. She came from a reputable family and had only been visiting their neighborhood with some friends when the drive-by happened.

She'd been only three months older than his sister, who was also out with her friends that day, but in a different place. That difference, which seemed like nothing at all at the time, became more significant with each and every passing day.

The reason he'd decided to work at the salon, beyond leaving the mechanic shop his father worked at, had been Vera. She didn't know he was at the park when her daughter had been shot. When he applied here two years after the incident, enough time had passed for him to grow some stubble and put on an inch or two. Even though he still wasn't all that tall.

Vera had always been open about her grief and the journey she made, and in a way, it had helped him, too, but that wasn't why he wanted to be close to her. He hadn't taken a bullet, his heart couldn't beat the same afterward. Even now, as he stared at a fragmented reflection in the blade of his scissors and then a complete picture of a less-than-whole man in the mirror, he couldn't shake the memory.

Someone out there had looked at him with the intent to kill, had almost stolen everything he had. He should have known— some instinct should have sensed they were coming. Wasn't bloodlust supposed to be palpable? Didn't death come with at least one warning, even if it was small?

But it didn't, and he hadn't known; there were still no answers.

The case went unsolved. The killer and their motives remained buried as deep as the caskets that held each of their victims. The story shook the local news for a month or so, with initial shock followed by outrage for justice, and after Vera's public candle-lit vigil, the incident concluded with her plea for healing and increased efforts for peace. She'd become a symbol in the community, and customers often commented on her strength as an inspiration.

Everyone moved on in their own ways, but he couldn't. On the surface, he'd grown into a responsible adult acclimated to normal society. But inside, he remembered the threat of death all too well. It could happen at any moment. Without warning.

The shooter might come back—out of a twisted sense of pride or even guilt, maybe even to finish the job. So he searched for signs. This time, he wouldn't miss them, not a single indication of danger.

For so many years, he'd felt the same way Ivory explained, as if no one was there but the heavens. As if no one truly saw what he did behind the pain. She'd said it so blatantly, so matter of fact, like anyone could see suffering and explain it in such simple terms. He could never forget it.

It's true that the only light that had come into his world was through tiny star-like pinpricks, the fullness of the sun hidden ever since he'd witnessed death. Truth had become a concept as mysterious as the inner workings of the universe.

The salon chime rang again, and he straightened as a young man stepped in, about in his twenties with a clean-shaven face and a coat puffing out his frame. Snowflakes shimmered on the petals of a bouquet of white flowers, soft and elegant as if they'd been carved from the fresh snow itself.

Vera's face lit up in recognition, and she stepped out from the counter to greet the young man. "Eli. You didn't have to come all the way out here."

"Of course I did," he said as they embraced and handed off the flowers. "For her."

Adrian clenched his jaw, pierced by a metaphorical thorn at

the injustice of it all. Flowers for a girl who was never supposed to die. For a woman who should be here to smell them herself.

"Thank you," Vera whispered, eyes starting to glisten. "These are..." She sniffed and clapped her hands. "These are just marvelous. I'm sure everyone who comes in will love them."

The young man gave her a somber smile. "I'm glad, and I wouldn't miss seeing you on this day for the world."

Vera turned to Adrian as she set the flowers on the counter. "Adrian, this is Eli—Eli, Adrian." They shook hands, and she continued, "Eli was Kassy's boyfriend at the time."

Another wave of emotion stirred in her face, but she marched onward. "He's kept in touch. I think last year you had class when he stopped by, but he normally brings me flowers on her birthday." She hummed and walked away to rearrange some supplies he'd already taken care of in the main room.

"That's wonderful," Adrian commented, genuinely appreciative to see their connection. Such dedication was rare. The world needed more people like that and fewer people who killed in cold blood.

"It's more for me than anyone else," Eli said, sticking his hands in his pockets. "Hard to believe it happened over five years ago." He took a deep breath. "But Vera reminds me to smile." The young man tried to enact his words, but his smile didn't reach his eyes.

That's something Adrian knew he couldn't do—cover his anger with a prettier emotion. If it meant he could get revenge, he'd march into hell itself. He held back a scowl and gave Eli a nod of acknowledgment. "That she does."

"When's the last time you got a line-up, dear?" Vera asked, directing the question to Eli.

Eli ran a hand over his tight curls and laughed. "Well, I did try to shave before stopping in today. Didn't spend much time with a mirror, though."

"Why don't you take a minute to get sharpened up? I'm sure Adrian wouldn't mind," she said. Of course, it wasn't really a question.

"Sure," he answered and motioned for Eli to come to the barbershop section of the salon. "Won't take long."

Both forced to accept Vera's kindness, Eli unzipped his coat and settled down, while Adrian took out a razor.

"You enjoy working here?" Eli asked.

"I do," Adrian replied. "It's convenient—Vera reminds me to get a cut before my mom can say anything." They both laughed. "Also, it's not far from the college."

"Oh nice," Eli replied. "That school shit is tough, man."

"Don't I know it," Adrian chuckled as he wrapped the styling cloth over Eli's shoulders. A red design carved into the tile hanging from Eli's neck instantly caught his attention.

"That's a unique necklace," he commented, wondering if it meant what he thought it did.

Last he knew, members of the Red Dragon motorcycle club identified themselves with tattoos on their skulls, not tiles on a string. Nor did Eli look like he came from the right side of the block, the side who came from Asian roots and worshiped the Yu family—though even inside their own community, most secretly despised the gang's influence.

"Oh," Eli said, twisting the necklace between his fingers. "This is uh—" He cleared his throat and glanced at Vera.

"You can tell him," she said with a wave of the hand. "Adrian's not one to gossip."

"I found it next to her," Eli said in a low voice, as if someone outside might hear. "I know I should have gone to the police, but it was just a piece of junk in a park, and I—I had to keep something. The red made me think of fate." He paused, then took a breath. "That maybe she's in a better place. It was weeks before we got her belongings back, and I haven't been able to get rid of it ever since."

Mind reeling, Adrian began to piece together things Eli must not have realized. Things that he'd been looking for all these years. He'd never gotten involved with the club, but Royal Flush wasn't discreet about their long-standing rivalry with the Dragons, either.

"I understand," he said, keeping his voice as calm as if they were discussing what angle to cut his hair.

It might be someone else's trash, simply a discarded game piece.

Or it could've been more. A signature. The link that had gone unaccounted for. As soon as he got off work, he needed to call Raptor.

And he was going to be late to Caspian's party.

NINE

"WHAT DO YOU MEAN YOU CAN'T TELL ME ABOUT THE DRAGON tile?" Adrian scowled into the phone. Bitter smoke tumbled from his lips as he kicked chunks of ice around the back of his apartment complex.

Maybe he should've followed his first instinct and barged straight into Beta Rho, demanding answers. Even if Jace hadn't become an official Red Dragon, he'd be the one to snitch. Cowards parading as tough guys always caved first. Besides, he had no issues roughing him up again.

"I mean," Raptor replied on the other line. "You chose not to be initiated. I can't discuss club business with anyone outside of Royal Flush, especially about the Dragons. You know that."

"Bullshit," Adrian spat, almost snapping the cigarette when his hand clenched into a fist. "You told me the shooting wasn't a club matter, and if it had been, President Cortez would've retaliated—Luke was his *son*, for crying out loud. This has to be something else. It means something, and I need to know."

Whatever triggered the events that led to the death of his father and childhood friend, he had to find out. Maybe it'd been something small, like a side deal gone wrong, or it could've been something worse, like a spilled secret. Whatever it was, however that tile had gotten next to that girl's body, it hadn't been a fluke.

Raptor hesitated. "Like I said—"

"I'm aware of the rules." Adrian cut him off with a scoff, followed by another drag on the burning roll of tobacco. He'd known Raptor since middle school, when he started working under his father at the club's mechanic shop. But ever since Raptor took the VP cut, they'd seen each other less and less. "You're telling me I finally found a piece of the puzzle—finally have a chance to avenge my family and get us some goddamn peace—and I need to become a criminal to get your help? That I need to sell what's left of my soul in order to heal the thing that broke it in the first place?"

Adrian exhaled, his vision blurring between the grey smoke and dirty piles of parking lot snow. Several streetlamps clicked on and chased off gathering darkness. "My sister may be able to deal with the club's activities, but I have to think further down the line, R. I have to make sure mom's taken care of. I need to be there to bail your ass out *when* things go wrong, and all I need is one damn answer."

"Stop. Look man, I shouldn't be so cold with you, it's just—" Raptor sighed. "I still stand by my advice to not join, and this discovery is fucking crazy, but hold on. Give me time to talk with Pres."

"Cortez will say the same damn thing you did. He's never given up on me joining, and that's why I cut ties in the first place." Ever since the President's son died, Cortez had treated Adrian like family—or so everyone else said—but the look in that man's eyes spoke less of fatherly concern and more like a patriarch who needed an heir. He wanted nothing to do with the fate attached to that title.

"Yeah, I know. I'll poke around on my own, okay?" Raptor grunted. "For now, you have to lay low. Seriously—don't start anything. Even members need to verify shit like this before any moves are made."

"Fuck," Adrian cursed and leaned back against the rough brick wall, the coldness of it seeping past his jacket and into his bones, cutting through the restlessness boiling in his veins. "Fine. I'll give you a few days, but after that, I'm following up on my own."

Raptor grunted. "You know Riley's going to make a fuss if she hears you called and didn't make plans to visit."

"I'll stop by soon," Adrian said, pushing back his hair. "I got a thing right now, so I gotta go."

"All right, I'll tell her, but you know what will happen if you don't show."

"Yeah, yeah." Adrian shook his head. What would happen was his sister biting both their heads off, but he didn't want to drag her into this shit. Her affiliation with Royal Flush put her in harm's way enough already.

"Stay straight, little man," Raptor joked, tone light but sentiment serious.

Adrian snorted. "Just because you're legally my brother now doesn't mean you can son me. In case you hadn't noticed, a few months ago, I turned twenty-one."

"Aw, look at that," Raptor teased. "Little man's finally old enough to drink without getting locked up."

"Like jail has ever been a concern of yours," he shot back.

"Hey, still ain't a place I want to be. Might be a part of the game, but doesn't mean the card'll end up in my hand." Raptor chuckled. "I'll let you go. See ya around."

"See you." Adrian hung up the call, letting his head tip back and hit the solid brick with a thunk. He puffed out the last of his cigarette, then tossed the burnt remains to the ground and smothered it with his boot. Sooty, blackened ash smeared into the snow and asphalt.

Raptor had taken the edge off his mood, but as soon as

the conversation ended, the sting of impatience only hit harder. Years of wondering. Years of nothing. Why couldn't he *act*?

He struck the wall with a fist, hard enough to feel the force of it break his skin and the metal rings to bruise his bone.

Fuck. Pain shot into his fingers, and he slumped against the brick.

This was no way to handle things. He needed to be smart, not impulsive. That's why he'd called Raptor in the first place. And this certainly wasn't the right mood for an engagement party.

His father taught him to fight, not to back down no matter the opponent, but also to see reason. To put family first—and Caspian might as well be family. When he heard Caspian was putting on a small party, he'd been happily surprised. It was no secret that his friend went through a rough patch in their first year, and this only showed how Nia helped him get back on his feet in more than one way.

Filling his lungs with icy air, he gathered all the thoughts about his father and the dragon tile, then shoved them into a box. He'd open that later.

Welcome warmth melted the frost clinging to his clothes and hair as he entered the building. Across the hall from his apartment, Caspian's door hung partially open. Trickles of music and conversation leaked out as if in invitation. It didn't sound like many people had come yet, but then again, it wasn't supposed to be a big thing.

He flicked a glance to his door, debating whether to try and clean himself up. Before he reached a decision, however, his friend's face popped into view.

"Hey puke hair, get your ass in here. We have cake."

The familiar greeting made him crack a smile. "Nice to see you too, dog breath."

Caspian still hadn't gotten the memo that pink hair was as

good as any other—but with the addiction to breath mints the guy had, it was easy enough to tease him back.

Half a step inside, the temperature in Caspian's apartment hit him full blast. It must have been between about 70 degrees because not only did he thaw out instantly, he started to sweat. Shrugging out of his jacket, he stepped in the rest of the way.

"How many bodies you got in this place? Feels like summer in the middle of fucking January."

Caspian chuckled. "That's from the oven and not leaving the porch open like someone I know." Adrian ignored the subliminal jab. "No, there's only four of us."

—Four?

Himself, Caspian, Nia, and...

His eyes moved over the combined living room and kitchen, and then, with a catch in his chest, he recognized the fourth guest.

His sweet little wanna-be-evil witch, working her magic in the kitchen. Ivory.

In all the mess earlier, he'd forgotten she'd likely be here since she was Nia's friend. But he didn't think she'd be the *only* other guest. He narrowed his eyes at Caspian. "More people are coming, right?"

Caspian shook his head. "I did say it'd be small."

Adrian groaned under his breath.

Nia came over to hover at Caspian's side and gave Adrian a polite smile. "Glad you could come."

He pursed his lips. Had this been some kind of girl pact, then?

"Thanks for the invitation," he said, nodding to her and once again dismissing his preoccupations. "Congrats on the engagement, you two. Truly happy that you found each other."

Nia beamed, then turned her face up at Caspian as he leaned down for a kiss.

Ugh.

He'd secretly been on team Nia ever since she got Caspian to be more self-aware, but he didn't need a front row seat to their sappy affections.

He spared another glance past Caspian, where Ivory hummed in the kitchen and piped decorative swirls of white frosting on a round cake. Her hips swayed as she spun the plate on the counter, lips curved into a delicate smile.

The heat must not have gotten to her, because a sweater bunched at her elbows and hung just below the curve of her ass, tights hugging her long legs.

Damn. She was achingly gorgeous. And the last person he needed right now. She'd see through his attempts to hide his underlying frustration in a heartbeat.

Yet, even as the thought passed through his mind, a sense of calm accompanied her presence. His worries were overshadowed by the light she radiated, like a personal northern star. Her happy mood was contagious, and as he turned back to Caspian and Nia, he realized his emotional immune system had been severely compromised.

"Thanks for coming, man," Caspian said, snapping him back to the conversation. "Means a lot." But he'd caught Adrian's wayward gaze and looked over to Ivory, then quirked an eyebrow at Nia, who blushed.

Well, now the cat was out of the bag.

"I'll leave you two to chat, or whatever guys do," Nia said and flitted off to Ivory's side.

Caspian pinned him with a presumptuous smile and a silent question swirling in his blue eyes.

"It's nothing," Adrian said. "I'm not interested."

Caspian laughed. "Sure. Whatever you say, man."

TEN

Adrian

HE SETTLED ON THE COUCH, BEER IN HAND, AND PRETENDED NOT to be bothered by the two sets of eyes staring at his back from the kitchen. Meanwhile, his and Caspian's conversation meandered through a traditional path of how-were-your-holidays, grumbling about how much homework had been assigned in the first week of classes, and then down memory lane, which circled back to what it was like not to be single.

Or, in Adrian's case, what it was like to still be single. He carefully avoided the topic of Ivory, not wanting to say something she'd overhear and get embarrassed by.

After a short while, she and Nia brought in plates of fancy appetizers, or what Ivory called *mini charcuterie*—a collection of cheese, deli meats, and fresh fruit that looked far better than anything he'd seen at any college gathering.

"It's simple, kinda plain, but I guess it does the trick," Ivory said, handing him a small plate.

"Looks good to me," he commented.

Nia cast a proud look at her friend and sat beside Caspian on the couch. "It was all her idea."

Ivory shrunk at the compliment, picking at the piling on her sweater as she mumbled that it was really nothing special.

Noting the limited space on the couch—the only comfortable seating option, which left a lot to be desired of Caspian's hosting etiquette—Adrian relocated to the desk chair and made space for the ladies. Caspian went about setting up a multiplayer video game while Nia happily munched on the snacks.

It took Ivory all of two seconds to notice the newest damage done to his knuckles, glancing over them with concern. Just when he'd managed to forget about it, too. Her gaze darted between her lap and his hands, between the television screen and back to his knuckles.

Hell, it was annoying. But what bothered him most of all was that her attention never lifted to his face. He wanted her to know he wasn't worth her time, not to make her uncomfortable in his presence.

Now that she wouldn't meet his gaze, he realized he missed the way she looked at him on Halloween. Like she'd hand him her whole world because she thought he could offer something better. Adrian forced his gaze away from her. He knew he didn't have anything good to offer her. Maybe it was better this way.

"Only found two controllers, but we can make it work." Caspian reclaimed his seat next to Nia with a fresh beer. "Who's up first?"

"I need to watch a round. I've never played before," Ivory replied.

Caspian looked over expectedly. "I'll give it a go," Adrian acquiesced, trying to ignore Ivory's persistent sideways stare.

Nia passed a controller to Ivory, who then gave it to him. She hesitated as their fingers brushed, and even from the slight touch, he relished the warmth of her skin, smooth where his was rough and broken. Today her nails were painted lavender with little jeweled snowflakes on the thumb. He wondered if she'd done them herself.

The first match ended in a win for him, meaning a loss for Caspian, per usual. He handed the controller back, but after Ivory insisted she needed to watch another round, Nia took over.

As the next match started, Ivory leaned toward him and broke her silence. "Is it really that hard to take care of yourself?" She focused again on his hand and finally lifted her jade eyes to his. "Or did you just get back from defending another damsel in distress?"

That's when he saw it—the annoyance sparking within the shadows of her pupils, challenging him to disagree.

Which he did.

"I appreciate your concern, but no maidens were involved," he replied. "And I'd say you should see the other guy, but I don't think the brick wall looks any worse for wear." A little scrape like this was nothing for her to get worked up over.

Her expression looked less than amused. She might as well have handed him nails and a hammer, set up a cross in the middle of the room, and demanded he pay for a mortal sin. Still, it'd be a lie to say he didn't like to see that fury rekindle in her eyes. So different from when she let him blow smoke in her face.

"Well, you should really get it disinfected," she huffed.

"They'll heal," he replied, keeping his voice low. "It's not the first time, and it won't be the last."

"All the more reason to take care of it," she retorted, unapologetic to how her stubbornness had begun to dominate the conversation. "They'll heal better without getting infected."

After all his wanting for her direct attention, the objection ate at his insides. No one else had noticed his scars, because his personal shit wasn't their concern. He wasn't about to go nursing wounds that were bound to fester later. Especially not to someone like her. Someone who cared enough to see through his facade.

Holding her stare, he met her defiance with his own. If it was that much of an issue, then he'd give her something else to gawk at. He reached between his shoulder blades and tugged the shirt off his back in one motion, wrapping it around his damaged knuckles. "I didn't want to make a big deal about it, but if it's too distracting for you, I'll cover it up."

Her eyes rounded into large saucers, jaw open. His physique wasn't cover-model worthy, but it was nothing to be ashamed of, either. At least now her attention was off his injury, although it still fell short of his face. He didn't know if that was better or worse.

Better, he decided, as the look in her eyes shifted from irritation to poorly masked desire. That was something he knew how to handle.

"I'll take care of it," he affirmed, aware of how his tone had lowered and how her eyes flicked up to his. Much better. Those beautiful deer-in-headlight eyes gave away more than she knew.

She closed her mouth, and the video game announcer declared a winner.

"Hey now—when did it become no shirt time?" Caspian asked, impervious to the room's shift in mood.

"Keep your clothes on," Nia hissed.

Adrian tore his eyes away from Ivory to mock Caspian. "You're a fucking exhibitionist. No one said they wanted to see you shirtless."

Caspian chuckled, raising an eyebrow at his fiancée. "What you don't know won't kill you."

"It's what I know that scares me," Adrian shot back.

Nia didn't look amused. "Caspian, if he needs a new shirt, he could borrow one of yours?"

"He needs a first aid kit," Ivory cut in.

Caspian looked him over quizzically, then zeroed in on the pseudo-bandaged hand.

"I, um...think we have one in the bathroom," Nia offered.

Ivory gave him a pointed look, and despite her scowl, the natural pink on her lips looked extra sweet today. He sighed. She wasn't going to let this go, was she?

Frustrated even by his slow response, Ivory got up to head towards the bathroom. "If you won't do it for yourself, then I will."

He caught her arm as she walked by, expecting her to pull away, but she didn't. Her breath hitched, and she stared down at him. "I'll do it," he said softly. "You don't need to take care of me."

"Clearly, I do." Though the words carried her attitude, they came out gentle and meek.

He chuckled and shook his head. "Why?"

He genuinely wanted to know—why did she insist on looking out for him? After rejecting her and making her ride on his big scary bike, and now showing a glimpse of the kind of disaster he really was, why would she care?

"Because..." She hesitated and pulled her lip between her teeth. "I want my hair dyed. That's why." With a glance down, one that lingered on his abdomen before settling on his hand gripping her arm, she added, "I need those hands in good shape."

In another scenario, he might have smirked, said something along the lines of *my hands aren't the only thing I can use on you*, but her words went deeper than that. They meant more than a shallow innuendo—not just to her, but to him too.

She rolled her eyes, and he had to bite his tongue not to reprimand her attitude. "Come on. Such a big baby, what happened to my knight?"

"We're just gonna play another match, cool?" Caspian said. Adrian gave him a nod.

He didn't protest further as Ivory pulled him into the bathroom, sat him on the toilet, and gracefully kneeled to rummage for the first aid kit under the sink.

The game's music started back up in the living room, but Ivory's position took his mind off everything else. The apartment's bathroom was tiny, and the only space left for her to sit was directly between his legs. He tried not to wonder what she'd do if he squared his shoulders, if he used that low, commanding tone and told her how pretty she looked on her knees.

No. This was exactly why he had to keep distance between them. Even though it would be twice as painful to see her walk away again.

"If you'd been this way around Jace, he would think twice about targeting you." He spoke quietly enough for the words to not carry outside the bathroom and unsuccessfully tried to distract himself from watching the line of her sweater inch up the back of her thighs.

"What way?" she asked, voice muffled by the cabinet.

"The mean, stubborn way. Jace doesn't deserve your kindness." Neither did he, for that matter. But the more she offered it to him, the more he wanted to take it.

"I'm not mean." She sat upright, pulling out a red and white bag and a bottle of rubbing alcohol. "Maybe *a little* stubborn."

Oh, she had no idea. He'd love to teach her what that kind of stubbornness would get her—if he reversed the roles and showed her just how well *he* could take care of *her* needs. He'd insist on giving her what he thought was best, even when she asked for less. Even when she begged that she couldn't take any more.

"So you're only like that when you want to help someone else?" he asked. "Not when it comes to helping yourself?"

"Something like that," she whispered. Her gaze found his belt, wavering as she trailed up his bare chest and landed on his face. She snapped her eyes back to his hand and carefully unwrapped the shirt.

His body stirred under the appraisal, her will alone enough to summon him to action despite his efforts to repress it. "Have you ever called him out? Told Jace to fuck off and walked away?"

She stiffened. "Not in those exact words. I'm hoping he'll forget about me. There are other girls who want to be around him."

"You're hard to forget, sweetheart."

He figured Jace would keep his distance after their little exchange, but that kind of guy rarely stopped. Once they found a target, they kept coming back like an addict. Taking away power from others was their drug, and she had to stop feeding into it. "I want him to see that side of you next time. You're more than capable of putting him in his place."

She didn't reply, instead picking out a cotton ball and dousing it with alcohol, then tenderly gripped his hand. Her movements were much too gentle—too gratifying—as she dabbed at the skin around his rings.

"Does it hurt?" She no longer hid how her eyes wandered from his knuckles to the trail of dark hair disappearing under his beltline, leaving his skin hot and heart pounding.

Dammit, he shouldn't have pulled that stupid stunt and taken off his shirt. "Yeah," he murmured with a twitch of his lips. "But I'll take the pain if it comes with the pleasure of having you care for me."

She scoffed, concentrating as she moved over the deeper cuts where blood had dried in the cracks. He watched her for a while, using the pain to keep his mind off imagining what else her hands could do—or what they'd look like tied to his headboard. She'd consume his every thought if he wasn't careful.

"I'm not made of glass. You won't break me," he added, then winced as she pressed harder.

Still, the alcohol stung less than the thought of Jace assuming he could get away with shit if he found Ivory alone. The mere thought of that asshole touching her again, *looking* at her, made him scowl. If he was about to get his hands dirty with the Dragons, he wouldn't be there to protect her. He had to know she'd be okay—even if he had to push her limits.

ELEVEN

THIS WHOLE THING HAD BEEN A TERRIBLE IDEA.

She could deny their history, block out the warm fuzzy memories of walking down dark October streets, but couldn't change how his presence called to her as he stepped through the door. How he wove into her mind without even speaking, the bitter tang of cigarettes prickling her nose.

Despite that, she had tried really, really hard to act normal.

She kept herself from constantly staring and hadn't been overly curious while they conversed. Didn't even ask why his hand was bleeding. Again. All she wanted was for him to take care of himself—something she wished equally for everyone she cared about. It wasn't because he was special.

Then he had to pull the ultimate trump card, that sexy thing men do where they're too lazy to use both hands yet talented enough to take off their shirt in one flawless motion. It made her want to slap him, and then maybe he'd bend her over his knee and teach her better.

Even when he called her out, riled her up, and amplified every bothersome feeling she'd ever felt towards him, she'd kept her focus. If she had to clean his knuckles herself, then so be it, but she wasn't going to let it go. For the principle of the matter.

She didn't like being mean. She didn't want him to think she was mean—did he? Wouldn't it have been meaner not to say anything?

"Pretend I'm Jace and tell me to fuck off," he prompted as she cleaned his wounds. His voice was firm, barely above a whisper.

The fabric of his black jeans rubbed softly against her arm, and a scent under the layer of smoke caught her attention—a smooth, rich aroma that reminded her of cinnamon and nutmeg. She couldn't look up from his knuckles, away from the rough, scraped skin, to see how his eyes would search hers. To let their golden stare take her breath away.

The fact that she hadn't hyperventilated at being this close and touching him so casually had been a miracle.

"Say it for me," Adrian repeated.

The words grated against her conscience, and she pressed on the alcohol wipe. Jace was the last person she wanted to think about. Sure, she could say exactly how pathetic and despicable he was in her thoughts, but to his face? With real words?

"I don't think I could ever pretend you were Jace." She sighed, glancing up. Adrian looked back with an unreadable expression. Besides, she didn't want him to see her like that. He wasn't the one who deserved it. "But I think you're right. Jace might get the hint if I was more firm."

So far, ignoring Jace had not equated to Jace ignoring her, but beating him up as her black knight did was out of the question. She'd have to learn to hold her own in some other way.

"Then start with something else," Adrian said as his fingers absently slid against her arm, "I pissed you off earlier, so give me a piece of your mind. Don't hold back."

The invitation sunk in as she inspected his wounds one last time. Up close, a small collection of scratches was visible on the surface of his rings—unpolished, opposite to the chrome accents on his bike.

How could he cherish one so much and the other so little?

She pulled away to throw the cotton into the trash and zipped up the first aid kit. Holding her breath, she tried not to linger on the trail of dark hair leading down his navel or how it disappeared under the snug fit of his leather belt.

"Can I just say the cuss word and phrase it differently?" she asked. "You won't take me seriously?"

"If that will help you stand up to Jace."

The first time she'd heard Adrian swear popped into her head. *Don't waste your time on me, sweetheart. All you'd be to me is something to fuck.*

She could do this. She could replicate his unfeigned attitude. Firm, but not overly abrasive. Squaring her shoulders, she put on a brave face and looked him straight in the eye.

"Fuck me."

As soon as the phrase left her lips, he froze. Oh no. This was bad.

Very bad.

Her heart hammered out of control like a terrified rabbit.

"I'm sorry, it was the first thing that came to mind," she whispered in a rush. The words only served to bounce around the bathroom walls and condemn her more. "I said it without thinking."

She hung her head as heat rose over every inch of her skin. Adrian's legs shifted in her peripheral vision. "I tried to not say please at the end if that helps," she squeaked.

Adrian cleared his throat. The deep hum resonated in her chest, and her thighs squeezed together.

"You did great, sweetheart." His voice dropped dangerously, *deliciously* low. Like a warning wrapped up in the shining foil of praise.

There was no way she could ever look at him again.

Ever.

He reached out to touch her shoulder and squeezed lightly, encouraging her to look up. Responding to the gentle touch, she lifted her eyes and straightened her spine, even though the confident position felt unfamiliar. He hadn't laughed or tried to demean her, but the truth had become painfully obvious.

She was weak. The moment she tried to pretend otherwise, her façade cracked. That's exactly why Jace knew he could toy with her—she'd practically told him as much—and by now, Adrian must have caught on, too.

"Your words carry more value than you think, Iv." He smiled. "No need to apologize for them."

The darkness encroaching on her vision vanished, and her breath hitched at the new nickname. *Her* name—from his lips. She wanted to hear him say it over and over.

"Now all you have to do is replace *me* with *off*," he instructed, back to being serious as he removed his hand.

She immediately mourned the loss of his touch and broke into a breathless laugh. "It does change the message quite a lot, doesn't it?"

He didn't look amused. "You don't have to say it like I did, but you need Jace to know you won't back down."

"I want to say it." Taking a deep breath, she cleared her mind. Then forced out the phrase. "Fuck off."

Adrian stared at her, and for a second, she thought he'd been offended for real. Maybe she'd been too harsh—

He broke out in a chuckle, a soft one that filled the room, but it irritated her nonetheless. Her previous exclamation hadn't made him laugh, but *that* did?

"Say it like you did the first time," he said, lips turned into a breathtaking smile.

"How did I say it the first time?"

"Like you meant it."

Oh.

Okay.

Pushing down another wave of insecurity, she summoned her best version of dark-witch energy and tried to remember how the phrase sounded when he'd said them. The confidence he reigned in so effortlessly.

"Fuck off."

On the second try, it came out firm, less of a plea and more like a command. The difference sounded clear to her, but the sight of Adrian's look of approval eclipsed her own pride.

"There it is," he praised. "Good girl."

Her insides turned into a puddle. Great. So much for keeping her cool. How could she go from mean to melted with two words?

"Let's get back to the party, shall we?" he asked.

"Yeah." She nodded, grateful he didn't seem to notice how his words had left her dazed.

She stood, and he pulled the shirt back over his head, the fabric stretching over his form in a way that only incapacitated her more. A part of her felt bad for how pushy she'd been, but she couldn't regret helping him. Or their conversation. Or getting close to him in general.

She felt a million times lighter, actually. Looking away, she mumbled, "Thanks for letting me patch you up."

One side of his mouth quirked up. "I didn't really have a choice, did I?"

Raising her chin, she brushed off the swarm of butterflies in her belly and walked back into the living room, where the video game's music had been on a loop for longer than usual. The screen had been paused on the results of the last match, and Nia and Caspian were curled up together on one end of the couch, whispering about something she was sure she didn't want to hear.

Behind her, Adrian cleared his throat. "I was lured here under the premise of cake, was I not?"

Ivory

Nia stopped mid-whisper and blushed, tucking herself closer to Caspian, who turned to look at them with raised eyebrows and a gleam in his eyes. "I offered cake before we knew your hand was broken. Can you manage to lift the fork?" Caspian teased.

Adrian's face returned to its perpetual indifference. "You wish. What kind of friend would I be if I let you get fat before the big day?"

"I think I'd manage to work it off somehow," Caspian replied, turning to Nia with a wink.

"Shut up," she hissed and smacked him on the arm.

The tension from earlier washed away, and Ivory laughed along with the others. Maybe she could do this after all. Despite how Adrian innately affected her, they could make it through one evening in the same place. He hadn't been as irritated at her as she expected and even handled her awkward conversation like a pro.

"I'll go bring it out with some plates," she offered, both relieved and disappointed that the trip to the kitchen took her farther away from Adrian.

Tiny rosettes lined the circular cake, with a cluster of three larger flowers in the center and *Nia & Caspian* written in her best cursive writing. It didn't look like a professional cake, but she was proud of her work. All the other times she'd baked had been for birthday parties, and she wasn't used to adding a romantic element. Hopefully, her design would be enough. As long as it tasted as good as it looked.

"All right," she said, excited all over again as she placed the cake on their small coffee table and handed Nia a kitchen knife. "You have to be the one to cut it."

"I thought that was only for the wedding?" Nia asked, looking equally adorable and dangerous as she precariously gripped the large knife.

"Then consider this practice," she replied, taking a seat next to Nia.

"Here, I got you." Caspian placed his hand over Nia's, and Ivory's heart all but burst. People deserved this kind of happiness. They deserved love, and watching these two come full circle was a privilege she cherished.

Maybe one day, she'd get to see Adrian fall in love, too. A sharp stab of emotion shot through her chest as the couple sliced through the cake. Ignoring it, she clapped her hands. "Hooray! Congrats!"

Adrian chimed in, and Nia brushed off the attention, cutting the rest of the slices and serving them on small paper plates. "I don't know how I'm going to do this with more people. Maybe I did need a trial run." She handed a plate to Ivory, the cake's scarlet color bright and rich. "Thanks for making this. The cake looks so good."

"You're welcome!" A genuine smile stretched across Ivory's face. "It was super fun, and I couldn't have done it without your kitchen. I should be thanking you."

"Let's dig in," Caspian said, already lifting a forkful into his mouth.

Ivory sectioned off a piece of the cake and took a tentative bite of the creation, hoping the compliments hadn't been premature. She'd been extra careful to follow the recipe, but that didn't mean she was accident-proof. Her mother never let her live down the one time she forgot to add sugar or when she mixed up tablespoons for teaspoons of baking soda.

"Mm, wow," Nia exclaimed.

Ivory hummed as a spongy texture graced her tongue. The cake turned out decent. The cream cheese frosting tasted light enough to balance the heavy chocolate flavor and not too sweet, either. Could've added another egg, though.

Caspian quickly served himself another piece. "This is one hundred percent worth every extra ounce. Feel free to use our kitchen whenever you want, Ivory."

"Thanks," she mumbled.

"It's delicious, Iv," Adrian said, lifting his eyes to meet hers.

That nickname again. She looked down and busied herself with another bite of cake, ignoring the heat creeping back into her face. Then she remembered. "Oh shoot, I did forget something!"

"What?" Nia asked.

"I wanted to bring a bottle of champagne, too." It would have been perfect, but she hadn't gotten around to asking someone old enough to buy it for her.

"I think we have juice in the fridge," Caspian offered.

Nia rolled her eyes. "It's all right, Ivory. You already did so much."

"Not champagne, but my sister dropped off some mixed cocktails the other day. Said she didn't want them anymore. Would those work?" Adrian asked.

Hope shot through her. That would be perfect! "You wouldn't mind?"

He shook his head and stood up from the chair. "I won't

drink them." Then he cast a glance at Caspian and Nia. "You both want one?"

"Not for me." Nia declined. "I have to drive Ivory to the dorms later, but don't let me hold you back." She gave a small smile to Caspian and then to Ivory. "It is a party, after all. You should enjoy yourselves."

"I'm good with beer," Caspian said, wrapping his arm around Nia and settling into the couch. "We can break out the board games and play the special *adult* version."

Adrian cocked an eyebrow. "And what would that be?"

Caspian grinned. "Take The Game of Life, for example. Instead of drawing a life tile, you have to finish your drink. I recommend small cups for that one."

"Ohh, sounds fun," Ivory said.

"Get the game set while they grab the drinks?" Nia asked, looking at Caspian with love-struck enthusiasm.

"Yes, ma'am," he answered and gave her a kiss on the forehead.

Adrian motioned to Ivory as he walked to the door. "It's just across the hall. Come pick what you want."

"Oh, okay." She followed, guilty about leaving Nia and Caspian alone for the second time, but it wasn't like they didn't enjoy each other's company. If anything, Adrian was the one who had to suffer being alone with her again.

Watching him silently as they crossed the empty hallway, familiar nerves crept in while he unlocked the door. Maybe if she kept her mouth shut this time, she wouldn't say anything embarrassing.

So much for forgetting—she still recalled his exact words to her from months ago. Then, on top of it, proved she'd clung to feelings she said she wouldn't.

The last thing she wanted was for him to see her as some desperate love-struck girl, and she thought of him as more than some guy who'd be a good lay. Good thing he hadn't taken her words as more than a slip of the tongue...right? But what if...

Dread clawed into her gut. Based on what Jace had said or what he'd been about to say, her actions could have been taken in a drastically different way. This wasn't an attempt to seduce Adrian against his wishes. She had to clear it up before Adrian started thinking she was something she wasn't.

The lock clicked, and the door swung open. Before she could say anything about the matter, Adrian stepped into the apartment. He flicked on the light and went to the kitchen, but her feet stuck to the ground, unable to follow. The threshold felt more intimidating than it should've been.

She shuffled hesitantly over the entrance like it was a holy grail. At first glance, the layout looked like a mirror of Nia and Caspian's, but instead of a desk, there was a wall lined with bookshelves. A round wooden table with a handful of matching bar stools connected the kitchen and living areas, where a couch with a gray fabric slipcover and a large recliner faced the television.

Across the room, the door to the bathroom hung halfway open, and the door adjacent stood sealed shut—she assumed it led to his bedroom. Or better, a dungeon.

"Here, take your pick. As many as you want," Adrian said, opening the fridge.

Hurrying over, she chastised herself for gawking. It wasn't her place to look around or take in the scenery. He wouldn't want her trying to pick out information about him from his living space, even though he gave out so little about himself.

She bent and inspected the shelves inside the fridge, reading the collection of brightly colored cans.

"Ooh, peach margarita?" she hummed and reached in. Picking out her favorite flavor and a couple of others that looked good, she straightened and turned around. A draft of air colder than the cans in her hands made a trail of goosebumps rise along her neck. She shivered as her sweater did its best to trap in body heat with its loose knitting.

Adrian had gone onto the porch and let in a blast of winter air. She set the cocktails on the counter and walked over to him, catching a peek at the top of his cigarette pack as he slipped it back into his pocket, hands empty. He'd probably decided to wait to smoke until the party was over. Until he didn't have to do it around her.

She swallowed, wishing the memories that had come flooding back didn't make her heart race.

He turned to face her, and the faint light reflecting through his eyes made them shimmer like liquid gold. In an instant, she knew he hadn't forgotten about their last night together. He hadn't forgotten her, just like she couldn't forget him.

"Iv," he started, a low hum in his voice she'd craved for far too long. He shifted closer, gaze roaming over her face. A pull tugged from deep inside her as if he'd switched on a personal gravitational field, and she was tuned to be drawn into it.

No. She forced herself to look away. She wouldn't let emotions overpower her logic.

Adrian reached out and slid his palm around the back of her neck, guiding her eyes back to his. Blocking her escape. Heat surged through her veins.

"Be honest with me," he continued. "Even with what I've told you, what you've seen, do you have feelings for me?"

THIRTEEN

HE WAS SO CLOSE. CLOSE ENOUGH THAT SHE COULD SEE EVERY curve and edge in his expression, to gauge the depth of his brows and measure the fan of his dark eyelashes. Close enough to study the pool of shadow under his lower lip and the round cut of his Adam's apple.

Close enough to kiss.

She took a step back, remembering exactly what happened the last time she thought Adrian was going to kiss her. "No, I wasn't trying anything. I promise." They didn't need things to get awkward between them when they'd just managed a normal conversation. "I really didn't think about what I said earlier. We can just be friends, and if you want, I can forget—again."

She wouldn't force him to keep rejecting her. He obviously didn't need a woman fawning over him. He didn't *want* that. These stupid feelings that kept flaring up only got in the way— but she was more than a girl with overactive ovaries, and she'd prove it.

Adrian stepped inside and turned to close the door, cutting off the flow of cold air. Goosebumps still clung to her skin.

"Unlike some men, I care about what you say, so I'll take your word for it." He looked at her reflection through the glass, golden eyes dark and murky. "I'd be a terrible friend, so don't think of me as one. But you don't have to think of me as a stranger, either."

Somehow, that felt like a big step for him.

"I didn't mean to give the wrong impression. I just—" She paused. "I can't not care, even if you ask me not to." Her fingers twined in a knot behind her back.

"I know," he whispered, then walked past her to the kitchen, pausing in front of the counter. "You're too good for me, anyway."

She followed, wondering how he could say that. He was *her* black knight. She was the one who needed *his* rescue.

"I'm not," she whispered, lowering her gaze.

Thinking back to that night let in a slew of emotions. The night she admitted to Jace what she could've never told her straight-laced ex-boyfriend. The night she agreed to submit. In her drunken logic, she had thought it would feel like freedom, embracing the hidden parts of herself, maybe even dull the ache of her breakup.

When Jace asked if she liked it rough, she said yes.

She told him to take control. That she wanted it.

But she didn't want her windpipe blocked off. She didn't want to choke on salty tears and a foul dick and stomach acid mixed with all the drinks she'd downed in the past few hours. She didn't want the night to end in her running away, too scared of what he'd do if the rest of her clothes came off.

Her desires had been wrong, so wrong. They were so pitch black that she hadn't seen what asking for them could lead to.

"Jace may be a jerk, but—"

"Iv." Adrian's voice cut her off, and she bit her lip. "Don't believe for a second whatever you were about to say. His behavior has no excuse."

She sucked in a breath and nodded.

If he knew all of what happened...If she wore her darkness as plainly as he wore his, would he still care about what she wanted? Or only what he could get from it?

"Can I explain something to you?" he asked, tipping her chin up to look at him.

The overhead light shone through his eyes, illuminating them like sun rays that chased away her memories. She wasn't in a dingy, dark room with a man who would abuse her.

She was with Adrian. She was safe, and that knowledge warmed her to the bone—calmed her heart and wound into her being enough to reignite her fire.

"Sure," she said, standing with more confidence.

"You don't need to hide. Nothing Jace did or said justifies being ashamed of yourself, even if you think it does."

She swallowed. "I'm not as sweet as you think I am."

"Oh, Iv." He smiled, tone tender yet rough around the edges like every other part of him. "I could show you exactly how sweet you are."

Her breath caught, and the familiar skip in her pulse spiked her senses. The room didn't feel cold anymore, and she didn't feel shy. She didn't want to hide from him.

Especially if what he said was true. "Show me," she whispered, the pounding of her heart loud in her ears.

"It won't be very friend-like of me," he warned.

"Just this once," she breathed.

He held her gaze, and when he spoke, he left no room for misinterpretation. "If you want me to stop, you'll tell me."

"Yes." She nodded.

A knot of anticipation tightened in her core. This static between them—this energy—came alive. It built her up, buoyed her until she was floating on a plane of him and her. Nothing like the stifling, repressive way Jace handled things.

With words alone, Adrian surpassed him as a god to a mere mortal.

"Face the countertop."

The words were clear and direct, and as he spoke, Adrian watched her with expectation. Her breathing slowed, breaths deepening as she followed his orders and turned her back to him. Every part of her stood to attention, the point of her nipples pressing against the cups of the bra. Obeying him came as second nature, almost too easy. Too innate.

"Perfect," he stated, as certain as if it were not a matter of opinion but fact.

She sucked in a sharp breath and relaxed her shoulders, a peaceful calm settling over her in the position. He stood far enough not to touch yet close enough to reassure her of his presence.

"You think so?" The question felt like a gamble, like she was asking him to take back what he'd said if he couldn't prove it. But he didn't disappoint.

"I do," he murmured. "You're responsive. You believe I can give you what you ask for, and that allows me to listen to you as I lead. This won't work any other way."

"Oh," she breathed. "It's easy because I trust you."

He hummed, and a shiver went down her spine. "As I trust you." He took a step closer. "You are truly divine, Ivory. Worthy of worship. Never question that."

She wanted to believe him—wanted to say she'd known it all along, but too many times, she'd been unable to live up to her own expectations. Much less those of others. "It's hard not to question," she admitted.

His palm slid into the curve of her waist, fingers splaying out as he moved up to her shoulder and down the other side. The touch was soothing, sinking past her clothes and into her skin. She could picture how his hand would look, the cleaned cuts and scarred rings against the soft cotton of her sweater.

"Even a blind man would be drawn to your voice, to your touch," he continued. "I want you to appreciate yourself. Can you do that for me?"

Her eyes fluttered closed. "I can try."

His hand traced up her spine, halting between her shoulder blades and then applying a touch of pressure. She bent with the silent command. "If we'd discussed rules beforehand," he started, voice crisp as he guided her down, "you'd know that's not an acceptable answer—and I'd punish you for it."

The laminate was cold, frosted over from the earlier breeze. Her cheek pressed down into the counter, fully flushed and relieved to settle into the chill. Chest flat against the hard surface, she was tempted to squirm as the hem of her sweater rose over her ass, but she stayed still, not wanting to inspire further need for punishment. The concept had once sounded attractive in her mind, but now the possibility of reprimand formed a tight pit in her stomach.

"It wouldn't be to belittle or exert force, but a reminder. A consequence you earned in order to learn. Do you understand?" His hand smoothed down to where her sweater stopped at her tailbone, and she became acutely aware of how her tights clung to each dip and curve. Comfort had been the only deciding factor of her current outfit, but at the moment, it had no such effect.

He'd be able to see everything. Every way her body formed to pair with his. The thought alone had her quivering, but she managed to breathe out a reply.

"Yes, sir." The words slipped out before she could stop them. He didn't seem to mind, though. It almost felt as natural as when she'd said it on their midnight walk.

"So try again," he prompted.

"I'll appreciate myself." Doubt still flickered in the back of her mind, but she was determined to do it because he asked—

even if it was small. Even if she could only appreciate one thing, she'd put in the effort.

"Good," he praised. "Because I appreciate you. And I don't like when others undervalue the things I appreciate."

Warmth blossomed in her chest. What did he see in her?

Adrian continued. "Not every man will know what to do with this—-your desire to submit, to please—but it is powerful. Sweet and good and desirable."

He inhaled slowly as if he was having just as much trouble breathing as she was. "You are powerful."

His hand moved up to the nape of her neck, gently brushing the hair out of the way so as not to tangle it and massaged away her built-up tension. The heat from their skin meeting sent a shiver down her spine, leaving in its wake a blazing trail of desire.

For a moment, she pictured them in the quiet stillness of the night, somewhere deep in the woods and away from prying eyes. On Halloween, with blood still on his knuckles and shimmers of moonlight kissing her skin.

A black knight and his witch, who only wove her magic for him. A man who prized his woman over his own life.

"Thank you," she whispered.

"You are very welcome," he murmured, then stepped away and his hand left. His warmth left.

Her body ached in protest as if she could summon him back with sheer willpower. With raw need.

"Come here," he said, and though it was still a command, his voice came out soft and reverent.

She straightened, tucked her sweater around her thighs, and turned toward him.

His eyes were molten. A bright, hot liquid gold. "Tonight was an exception, but before a man should even get to think about that part of you, he should care about this."

He brought his finger to the center of her chest.

She took a deep breath, steadying herself with the words that she'd known all along but needed to hear.

"Not for one second do I take for granted the trust you've given me, sweetheart." His hand dropped, and she saw the change in him, how his face fell, and his tone turned gritty and dark. "But I don't deserve it."

She wanted to argue, to deny his point, but she had no good reason. She knew so little about him. Now, all she wanted was to find out more. He'd reassured her of her insecurities, and it was fair that she did the same for him. Regardless of what she did or didn't know, one thing had become clear. She wasn't the only one giving mixed signals.

He picked up two packs of beer and turned to the door, but she had to know one thing before they went back.

"Did you ever find what you were looking for?"

His shoulders rose as he inhaled, then they slumped. "Yeah, I did find something." He paused. "But I still look up at night and find myself alone with the stars."

FOURTEEN

Adrian

LAST NIGHT HE'D MADE IT THROUGH ONE ROUND OF CASPIAN'S shitty version of The Game of Life before calling it quits.

The only thing more fucked up than hitting every event space and getting more drunk than he planned was remembering how fucked up his real life had become. A steady ache grew in his chest from stealing glances at his sweet witch and knowing that even though she cared, even though she'd felt like perfection under the palm of his hand—Ivory wasn't truly his.

Moreover, she'd told him she didn't want to be. Not like that.

Her dark desires may align perfectly with his, but a lot more mattered in a relationship than sexual compatibility. He'd been in the underground scene for a while, starting when he was young enough to lie about his age, and knew despite consent being the cornerstone of kink, some people—pathetic wastes of particles like Jace—would use her regardless of whether she gave mixed signals. He needed her intentions to be crystal clear. So that was that.

Unfortunately for him, Ivory had loosened up more and

more with a few cocktails, and by the morning, her musical laugh still echoed in his ears. Her smile still blinded him when he closed his eyes.

Sunlight poured through the window in his bedroom, and he covered his face, preferring the memory of her to the reality of today. He'd almost asked what she would've done in his position. What path would someone with such a kind heart choose if they knew what he did, if they saw what he'd lived through?

Would she choose to face her father's killer? Would she want revenge? Would it eat at her the same way it did him?

But it'd be far better if she never had to endure such circumstances, never had to question if her very life was in danger. Never need to even think about it.

She didn't need a man intent on vengeance, someone so consumed by the past it blinded him to the future.

She deserved so much better.

The way she listened, not only when he showed her the kind of respect a proper man would give her, but when he wasn't even speaking.

He swore she could tune into his very heartbeat, hear all the little flaws and fractures that made up who he was.

She cared enough to ask, to notice what others missed.

It was going to kill him, this sheer drive to wrap her up and never let go. So first, he had to get his own shit together. After he finished tying up the loose ends and cutting off all the rotten, mildewed parts of himself, he'd rebuild.

And then, maybe then, he'd ask her again—if he was someone worthy of her feelings.

Groaning, he pulled his arm off his eyes and reached over to fumble around his bedside table for the phone, knocking off a half-empty glass of water in the process.

"Shit," he cursed and rolled off the bed to pat the damp spot with the nearest cloth he could find.

The room wasn't *messy*, but he didn't have the energy to keep it spick and span like the rest of his apartment. Laundry he hadn't bothered to fold ended up piled on a chair, and boxes of old CDs along with motorcycle magazines he'd collected over the years were scattered around. He sequestered away all the disastrous parts of his lifestyle—a habit of convenience. A habit that paid off because he wouldn't have been able to bring Ivory inside, much less bend her over the counter, if his place hadn't been clean.

One day, he wanted to bend her over every available surface and then go find more.

Sitting back on his bed in nothing but a pair of sweatpants, he located his phone next to an empty beer bottle and unlocked it.

10:23

Good thing he had the day off work. He stretched, calculating if he could risk calling Raptor again without incurring his wrath. Or if he cared. He also wanted to call his mom, make sure the cold wasn't bothering her.

Swiping through emails from the school and a slew of new posts on social media, he saw an unread text Caspian sent late last night.

DOG BREATH

Better watch all that smiling, puke hair. Or that girl's gonna think she's the reason behind it.

He scowled. Stupid drunk Caspian. He shot a quick text back and hoped it woke up his friend's hung-over ass, no doubt trying to sleep in as long as possible.

None of your business.

Fuck it, he might as well send a text to Raptor, too, even

though it hadn't yet been a full 24 hours since their last conversation. Maybe he'd drop by tonight, for Riley's sake.

By the time he was done, Caspian had sent a reply.

> Shit, so it wasn't the alcohol making me see heart eyes all over you last night?

Adrian groaned and ran a hand over his face, prickly stubble scratching his palm. When had Caspian gotten so perceptive? Or was it him who had been slipping, getting too easy to read? Dammit all.

Another string of messages came in.

> Just joking, man.

> I haven't talked with Ivory before, but last semester, she low-key threatened me if I ever broke Nia's heart.

> Still think that's valid, too. I know Nia would return the favor, and since she's my future wife, you know what that means.

> Don't mess around unless you're serious.

As if he needed the warning. He'd never intended to mess around, didn't take pleasure from playing with women's hearts in the first place, but the thought of *anyone* toying with Ivory riled him up. If he ever hurt her, before Nia or Caspian found out, he'd take care of the problem, even if that meant castrating himself.

> I'm not messing around.

He'd left off the most important part, though.

Being serious.

He couldn't promise that—not yet. Not until he got the

information he needed and put this behind him once and for all.

Yesterday's flurries left the side of the streets piled with dirty snow, but the sun had poked its head through the thin veils of clouds and dried the roads well enough.

Adrian pulled his bike over by a suburban house. The tang of sap filled his nose, and a sharp cry sounded from above as a bird fled its nest. He took off his helmet and shook his hair loose.

This neighborhood showed signs of life, but the chill of winter deterred most residents from venturing outside their comfy homes on a weekend.

Back at his parent's place, he knew even the weather wouldn't stop street business. Most travelers would walk the crumbling sidewalks—the ones the city decided twenty years ago would look better as poorly maintained cement than plain dirt—and an occasional low-riding sedan or loud-mouthed motorcycle would whiz past.

Most of those people didn't have money for nice cars, and when they did, they were either smart enough to get the hell out or dumb enough to get caught up and land themselves in either jail or a casket.

Raptor had been the smart type, bought Riley this place, and gave her the life she deserved. For that, he'd earned Adrian's permanent respect, but they all knew it cost more than a lump sum of cash. Royal Flush gave Raptor his life, and whether they wanted to admit it or not, the club would take it back one day.

He trudged up the shoveled front walk and rang the doorbell, shuffling around the porch where Riley had put out a tall ceramic pot of faux bushes with red berries. It looked good, charming.

"Aw, look what the cat dragged in," his sister cooed as she opened the door, tone unusually nice. He narrowed his eyes but wasn't about to point it out. Clothed in a pair of baggy black sweatpants and a Harley t-shirt, she almost looked like a normal housewife.

Almost.

He smiled, glad her eyes shone with the same fire they always had. Thick, dark chestnut hair swished down to her waist, half tied up with a black ribbon, and she rested a hand on her hip. Society may see Raptor as a rebel, but compared to Riley, he was tame.

"I'll take my chances with the cat over you," he replied.

"Get your ass in here. You're letting out the hot air." She rolled her eyes and ushered him into a cinnamon-scented entryway.

"What's with the fancy hairdo?" he asked, bending to remove his boots. Ever since they were kids, she'd worn a messy bun or long braid—hence his first lessons as a stylist—but a ribbon would hardly have been found among her plain hair ties.

"Oh, shut it, a girl likes to look nice every now and then," she quipped, then nodded towards his shoes. "Leave 'em. Raptor ruins the carpet enough as is."

He straightened, grumbling that he didn't want to be blamed for ruining the carpets, either.

Then her arms wrapped around his waist.

...a hug?

He returned the sentiment, drawing her close. The memory of a little girl with pigtails and a toad in her hands flashed in his mind, her face splattered with dirt. He held on a little tighter, a little longer.

Back when they were kids, she'd been the one who taught

him to be brave, the one who held his hand as they crossed the street and took the blame when he accidentally broke their mom's favorite vase.

Now he had a solid inch over her, and even though Raptor would tear through any threat she faced, he would be right beside Raptor to back her up.

Younger or not, he was gonna be her big brother forever.

"Everything okay?" he asked as she let go.

She answered by punching him in the arm. Fuck, she still didn't know how to hold back, did she?

"Don't tell me you've gone soft," she teased. "I had to get it out of the way, so you can't use a bullshit excuse like *I'm mean* not to visit."

"I was here at Christmas," he complained. "Don't tell me you want to see this ugly face more than once a month."

She scoffed and led him past the living room into the kitchen, where a pot on the stove smelled like god had made it herself. "Yeah, you're right. Better keep the fact we're related on the down low. Might scare Raptor off," she said.

He sighed, shoes squeaking as he made his way across the kitchen and helped himself to a soda. "I think that ship already sailed. By a long shot."

After all, he had known Raptor for years before Riley stole him. Poor guy had been a goner from day one.

"He's in the garage if you wanna chat until this is ready." She waved toward the garage door and picked up her phone, typing as Latin pop started blasting his eardrums. "You got about half an hour."

"Need any help?" he asked, noticing that the dark wood cabinets and granite countertop shone like new, except for one spot that was dusted with flour, scattered with several bowls and utensils. She must've spent all morning cleaning and the afternoon cooking.

Her hips swayed as she stirred the pot, and she had to raise her voice to talk over the music. "The kitchen is clean for once, so I'd rather you not contaminate it. Just make sure Raptor finishes up in time to eat."

"Uh-huh," he hummed, wondering what was going on.

Yesterday, Raptor sounded tense over the phone, and now *hair ribbons* and *cleaning*? Something had to be stressing them out.

FIFTEEN

In the garage, Raptor held a beer in the middle of what looked like a miniature junkyard. The temperature fluctuated somewhere between the tropical warmth of the house and the numbing cold outside, and natural light blended with a fluorescent bulb hanging directly over a folding chair.

Miscellaneous engine parts encircled him like a pack of ravenous wolves, their leader a bike that might've been healthier before it got dismantled. Not that Raptor looked much better—his short brown hair spiked and dirtied from running his hands through it.

It felt just like old times when they'd help Adrian's father with a particularly challenging project. Or after his death, when they'd pull all-nighters just to take their minds off what happened.

"Sup," Adrian said, stepping through the familiar mess to rescue his friend. Tattoos curled around Raptor's neck, disappearing under his grey sweatshirt and returning to flicker their permanent shadows down his forearm, around his wrists, then up weathered fingers.

Raptor responded with a nod and finished off his beer.

"Before you ask," he started, wiping his face with an oil-stained sleeve. "I don't have answers for you yet. Not solid ones, at least."

He figured. No answers meant he'd take things into his own hands, simple as that. He'd warned Raptor of his intentions and wasn't the type to speak twice.

"What year is it?" he asked, motioning to the skeleton of a bike.

Raptor sighed. "She's an original from sixteen years ago. Man, it takes me back, but some of the parts are a bitch to find. A side project until the damn snow melts."

"Or a side project for when Riri turns into a hurricane and kicks you out of the house." He cracked a knowing smile.

Raptor chuckled and shook his head, then pulled out a case of cigars. "Want one?" he asked, words muffled as he stuck a thick roll of paper and tobacco between his lips.

Adrian frowned. "Naw."

The earthen bitter-sweet scent of the smoke filled the garage, air warmed by the burning chemicals that brought nostalgia and a false security blanket he knew all too well. With a deep sigh, he pulled out a cigarette and tried to rationalize why the things had ever been beneficial.

"You know all this does is kill us, right?"

"Stress will kill ya, too," Raptor replied through a cloud of smoke and handed him a lighter.

They smoked in silence, hot breath and cold air mingling with unspoken thoughts and a graveyard of memories.

Raptor finally broke their meditation. "Whoever left that dragon tile at the scene was sloppy, at best. Even if they meant it as a signature, they must have been a coward with no intention of claiming the kill."

That, too, he'd figured out. If it had been a proper hit, the tile would've gotten into the hands of someone who knew what it signified, not picked up by some poor kid who wore it like a bad luck charm.

Red Dragon had too much pride for that.

Raptor continued, "Could've been a set-up, and that's the problem."

"It's why I went to you first," Adrian replied. "Forcing bad blood between Royal Flush and Red Dragon is one thing, but why involve my family? Why shoot an innocent girl?" He clenched his fists.

Raptor's shoulders slumped. "Shit, man, why does the world spin one way and not the other? We're only humans, and humans do fucked up shit."

"No." He took a final drag of the cigarette before stomping it out on the floor. "Murdering innocent people for no reason isn't just fucked up. It's unforgivable. I need to know who pulled the trigger. Look them in the eyes."

Raptor exhaled, the smoke as thick and heavy as the tension in the room. "Problem with that is, half the Dragons from five years ago are retired—or dead."

"Won't they care if it *was* a setup?" Adrian asked. "Either their club was in on it, or their name got used without permission. They'd care about shit like that."

Raptor scratched his beard, considering the words. "If it just happened, you might have something, but digging up old dirt now will only earn you a can of worms." He tapped the end of the cigar, ash crumbing to the ground. "Like it or not, you're affiliated with Royal Flush, and we can't risk starting a war when things have been smooth for a while. Bad for business." He took another drag as if that point would end the conversation.

"The last thing I want is to put the family or anyone else in danger," he said, looking Raptor in the eye. "But I'm not giving up. I'll find something, even if it takes me another five years to do it."

Raptor held his stare, steel against gold.

"There are better things to hold on to than death and revenge," Raptor said at last. "I won't tell you what to do, but I will warn you—" He sighed, looking away. "I'm grateful for the life I have—my wife, our home, our livelihood, but not a single day passes that I don't think about what it would be like if I didn't have to be married to both her and the club. At one time, it seemed like the only way out. But I'm not sure it was for the best anymore."

Adrian hung his head, the words hitting a place he'd hidden from himself for a long while. Fixating on one solution didn't mean it was right. "You know I'd do anything for the both of you."

Raptor grinned. "You could take out the trash on Thursdays."

Adrian scoffed and shook his head. "Should I tell Riri you're shirking out on the chores?"

"I call it delegating," Raptor said, and they both laughed.

"Seriously, man, everything good?" he asked.

Raptor nodded. "The woman drives me fucking crazy, but I wouldn't have it any other way."

"Crazy suits you," he replied. They both knew full well Riley grounded Raptor. He hadn't earned the name for nothing —man was a beast on a bike, could and would surpass anything on two wheels—but outside of his element, he needed her to stay sane.

"Crazy would suit you too, little bro," Raptor said with a sideways glance, a smile curling up one half of his mouth. "One day, you'll find a woman who's worth more than all this." He motioned to the spread of manufactured metal and swirling leftover smoke. "That one person who can see and appreciate even the broken parts of you, who makes you think, *damn, that's why I'm here.*" He threw his hands up. "Life means nothing without her."

Adrian swallowed and ground out his cigarette.

Yeah, he might know what Raptor was talking about.

Jade eyes peering at him in the moonlight, strawberry sweet lips and a laugh that haunted his best dreams. A woman who saw him as more than a man, who could shine brighter than any star. Bright enough to illuminate his permanent residence of dread and regret.

"Shit," Raptor said, drawing out the word in a low hum. "What's her name?"

Fuck. Those heart eyes must've returned.

"Too good for a guy like me," Adrian said. "That's her name."

"Ah, yeah." Raptor chuckled and stood from the chair to clap him on the shoulder. "I used to call Riley that, too."

He shouldn't need revenge. He knew that.

A week and some change had passed since dinner with Riley and Raptor, and he'd mulled over what to do again and again. Threaded his hands back and forth around that ribbon Riley had sent him home with. Over and over. She told him to use it on someone at the salon and teased that'd be the only place he could find a girlfriend. The pack she'd bought came with plenty of colors—black and pink being her favorites, but he took the purple one.

For a wannabe purple-haired witch, if he ever got to talk to her again.

He didn't know how to fix himself without getting closure on the past, but the problem with chasing vengeance was that it would inevitably fuck with the future.

So, for the present, he worked. He went to class and rubbed the fading cuts on his knuckles. Came to terms with the fact that the violence connected to the Dragons, indirect or not, had ended his father's life. Almost ended his, and took his best friend, too.

Daylight passed as he traveled from one place to another. Nighttime stretched between pages of his textbook and breaks like the one he took now, smoking out on the porch as he gazed up at a web of constellations and the dark void that stitched them together.

He crushed a half-used cigarette in an empty sardine can and sighed. Instead of smoke, hot vapor fogged from his lips before disappearing into the chilled air.

The one person who'd been able to move on from all this had been his boss. Vera helped countless others to find peace, but the longer he searched for it, the more elusive it became.

Forcing himself into a domestic life felt like a lie, a disgrace to his father's legacy of finishing what he started. Someone had stolen it—taken their father's chance to walk his daughter down the aisle, to attend his son's graduation, to watch his wife age into a graceful old lady.

No. He couldn't forget, much less forgive.

Even if he didn't act on it, he had to know who pulled the trigger. A name, that was all.

He wouldn't stir up shit and cause trouble for Raptor or Riley. He wouldn't pick up the pistol in his dresser drawer like he'd planned.

For the first few years, all he'd thought about was an eye for an eye. Three bullets for three lives. He'd roll them around in his palm, the metal heating to the boiling point of his blood as he planned his revenge.

One shot to the knee, so they could never stand straight again.

One shot to the shoulder, so they could never pick up another gun.

Then one shot between the eyes, so they'd be forced to face death themselves.

Except, life was priceless. Taking one could never replace another.

The stars twinkled above him, shining what little light they could on his misery. If all he got was a name, if all he could hold on to was knowing where to place his grief, then he'd do his best to move on.

He turned and walked inside, shutting the porch door and the night sky out along with it. How late was it, anyway? Picking up his phone, he tapped to check how much time had passed but instead saw a message from a new number.

The sender had included their name, but her personality came out plenty in a handful of words. Of course, she'd reach out now, when he needed her kind heart as much as she needed a less-than-chivalrous knight.

His sweet witch, Ivory.

SIXTEEN

She swung her legs back and forth, kicking the rubber heel of her shoes against the old brick building with small, dull thuds. Most of the school's structures were newer, but some had been around long enough to outwit modern safety protocols.

Tucked away in a corner of campus bordering the woods, a three-story building sat with a rusted metal escape ladder hanging down the side that cut off just above an industrial dumpster. She was barely tall enough to reach the bottom rung while balancing on the dumpster's icy rim, but pulling herself up to the roof had been worth it.

After a conversation with her mom about another mediocre test score, she needed space, not the suffocating stuffiness of a dorm room. She needed the open sky, to see something other than a projection of who she was supposed to be.

Between avoiding everyone at Beta Rho, namely Jace, Jewelle, and Serena, and convincing her parents she didn't go out partying every night, life had become a tightrope.

Reaching for success had begun to taste so bitter.

Even worse, she couldn't obtain it. She didn't know how to

patch things up between her friends, she wasn't getting grades good enough to maintain the Monroe legacy of becoming valedictorian, and the harder she tried, the more she sunk into a pit that sucked away her joy.

She'd never cared about being average, but now her identity had begun to fade away entirely, and it became harder and harder to keep her promise to Adrian—to appreciate herself.

So she finally made up her mind to dye her hair. Not out of desperation to see him again, though that was a plus, and not even to make Nia's drunken excuse at the Halloween party more valid. Because she wanted it. For herself.

Such a trivial thing shouldn't take much effort to decide— either leave it or try a change. A new hair color would hardly be life-altering, and it would grow back naturally, but precisely because it was trivial, she hadn't pursued it.

It wouldn't really matter in the long run. It didn't change who she was or wasn't.

Everyone else wouldn't care one way or the other—but more importantly, the last time she tried to ask for what she wanted, Jace happened. All it took was one foolish, naive slip-up, and now even the thought of making a tiny off-route decision felt daunting.

But after hours of debating, getting up the nerve to send a text, and now no reply from Adrian, she still hadn't rescinded her request.

She wanted to look in the mirror and see someone different. Less of a little lost girl and more of a witch capable of casting her own magic. Maybe a hint of what Adrian said she was —powerful.

Even if she'd never felt that way her whole life.

She was a sidekick. A pedestrian in passing. An onlooker to a galaxy much bigger and much more significant than herself.

Above her, stars peaked out from darkening skies. The last of the sun's red rays had long since glared over campus before dipping below the horizon, and she lay nestled in her hoodie, tracing familiar constellations. The wind whispered incomprehensible secrets as it passed over, and the skirmish of animals in the woods let her know she wasn't alone. Despite wearing decent socks, her toes had gone numb, and her breath now fogged out above her frozen nose, but she didn't move.

People used to make fun of her for staring at the sky for so long. She'd watch for hours on end—after the eclipse or meteor shower ended and everyone else finished their cup of hot cocoa, she'd still be looking heavenward. They didn't know she did it even when there wasn't a reason to look. From her bedroom window, or on a blanket out in the yard when everyone else had gone to sleep, she'd always made time for the stars.

During the day, she got absorbed with looking out for everyone else, but when she was alone with the stars, she didn't need to hide from herself. She could worry and cry and think without bothering anyone else.

Her phone buzzed, and she jumped. It vibrated from the center pocket of her sweatshirt, tickling her belly. Casting a quick glance around, she reassured herself that, indeed, no one else was out on the abandoned rooftop to witness her overreaction, then relaxed and pulled out her phone, holding the screen above her face.

She blinked, and her heart did a little flip.

He finally replied.

To ensure her first message had sounded clear, she read it over again.

> Hey, it's Ivory. I don't mean to bother you.

> Caspian gave me your number because I mentioned wanting to dye my hair purple. Not sure if you remember, but I'd like to take you up on your offer.

Nothing about that seemed too awkward. But Adrian's response had multiple lines—too long to be a simple "no." Her apprehension magnified as she opened the text.

BLACK KNIGHT

Offer is still good. You can set an appointment up at the salon or come over to my apartment. Either way, it's free of charge.

She read his words a second time, then a third, and slowly digested his lack of rejection. He'd upheld his promise to be professional. Did this mean he was being polite even though he didn't like her? Or was his professionalism in spite of deeper feelings?

At first, helping him find whatever it was he needed had been her only goal, and she still wanted that with all her heart, but her desire for his well-being no longer outweighed the possibility of losing their connection. Nothing she'd ever experienced before had come close.

Watching him leave the party that night, content to leave her behind while she clung to his memory, had left a heavy imprint on her chest. When had the scales tipped? The moment she'd outright asked him to fuck her? Or when he'd given her a taste of what exactly that would feel like?

Or maybe it was when she'd believed what he said—that she was good.

Not good *enough*, just good. A good girl.

She read the reply a fourth time. He gave two options: go to the salon, where she could request any stylist, or go to his apartment.

One held true to their non-stranger pact. Formal, but not outright avoidance.

The other would be more than that. She highly doubted it would lead to a repeat of the last time, even though she'd gladly bend over any surface he wanted, but it was clear that being in his apartment led to conversations they couldn't have elsewhere.

In the end, she knew she'd made her choice the moment he offered all those months ago.

> Your apartment will be fine since I already know where it is, but I'll pay for the dye.

She didn't want to take advantage of his generosity, even though he had a job and all she had was her summer savings. His reply came faster than she expected.

> Okay. You only need to pay if you want to—it's not an issue. Did you have a day in mind?

They discussed schedules and settled on next Thursday evening. As the conversation neared its end, she put her phone down on her chest and looked at the night sky. Then reached for the phone again.

> Can you see the stars right now? The sky is clear tonight.

> No, I'm inside. But I can go out on the porch.

The memory of him standing with the glass door open in his apartment rushed back. The air was just as frigid now as it had been then. Inside, it had smelled clean, like fresh laundry and Pine Sol. If he didn't smoke indoors, the only place for him to go would be on the porch.

> That's okay. I don't want to think you're out there to give yourself lung cancer.

> I already smoked tonight, no worries.

She rolled her eyes, grateful he couldn't see it. The action wouldn't earn her a reward. She was sure of that.

I'm outside now.

She giggled—he'd really gone outside! Carefully, she selected her next words.

If you ever wanted someone to listen…I wouldn't judge or try to fix anything. I won't even say anything back if you don't want me to.

That way, we could both be alone, under the stars.

With a deep breath, she pressed send and hoped it hadn't been too soon to breach such a topic. Still, she half expected him to ghost her.

He didn't.

I know you wouldn't, sweetheart.

You study space, right?

He remembered. All those months ago, and he remembered a tiny detail like her minor. If only the warmth bubbling up in her chest would travel to her toes.

Yeah. Astronomy.

Her eyes roamed over the constellations, and she tried to summon patience while he typed a response.

Then I have one question for you.

Does the world rotate in a specific direction for a reason? Or is it a coincidence?

Her fingers tapped across the keypad with a rush of excitement. Finally, something she could help with. He could've easily looked it up for himself, but she was proud to supply the answer. One less thing he had to search for.

> The Earth spins counter-clockwise, like most planets in our solar system. When the planet was forming, clouds and dust collapsed on themselves and caused it to spin in that direction.

> It could've gone the other way, but there is a definite reason for it. Everything has an answer, though I think some are more important than others :)

Damn, you knew that off the top of your head?

> I've looked up random facts about outer space for years. It's not that impressive lol.

She bit her lip, feeling more Ivy League than she really was. His next response caught her off-guard and reminded her of who he was.

Don't sell yourself short. Remember what I said about your words?

> ...that my words carry more weight than I think.

Yes. You said precisely what I needed to hear, and no search engine could've done that.

:)

A lot of things made her smile about his message, but most of all, it was the emoji at the end. He sent it separately, like he'd taken time to think about it and knew she'd like to see it.

I'll let you sleep now.

In truth, it was getting too late to be out, but she hadn't wanted to start walking back until their conversation ended.

> It's okay. I'm actually not at the dorms… although it's freezing outside, and I should head back soon.

> Are you okay? Do you need a ride?

> No, I'm fine. I can walk—seriously, this time I'm not far away.

Her cheeks hurt from smiling so much. She sat up and brushed herself off before reading his next message.

> Please be safe. Call if you need anything.

> Yes, sir :)

> Good girl. Let me know when you get home.

She sighed, her breath swirling in front of her face. As always, her dark knight extended his protection. Maybe one day, she'd take him up on it.

Between him and the stars—that's where she wanted to stay.

But her body had other plans, and she really wouldn't want to explain to him why she had frostbite next week. So, she tucked her phone back into her pocket, pulled on her gloves, and started her precarious descent.

In retrospect, this had possibly been one of the most dangerous places to hang out in the dark when no one knew where she was, but as she jumped down from the ladder, she knew she'd gotten what she came for.

A glimpse of her true self.

SEVENTEEN

Why hadn't she checked the date?

Why, why, *whyyy?*

Every other year, this day had been marked on her calendar for weeks, but now that she had no reason to celebrate it, she'd unknowingly set up her appointment with Adrian to be the most awkward recorded in history. Ever.

It was Thursday afternoon, the day he agreed to dye her hair—and Valentine's Day.

Adrian probably didn't have anyone special, or she hoped he didn't. His blatant anti-relationship stance made any love interest hard to imagine, but that didn't mean someone else wasn't trying to win over his affections...besides her.

She wasn't naïve enough to assume none of the girls at all those parties wouldn't try something. What if they showed up when she was at his apartment?

She groaned and tugged her scarf closer, tiny clouds of breath puffing out between the layers as she pulled open the school library doors. Nia's class got out in an hour, which meant she had plenty of time to figure out how to approach the situation. Or to stress about it. Competing over a man just wasn't her style, and she hated drama, but could she really give up if it came down to it?

He was *her* knight, after all.

Huffing, she shuffled her boots on the welcome mat inside, which only added to the puddle of melted snow, but it was better to leave the outside elements here than trample it around the books.

The main floor of the campus library was abuzz with the low hum of computers and pieces of conversation drifting from the cluster of tables in the group study area. To her left stood the main desk, and beyond that stood a colorful display of new and popular mainstream titles. The theme: Romance, decorated with paper hearts and plastic arrows.

She wondered who on earth had time for leisure reading in school—between assigned reading and speeding through lecture slides, her brain lacked any motivation to see more words on a page than necessary.

Turning to the right, she passed a row of computers and searched for an empty seat among the polished oak tables. Most were occupied by small groups or couples, but a familiar face caught her eye.

Avril must have noticed her, too, because the brunette turned and waved. Her easy smile held no trace of their falling out last semester over Jewelle's drama. Unsure of what to expect, Ivory waved back and walked over.

"Hey, where have you been?" Avril asked in her usual cheery tone. "I swear you disappeared on me after winter break."

Ivory didn't recognize any of the others at the table but gave them a wave and replied, "Yeah, I've been focusing more on studies, I guess. Honestly, I'm not a fan of Beta Rho, even though I know everyone hangs out there."

Avril laughed and rolled her eyes. "You mean the Beta Boys?"

...The Beta Boys? A surprised laugh bubbled out, followed by more around the group, and she was relieved they didn't seem to share the same opinion as the rest of campus.

"Trust me," Avril continued. "Not everyone's a fan. I know Serena and Jewelle cliqued up, and don't get me wrong—they're cool, but even I get tired of being around so many guys."

Ivory took a seat across from her. "I get what you mean. But I thought you three were a trio...especially after the end of last semester."

Avril waved her hand as if to dismiss the point. "I can't stick with one crowd too long anyway." Lowering her voice and leaning forward as the others resumed a previous conversation, she added, "Listen, all I'll say about what happened is Nia shouldn't have slapped Jewelle. Whatever went on between her and Caspian should stay between them. I don't know why everyone else got involved."

"Well, Nia's in love with Caspian. They're engaged," Ivory said, furrowing her brows. "What Jewelle said was out of line." She understood why Avril wanted to stay out of it—Nia hadn't been completely right, either. But Jewelle took advantage of Caspian and got off the hook too easily.

"Oh, they are?" Avril replied. "I had no idea. Tell them congrats for me."

Ivory eyed her with disbelief. "Sure, I can pass it along, but last time you spoke to Nia, you said some mean things, too, you know."

Avril's smile faded. "I guess...Yeah, I should apologize for that. She can be pretty sensitive."

"We're all sensitive when it comes to what matters to us," Ivory replied. But she didn't want to linger on the topic. "What have you been up to?"

Avril's cheerful tone returned, and she introduced Ivory to the others. They extended an invitation for her to join, and she graciously accepted, chatting about classes and campus events until her phone buzzed.

Slipping it out of her pocket, she read the short message from Nia and then said a quick goodbye to the group, exchanging the warmth of indoors for windy, grey skies. A particularly cold gust pummeled her in the chest as she fought to open the library's door.

Nia huddled in an alcove nearby, taking shelter from the wind. Her red hair wisped out from under an oversized jacket as she looked down, typing on her phone.

"Hey," Ivory said, shivering as she rewound her scarf tighter.

Nia opened her mouth to respond but sneezed instead.

"Bless you!" Ivory offered with a giggle.

"Thanks." Nia stuffed her phone away, and they began to walk towards the street where Caspian would pick them up.

Nia groaned and sniffled again. "I think I'm getting a cold."

"Looks like you might already have one," Ivory said, noting her puffed-up eyes and extra red nose. "It must suck to be sick on Valentine's Day."

Nia shook her head. "It's fine. We decided to celebrate it over the weekend, so we don't have to worry about classes." She pulled out a tissue. "I told Caspian not to overexert himself since the day is just a ploy to get money out of people, but he's insistent."

Ivory gave her a knowing side-glance. "From what I've seen, he's not one to give up easily."

A smile took over Nia's expression, though she still looked rather miserable. "He sure doesn't."

"I saw Avril today," Ivory mentioned as they passed the clock tower, the bell ringing over the wind. "I told her you guys got engaged, and she said to tell you congrats. Seems like she's not hanging out with Serena or Jewelle anymore."

Nia huffed. "That's good, I guess."

"Still a sore subject?"

"Not really," Nia replied. "It's not something I think about, but I haven't forgiven it, either."

She hummed. "I don't think it's something that can be forgiven without some kind of closure."

"What do you mean?" Nia asked, stuffing the tissue and her hands into fluffy pockets.

"It's not like Jewelle's tried to make amends—she hasn't even admitted to doing wrong in the first place. Of course, you and Caspian being happy is what matters in the long run, and moving on is the important part, but is that the same as forgiving?"

"I don't know," Nia replied. "If she does ever admit to it, I'd like to see that." Caspian's car pulled up as she spoke, and their conversation got cut short. She climbed into the backseat and moved into the range of the heater, which Caspian had turned on full blast.

"Hi, Caspian," she said, wiggling her fingers as numbness from the cold faded.

"Hey," he replied, eyes locked on Nia as she buckled her seatbelt. "You look even worse than this morning."

"I'm *fine*," Nia insisted. "Either way, I can't afford to miss class."

"Either way, you're staying home tomorrow," he countered.

"Caspian," Nia hissed. "Not now."

He gave her a hard look, to which she responded by leaning over and giving him a peck on the cheek.

He chuckled. "Not gonna work, by the way. But thanks for the kiss, baby girl."

She rolled her eyes, and he drove off without further argument.

"You two are adorable," Ivory sighed, enjoying the scene as it played out. Their banter sounded like her own parents, just younger and more impulsive. It made her smile.

"Don't think I'm not gonna ask about Adrian," Nia warned,

turning around from the front seat and pursing her lips. "Are you two a thing yet?"

"No, not at all," Ivory tried to laugh off the butterflies fluttering in her chest. "You're the only couple around here."

Caspian said nothing, but his Cheshire grin gave away more than enough.

"If anything, I bet your cookies will change his mind," Nia suggested, turning back to face the front.

"They're for payment, not a bribe," Ivory said, pouting, then turned to Caspian. "You're sure he doesn't have allergies, right?"

"No allergies," Caspian affirmed. "Full disclosure: I suggested chocolate peanut butter because they're my favorite. I have no idea what Adrian prefers."

"I guess that's only fair, seeing as you get half the batch," Ivory replied.

"And I'm looking forward to it."

The drive to their apartment building didn't take long. When they arrived, Nia apologized for being sick and unable to help with the cookies, but Ivory didn't mind. Her nerves had kicked in again, and she threw herself into baking. Whatever conclusions Adrian might have drawn about it being Valentine's Day couldn't be that bad, right?

Either way, it wouldn't be long until she found out.

EIGHTEEN

MOTIVE.

He'd gone over it a thousand times. A thousand and one reasons could—and had been—used to justify murder, but in the end, it boiled down to four categories: lust, love, loathing, and loot.

Adrian rubbed the stubble on his chin, unaware of the ticking clock on the wall or the hardness of his chair as he ran through everyone involved in the shooting.

Eli picked up the dragon tile by Kassy's body and kept it a secret all these years, but it was obvious neither of them had connections to Red Dragon or Royal Flush. And though it was possible Kassy had attracted a stalker in one of the clubs who acted out of a fit of jealousy, they wouldn't have dropped the tile for such a personal matter. That theory also didn't explain why his father and Luke had been shot, but not Eli.

That left him, his father, and Lucas Cortez as the true targets.

Luke had been a good kid. He'd rarely been home—either out riding, playing ball, or hanging around the schoolyard with some girl. He was hardly one to start something so serious it had to end with blood.

Luke's father was a different story though. For a long time, Adrian assumed Royal Flush had done something to spark the shooting, but there had been no proof and then no retaliation. He'd asked Raptor about it, but all he said at the time was that President Cortez felt just as blindsided by his son's death as everyone else. The club couldn't make a move without solid evidence, and even now that they had it, something tied their hands.

To that end, he had to admit Raptor was right. Involving the club would only lead to more death. Not to mention, it would put Riley in danger, which was the last thing he wanted. But Raptor had still managed to call in a favor and stopped by earlier in the week to drop off an envelope, mentioning it was the best he could do for now.

The favor turned out to be a USB with the official police records on the case, including details not released to the public.

Adrian hunched over his desk, the glare off the computer brighter than the fading sunlight outside as he read through the report, reliving the story that haunted him all these years.

—Three shots heard around 7:23 pm at Avendale Park.

—Witnesses claim the shots came from a nondescript four-door sedan, some specified a Corolla, with a dark or black paint job. No license plate.

—Shooter described as a light-skinned, young adult male in their twenties wearing a black hooded sweatshirt. One witness later claimed the shooter had a large silver ring on their right hand, the same hand that fired the gun.

—A car fitting the description was found later that night in a back alley, burnt to a crisp. Forensic results came up blank.

—Ballistics on three shell casings found at the scene and bullets removed from the victims confirmed the weapon used was a Glock-19. No cartridge with matching markings had yet been cataloged.

There wasn't much to go on.

Despite the tile signature being sloppy, the hit itself had been clean. The shooter had to have enough skill to hit a target, but they let nerves get the better of them at the last second.

An unsanctioned hit?

Churning over the information, he reached for the pack of cigarettes when his phone buzzed on the desk, its vibration rumbling over the wood. Looking away from the computer screen, he read the preview text.

I'm at Nia's place, let me know when you're ready.

Ivory.

Right, he was supposed to dye her hair today. He'd taken the supplies back with him from the salon, but then got sidetracked digging into the case file.

His pack of cigarettes got tossed back inside the drawer, and he clicked off the report.

When she asked about getting her hair dyed, he'd been almost too glad to have a reason to see her again. Even more so when she agreed to come to his apartment. The more he saw of her—the girl who couldn't help but care more than she should —the more he understood how selfless she was.

Despite his refusal to let her get close enough to unravel the root of his problems, she still wanted to help. She still tried to be there when he'd given her no reason to.

Her patience for him was an unsolvable puzzle in its own right. It would be far easier to give up. He wasn't the most conventional person to hook up with and was even harder to care about. Yet she kept pushing aside her attraction for the former to persist in the latter. At this point, he had a lot of catching up to do to be worthy of her, but he was going to try.

Closing the laptop, he shoved grim memories of the crime to the back of his mind. Even before it all happened, he'd been good at compartmentalizing. Now, that gift had become more important than ever. The less she got involved in this whole thing, the better.

Not getting involved hadn't stopped her from helping, though. After their text conversation, he'd been able to focus on what mattered. He didn't need every answer, just the right one. The important one—like knowing justice had been served. He may never understand why it happened, but he'd sure as hell find out who and make sure they'd never target him again.

He shot a text back telling her to come over and went to get a plastic sheet to cover the counter and floor. The apartment's bathroom would be much too small, and being so close to her always seemed to lead to unintended side effects, so he planned to use the kitchen. It'd be easier to clean up, and he'd be able to think more clearly. Hopefully.

A small knock came at his door, almost too quiet to hear, and he set down the folded plastic to let Ivory in.

She stood waiting in the hallway, her sweet smile paired with purple pants and a paisley top that fit her personality perfectly—topped off with a plate of what smelled like freshly baked cookies.

Shit. She was really trying to kill him.

"What do we have here, a sweet girl bringing treats over to the big, bad wolf?" he teased, lowering his voice with a wicked grin.

She laughed and played along. "You do have rather sharp teeth."

"All the better to eat you with."

Her expression faltered, and he didn't miss how her eyes lingered on his mouth.

Fuck, what was he doing? She hadn't even stepped inside, and all that had already slipped out. Just as he predicted, he'd be a terrible friend—because there was nothing friendly about his thoughts at the moment.

He cleared his throat. "Come in."

Without waiting around to close the door after her, he walked into the kitchen and continued to spread out the plastic.

"Thank you for bringing cookies," he said, this time avoiding any Little Red Riding Hood comparisons.

"You're welcome," she replied in her signature meek tone. "I know I didn't have to, but I wanted to pay you somehow."

She set the plate down on the far end of the counter, away from the sink where he was setting up. "I'm not sure what kind of cookies you like, so I hope chocolate peanut butter doesn't sound too bad?"

It sounded amazing, actually, and they smelled even better. "I'd be happy with anything you baked."

A small smile danced across her lips as he walked over and picked up a cookie, the middle warm and fresh out of the oven.

One bite was all it took.

She'd stolen his soul, and quite frankly, he didn't want it back.

"Have you tried these?" he asked after finishing the bite. "They're amazing."

She giggled. "I'm glad you think so. Caspian and Nia also said they approved, but I haven't verified for myself."

He motioned to the plate. "That's cruel. Have some while I finish setting up."

"No, these are all yours," she protested, waving her hands, but he shoved the plate towards her and walked away.

"I don't trust someone who won't taste their own cooking, so eat up," he ordered.

She picked up a cookie like a good girl.

A glance in her direction revealed the look of contentment on her face, and that in itself was a far better treat than hoarding all those delicious cookies for himself.

"See?" he said. "How selfish would I have been not to share?"

She shook her head and tried to hide her smile. "It's okay to be selfish with some things. This was a gift."

"Oh, Iv," he murmured, once again unsuccessful at filtering his thoughts. "I can be a very selfish man, but only with gifts that aren't meant to be shared."

NINETEEN

Adrian

Grabbing dark purple dye, a brush, and clips to separate her hair, he washed his hands and set everything next to the sink. "Ready to start?"

"Mhm." Ivory popped the last of a cookie into her mouth and gave him a guilty but cute-as-hell smile.

"Do you want everything dyed or specific parts?"

"All of it." She settled on the stool placed in the center of the plastic, sitting awkwardly and shoving her hands under her thighs. "Unless you think that won't look as good?"

"It'll look great," he replied, then added, "You can leave your hands in your lap." Tucking them away would get uncomfortable later, and it wasn't helping him to ignore how good she'd look bound in a similar fashion, her breasts pushed together and peaked in arousal.

Ivory fixed her hands, seemingly more at ease after receiving directions, and then listened as he showed her the dye and explained the process before getting to work. This particular dye was made for brunettes, it would lighten her hair slightly to give a more vibrant result. He'd also brought a color-

131

preserving conditioner that should help fix the damage done by the cold weather.

"How was your day?" he asked, slipping into casual conversation as he moved behind her to clip up the top layers of hair.

"It was good. Nothing out of the ordinary. I was, um..." She sucked in a quick breath. "Hoping I didn't ruin any plans you had."

"Don't worry about it," he replied. "This is a welcome break before I have to start a ten-page history paper."

"Oh." She paused. "I mean, it's the fourteenth and all, so I didn't know if..." She trailed off, and he glanced over to see her bottom lip pulled between her teeth.

His witch looked much too worried. He couldn't have that. Walking around to face her, he gently tipped up her chin and looked her in the eyes. "Is there something special about the fourteenth?"

She relaxed into his touch, her skin soft and warm in his palm, and he hated having to pull away before he lingered too long.

"It's Valentine's Day," she whispered at last, then glanced away. "I thought you might have someone special."

He frowned. Surely she knew he wouldn't hide something like that. "I did tell you I don't do relationships, right?"

"Yeah, but...it's hard to imagine no one chasing after you." She gave a little shrug and another cute smile, meeting his eyes as a blush spread over her cheeks.

Fuck, he wished he could kiss her right now.

Kiss those strawberry lips until they were swollen and red, then let her beg him to kiss more of her. Ask for him to leave his mark before he gave her the sweetest pleasure she'd ever tasted.

He studied her jade eyes before stepping away and averting

his attention to mix the dye. "I'm glad you think so, sweetheart. But even if someone else wanted to chase me, it would be against my rules."

No one would be able to compete with her, anyway.

"Oh," she said again. "I'm sorry. I didn't know."

"It's nothing you need to apologize for." He grinned, glad he stood outside of her line of sight. Her disappointment at not knowing rules he'd never given her was heartwarming, a sign he still had a chance. She wanted to be good for him so bad, and she was—her efforts were so very sweet—but he decided to test the waters and tease her a little.

"Are you worried you'd break those rules?" he asked. "Or have you already?"

He secretly—selfishly—hoped she had. The first night they met, she denied wanting a relationship, but she also hadn't settled for less.

She hesitated, tensing up. "I..."

"I'm only teasing," he added before she took him too seriously, noticing her discomfort. "You don't have to answer. When I set rules, I make sure they are clearly understood. Those are only for my arrangements."

"Arrangements?" she asked, dropping her previous concerns as curiosity colored her voice.

Traditional hook-ups had never appealed to him. They were chaotic, based neither in consistency or kink, and he required both. During the year he'd taken to save up between high school and college, he developed a different approach.

He painted on the first stroke of deep purple and explained. "It's still true that I don't do relationships, but I don't do spontaneous one-night stands, either. Instead, I set up arrangements where everyone involved can have an open discussion before anything happens. That way, we both know what to expect. I won't lead someone on when I'm not putting in the right kind of effort or try to force something I'm not willing to give. So, I can guarantee no one is out there buying me a Valentine's gift or planning a romantic date."

She hummed, thinking over his words. "You avoid emotional attachment."

"Close, but not quite," he replied, not at all offended by her conclusion. "I care about my partner, even if it's in a predefined capacity. I need them to know they can trust me and vice-versa. You'd be surprised what emotions come up in intense play."

Content that the current section of hair had sufficient dye, he clipped it to the side and moved on to the next before continuing. "In fact, I don't think I could enjoy sex without any form of attachment, but plenty of people have told me they prefer this type of arrangement to being kept in the dark or feeling like it's difficult to communicate. This allows them to ask for what they want. Anything they want."

"Makes sense," she said, then added after a pause, "What kind of things do people ask for? If you can share."

He glanced over to see her nibbling on her lip again. With his hands occupied with the dye, he could do nothing about it except try not to get too turned on.

However, she didn't look shocked by the topic, her eyes turning bright and inquisitive. Another good sign, although it was one he anticipated.

"Sometimes they have specific requests, sometimes they don't," he answered. "Most of the time, it's spanking or bondage, maybe a role play or new toys. Once I know what they're comfortable with, I suggest other things."

"And what about you?" she asked, crossing one leg over the other. "What things do you ask for?" Her voice came out soft but firm, the hesitation slowly giving way to genuine curiosity, and he happily answered.

"Besides a willing submissive, I enjoy most types of play. I'm not a sadist who enjoys inflicting pain for pain's sake. There has to be a purpose to the suffering. A reward for each sacrifice." He didn't need to inflict pain or humiliation to get off, but nothing compared to a woman on her knees, handing him the power to control her mind as well as her body. Nothing could replace the rush and rhythm of peering into a person's soul, of peeling it apart layer by layer.

Except, as he explained all this to Ivory, it felt as if she were the one peering into his soul. It always had. The grace and eagerness with which she responded to him was like a secret trigger, a switch programmed into his psyche he didn't even know he had. If he ever got lucky enough to do a scene with her, he knew it would far surpass the sinful images conjured by his imagination.

"That's why having rules is crucial," he continued. "One oversight can cause serious harm or break my partner's trust." Coating the brush with more dye, he repeated the same words he'd told everyone else. "I have three rules, but more might be added based on the scenario."

"One, neither of us shows up at the other's residence without an invitation. So you won't have to worry about any awkward encounters. And although this isn't technically a rule, I also don't take girls into my bedroom. It's too informal."

"Two, if they don't wish to be exclusive, I need to know what else they're involved in. Complete transparency. That one is mostly for safety, and I use protection regardless."

"Three, once we end the arrangement, for whatever reason, it's over. No second chances, especially if any rules were broken."

She nodded and uncrossed her legs. "Then do you..." Her voice faltered, betraying a hint of concern. "Can I ask how many arrangements you have right now?"

"None," he answered, more than pleased as her shoulders dropped when she released a breath. Investigating the Dragons had taken up too much of his time and energy to do anything on the side.

Of course, it was also because of her.

It didn't matter how many girls had been in his living room before. All he could see was her. All he wanted was her.

TWENTY

SHE KNEW COMING TO HIS APARTMENT WOULD LEAD TO something unexpected, but she hadn't planned on a full discourse detailing how perfect he was.

Every word that came out of his mouth made this whole situation more unbearable, and not in a bad way. In a way that would have her crawling at his feet if he asked. A willing submissive—she certainly met his requirements.

And since he worked out of her line of sight, it forced her to rely on every other sense to feel him. The heat from his hands contrasted with the cool touch of the hair dye, the smooth baritone of his voice combined with the gentle boldness of his words, and the rich, spicy scent of his cologne. All of it brought to life fantasies she couldn't keep locked away, no matter how hard she tried.

"But I haven't done anything in a while," he continued explaining, then cut off with a sigh. "Haven't been in the right mindset."

There it was. The reason she hadn't accepted his offer that first night. The reason she never even got to find out that he had arrangements and rules from the beginning. The reason she couldn't let herself be just a stranger or an arrangement—even if as only a friend, she wanted to help chase away whatever darkness haunted him.

"How are things going with that?" she asked, biting down the rest of her questions about his sex life. "Is your mindset getting better or worse?"

"Depends on how you look at it," he replied, working through her hair methodically. "Better, for the most part." He paused, then asked, "What about you? Has Jace bothered you anymore? I haven't heard any gossip about you cussing him out."

That was because she'd made a point to avoid him, and finally, he'd left her alone. Which meant their one night together could remain buried in the dark—exactly where it belonged. Along with the part of her that had secretly hoped to find something in that darkness.

She thought back to her awkward "fuck me" moment at Nia and Caspian's party and felt her spirit lift. From the sound of it, Adrian wasn't unfamiliar with blatant requests. Maybe things would have been different if Jace had set up rules. Or maybe it wasn't the rules but the person making them.

"I've been hiding in the dorms, so Jace can't find me," she replied, unable to see his frown but knowing it'd be there. "*I'm kidding.*"

Adrian scoffed, and she couldn't stop herself from smiling. Getting under his skin never got old.

"Really, though," she continued. "I haven't seen him on campus and that's where I spend all my time now, either going over class notes or getting extra office hours with the professors." She sighed. Discussing her issues hadn't been in her plans, either, but maybe if he saw her flaws, he'd be more accepting of his. "My grades aren't looking so good. I thought last semester was bad because of the new environment, but now I think maybe it's because of me."

"What makes you think it's you?" he asked, switching sides to work on the other half of her head.

Excitement bubbled up to see the full effect of the new color, but she tried her best to be patient. "I enjoy my classes, and it's not like I don't study. I'm just...not as smart as I thought I was."

"By smart, you mean getting a 4.0?" he asked. "There's a lot of other ways to measure intelligence."

"Yeah, I know," she said. "I know I have to put in the work, too. I expected college to be a bigger challenge than high school, and I've tried to work extra hard, but it's not making a difference. My mom was valedictorian at her graduation, and it's kinda expected that I'll be the same."

"Do you want to be valedictorian?"

"I don't *not* want it." She thought it over, admitting what she hadn't dared to tell her family. "I don't mind being average, either. That's all I've ever been." Her hands curled into balls in her lap.

"You're anything but average, Iv," Adrian murmured. "I haven't met anyone else who cares about others the way you do. Look at what you've done for Nia. I doubt she thinks you're average."

He paused to unpin a section of hair and applied more dye on the brush. "You got accepted here, so I don't think you aren't smart enough. Most people decide to give up instead of working harder. Be proud of what you've achieved. Plus, you're an amazing baker and by far my favorite person to talk to."

Her heart swelled. All that came so easy to him, like it was so obvious, but she'd never thought of herself that way. "You really think so?"

He chuckled. "Even from the first night we talked, I didn't want to sell you short with an arrangement when you deserve so much more...however it seems that showing you how harsh I can be didn't scare you away." She caught his eye from the corner of hers, but then he glanced away. "I can't say much about the importance of good grades, but from what I've seen, you have an amazing heart. Don't dismiss your strengths for one moment of weakness."

Speaking of hearts, hers was racing a thousand miles a minute. This suddenly got much deeper than she thought possible. All those words couldn't really be meant for her.

On top of that, this meant he'd thought about her—as much more than a stranger or friend from that first night. What would have happened if she agreed to follow his rules? What would he have wanted?

No, being his friend meant more to her than regretting what could have been. Knowing him on a personal level wouldn't have been possible if she'd been bound by the rules of his arrangements. She wanted access to more than just his body.

"Thanks," she mumbled, uncoiling her hands. "I think you're pretty amazing, too."

He paused as he put down the brush by the sink. "Thank you," he said at last, as if her one sentence meant more than his entire speech. Then he cleared his throat and announced, "All done."

Her heart did a little flip. It was done. If only that meant she could see the final product right now. "I have to let it sit for a while, right?"

"Yep," he answered. "You're welcome to wait here, or if you want to spend time with Nia across the hall, come back in an hour."

In the thirty minutes it took to put on the dye, she'd learned so much. She wasn't about to give up a whole hour with him. "Could I stay?" she asked, standing to stretch her legs.

"Of course," he replied, back turned as he rinsed out the brushes and put away the dye. A Harley-Davidson shirt stretched across his shoulders and biceps, black jeans hanging around strong hips and thighs. His touch had been so careful, but his physique was nothing but power and masculinity.

What could he have been through to impact his psyche so much?

"You could tell me more about yourself," she added. "I like talking with you."

He turned to her with a smile, a few loose strands of his bun falling to his neck. "Me too."

She blushed.

"Here, put this on." His fingers feathered a trail of heat around her face as he helped her out on a plastic hair cap. "There. Feel free to make yourself at home."

Moving cautiously so as not to let her hair slip out, she grabbed the plate of cookies and followed him to the living room, then curled into one end of the couch as he sat on the other.

He reached over, picked up a cookie, and arched his eyebrows. "What do you want to know?"

She shrugged. "What was your life like before college?"

They passed the rest of the cookies back and forth as he told her about his childhood. How his dad loved to play ball with him and his friends, and all the times he covered for his sister when she was up to no good. Most of his stories were from when he was younger—everything after that was reduced to short answers, but that was okay. She didn't want to pry when he'd just begun to open up.

Even the smallest details, like his favorite band or the scars he got from falling off his first bicycle, felt significant. Almost like he was telling someone else for the first time. Maybe he was.

She could listen to him talk for hours, picking up on the inflections of his voice and watching shadows move across his jaw and cheekbones.

When he asked her the same questions, it didn't feel forced

or insincere. His eyes shone as he listened, and instead of laughing at the stories where she embarrassed herself, he was polite enough to say she'd been cute—even though walking around with her shirt inside out in high school was *not* cute, more like ridiculous. It ruined any chance she had at a decent reputation when her mother posted it online.

She explained how she'd decided to be a teacher, recalling all the names of the students she used to tutor and some who still sent her Christmas cards. Helping others had brought her joy, and now it'd become her purpose.

Adrian smiled when she told him she'd been sticking glow-in-the-dark stars on her bedroom ceiling in precise constellations since she learned what they were and once spent an extra hour talking about deep space objects with her physics teacher after school.

When her ex came up, it didn't feel as weird as she thought it would be. For the first time, the ache that came with that particular topic felt more like a sour memory, not a parasite gnawing into her chest.

"He broke everything off the same day he got accepted," she explained. "It hurt—a lot more than I wanted to admit, but I think it was better that way. I wasn't left holding onto false hope of him being faithful in a long-distance relationship."

Adrian scowled. "See, that's a prime example of someone who claims to be smart but clearly lacks intelligence."

She laughed. While it was soothing to think her ex was the one who truly lost out, that hadn't made the breakup any easier.

The conversation continued, less one-sided than she'd gotten used to with other guys. It felt good. By the time he'd learned about her family and all the things she missed away at college—how she couldn't stress-bake like normal, and sometimes it felt weird not being able to bug her brother— their hour had run up.

TWENTY-ONE

"Should be time to rinse your hair out," Adrian said, standing. "Shall we?"

"Yes!" she squealed, jumping up. "I'm so excited to see how it looks." Now that he'd allowed her to open up without the aid of tequila, her exuberance spilled out in full force.

"Glad to hear it." His lips tipped up as he dragged the stool over to the sink and motioned for her to sit with her back toward the counter. "This isn't the most ideal setup, but it's the best I got."

"I don't mind," she said, straddling the stool.

"Okay, lean back for me," he instructed, setting a hand on her back for support. "Let's see if we need to adjust anything."

Bracing her toes on the floor, she let him guide her backward until the nape of her neck hit the plastic-covered counter.

"Look at that, perfect," he murmured, withdrawing his hand as his gaze roamed over her face. She wasn't sure if he'd been referring to the placement of the stool or something else. Her chest rose as she took in a breath, and the coincidence of their position sent a thrill through her system.

Him standing over her, with a view of everything from the tip of her toes to the crown of her head. Her breathless and eager for his touch.

Is this how being his submissive would feel?

"Are you comfortable enough?" he asked, eyes still fixed on her so he could read any trace of apprehension.

"Yeah," she replied, anticipation sparking across the surface of her skin.

The stool offered little to no support, and it wasn't a pose she could maintain for long, but something about being exposed like this, restricted and vulnerable while he watched, made it worth the slight discomfort.

"The water can't be hot, or it will dilute the dye," he said, reaching over to turn on the sink. "I'll try not to make it too cold, though." His stomach brushed against her shoulder, and the thin shirt did nothing to hide the firmness of the muscles underneath. A woodsy scent wrapped around her, the pungent tartness of smoke mixed with a lighter fragrance of laundry detergent and fresh deodorant.

"Okay," she whispered, her earlier energy funneling lower in her abdomen as he slipped the cap off her head.

Chilled water began to flow over her scalp, and his fingers wove into her hair, cradling her head and lending some of his warmth. Her eyes drifted closed as he began to work at rinsing the dye down to her roots.

"Not too cold?" he asked.

"No." She sighed and relaxed further into his hands. "I can handle it."

"Good girl," he hummed, his voice a low rumble from his chest.

Her breath hitched, body thrumming with pleasure at his dark tone. Despite only being able to set her toes on the ground when she sat down, her heels now rested on the floor, and her knees fell to either side of the stool. Here with Adrian, she felt no different than being wrapped in a cozy blanket of stars and galaxies. This was right—whole. With her black knight by her side, nothing had the power to drag her down. His darkness became a sheath, a defense against the world.

When she'd knelt in front of Jace in his dingy frat room, a dark void of the unknown loomed overhead and threatened to swallow her whole. She didn't know what Adrian would ask for if she handed over control, but she had no doubt he respected her. He'd give her the space to speak her mind instead of enforcing his will alone. Without question, she knew he could take her to hell and bring her back in one piece. The thought itself was all too tempting, too good not to consider.

He'd been nothing but honest, and this was her chance to do the same. She couldn't expect to learn his truths if she hid hers, especially the ones involving him.

"I think," she whispered, delving into that part of her that she hoped out of all people, he would understand. "I could take anything if you asked me to." She hesitated but continued under her breath. "I'd want you to ask me for the things not meant for a friend or a stranger. Things you'd ask from one of your arrangements."

Her very existence hung in the air, and she stopped breathing altogether. Surely, this time, she'd gone and said too much.

Adrian's movements paused. "You mean that?"

Glad her eyes were closed and sealed off from his reaction, she admitted the truth. "Yes."

"Oh, Iv," he murmured, tone warm and low as his fingers resumed stroking her scalp. "My sweet little witch." Her heart hammered at his words, begging him to say more. Then, his hand tightened around the roots of her hair. "Hold still for me, sweetheart."

Moving wouldn't be an option even if she wanted—tilting her head to the side was impossible with his iron grip, harsh enough to ensure control yet attentive enough not to cause damage. It made more heat flush through her veins, and adrenaline quickened her pulse. She was sure he saw the flutter of her heartbeat on her neck, though that wasn't the only place she felt his effects. Her jeans felt as thin as lace as her sex swelled, spread open and slick.

"I'd like nothing more than to teach you how much you can take for me," he rasped in a whisper. "To ask and know you want to obey, no matter the cost. Would you want that? Would you let me?"

She would—she knew in an instant. Even if what he asked for was difficult, even if he offered her as much pain as pleasure, she'd take it. "Yes," she said. "I'd want to obey, to please you. I'd do my best to follow all your rules."

Except for the part where she'd already fallen for him, but that thought didn't have time to take root as he released one hand and reached across her chest to the counter, letting cold droplets of water run from his fingers onto her chest. They dripped down her shirt, rolled over her breasts, and pooled in her navel.

Her lips parted in a silent gasp. A prayer of gratitude to her dark, godly knight. The ache inside her grew almost unbearable, and she reveled in it. She wanted to be on edge, to be held there at his command.

"I promise to give that to you," he said, retracting his hand and relaxing his grip on her hair. "To give you everything I can —but first, I need to take care of some things."

Everything.

The word echoed inside her, expanded until she all but burst. He'd promised her everything when before he'd mentioned his partners could ask for anything. The shift in words was too significant to ignore. Maybe that meant she could ask for something he hadn't been willing to give before.

"Until then, will you do me a favor?" he asked. His fingers

began to work another liquid into her hair, making suds and filling the air with a sweet aroma. Must be the conditioner he showed her earlier.

"Of course," she whispered. Her desire went beyond fulfilling their pleasures; she wanted him to find happiness. To be as whole as he made her.

When he didn't respond after a moment, she opened her eyes and focused above her head, his hands rinsing her hair for the final time. Something in his expression looked soft—maybe it was how his mouth didn't tip down in a frown or how his eyelashes fanned over his irises and left thin lines of shadow over his cheekbones. Maybe because he wasn't thinking about all the things that dragged him down.

"Don't stop believing in me," he murmured at last.

She smiled, grateful his request was so easy. "I could never."

He brushed his thumbs over her temple to wipe away traces of the conditioner, then bent down, warm lips hovering over her chilled skin.

"Don't stop believing in yourself, either," he whispered, and kissed her forehead.

She crumbled beneath him, overwhelmed by the too-good-to-be-true promises in his words and the confidence he not only personified but built inside her. She'd wanted all of it from the beginning—and he was willing to give it to her.

Believing in both of them was the least she could do in return. "I won't," she managed to whisper back. "Promise."

TWENTY-TWO

Adrian

This feeling...a lightness eerily similar to hope.

It was too soon to be giving out promises, too soon to pretend to be someone he wasn't, but he couldn't leave Ivory with nothing when she'd laid herself bare.

When he truly wanted to give her everything.

It'd been so long since he looked forward to something like this. To be done with his past. To remove the lurking presence of an unknown killer in the corner of his thoughts and replace it with someone as good as her. With someone as sweet and responsive and beautiful beyond words arched underneath him as if it were the most natural thing in the world. If it came down to it, he'd burn down the world to earn his place at her side.

For now, at least she'd been upfront about her desires. Showing her the kind of pleasure she asked for would be all too easy and more than rewarding. Ivory was too compatible, too eager to be molded into a perfect doll, one he'd make sure to shower with praise well into the night.

Before they got to that point, he had to be in a position to keep his word. His burdens couldn't get in the way when she needed him, when her insecurities felt too daunting, or simply when she needed to laugh if the world got too grey. She shouldn't settle for anything less.

"You can sit up now," he instructed, breaking their trance as he helped her straighten out on the stool and wrapped a towel around her shoulders.

"Thanks," she said, cheeks flushed crimson.

He turned away and grabbed the hair dryer. "Almost ready to reveal the final result. I won't keep you waiting much longer."

"Finally." She twisted her hands in her lap. "I'm a little nervous. It's such a big change."

He chuckled. "I can always dye it back if you want, but let's see how you like it first."

Minutes later, her locks were blow-dried with a healthy sheen—and very purple. Ivory no longer needed a pointed hat to look like a magical witch. For the reveal, he had her close her eyes and stand with her back to the bathroom mirror as he got a smaller one and placed it in her hands.

He paused, admiring the trust she placed in him and the subtle way she tried not to bite her lip or the tiny movements under her closed lids as she fought the urge to peek. Would there ever be a moment when he didn't want to see her face?

"All right, open," he said.

Her eyes lit up, and she let out a little gasp, twirling to take in the new amethyst shade tumbling down her shoulders. "This is...amazing." She swirled left and right, running her fingers through her hair, then turned to face him. "I love it."

Unable to control himself, he smiled. That lightness from earlier magnified tenfold. "I'm glad you like it so much, and you do look rather amazing." Then he remembered one last detail. "Would you mind if I add something else?"

Her eyes widened like a little kitten being brought a new toy. "Sure, go ahead."

Nudging past her, he opened the cabinet to the right of the sink and brought out the ribbon his sister sent home with him.

It looked a few shades lighter than the dye but matched the hue and complimented her eyes.

"Turn around," he instructed.

She did as she was told, letting him gather a few strands from her face and braid them at the back, weaving in the ribbon as he went and tying it off with a neat bow.

The few perks of dealing with a sister when they were young were that Riley taught him to style hair—or rather forced him to help do hers—even before he started work at the salon. Of course, she experimented more than once on his own locks, but after she reached for the scissors the first time, he quickly learned to avoid such requests.

"Ah," he breathed, marveling at his work. "That's it. Here, take a look." He stepped out of the way so she could inspect it properly.

Ivory remained quiet as she tilted the mirror this way and that, her lips parted in what he hoped was a pleased expression. "It's perfect," she said at last.

Damn. How could she make him feel this proud over something so simple?

"It's so soft, too," she continued. "How did you do it?"

"Cold winter air and dry indoor heat will damage your hair. The conditioner I used helps and hopefully can prevent most of that." He walked into the kitchen to get the bottle. "The main ingredient is avocado oil. I use it myself."

"Oh," she said, following and taking the bottle to read the label. "Is your hair as soft as it looks?"

"Well, it should be," he replied, rubbing the stubble that had appeared over the last few days. Past time to take a razor to it.

Before he could catch on to her intentions, her fingers brushed up against his as she stroked the side of his jaw. Fuck. He forced himself to breathe normally—her touch felt feather-light, but it might as well have been an electrical shock with how it sparked through him.

"Ah," she hummed. "It must work if your stubble is that soft. I've never felt anything like it."

He turned away to resist the urge to put those hands of hers to better use. Show her that not every part of him was so soft. Clearing his mind, he started bunching up the plastic and cleaning up the rest of the supplies. "Take the rest with you. I can always get another bottle."

"Well, I—" She cut herself off and sighed. "Thank you again. I'll just have to bake you more cookies."

"I can't say no to that." He tossed everything except the brushes into the trash. After rinsing them, he turned to bring them to his desk, where he'd hopefully remember to take them back to the salon.

"Do you need a ride?" he asked when he saw her hovering by the door.

"Oh." She pulled her bottom lip between her teeth. "No, you don't have to go out of your way. Nia already agreed to drive me to the dorms."

"Didn't scare you off from riding the bike, did I?" he teased.

She looked down and laughed. "No, well...no more than I already was. Bikes and I don't usually mix. As in never—we never mix, and I didn't think I'd ride one again after..." She sucked in a quick breath. "After causing all those problems at the party."

Something similar to sadness, maybe longing mixed with guilt, flashed in her downcast eyes. One day, he'd make sure to chase away all those doubts, replace them with the pride she owed herself and with confidence that would let her shine even brighter.

"We'll have to remedy that someday," he said, lifting her chin with the pad of his pointer finger. "Get you and the bike more acquainted with one another." She didn't look thrilled at the idea but didn't refute it either. "Maybe you can teach me more about the stars, too?" he offered.

At that, she smiled. "Sure, I can do that."

"Sounds like a deal. Have a good evening, Iv." He nodded, expecting her to show herself out. Retreating to his bedroom, he set the brushes down and accidentally nudged the side of the mouse, waking the computer screen.

The police report flooded his vision and took over again. Now more than ever, he had to end this and find closure. No more digging until it was time to bury the past for good. He couldn't waste any more time in limbo.

Taking action was the only option left.

Skimming the details over again, one in particular stood out. One person had noticed a silver ring on the shooter's finger. Could've been a flash of the gun. Witnesses weren't the most reliable, but that didn't mean there was no credibility to it, either. How big would that ring have to be to be so noticeable? Hadn't he seen something like that before?

Sliding open the drawer, he grabbed the pack of cigarettes as familiar tension rose inside him and snuffed out Ivory's lingering effects. Damn, it would feel so good to let all the darkness out. To give it to the person who earned it instead of using cigarettes as artificial suffocation. To breathe in order to live instead of chasing death.

He snatched a lighter and walked out of the room to the porch but came to a stop mid-step as he closed the bedroom door.

Ivory was still here, looking at him as she shuffled on her feet.

TWENTY-THREE

Adrian

"Need something else?" he asked, torn between wanting her to stay and knowing she probably shouldn't.

Her face scrunched and then bloomed bright red as if he'd caught her doing something wrong. "I—uh, no. Unless there's something I can do for you? I mean—" She sucked in a breath, fiddling with the bottle of conditioner. "Let me start over. Can we be friends instead of not-strangers?"

From her guilty expression, she looked like she had just asked for his left kidney. He almost chuckled. Only a fool would turn down an offer like that. Then he groaned inwardly. *He* had been that fool. That's why she'd been nervous to ask.

"Yes, we can call it that," he answered and closed some of the distance between them, hoping the expression he wore looked nothing like the rejection or anger she'd expected. "As long as you know, I don't want, or intend, for it to stay that way."

If possible, her face flushed a shade brighter. "Yes! I don't, either—want it to stay that way. If that's okay with you." The rush of her words was too cute to bear.

His fingers tightened around the pack of cigarettes and crushed them. Why did he have to be trapped like this, unable to embrace her the way he desperately wanted without mixing her up in his shit?

Taking one dangerous step closer, he clarified, "I'll never be mad at you for asking a question or saying what you want. Don't hold that back from me, okay?"

She nodded. "Okay." Then she smiled. "I only want you to be as happy as you make me."

He froze. The air in his lungs vanished. Nothing could have prepared him to hear that.

He tried to regain the ability to function, unaware until after the fact that his thumb idly traced over her bottom lip. So plump and pink. Unimaginably soft.

Not touching her wasn't an option, apparently. But it wasn't helping—her silky skin and that expression written on her gracious features, the delicate dip of her cupid's bow in the sweetest strawberry shade—his thoughts rapidly collapsed into an utter train wreck, and worse, he couldn't bring himself to stop.

But the next thing she did incinerated the last of his restraint. Her tongue swept out to lick his thumb, tasting his skin before it disappeared back into her mouth.

The effects were intense and immediate. He'd never gotten this hard so fast. His gaze snapped up and honed in on hers, the same delicate jade doe-eyes he'd seen roaming over him much too often to be ignored. She knew exactly what she'd done, and it pleased him to see no trace of regret this time.

He tsked and whispered, "Soon, I'm going to put that tongue to good use." His tone deepened, low and measured. "But first, let me make one thing clear, sweetheart. Open your mouth."

Her eyes widened, pupils dilating, and ever so slowly, she parted her lips until that troublesome tongue of hers came into view. Fuck, if he got any harder, his dick was going to tear through his pants. And if he wasn't careful, he might just let it.

"This mouth was made for me, so perfect," he mused, pressing his finger inside and gliding over the back of her tongue, careful not to make her gag but intrusive enough to make her drop her jaw. She felt hot and slick, the ultimate temptation wrapped in the most beautiful form. "Made for my pleasure, just like the rest of you."

Her expression melted as he continued. "You already make me happy, sweetheart. I could spend hours listening to you tell me about the little things you think are insignificant. Watching your smile, seeing you get all hot and greedy for me—I'd gladly do it every day for the rest of my life. You could tell me I'm a piece of shit, and I'd thank you for it."

Giving her tongue one final caress, he slid out of her mouth to let her respond but didn't take his hand away. Not yet. A wet trail of saliva followed the path of his fingers to the curve of her neck, where he rested his palm around her throat so she'd feel the weight of his desire, of what it would be like to be his. "Now, do you realize what you do to me?"

She closed her mouth, swallowing before she spoke. Her throat moved under his hand, and his fingers danced over her skin to soak up every reaction.

"Yes," she said in a broken whisper, all her need and desire pouring out in that single, penetrating word.

He hardened his grip at the sides of her neck, her pulse steady as it thrummed into the tips of his fingers.

"Yes, what?" he growled, loosening his hold to release a rush of blood.

"Yes, sir," she corrected, a lilt to her voice that resonated deep inside his chest and took root in a place no one had reached before. Every part of her expression became etched with the same yearning and awe he'd felt for her from day one.

Leaning in, he hovered his lips over hers and spoke the only words she deserved to hear. "Good girl."

Then there was nothing. Nothing and everything all at

once. Nothing between their fervent mouths, no space nor air to breathe in the wake of their lips as they joined at last, while everything about her consumed him—the sugary sweetness on her breath, the supple texture of her lips, the heat of her tongue. The uninhibited moan as he claimed her mouth as his, biting into the forbidden fruit without a trace of remorse.

She kissed him back and parted like a flower in full bloom. The urgent press of her lips ebbed and molded with his own, both insatiable, both lost in a void of time that stretched on and on and on until his lungs burned and his lust burned hotter.

"Fuck being friends," he rasped, out of breath. "You're more than that. You're mine, Ivory, and I'll make damn sure you never forget it." Pulling away, he released her as she stared back at him, lips a dark red. "As soon as I'm certain I won't put you in danger, it'll be my turn to return all the care and happiness you granted me."

He released her neck and traced a finger over the rosy blush on her cheeks. But her eyebrows knitted as she searched his face. "Danger?"

Shit. Of course, that would make her worry. "It's nothing you have to be concerned about," he assured. "When it's all over, I'll tell you everything."

When he could finally be the man that she thought he was.

She frowned, but conceded. "As long as you're okay."

He gave her a confident nod.

"One more thing?" she asked.

"Anything." A dangerous answer, albeit a truthful one.

She smiled, still shy about speaking her mind but at least a little more inclined to do so. "What about those?" she asked, looking down at the crushed and forgotten box of cigarettes in his other hand. "Do they help...or make it harder to deal with things in the long run?"

He sighed, admitting the truth. "I've wanted to quit for a while. Then this thing came up, and I lost my momentum."

"Let me help," she offered, the hopeful spark in her eyes igniting.

"How do you plan to do that?" he asked.

"Use me instead." She wrung her hands around the bottle of conditioner, and he frowned. While he fully intended to use her, it wouldn't be as a method to dull his senses. Quite the opposite.

She hurried to explain, "Like, whenever you want to smoke, text me."

He hummed, considering her suggestion. "You're offering to become my new addiction?" he asked, choosing the words intentionally. "To clarify."

"Yeah," she breathed. "If you'll let me."

This woman.

He took in a deep breath, then picked out a single cigarette and handed the rest of the box to her. "I get my last supper," he said, looking over regretfully at the new box. "After this one, I'll text you. Don't answer if you're in class or if it's going to distract you."

Her face lit up. "Okay! I'll make sure to check between every class. You won't have to wait more than an hour, tops. Unless I'm sleeping, but then..."

"I won't text after midnight. Sound good?" All this excitement over something so small and mundane. It was adorable.

"Deal," she confirmed.

"All right, what about you?" he mused. "Do I get to choose a reason for you to text me?"

She peered up at him, awkwardly fitting her fingers around both the paper box and the bottle of conditioner. "If...you want to." She shrugged, but he saw how curiosity sparkled in her eyes. Any chance he offered to please him, she took it without question.

Such a very good girl.

He smiled. "This will certainly be helpful on my end, although I won't make it mandatory. Only if you're comfortable with it." Giving her a stern look, she nodded, and he continued. "Every time you think about me making you come, text me... and if you can, send a photo with it."

"I—" The rest of her words failed to form. By the look on her face, he could tell she'd already thought of him that way on multiple occasions. About time he got in on at least some of the fun.

"Okay," she said at last. "I agree."

"I'm looking forward to it." A little too much so. "Are you sure you don't need a ride?" They'd spent more time together than expected, and he didn't want her trying to walk back to avoid causing trouble for her friend.

She glanced past him out the window, where darkness had crawled over every part of the town save a strip of deep blue sky. "It's not a bother? I don't want to disrupt your studies."

He shook his head and reached for his jacket. "Another thing we have to work on. If you want me to use you, you have to get used to using me too, okay?"

She laughed. "Well, when you put it like that, it sounds reasonable." She turned to look at him from under her lashes, watching as he zipped up the jacket and grabbed his helmet. "Also...this might lead to me having to text you as soon as I get back."

Having Ivory on his bike again, their proximity paired with an acute awareness of her warmth and the depth of her desires, made a cold shower imperative before he sat down to write that stupid essay.

Not getting the text had made it even worse.

Closing the five-page document he had managed to grind

out in two hours, he gave up on finishing the essay and started browsing the web for purple bike helmets. The distraction only lasted so long, and as he checked his phone again, he noticed how late it had gotten.

11:11. A good omen? Maybe, or maybe that was a myth, but he decided it was as good of a time as any to text his little witch.

> Sleep well, Iv. Thank you for today.

He didn't wait for an answer and instead went out on the porch to smoke his last cigarette while gazing up at the stars.

Stepping out of her comfort zone wasn't going to be easy, and he hadn't fully expected her to agree to his proposition, but now that she'd gotten cold feet, he couldn't help but be disappointed. Not in her, but rather in the fact that he wasn't more available. This would be so much better if they could spend more time together in person.

Tomorrow night, he'd take care of all that. Get to the bottom of his need for closure and rid himself of this curse for good. He knew he'd seen an obnoxiously large silver ring recently, and when he placed it with a face, the owner happened to be the one person who conveniently had ties to Red Dragon. Someone he had no issue beating up.

Jace.

Which meant that for a little while longer, it was crucial he didn't hang around Ivory where Jace or his friends would see. Anyone trying to get in his way would pick her out as an easy target, which was the last thing he wanted.

TWENTY-FOUR

Adrian

The next morning, he woke up to several texts from Ivory.

He smiled, wondering if she knew how much she'd revealed. *Some* punishment, but not all of it? Whether she meant it as a subtle hint or not, he wasn't about to miss the implication. Being a good girl all the time was difficult—even for his sweet witch, who he had no doubt could be just as naughty as she was nice.

The photo she attached looked like it'd been taken in her dorm, presumably before leaving for class that morning. She'd used the ribbon to tie back a section of side-swept bangs and done her makeup with sparkly eyeshadow. Even with foundation, faint dark circles hung under her eyes. Perhaps it was better that he hadn't had the chance to keep her up.

However, her smile looked more radiant than ever, and whether that had something to do with the new hair color or their new dynamic, he loved to see it. He saved the photo to his phone and sent a reply.

> Good morning, beautiful.

> I hope your studies were fruitful, remember to reward yourself.

> I also see you're eager for punishments, that's good :) The picture you sent is particularly sweet, so I won't be harsh. Answer this, and you'll be in the clear: what about riding my bike turns you on?

Of course, a punishment wasn't really called for. Her end of the deal hadn't been mandatory, but since she mentioned it, he decided to play along.

Either way, he'd planned to ask her about the bike. He'd been surprised when she admitted it had such an effect on her, but he suspected something from the beginning. Could be the adrenaline, or maybe she enjoyed being afraid and knowing he'd still keep her safe, but he wanted to hear it in her own words.

She was probably in class at the moment, so he set the phone aside and started getting ready for the day. His only lecture would begin in an hour, and after that, he had work until dinner time. Then, once it was nice and dark out, he'd set things into motion.

A text came in as he sat down with a fried egg and some toast for breakfast. Luckily, it was from the only person he wanted to hear from.

Good morning yourself, handsome <3

For the reward, (since you insisted) I bought a hot chocolate. Hold on, I'll send a pic. They made a cute design with the creamer. And I'm not…eager. Maybe a little, but only because it's coming from you.

Forget I said that.

About the bike thing…I like being close to you. It's like my fate is in your hands.

His lips twitched. Forgetting was the last thing he'd do when it came to her.

He pondered the last message she sent. So, she was a true submissive—aroused by letting go of control. She also wanted the chance to be obedient and know the rules would be enforced. Several scenes came to mind, and he stored them all for later.

Giving her his full attention was going to be fun as hell.

But it was important that she got over being so strict with herself. Trying to live up to impossible standards would only make it harder for her to excel, and he'd rather she worked towards her own goals instead of what she thought others expected of her.

A photo of her hot chocolate came in; a fancy heart swirled into the froth like she'd mentioned. He wished the picture included more of her than a gloved hand, but he saved it regardless and then snapped a photo of his boring plate and sent it along with a reply.

I like to hear that, all of it. My food is less cute, but it does the job.

I'll make you cute food someday.

> You'll be my cute food someday.

Her response had made him smile, and his chest warmed when she sent a blushing emoji.

> Have you had any cravings to smoke?

> Nothing too bad.

> I'm going to keep myself busy tonight to keep my mind off it.

Or to let off some steam. It was a win-win as far as he was concerned. Not so much for the other party involved, though.

> About time for me to leave for lecture. I might not be able to talk much for the rest of the day, but I still expect you to hold up your end of the deal.

> Okay. Stay warm, it's freezing outside!

> Will do. You too.

> <3

She sent a purple heart back, and a weight settled on his chest as he closed their messages.

Cold or not, he had no choice but to ride his bike to campus. He'd used all his savings to buy that beauty, and nothing had been left over to maintain a car. No regrets.

Heated seats would've been nice, though.

As the sun set and dusk took over the snowy roads, even his

thick leather felt more like a piece of paper. He cut the engine off a block away from Beta Rho and rolled his bike behind a cluster of evergreens, careful not to leave a scratch.

The snow sparkled and his footfalls crunched on the unshoveled sidewalk. Most of the lights were on inside the house, but it didn't look like they had a crowd tonight. It was probably a casual evening full of the brothers and their personal guests. The back porch had been abandoned to drifted snow piles, much less inviting than the last time he'd been here. A handful of voices drifted out of cracked windows framed with red string lights.

He wondered why Jace would waste his time with a bunch of privileged brats who didn't give a shit about true brotherhood—but then again, this was Jace, the precious baby who could inherit the Yu legacy without lifting a finger.

Everyone knew their father gave Jun all the real work, which left Jace with enough freedom and leniency to wind up here. Flaunting expensive jewelry and wearing the club's symbol like a runway model was clearly more important to him than learning the family business. With all that partying, Adrian doubted a college degree would teach him what he actually needed to know, especially with the underworld.

All the better for him, though. Jace was close enough to the Dragons to know things he shouldn't and foolish enough to spill details he didn't realize were significant. Like who gave him that ring.

It might not be much of a lead, but it was something, and at the moment, that was all Adrian needed.

Creeping around the side of the house, he spotted Jace's uncovered bike parked next to the red Mercedes he drove in the winter. What a waste. The bike would be rusted by spring. Silver skull accents on the handlebars were unpolished but still gleamed in the faint light, and the dark red stones set into the eye sockets glared back at him. Red and black leather covered the seat and a small pack on the side, protecting at least some of it from the elements.

A damn nice bike, one that must cost twice as much as his.

With a solid kick, he sent it crashing to the ground. The metal clanged against the Mercedes and left behind a decent-sized scar. Someone shouted from inside, and the blinds rustled on a nearby window.

Ducking behind a tree trunk, Adrian hid out of sight and waited.

"Shit, man, it's the bike," a voice called out from the back door, cracking it open enough to let out a sliver of light.

"Fuck," another replied. "Jace! Someone fucked with your shit!"

"Hey man, I'm not sticking around to catch the blame," the first said. The second cursed and replied something indiscernible, then their heavy footfalls raced up the stairs. Left hanging on its hinges, the door swung open as a gust of air swept through the yard. Snow blew across the deck and whipped past Adrian's face.

Then the door slammed against the siding of the house, and Jace marched outside with a string of curses. His hands balled into fists, displaying three silver rings, one bigger than his largest knuckle and plenty easy to spot despite the dim light.

A tall blonde appeared in the door frame, pulling a sweatshirt down her arms. "Jace, what happened?"

"Fucking hell, Serena. Get inside," Jace spat, squatting down in the snow to right the fallen bike. "I didn't ask for your help."

She huffed and slammed the door shut, leaving him alone.

Just what Adrian had been waiting for.

"Aw *fuck* no," Jace hissed, his attention now on the Mercedes. "Fucking dammit, he's gonna murder me."

"Looks like someone's toys got a little damaged," Adrian

said, moving out of the shadows enough for Jace to see half his face.

"Son of a bitch," Jace cursed, turning away from the vehicles to stomp over. Razed hair exposed a vein on the side of his temple. "You're gonna fucking pay for this."

Jace cracked his knuckles. Adrian laughed under his breath. A flash caught his eye, the details of the large ring now clearer. A serpent clinging to a red gemstone.

"No one touches my property," Jace snarled, curling his lip. "Especially not you."

Adrian stepped back and led them both further under the trees. "Too bad. Looks like I already did."

"Don't think I forgot about last time—payback's a bitch." Jace lunged forward with the first swing, but Adrian dodged. Fighting blinded by rage wasn't much better than being drunk and high.

"Pretty boy thinks he can have anything he wants, doesn't he?" Adrian taunted, ducking to the side. A little fun before the real questions never hurt anyone.

Jace's eyes narrowed. "You think because you got my sloppy seconds, that makes you better than me?"

Damn.

Him.

Jace threw another punch, but this time, Adrian moved faster. He took a minor hit to the side of his face and his own fist collided with Jace's front teeth. He hissed, lungs filled with frigid air.

That felt good.

They both took a step back before swinging again. With every punch, Adrian made sure to hit harder than the last. But Jace refused to back down, as he'd expected. Hot blood dripped from his nose, the metallic taste settling in his mouth as they exchanged blow for blow. Soon, both were panting, pain radiating up his fingers to his arm. Adrian tightened his fist and went for an uppercut.

Using the shadows as cover, Jace twisted and grabbed Adrian's arm before the hit could connect.

The air got knocked from his lungs as Jace threw him to the ground. A flurry of snow scattered at the impact, the cold biting into his neck and back. Another searing pain exploded in his abdomen, and he struggled to regain his bearing.

"Pathetic fucker," Jace growled, unleashing another brutal kick. "Know your damn place."

Adrian coughed up blood and turned on his side, fingers clawing into the ground. He had enough strength to stand but didn't waste the energy. This was the perfect time to get the information he came for, right when Jace thought he had the advantage. Men became their weakest when they thought they'd won.

"Your ring," he rasped, forcing one knee underneath his body and moving a hand closer to the top of his boot, where he kept his blade. He didn't intend to use it and would rather walk away like last time, but he didn't have to worry about Ivory getting hurt and wasn't about to take any chances if things got ugly. "Where'd you get it?"

Jace snorted, inspecting the silver that decorated his hand. "Can't help but grovel for what you'll never have, I suppose."

"Who gave it to you?" Adrian demanded, earning him another kick to the side. He grunted as he dug the heel of his boot into the dirt, bracing against an exposed tree root.

"Shut up," Jace ordered. "You want to know about the ring?" He bent down, sneering as he waved the silver dragon in front of Adrian's face. "It's a symbol of who I am, of my family, and what we've done—what we can do. Our rule is ordained, and anyone who gets in our way will pay with blood. It means I could kill you right now, and no one would know. No one would care. I bet they wouldn't even find the body."

So that's what the ring meant—a family emblem. The killer hadn't been just a Red Dragon. They'd been a Yu.

Adrian's fingers brushed the handle of the knife, but he had to hold back. Better to let Jace think he won. Lose the battle, win the war—pride was a small price to pay for knowledge.

"Too bad you're not worth my time." Jace tsked and stood up. "Freeze to death for all I care, but the next time you try to fuck with me" —another hard kick came toward his face, but Adrian moved his arm to block just in time— "will be your last."

Snow crunched as Jace walked away, then the bike rattled as Jace set it upright, and finally, the back door opened and shut.

Steam curled from Adrian's cracked lips and melted the ice crystals in front of his face. After another minute, he got up and brushed himself off, then turned to walk back to his bike. Pain shot through every cell in his body. He let out a gruff laugh.

Fuck.

Everything hurt.

One thing was certain—when Ivory found out about this, she might beat him up worse than Jace had.

TWENTY-FIVE

SHE WASN'T GOING TO CHICKEN OUT AGAIN.

Homework had been a priority last night, but today she had no more excuses. Time to hold up her end of the deal.

She hated to admit it, but thinking about Adrian had become a nightly occurrence. Not that all her thoughts were explicit, but after their most recent conversations...a lot of explicit things had been on her mind.

As he'd said, Adrian didn't reach out again after their mid-morning texts. But that hadn't stopped her from picking up her phone the whole day, then promptly putting it down. The goal wasn't to disturb him, even though she felt the need to ask if he was okay.

She didn't want to bring up his lack of cigarettes if he'd purposely kept himself busy. Then there was how he mentioned putting her in danger. It'd been floating in the back of her thoughts since yesterday. Did that mean *he* was in danger? What kind?

Whatever it was, he could handle it. Or so she hoped.

Ivory sighed, closing out all the open apps on her phone and set it aside. Enough lazing around. Using some of this pent-up energy to pick out a good outfit might help. If she wanted to send an actual, *sexy* photo, it would take a little forethought.

Her current choice of clothing, sleep shorts and a tank top, didn't look bad, but they didn't have the wow factor she wanted.

This couldn't be just any photo. It had to be *the* photo. The one *he* looked at if…if…

A flare of heat rose on her face despite the dorm's overactive furnace. The mere possibility of Adrian getting himself off to the thought of her felt unreal.

Not that she wasn't aware most humans masturbated, but the thought of his rough, scarred hand dragging down his zipper and wrapping around his dick, his deep moans while picturing her in his mind—

She rolled off the bed, the heat from earlier now blooming between her legs. Better get the logistics out of the way before she got too worked up. Even though he'd given the okay to fantasize about him, encouraged it even, she shouldn't get too carried away.

It would be fair to ask for a photo in return, right?

Shuffling across her fuzzy purple rug, she walked over to the dresser and slid out her underwear drawer. Nothing extraordinary there.

The closest thing she owned to 'sexy' was a bra that had little jewels sewn between the cups and a thong she'd gotten as a white elephant gift. Her top half didn't have much to offer in the boob department, and that bra in particular dwarfed what meager assets she had, so she opted for the thong and decided to focus on the waist down.

Did people pose for this stuff? What about proper lighting? Being an amateur model took way more work than she anticipated. Then again, she shouldn't overthink. He hadn't specified what to include in the photo, and this may already be going a bit overboard.

Ugh.

She grabbed a pair of purple nylon knee-high socks and one of the shortest dresses she owned, a dark sundress that flared at her waist and threw it all on the bed. Whatever. Just because she'd never found out what Victoria's special secret was didn't mean this couldn't work out the way she wanted.

After dressing up, she clicked off the main overhead light and plugged in the string of purple bulbs she'd gotten on sale after Halloween. They glowed around her floor-length mirror, casting a mystic hue over her skin. Her skin had always been chalk-white, but she looked downright supernatural in this light.

Pulling her hair out from behind her shoulders, she made a few mock expressions using the shadows to twist and distort her features. Ah, yes, much more witchy than before. The lights accentuated her new hair color, almost as if she had become a monotone of purple. She smiled and couldn't help but laugh out loud at her antics. Maybe being a cute witch wasn't so bad after all.

The ribbon Adrian put in her hair hung off the side of her desk, and she reached over to grab it. Biting her lip, she threaded it between her fingers, remembering how his hands felt as they weaved through her hair. How secure she'd felt with them wrapped around her throat and the fresh taste of his skin on her tongue.

She thought Jace had ruined the act of guys taking pleasure from her mouth, but Adrian had been so gentle, so authoritative without overstepping. One finger almost hadn't been enough.

Caught up again in dark thoughts, she tied the ribbon around her neck like a choker and took a few photos for herself. Her old profile photo looked outdated anyway.

With a deep breath, she settled into a comfortable position on her knees and spread her legs a few inches; enough to see where the thong curved over her pussy lips, but leaving ample shadow to cover the details. She giggled mischievously—he'd just have to undress her in person to see the rest.

The best method turned out to be using a timer and propping the phone against the mirror. After a few takes, she got a photo that turned out decent enough. Of course, then she tried to adjust it with filters but gave up after five minutes of wasted time. If only she could find a way to see his reaction when she sent it.

But first, something else needed to be taken care of.

She squirmed as she set her phone aside and slipped back into bed. All this prep had done the trick, and it wasn't hard to tell how wet she'd gotten. The sheets were soft and cool as she leaned into her mountain of pillows, then she closed her eyes and relinquished her mind to the darkness.

A fantasy formed in her subconscious. Her hands became bound above her head, tight enough that she couldn't wiggle or turn her wrists. A breeze caressed her skin, hardening stiff nipples and revealing a slickness dripping down her thighs— arousal from being stripped, bound, and blindfolded, strung up from the ceiling for her Sir to inspect.

Slow, steady footsteps echoed in a circle around her, and Adrian's quiet hum filled the air. She breathed him in, nutmeg and a warm, light musk that wound through her core.

His hand brushed down her side, the metal of his rings cold as he stroked her hip. "Very good, Iv."

Her real hand followed the movement, then traced back up to pinch her nipple.

"Thank you, sir," her alternate self replied, gasping as he pinched her harder than she dared to do herself.

"Will you be a good girl for me?" he asked, continuing to play with her breast in tantalizing movements. His mouth closed over the other nipple, teeth pulling taut before using his tongue to soothe the ache.

"Yes, sir," she moaned, trying her best not to writhe under his increasingly teasing touch.

He withdrew, and she wanted to scream and beg for more—but she didn't. She waited, breath bated, listening for the slightest clue.

"Let's find out." He thrust a finger inside her, and pleasure shot through her core. Her legs buckled, but she didn't dare squirm, didn't dare make a sound for fear of punishment. Her real finger moved inside herself as fantasy Adrian pumped in and out, increasing the intensity to test her breaking point.

"Don't you dare come," Adrian growled.

He circled his thumb around her clit, spreading her open as her real hand did the same. She'd barely begun to touch herself, and already, she'd gotten soaked. Every touch grew more intense, her body trying to arch off the bed as she forced herself to stay still.

Adrian hummed in approval, the sound sliding over her skin and resonating in her bones. "Excellent. You are marvelous. Take your reward."

Yes...so close...so very, *very* close.

Wait. She stopped. Was she supposed to text him before or after she came? Was she supposed to come at all? Did she need permission from the real Adrian?

It was almost too painful to retract her hand, but she did. Opening her eyes to break the illusion, she looked around for her phone.

Better to ask.

Her clit throbbed in protest as she hurried to select the best photo and then sent it off along with a quick caption.

> May I please come, sir?

TWENTY-SIX

As soon she hit send, panic flared in her gut. She'd really done it.

Oh no, what if she'd gone too far? What if she wasn't supposed to ask without a proper agreement?

She groaned and tossed her head back into the pile of pillows. What a self-sabotaging decision. Now, she had to wait for a response before she got any relief.

Finishing the job would be easy enough, but now that she'd gone and asked, she couldn't. Stupid inner masochist, making up her own rules.

She glanced at the clock. If five, no—if ten minutes passed without a reply, she'd assume he didn't see the message. That should be reasonable.

Just as she took note of the exact time, her phone buzzed. Scrambling, she almost flung it across the room as she opened the message.

SIR ADRIAN

No.

...No? What did he mean, no?!

Adrian had never been brief when texting, and *this* had to be one time he decided to give a one word reply?

Anger boiled under her skin, mixing with confusion and the unbearable ache between her legs. Seconds ago, she'd been prepared to wait a full ten minutes. But now that he'd outright denied her orgasm, she wanted it all the more. Her fingers hovered over the screen, utterly lost about what to type.

Then, her phone lit up with an incoming call.

A hint of relief flooded through her, followed quickly by a tidal wave of adrenaline. If she didn't know how to respond to his message, a live call would be ten times worse.

But need outweighed uncertainty, and she swiped the answer button.

"Um, hi," she whispered, letting her eyes adjust to the dark room as she held the phone to her ear.

"Did you come yet?" The smooth tenor of Adrian's voice accompanied his demand and reignited the embers that had dulled during her moment of shock.

"No," she answered, grateful her patience held out.

"Good girl."

She let out a breath and melted into his praise. Every bit of self-induced anxiety had been worth it.

"What do I do now?" She squirmed, unable to lie still but not having gained the permission she needed.

"Do you mind staying on the phone?" he asked. "I've been dying to talk to you all day, then when I saw that photo..." He groaned, a low, broken whisper of a curse, but it was ten times better than she'd ever imagined. "I needed to hear your voice. If you prefer to talk after you finish, I can do that too."

"It's okay," she whispered, stretching her legs back out under the sheets, even wetter now from hearing his voice. "I want to stay on the phone. It's just...I've never done this before. The whole phone-sex thing."

"Neither have I."

His admission came as a surprise, but when she attempted to laugh it came out as a whine. Thinking was next to impossible in her current condition. She reached down to trace slow circles over her swollen clit, throbbing for release. "I'm so close."

"Tell me what you were thinking about," he rasped, breaths heavy on the other end of the line.

She wished she could see him, could do more than helplessly conjure an image that did his real form no justice. "Are you..." She paused, blushing at her next words. "Are you touching yourself too?"

"Yeah," he whispered.

She stifled another moan and pressed against her walls until a fresh wave of lust consumed her. "I thought about that, you getting off. What your dick would look like in your hand, how hard it would get just before you come."

"Shit, Iv. It's taking all I have not to," he said. "When I finally have you to myself, all my pleasure will be yours and yours alone. I'm saving it all for you."

"Wait, you're not going to come?" she gasped, trapped under the weight of holding herself back.

He chuckled at her bewilderment, then groaned as if he were really in pain. "I'll survive. You're the one who earned it, sweetheart. Not me. But when I do come, I'm going to fill you. When I'm done, you'll be so cum-drunk and so full, bursting at the brim for me. I'm going to claim every inch of you and leave a mark no one else can undo."

The scene filled her mind, spilling out into physical sensation as vivid as he painted it. Would he really save himself for her? Wait until he couldn't bear it and give her all of him when she was ready?

Her body pulsed, reacting to the idea of his release deep inside her. She rubbed harder at the ache.

"What else were you thinking about?" he asked.

"Being tied up," she breathed. "You wanted me to behave, to be good, and earn my rewards."

He groaned. "You did so well today. Sending me a sexy as fuck photo and sharing your dirty secrets. I'm so proud of you."

"Adrian," she pleaded, unable to stop herself a second time as her clit swelled under the stroke of her finger, her walls clenching down like a vice. The desperation in her voice rang out embarrassingly clear, giving away exactly how helpless she'd become. If he didn't let her come soon, she might break for real.

"Come for me, Iv," he ordered. "And let me hear your pretty cries as you do."

"Ah, Adrian—" Her words flowed out in an incoherent string. The climax hit like a freight train. Her body hummed, vibrating as her thighs snapped shut around her hand. She dropped the phone amidst the onslaught of pleasure, and it landed on the pillow as Adrian talked her through it.

"That's it," he praised. "Don't stop, ride it out." He whispered unending praises in her ear, told her how hard he'd gotten from her voice and from picturing her sweet cunt, how perfect she was, how good she'd taste when he buried his face between her legs.

A final sigh left her lips as the torrent of sensation ended, and she floated back to earth, limbs heavy and sinking into the mattress. She let out a soft giggle, caught in the afterglow and the reality that Adrian had not only called her but given her the best orgasm of her life—without even being here.

"Your laugh is so beautiful," he murmured.

Goodness gracious, this boy. He was going to make her heart burst.

"So..." she whispered. "What now?'

"Now I burn the sound of you coming into my mind and find a way to survive until I get to experience it in person."

She groaned. "How is that just as embarrassing as it is sexy?

Let's talk about something else—how was your day? Did staying busy distract you?"

"It, uh..." He paused, searching for words. "I'm pretty sure the best part of my day was the past five minutes."

She rolled her eyes, glad he couldn't see. But she had to admit that the past five minutes were also the best part of her day. "You haven't bought any more cigarettes, have you?"

"No, I'm clean," he replied. "And I don't think I'll be going to the store anytime soon, either."

Relief fused with the endorphins flooding her brain. "Why not?"

"Gave myself a bit of a workout tonight," he answered, then grunted as she heard him change positions. "I'll be feeling it for the next few days, at least."

She sighed. "Endorphins do help, I guess. Just don't push yourself too hard."

"Tell me about your day," he asked, changing the topic. "I want to know everything I missed."

Smiling, she began to tell him about her mundane classes and study routine, then got interrupted by a huge yawn. "You drained all my energy," she teased.

He hummed proudly. "We both need some rest. Call me tomorrow when you're free."

"Okay." She hated to go, but sleep was going to happen whether she liked it or not. "Sweet dreams," she whispered.

"You too," he whispered back. "Goodnight, Iv."

Reaching over a pillow, she went to set the phone on her desk but noticed he hadn't hung up. Her eyelids began to slide closed as she waited, watching the phone screen.

If he wasn't going to hang up, then she wasn't either. And as sleep descended, it felt a lot like being cradled in his arms.

TWENTY-SEVEN

Ivory

> You can spot this one—Orion the Hunter.

> He's one of the brightest constellations this time of year, or at least his belt is pretty clear. Look southwest for three big stars in a line.

> On dark nights, you can even see a blob underneath. That's the Orion Nebula, the closest active star formation area to our universe.

SIR ADRIAN

Looking for a heavenly belt, are we? Is that a hint?

> Maybe. I've heard it can make a girl see stars.

FYI, my belt can do the same thing.

Okay, I think I found it.

SHE SMILED AS SHE REREAD THEIR CONVERSATION FROM LAST night, especially Adrian's response.

Almost every other day this week, she'd fallen asleep

talking to him—and, as a consequence, had overslept this morning and nearly been late for the first lecture. Now that class was over, she sent him a quick message but knew he wouldn't reply immediately.

Turned out that telling him about her schedule meant he wouldn't distract her during Avril's study group. It *had* been helpful to meet up with them twice a week, and some of them even took the same courses and could explain things much simpler than the textbook. Unfortunately, today, her mind was somewhere else.

Adrian had officially gone six days without smoking. With each new day, she grew more concerned about an impending crash. Quitting wouldn't be as easy as he made it seem, and she wouldn't let him do it all alone. If nothing else, she'd show up at his door this weekend armed with a plate of cookies.

But for now, she stuffed her phone into her coat pocket and geared up to brave a blizzard. Unlike grade school, college didn't offer leniency for inconvenient weather, and an inch of snow had accumulated so far this morning, with more on the way. Pulling out her gloves, she shuffled out of the lecture hall, took a shortcut behind the main buildings, and headed for the library. She missed the days when Nia and the others would study together at the dorms.

Thick, wet flakes stuck to her forehead, and streaks of purple hair whipped past her nose as she bowed her head to avoid the worst of the wind. Why did the biggest storms always hit right before spring—as if winter wanted to leave one last impression before releasing its iron grip? Trails of slush replaced the sidewalks, filled with imprints of boots that would freeze by nightfall.

The library finally came into view as she turned the corner. Curling her fingers, she puffed out a breath and quickened her pace. Then something—someone—grabbed her arm and yanked to the side.

Her back slammed against a brick wall, and the textbooks in her backpack dug into her spine. For a split second, her body refused to function, lungs frozen mid-breath as she tried to process what happened.

Jace's repulsive face came into focus, and the trance shattered. She wrenched her arm back, only for his fingers to dig in deeper. Fear rippled through her.

"Chill out, Ivory," he chided, a lazy smirk curling his lips from under a dark hoodie. He kept a jovial tone to sound friendly, but the glare from his black eyes told her he hadn't come to play. He wasn't going to just mess around this time. Something felt off—he had hurt her on purpose.

A half-healed cut above his eyebrow gave his face a sinister look, hair still shaved into the shape of a dragon. When he smiled, she noticed one of his front teeth had been chipped.

"Leave me alone," she hissed, wiping the hair out of her face as the wind whipped it right back.

"Let her go, Jay."

Ivory snapped her eyes over his shoulder to see Serena, a sympathetic look on her face as she shivered from inside a fur-lined jacket. "It's not like she's gonna run."

Jace seemed to agree, scoffing before he let go and crowded her against the wall. As he withdrew his hand, scars similar to the ones Adrian had crisscrossed his knuckles, the skin cracked and red from what must have been a recent fight. The imprint from his fingers throbbed, and she rubbed her arm furiously to get rid of his touch.

"Why'd you do it?" Jace asked, drawing her attention and pinning her with a cold-as-steel gaze.

"Do what?" She glanced over to Serena, pleading for help. Snow began to settle in a layer over her clothes, and she shivered down to her toes.

"Send your new boyfriend after us," Serena clarified.

"What?" Ivory asked. Surely they didn't mean Adrian, why would he—

"Don't play dumb." Serena stepped forward. "I know you and Nia have a vendetta against Jewelle, but sending Adrian to torment her cousin won't change the past with Caspian."

Was she talking about last semester? Hadn't that all been settled? Adrian would have told her if something new came up, wouldn't he? Ivory pressed herself into the wall, wishing she could disappear.

"I don't know anything," she said, glancing around. Most other students kept their heads straight due to the storm, unable to hear or see what was happening.

Serena clicked her tongue. "Well then. Maybe they left you out of it after all. I knew all along Nia coerced you into standing up for her."

"Nia and Caspian aren't out to harm anyone," Ivory insisted. "Despite confronting Jewelle, they don't want more drama, and neither do I."

"I couldn't care less what they want," Serena sneered. "But I'm just as capable of standing up for my man as Nia is."

"I'm sure Adrian got the message loud and clear when I left him bleeding out in the snow," Jace gloated with a smirk. "But you better tell your friends to back off."

Time froze. She couldn't breathe, couldn't think. When did —how long ago had Adrian been—oh no, was he still out there? Balling her fists, she choked down a sob and forced it to stay lodged in her throat. Jace didn't get to see her weakness.

But despite her restraint, his eyes tore into her, and his smirk grew as he saw behind her façade. Leaning forward, he whispered, "And if it happens again, I'll tell Serena just how much of a *friend* you and I were. I'm sure she'd love to know what you did behind her back."

No. No, he wouldn't—

Bile rose at the memory. The one night between them

happened long before Serena even wanted to get with him. They'd hardly met...

Serena's eyes shifted between them, and Jace leaned away. "Nice hair, by the way," he said, putting an arm around Serena. "You're welcome to show it off at Beta Rho, and we can teach you how good girls are supposed to behave."

Hot, searing anger melted the icicle of fear lodged in her chest. Of all people, *he* didn't get to use those words. Especially not with her. "I said *leave me alone*," she repeated, raising her voice and stepping closer to the main path.

Jace laughed, holding Serena close when she tried to turn away. "Actually, I think I like you better this way. A little feisty, like an adorable kitten with miniature claws."

"*Fuck off*," she shouted. His jaw clenched before she spun, putting as much distance between them as she could.

The exclamation caught the attention of a group of students heading into the library, and they all stopped to stare in her direction. She shrunk under their gaze, hating how vulnerable Jace made her feel.

A familiar brunette in a beanie separated from the rest and walked over. "Woah, are you okay?" Avril asked. "Was that Jace and Serena?"

"Yeah," Ivory replied numbly, rubbing her arms. She couldn't feel the cold anymore. Couldn't feel anything but Jace's eyes lingering on her back.

"It looked like he was harassing you. Should I call campus police?" she asked, looking over her shoulder.

"No—he was, but I'm sure he'll be gone by the time they get here." She hoped he had left already but wouldn't let herself look. Her fingers were trembling, curled into tight balls as her nails dug into her palms.

"Seriously, I don't know what Serena sees in him," Avril muttered as she started towards the library. "And it's freezing out here. Why would they want to talk outside like that?"

"Actually," Ivory mumbled, hesitating as Avril opened the door. "I have something else to do right now. I don't think I'll make it to the study session." Her chest constricted as if Jace physically reached out and hit her.

He'd certainly wanted to.

"I'll have to skip out on this one if you don't mind," she finished.

"Sure, no pressure." Avril looked her over with concern. "You take care of yourself. We'll see you next week."

"Thanks. See you then," Ivory put on her best smile and hoped it would put everyone else at ease. Avril didn't look convinced but stepped into the library with a final wave.

Ivory turned and walked the opposite way, sucking in a deep breath of ice-cold air. But soon the smile faded and tears resurfaced, hot and sticky on her cheeks. Her vision blurred with every step, the wind snapping at her face as she blindly navigated away from the crowds.

How pathetic. Jace was a jerk, the lowest of low. Yet he'd still gotten to her. He'd gotten to Adrian.

Little shudders from her chest grew into uneven gasps, and once she was alone, the brave exterior crumbled. She bent over and braced her hands on her knees, hating Jace and hating how he'd treated her like he could do whatever he wanted because she'd let him. Because he thought she was weak.

Maybe he was right. She certainly didn't feel strong.

His words replayed over and over, reminders of that awful night like a dark stain in her memory. And worse, the image of Adrian's blood seeping into the snow.

Nia and Caspian would never go out of their way to start trouble, and even if they did, they wouldn't send Adrian on their behalf. This only made sense if Jace made up a story to tell Serena, and his real goal had been to prove he could get anything he wanted—even her.

She ripped off her gloves and fumbled in her pocket for her phone, needing to see if Adrian had tried to contact her.

No notifications.

She hiccupped, fingers shaking as she navigated to his number. If she could only hear his voice. Just one word. Even if something bad had happened, she'd know it would all be okay if he picked up the phone.

The moment she dialed, the phone shut off. Her fist nearly crushed the useless device. Now was not the time for this! She pressed the power button harder, and the charge symbol appeared. The cold must have drained her battery.

Great. Flipping fantastic.

She swallowed, unable to break the lump in her throat. Then again, she had no reason to panic. The story could've been made up to scare her. Adrian wouldn't go down without a fight. Jace couldn't have beat him up and walked away with only a chipped tooth and some scratches...right?

Wrong. Jace would never fight fair, and Serena might be easily swayed, but she wasn't a straight-up liar.

She needed to see him. Now.

Where was he? Work? Class? She couldn't remember his schedule. What if he ended up in the hospital? She wiped her eyes and stood up straight. Glancing around, she spun in a circle as a pit formed in her gut. Nothing looked familiar.

Snow blew in every direction. Tall buildings in the distance became barely distinguishable, and a flat patch of land sprawled just ahead. Everything looked white except for a menacing iron gate that enclosed whatever was across the street.

Freezing *and* lost—what could she really do like this? She couldn't help anyone. There was no point in pretending she could make a difference. Something terrible had happened, and it was all her fault.

Her heart fell and then shattered into a million bleeding shards. If Adrian had been hurt, he wouldn't want to talk to her.

The storm blew her sideways with snow and ice, but she couldn't go back. She forced her legs to move, carrying her away from where she'd come. Away from her comfy dorm, away from the threat of Jace, and away from everyone she'd only disappoint in the end.

TWENTY-EIGHT

Adrian

D AMN WEATHER WAS COLD AS BALLS.

At midday, the sun should be bright overhead, but outside looked dark enough to be evening. He couldn't shake the constant chill even with a hoodie under his jacket. Large white flakes plummeted sideways before the wind swirled them up and blew them right back in his face.

How had he stood outside to smoke for the past five years without a care? How had he accepted being so numb?

Adrian rolled the last cigarette around his tongue—unlit— and looked down at a snow-covered grave. His father's headstone was newer than most, but it blended in all the same. A forgotten tick in an endless parade of departed souls.

On the other side of the cemetery, towering stone mausoleums and proper headstones rose from the barren field. Here, however, there were only small rectangles laid flat with the earth, some with engravings so worn they could hardly be made out.

He flexed his hand against the cold, mostly healed from the fight and marred by a few additional scars. Vera kicked him out of the salon as soon as she spotted his black eye. Apparently, customers didn't want to see an ugly stylist—but he knew she only wanted to look out for him, and his body needed the days off to heal.

In the end, he decided to get most of his classwork done from the apartment and hadn't left in a couple of days. Today, he woke up restless, and although this storm was brutal, a visit to the cemetery was long overdue.

Now that he'd obtained the right information, he didn't know what to do with it.

The way Jace talked about the ring...it sounded like an heirloom. Meaning that the ring meant more than a tie to the killer; it represented the Yu family itself. That shooting hadn't been a hit by the Dragons. It had been an assassination.

Family versus family, blood versus blood.

Cortez must've become a major threat, not just to Red Dragon, but to the family at the organization's core. Maybe his son had been his biggest weakness, the ultimate checkmate, or maybe Luke had shown enough potential to be as formidable as his father.

Maybe the shooter thought it best to take Luke's best friend out of the picture, too, just to be sure. But that boy had a father who actually paid attention, and he paid the price for it. Kassy had been an accident, her death as insignificant as an afterthought.

Maybe there wasn't any more sense to it than an exercise of power.

He hadn't expected a valid reason—he knew he wouldn't feel any sympathy for the one responsible, but this was bigger than he anticipated. Everyone else had come to terms with it, and now it all made sense. Who in their right mind would go up against the Yu's? Their wealth, combined with a throne of illegal drugs and weapons, meant they were unbeatable.

Knowing was as much of a burden as ignorance.

He puffed out a cloud of vapor that quickly vanished, then

removed the placebo cigarette. Maybe it was time to let go, whether he thought he could or not. People cared about him— even a sweet little witch who had no reason to. Surely, he could find purpose in that.

But if he spent any more time in this storm, he'd freeze to death before he got the chance. So he started the long walk back to his apartment.

Movement near the edge of the cemetery caught his attention. A lone figure staggered between graves; head held down as they almost tripped over a headstone. Who would be out walking in this? Chastised by its relentless frenzy, the snow and wind buffeted him forward. Whoever it was, they weren't his concern.

But something felt off.

He stopped to watch a little longer. It looked like a student, a backpack strapped over their hunched shoulders. Then, a gust of wind roared through the field, and purple hair whipped out of their hat.

Worry sliced through him like a blade, fast and deep.

"Ivory?" he called and took a step closer. Could it be? What on earth would she be doing—and why did she look like that?

His pace quickened. The figure turned toward him, and even from this distance, he recognized those jade eyes. But they were red and swollen, her whole face on the verge of frostbite.

"Fuck," he hissed, closing the gap between them. "Ivory!"

He grabbed her shoulders as she stared up at him. Then she burst into tears.

"It's true," she sniffed.

"Hey," he murmured, cupping her cheek and wiping away the wetness as it poured out. Shit, she was nearly frozen solid. "Talk to me. What happened? I swear if anyone hurt you—"

She broke out in a sob, unable to form proper words. "He really did it..."

Adrian pulled her face into his neck and tried to warm her

up. "I'm here. I'll keep you safe. Just tell me who did this to you."

"Jace said—"

He held his breath. That damn son of a bitch. He was going to pay for this.

But Ivory came first. Unzipping his jacket, he drew her into his chest and let her arms slide between the warm layers. "It's gonna be all right." He rubbed her back while shielding her from the storm. "Are you hurt? What did he do?"

She shook her head and clutched the fabric of his hoodie in her hands. "I'm okay."

"Oh, Iv," he muttered, holding her tight. How could he have let anything happen to her? Why had he been so focused on his own issues and left her to deal with hers alone? "I'm sorry," he whispered, rocking her back and forth as he stroked her icy hair. "I should have been there."

She shook her head again and pulled away to look at him. "No, it's my fault. I—" Her expression wilted, lips quivering as she raised her hand to trace his black eye. "You're the one who got hurt. He did this to get to me."

What?

"No, this had nothing to do with you, sweetheart," he reassured, pressing her hand to his cheek and warming her fingertips. "I promise I'm the one who provoked him. This was my fault."

Her face twisted. "Then did Nia and Caspian really—?"

"It had nothing to do with them either." Hell, what had she heard? "I'll explain, I promise, but after we get you warm and safe, okay?"

She searched his eyes, lingering over his bruise, and then nodded. "I just want to stay here a little longer."

"Okay," he said. "You're going to be okay." Her head fell to his chest, and she drew her first steady breath. At least that calmed her down. He let her relax, stroking her hair down to her back and focusing on the puff of hot breath on his skin.

She felt so good. Her heart beat against his, arms wrapped around his back, and sweet face nuzzled into his neck. So much better than anything he'd felt in the past five years.

"I've wanted to hold you for so long," he admitted quietly.

Her arms tightened, and he tried not to wince at the pain lingering in his left side.

"Why didn't you?" Her question sunk into him like barbed wire, so much more painful than the cracked rib.

"Because I'm a damn fool." He buried his face in her hair. "Because I knew once I did, I'd never be able to let go."

"Then don't," she whispered. "I don't want you to let go. Not ever."

"I won't," he whispered back.

Anger boiled like hot lava under his skin. The next time he saw Jace, there would be no talking. No discussions, not even a chance for a snarky insult.

He was going to ground that scumbag to a pulp.

"So that's why I thought it was my fault," Ivory finished, blowing on her cup of steamed milk and taking a delicate sip.

Adrian set his mug on the table, resisting the urge to chase down Jace right this minute.

Before leaving the cemetery, Ivory asked who he was going to visit and then made him stop at Luke's grave despite his insistence on getting inside. They paid their respects, and while they walked, he explained everything from the beginning. Everything about his dad, the shooting, and the dragon tile, including his fight with Jace.

Back at his apartment, she'd finished recounting the events that sent her spiraling. Color returned to her face, and now she sat snuggled on the couch against his side, warm and happy—just the way she should be. He'd held fast to his promise and hadn't let her more than an arm's distance away since their embrace in the graveyard.

"Do you really think he has the same ring as the shooter?" she asked after a pause. "Could it have been Jace who…"

He shook his head. "I doubt it. But there's probably more of those rings for different family members. Besides, Jace would have been in middle school when it happened, and while I'm sure he had access to a gun, he'd have to be a real prodigy to pull it off and not get caught."

Ivory snorted, then caught herself. "Sorry—it's not—nothing about this is funny." She sighed and looked away as her fingers circled the mug. "I don't see Jace being any kind of prodigy."

He wished he could laugh with her and take the whole thing as a cruel joke, but right now, all he wanted to do was teach the son of bitch a well-deserved lesson. Forcing himself to exhale, he rubbed at the permanent furrow in his brow. "As much as I want to storm over there and rip him into shreds, and as much as I wanted to get the bottom of my fucked up life history, I need you to know something."

Turning to face her, he took the mug out of her hands and set it down. "None of that is worth putting your safety at risk."

She met his eyes, the corner of her lips pulling into a frown he wished he could kiss away. "I was perfectly fine—"

"You weren't." He brushed a strand of hair back from her precious face. "Jace acted out of line because I provoked him, and you got hurt." If fate hadn't led them to each other in that graveyard, she could have ended up in a far worse situation. "I was trying to get this all taken care of before we got too involved. I didn't want my issues to become yours, but it's clear to me now that it's too late."

Her hand circled his wrist, warm and reassuring as she kept

his hand pressed to her face. "So what now? I can't ask you to abandon your search. Not when you've gotten so close."

He sighed and pulled her against him, bringing his lips to her forehead. "Sweetheart, I have to stop. We both know it."

"No." She pulled away. "I'm not going to let you do that. You can't give up because of me." Her words were as sincere as her undaunted expression, the same one she wore so many moons ago when he tried to walk away from her—and failed.

Conflicting desires warred inside him. On one hand, abandoning his quest for revenge would feel worse than getting punched by Jace. But he'd take it if that would protect Ivory.

"We just have to be more cautious," she continued, barreling ahead. "Before you say anything, I'm not making this out to be a glorified hero mission or pretending it's a movie where the good guys are guaranteed to win. But I can't live with the guilt of holding you back. I know there's a risk. I know I'll need to let you do all the work. Just pretend like I'm only here when you need me."

He leaned into the couch and dropped his hand to her waist, playing with the hem of her shirt. "First of all, I would never treat you that way." He switched to drawing small circles on the soft skin on her hip. "And second, if you weren't here, I wouldn't have had a future to look forward to. The things I'd be willing to do out of disregard for my own life aren't something I'm proud of."

"There has to be a middle ground," she argued, reaching for the free hand on his lap. He let her take it, much like he'd let her take almost anything if she asked. Her fingertips tenderly traced around his nicked rings.

"We don't have to come up with an answer tonight. Being smart means taking a step back and giving it proper thought." He wove his fingers between hers. No more unnecessary risks.

"All right." She leaned into his shoulder, eyes fixed on their hands. "As long as we find a way."

"I'll try. But I'm serious, Iv." He turned her chin to face him. "No matter what plan we come up with, the moment you tell me to stop, I will. I'm counting on you to say something before I go too far."

She nodded. "I will."

"Promise me."

"I promise." She began to roll her eyes but stopped halfway and bit her lip.

He pulled it free and ran his thumb along her jaw. "Good."

She held her breath, perfectly still under his touch. Perfectly obedient. Perfect in every way and then some. Dipping his head so their noses brushed, he inhaled her taste and let it tingle on the tip of his tongue. Let it override everything else on his mind until there was only Ivory. Then he closed the gap. Her lips melted like sprinkled sugar, sweeter than he remembered.

Fingers twisting into his hoodie, she pulled him closer as he deepened the kiss. This time, it wasn't rough or crazed but passionate and scorching, leaving a brand that cut to the very core. There was no part of her that didn't belong to him. No crime against her that would go unanswered. No hole in her heart that he wouldn't fill.

Her spine arched, and he pulled her onto his lap, pushing his fingers under her shirt and stretching them against her stomach. She shuddered underneath his touch.

He chuckled, leaving a sharp nip on her lips. "Next time you try to roll your eyes, I won't let you get away with it. You're lucky all I want is to enjoy being next to you until we have a proper discussion."

She sighed and snuggled into him after a few more lingering kisses. "And when will that be?"

"Soon," he answered. Things were already so different with her, but he still wanted to do it right. He always went over rules and limits before getting involved.

The light from outside had grown even darker. Outside, the snow started to drift against the porch door. "Hey," he said, breaking their momentary silence. "I don't think I'll be able to drive you to the dorms in this storm."

"I know," she replied. "I don't want to go back anyway, not yet. Is it okay if—" She paused, then hid her face.

"You're more than welcome to stay here if you'd like," he offered, answering her half-spoken question. As if he'd let her stay anywhere else.

"Thanks," she hummed, a smile peeking out as she looked at him through her lashes.

"In that case, let me put some food together," he offered. "Did you eat lunch?"

"No," she mumbled. "But I can cook. It's the least I can do for letting me stay the night. What do you have on hand?"

"I'm cooking," he affirmed in a tone that left no room for argument. "Let me take care of you for a change. Besides, you enjoy being taken care of."

"No," she protested, voice muffled in his arm as she shrunk into him. "I'm the one who enjoys taking care of *others*, remember?"

He knew all too well how insistent she could be. "I never said you didn't, but if you spend all your energy watching over everyone else, who's there to watch over you?"

She huffed, then stretched out and put her legs up on the couch. "Okay, fine. I should plug my phone in and see if I missed anything important. Do you have an extra charger?"

"Yeah, let me grab it." He started to get up, but her weight kept him from moving more than an inch. He smiled. "In a few minutes."

She groaned, snuggling into him again. "Yeah. In a few minutes."

TWENTY-NINE

AN HOUR LATER, CHICKEN SIMMERED ON THE STOVE, AND ITS delicious aroma wafted from the kitchen. Snow fell out on the balcony in thick flakes, but the apartment felt cozy, lit by a warm hue from the table lamp next to the couch.

Ivory tightened the blanket around her shoulders, one Adrian had pulled off his bed and stared at her phone screen. His scent washed over her, smooth, rich, and spicy. But distress knotted her insides.

She hadn't expected to see anything when her phone turned on. It'd only been off for a few hours, and people rarely texted her anyway...but it turned out those few hours were more important than she'd thought.

Three missed calls from her mom.

If that didn't have her sweating, it was followed by a text that sunk her spirits to a new low, accompanied by a screenshot of her latest profile picture. The one with her purple witch hair.

Adrian walked in from the kitchen, hair in a messy bun and holding one of the flavored margaritas she liked so much. But instead of perking up at the sight, she looked down at her lap.

"Everything okay?" he asked, setting the drink beside her.

"Yeah," she said but then shook her head. She couldn't lie to him.

Fitting himself into her cocoon, he wrapped her in his arms. That simple touch cast away some of her dismay, no longer stranded in a tower without a knight to save her. "What happened?"

She sighed. "I missed a call from my mom while everything happened earlier. Then she sent this."

She showed him the screen.

MOM

Too busy to answer a call from your mother, I see. I hope that means you're studying and not fooling around—especially not with whoever convinced you to do this to your precious hair! We are going to talk about this.

Adrian's brows knit as he read the message. "Iv, she shouldn't guilt you for dying your hair, even if she doesn't approve. Does your mom really think you'd neglect your studies when you've been working so hard to do well?"

She shrugged. "I don't mind her worrying about my studies. She's always been that way. I just don't know how to tell her I needed a change. Or explain that it was my idea in the first place. She wouldn't get it."

"She doesn't have to get it. It's not her choice to make," he said. "If she reacts this way to a photo, I can understand how bringing it up would be hard. Has she always pressured you so much?"

"Mom pressures everyone." She didn't mean it as an accusation. That was just the way things were. She rested her head on Adrian's shoulder. "It's because she sees potential in me, and it's pushed me to be a lot better than I would have been otherwise."

"I assume you haven't told her about Jace, and she wouldn't understand why you couldn't answer the call."

She shook her head. "No, my family are the last people I'd want to know. Mom would..." She cut herself off. If her mom knew all the details, she'd be outright disowned. Her straight-laced Ivy League ex had been the only kind of guy her parents approved of. Not that she would vouch for Jace, but the things she'd asked for, or the reason she'd entertained him in the first place...

Her mom would blow a gasket if she knew the kind of things her daughter wanted in a relationship. Cutsie girl talk had never been a part of their dynamic.

"I don't want them to see me as a failure," she whispered into Adrian's sleeve. "Not that the color of my hair matters, but I've never been able to bring home first place or win a scholastic competition or been good at literally anything other than taking up space."

"Ivory."

She looked up, eyes beginning to swell with the threat of another round of tears.

"You're good at a lot of things." He leaned over, caging her in with his arms. His stance left no room for her insecurities, and her frantic heart slowed down. She sucked in a deep breath. He leveled his gaze to hers. "You may not see the value in who you are—in everything you do—but I've seen it. You're smart and strong and sexy and one of a kind. There's a million reasons why I don't want to be with anyone else."

The gold ring around his pupils gleamed before he ducked his head, lips skimming along her neck. "When I think about making you mine, it drives me wild. Not because I want the sex—I want that too, in every way imaginable—but more than anything, I want *you*."

Her pulse heated against his mouth, the rough scratch of his stubble igniting her senses.

"One day, I'm going to make sure you never question yourself again," he whispered.

With him, she believed it. He could make her feel things no one else had, help her see things no one else could. Nothing seemed out of reach in his arms. Her deepest desires weren't a threat anymore, rather a promise. He made her entire being come to life, and instead of guilting her for trivial things, he praised her for earnest qualities.

She turned into his touch, wanting to drown in it until the only air left to breathe was what he granted her.

The kitchen timer dinged, and she nearly jumped out of her skin. Adrian let out a low, rumbling chuckle. "Talk about being saved by the bell."

She exhaled, heart pumping out of control. "Yeah..." Her voice dissolved into a trembling mess, and she steadied herself. "Except this time, I'm not sure I wanted to be saved."

"Don't worry, sweetheart," he groaned into her shoulder. His teeth grazed up her neck, then sunk into her earlobe. "You won't be safe for long."

She shivered, and he pulled back with a darkness in his eyes that could devour her whole. "Time to eat."

She gulped, nodding. "Yeah."

A grin curled his lips—predatory like his appetite had brought him to the brink of starvation—and she was his next meal.

He turned and went into the kitchen. "We can eat on the couch if you like. Watch a movie. It's been a long day, and you deserve to relax."

Relax wasn't what she wanted to hear at the moment, but he'd said the magic word, so she reached for the remote. "I know the perfect movie."

Adrian returned with two plates in hand and set one on her lap. Her stomach growled at the sight—chicken piled over a bed of rice covered in thick, spiced sauce. She'd forgotten she never had lunch. "This looks amazing."

"I should record you saying that and send it to my sister."

He grinned as he sat next to her, a boyish expression that she wouldn't have expected but instantly wanted to see more of. "She'd be astonished that I cooked anything worthy of eating."

Ivory laughed. But then the thought of meeting his family stuck in the forefront of her mind. Would that ever be a thing? Would he ever get to meet hers? "Has your family ever met your...arrangements before?"

"You mean, have any of them lasted long enough to meet my family? No. But I want you to." He leaned over and kissed her, fizzling out all her thoughts except that one word.

Want. It felt good, skating over her skin and diffusing into giddy excitement. "Does that mean I'm one of them now?"

He took the remote and brushed his thumb over her knuckles. "I don't want you to see yourself as just another arrangement. I want both of us to think of what we want out of a relationship and discuss it before going too far. I should have been more open with you from the beginning, and I'm not going to make the same mistake."

She nodded. That sounded like a good start.

He continued, "I put a lot of new information on your shoulders today, and you had enough stress to deal with already. I understand if you don't want to go into this until I'm in a better place—"

"No, it's...I want it." They'd kept their distance long enough. By now, all of her concerns had been answered.

His lips twitched. "I thought you'd say that. How about we talk things over this weekend? It gives you time to get your thoughts together. Plus, there's something I want to show you on Saturday."

"Oh?" She perked up.

"It's a surprise." The grin on his lips took form, curling with a secret she was desperate to discover.

She decided she liked surprises, especially ones from him. "Okay. I can do that."

"Good." He turned back to the TV and pulled up the selection screen. "Now, what movie did you pick?"

"Don't laugh," she mumbled, scooping up some food.

"Why would I?"

"I picked it because the hero reminds me of you."

THIRTY

Ivory

"Are you asleep?" Adrian whispered as he turned off the TV.

Her eyelids refused to open—each must've weighed at least ten pounds—and the comfort of Adrian's chest felt better than the plushest pillow as it rose and fell under her head. "Mmm, no," she mumbled. "I think I will be soon, though."

"Do you want to borrow something comfier?" he asked. "You don't have to sleep in those clothes."

She smiled, in love with the thought of wearing anything that belonged to him, but doubted her limbs would cooperate enough to change. "No, it's okay. I'll stay like this."

His couch felt perfect, especially with him in it. She must be the luckiest girl on the planet, fed, warm, and cared for.

"All right, if you say so." Her chest pillow shifted, and to her disappointment, he slowly untangled himself. She clung to the blanket with the little strength her body had left, not wanting to lose that, too. A sleepy haze washed over her mind, and she became faintly aware of the bathroom faucet running in the background. Then, the hinge of the bedroom door creaked before everything faded to black.

"Time for sleep," her knight whispered, watching over her even in the realm of dreams. A set of arms scooped her up, and she blinked back into consciousness.

"Where are we going?" she asked.

"To bed, silly." He didn't look down at her, too busy navigating in the near dark, but she stared up at his face all the same. The sharp angle of his jaw was jagged in the shroud of night, his stubble outlining two perfectly shaped lips and the slender rise of his cheekbone, feathered with thin stripes of his eyelashes. The solid hardness of his arms banded around her, but his strength didn't come as a surprise.

"I thought—" She paused, focusing to remember correctly. "I thought you don't bring girls into your bedroom."

He sighed and cast a glance down as he stood at the side of his bed. "How many times do I have to tell you that you're not some girl, Iv? And what am I supposed to do, sleep without a blanket? You're currently wrapped in the only one I have."

"Oh."

He set her down on a cool mattress, and she sat up. It was too dark to see much, but she could tell his room wasn't nearly as barren as the rest of the apartment. Silhouettes scattered the room, CDs and knick-knacks were stacked on his dresser while clothes were strewn across a pile of boxes next to his desk.

Looking at his personal space felt forbidden. Like she might find out some scary secret he kept from the rest of the world. But he'd already told her all his secrets, even though they had been scary. She didn't know how to feel about all of it, or more accurately, how he wanted her to feel about all of it. About knowing his past and being the reason he'd almost given up on finding out the truth. About seeing a side of him he'd tried so hard to eradicate.

Her gaze honed in on the most important part of the room: her black knight. Broad shoulders rippled as he balanced against the dresser to take off his socks, then turned and stripped off his shirt.

She gasped, now wide awake.

"Adrian!" He faced her, and more of the sickly blue-green bruise wrapping under his arm came into view. "What the heck is that?"

Another bruise ran up his forearm, skin dark and mottled like spilled ink. It was the most painful thing she'd ever seen. "Are those from Jace?"

"*Shh*," he whispered, switching off the light to hide his wounds and crawling into bed next to her. "Don't worry about it. I'll heal."

"That," she emphasized, "has to stop. You can't put yourself at risk, either. It's not how this works." Her hand tenderly moved along his side, eyes adjusting to the dark. The ugly mark remained visible even in the shadows. "Did you get it checked out?"

He gave a resigned sigh as if remembering how stubborn she could be and placed a hand over hers. "No. All a doctor would tell me to do is get rest. There's nothing else to do for a cracked rib."

She groaned. "I hate seeing you like this. What if it was me who'd gotten bruised?"

"If Jace gave you a bruise, I would kill him," Adrian said, suddenly not dismissive at all.

"Exactly. Now, what am I supposed to do? Go beat him up for you?" She was joking. Mostly.

He pulled her down beside him and drew her against his muscled chest. Furry wisps of dark hair tickled her cheek. "I explained he had to think he won, didn't I? That means I took a few hits here and there. It's nothing I wasn't prepared for."

She huffed against him, still annoyed, but his skin felt warm, and cuddling sounded much better than fighting. In the end, there was nothing else to do but let it heal. "I know," she whispered.

But—one way or another, Jace had to pay. They couldn't put this behind them. Not for his father's sake or for his friend's. Or for Adrian's.

"You know how Eve was made from Adam's rib?" he murmured, dipping his nose into her hair.

"Yeah," she replied.

"Well I have you now, so I get an extra rib. No need to worry about my old ones."

She scoffed and laid her head on his arm, careful not to pressure his side. "You only get one extra."

He smiled. "I know. Ribs are pretty important. Do you know why?"

"Why?" she asked.

"Because they protect your heart."

Hers gave a profound thud of its own at his implication, and she curled into him, moving her hand over his heart. She let her fingers run through the patch of coarse hair between his pecs, hoping her touch reached deeper than mere flesh and blood. "Then I'll do my best to protect yours."

"Thank you," he whispered. For a moment, his hard exterior cracked, and the strong beat of his heart resonated under her hand. It reminded her of all the sorrow he'd held in for years, all the grief he didn't know where to put, all the anger he'd tried to keep at bay. He'd been alone, too. He didn't only need someone to hold, but someone who wouldn't let go.

"Remember what you said about holding me?" she whispered. "That you wouldn't be able to let go?"

"Mhm," he hummed, wedging them closer with a strong pull of his arm. When she hesitated, he tipped up her chin, eyes black diamonds in the dark.

"You make me feel the same way," she finished under her breath.

"Oh Iv..." His hand moved to her jaw, thumb dancing at the corner of her mouth. "I know. I've always known. And because of that, you have no idea what else I want to make you feel."

The metal of his rings stroked down her cheek, warm and smooth, sparking her nerves to life. She could barely see, but every other sensation prickled with awareness. The heat of his skin against hers, the roll of his muscles as he leaned in, the way his breath teased her lips and the sound of his barely-there inhale. The softness of his lips finding hers.

Her world shattered—the same way it did every time they collided. The same way a collision of two neutron stars sent ripples through space and time, his possession rippled through her and left in its wake a mine of precious, elemental revelations. Her submission. His dominance. Power that was hers to claim. Control that was his to take. All of it coiled with a dense emotion that tugged on the fabric of her being.

There would never be enough kisses between them.

But tonight, it didn't end there. His hand threaded through her hair and tipped her head back as he licked along the seam of her lips, then entwined their tongues. She let him press her into the pillows, arched her back as he bore down, caging her in.

Her hands roamed over his chest and abdomen, around the flex of his obliques and the bunch of biceps on his arms. He held himself close enough to let her feel his heat but far enough so her breath could expand into her chest with rushed gasps. Her nipples pebbled under her shirt, and she melted into the kiss.

"I never want you to stop," she said, parting long enough to say the words before letting him continue his ministrations.

"Then I won't," he mumbled. "I'll kiss you until you forget what it ever felt like not to be kissed. Then I'll fuck you until you forget what it ever felt like not to be mine."

As if that already wasn't true. As if she could even recall a time *before.* Before he saw her. Before her name passed from his lips. Before she'd burned under his touch and bloomed under his praise.

She couldn't help but squirm, panting as she kissed him back. Her heart pounded so hard it hurt. She'd waited so long for this. Waited for him for what felt like her whole life.

"Don't stop," she breathed, repeating it over and over again like a sacred incantation.

Don't stop. Don't stop. Don't stop.

Her legs fell open as he settled himself between them. His lips explored hers, teeth greedily nipping until her skin stung and then licking away the pain. His erection twitched against her pelvis, fully hard and perfectly placed to rub her clit. Even through their clothes, she could tell he was big and delicious, her core eager and greedy to be filled with pleasure.

"I should wait," he said, even as his hand grazed down her side and inched up her shirt, tracing the curve of her breast. "We should talk first—"

"Yes," she interrupted. "We should wait but don't. Please don't stop."

He groaned, scraping stubble and teeth along her jaw, burrowing his nose in her neck and smelling her hair against the pillow. "Just a little, to make you feel good."

His fingers dipped between them, hot and sure, finally slipping into the secret place between her hips and under her clothes. Then they were there, right where she needed them. Right where every emotion blended into the next, and nothing was *his* or *hers* or *wrong* or *right.* It just was. And hell, it was good. So good that she moaned under her breath, so good that he bit her neck in response and then pulled her into another searing kiss.

He parted her folds that were already wet and slippery, perfect for him to find the rhythm and pressure that sent her to the brink in record time. Their breaths mingled, catching as he twisted inside of her and teased out a kind of pleasure she'd never experienced.

"So soft. So sweet." His thrusts deepened to reach an impossible place, and she whimpered. "Just how I knew you would be."

His thumb rubbed her clit with precision while his fingers stretched her pussy, curling and thrusting until she cried out beneath him. Her body wanted to break, but she wouldn't let it. Adrian wouldn't let it, forcing her to take as much as he could give. Inevitably, her climax grew closer until she couldn't contain herself, until it filled and consumed her.

"I'm—I'm going to come," she whimpered through their kiss.

"Good girl." His lips grew more demanding, teeth grazing her with a ferocity that matched the onslaught building in her abdomen. As if for all this time, it wasn't her that had been denied the pleasure, but him—he who had been denied the right to feel her come, he who was punished by not touching her, by not claiming her.

A second finger joined the first, picking up the pace until her legs shook and her hips bucked into his hand. Her nerves frayed as her mouth opened in a silent, desperate cry. Bright spotlights of color scattered over her vision, and then pleasure tore through her body.

Wave after wave, she resonated like a well-tuned instrument. But instead of slowing down, his two fingers sunk further into her pussy, fighting their way through the contractions and shaking her to the core. They plunged in and out, curling and scissoring and pushing, pushing, pushing, until she almost burst from the pressure.

Once wasn't enough. He was going to make her come again.

"That's it. Give me another." His palm ground into her already sore and sensitive clit, coated with the residue of her first climax, and she moaned into his insistent mouth. "Hush, you can take it," he mumbled, kissing her all the while.

She tried, focusing instead on his warm lips and the erotic dance of his tongue. The reprimand of his teeth. His firm arms and legs and torso that overshadowed her own.

A second orgasm crashed over her, shaking each cell until it hummed with a stream of endorphins. If she cried or screamed or both, she didn't know. All that mattered was clinging to this one singularity in time, this one paradox where she felt more alive than she'd ever been and, at the same time, had ceased to exist.

"Rest now, my sweet witch," he whispered, withdrawing his hand and laying back on his side, pulling her into his chest as she regained a sense of reality. "I have so much more planned for you."

Her lids were too heavy to open, limbs too relaxed to move, but even so, she didn't want him to take the honorable route now. She didn't want him to think she'd take a single thing from him and not give a piece of her in return.

"I want you to feel good, too," she mumbled. His dick was still hard, conveniently wedged between her thighs, and she gave it a little nudge. Reawakened, it pushed back through his pants.

"For *that*, I do insist we wait," Adrian chuckled, tucking himself away so she couldn't keep teasing. "Don't worry. As long as I can feel your heart beating next to mine, I'll feel good."

There were no words she could utter in response save a contented sigh and all the adoration in the world.

THIRTY-ONE

Adrian

Soft, heavenly heat ensnared him. Consumed him. He'd perish in it, and that was the only death he wanted to live for.

Sometime during the night, his hand had crept under Ivory's shirt, and the plush swell of her breast rested in his palm. His fingers stroked her nipple on their own accord, circling the small bud until it peaked and hardened. So responsive. He couldn't wait to tease her to oblivion on Saturday. To finally let them have what they both wanted.

He curled closer, and his dick gave a pitiful throb as it nestled between the swell of her ass. Somehow, he'd gotten even harder than when they'd fallen asleep. But more impressive by far was having her here. In his bed. In his arms. It all felt too natural—familiar not to memory but to something far deeper.

Her shoulders rose and fell peacefully within his embrace, heat radiating off her skin and gathering in his chest before it spread out to every cell in his body. A feeling that made him want all the lazy nights and crazy nights and everything in between. For the rest of his life.

For the rest of forever, if she'd let him.

He guarded himself with a measured breath. She may be willing to invest her body and a section of her heart for now, but that didn't mean long-term commitment. There was no guarantee she wouldn't see reason and decide it was better to cut her losses.

Not slipping inside her last night had been the cruelest form of torture, but after everything that happened, he needed to know she accepted what would come with it. The things that came with knowing him as a friend as well as a Dominant, something he'd prevented with everyone else.

She'd have to face the same risks that went hand in hand with the life he'd been given. A loss of her innocence, not only in a sexual sense but the brutal truth of the crimes he'd witnessed...and those intended to commit himself.

He rolled over to glance at the clock—*6:00*. No wonder he felt wide awake. He'd slept for more than eight hours. Already restless from the extra energy, he carefully slipped out of bed and pulled on a shirt, fixing the blankets before meandering into the living room so as not to wake his sleeping witch.

Through the windows, the sky was barely a shade above black, cloaked in the deep darkness of morning, but he could tell the snow had stopped. He switched on a lamp and went to his jacket hung by the door, pulling out his final cigarette. The one he still hadn't justified lighting up.

Not that he hadn't wanted to. Each time he tried, Ivory's disappointed face would pop into his mind. Even as he craved the bitter taste and dependable wave of nicotine, he set it unlit between his lips. Walking to the porch out of habit, he cracked the door and let in a blast of freezing air to clear his mind.

Other than the alarming intensity of his attraction to Ivory, he had a lot to think about. The Yu family, for one, and in particular, making Jace's life a living hell.

That nuisance had racked up enough reasons to take the

blame for all of his family's sins—Jace had become the perfect target to rid himself of the lust for revenge. Chances were he'd never get to prove who exactly set up Luke or who murdered his father, but he could rid the world of the one evil within his reach.

As he let the frost nip through his clothes, the bedroom door creaked, and his sweet, sleepy witch stumbled out. Wrapped in the blanket, hair a mess of purple strands, she shuffled over and shivered. "It's cold."

"Good morning," he murmured as she laid her head on his chest. He turned his back to the porch door and smoothed her hair, tucking the blanket over her shoulders. "I didn't mean to wake you."

"It's okay." She tipped her face up to blink at him. Then frowned, brows furrowed. "Hey!" She reached out and snatched away the cigarette. "Didn't I say no more of these?"

He grinned, for some reason pleased to be scolded by her, even when he knew he hadn't done anything wrong. The way she pursed her lips was more than adorable and much better when she wasn't a figment of his imagination. "I got to keep one, remember?"

"You haven't used it yet?" She inspected the end of the cancer stick, holding it backward.

"Nope."

"Well, you don't get to keep it anymore," she declared. "Time's up."

"You didn't say anything about a time limit." He reached over and closed the door, but when he looked down again, she had figured out which end went in her mouth and was testing the best placement for it.

He scowled and snatched it from her, crushing the paper. "Don't do that."

She pouted. "It was in *your* mouth."

"It was." He tipped up her chin with rough fingers, forcing

her to meet his gaze. "But I have much better things to put in yours."

Her eyes widened as she bit down on her bottom lip, smiling in that innocent way of hers. Which really wasn't innocent at all. Damn, she could already shackle him with one look. He dropped the cigarette and crushed his mouth to hers, kissing every inch of it, savoring her sweetness and how pliable she became at his slightest touch, only able to stop when they were both short of breath.

"So that's better than a smoke?" she whispered.

"A million times better."

She laughed and set her head on his shoulder. "You should've done that from the beginning."

"Mhm." He wrapped her in his arms. "If I recall, you said you weren't looking for a relationship the first time we met."

"That's only because I knew you'd say no." She paused, then added with a thoughtful sigh, "I could tell you kept everyone at an arm's distance, but I wanted to help despite that. I didn't want you to push me away because of my feelings."

Yet she called him the honorable one. "What about now?" he asked dryly. "Do you still worry about catching feelings?"

"I think it's a little too late for me," she whispered, smiling into his neck.

"Me too."

Her smile widened.

He rested his chin on her head, wishing the world would stop spinning if he held her close enough. That she could rewrite his life the same way she'd restructured his heart. They stood in silence for a while, speaking without words or movement. A certain stillness enveloped the air—a predestined bond, if such a thing existed.

Ivory stirred in his arms. "I think you should know about what happened with Jace." Her voice waived, and he tensed, already half convinced to throw out his plans for the day and give Jace what had been coming for a long time. One word from her was all it would take.

"Did he do something else yesterday?"

She shook her head. "No, I mean, you should know why he acts this way around me in the first place. You've been so open about your past. It's about time I faced mine, too."

"Okay." He rubbed her through the blanket, proud of her being brave enough to face this. He had no right to know, let alone ask, but he'd do anything in his power to help her heal if she offered the chance. "If you want to share, I'll listen."

She swallowed as if the words didn't want to leave her throat. "Last semester, Serena, Avril, and I met Jewelle outside the club. She gave us a ride back to Beta Rho, and that following week, we were over there almost every day." She let out a hollow scoff. "College was still so new to me. The parties. Greek life. The freedom to socialize with people from so many different places."

"One day, we were playing a round of truth or dare— nothing scandalous. Stupid things like '*Who was your childhood crush?*' and '*Have you ever cheated on a test?*' The dares were mostly to drink shots. By the time we got too drunk to play, everyone just...disappeared."

Her fingers curled into his shirt. "I remember Jace offering to give me a tour of the house, so he took me to his room. It felt dangerous, sinister in a wrong way. I was naive to fall for it, but I was also heartbroken from my ex breaking up with me over *Harvard*—imagine that, being dumped for an ancient brick institution." She stopped to breathe, and he massaged the base of her neck.

"Jace said he knew deep down I wasn't an innocent good girl; I said he was right. Then he shoved me to my knees, and I didn't even put up a fight. I told myself I wanted it rough. I wanted it to be abrasive. Ugly and demeaning. But when he forced himself past my lips, I started to cry." She shuddered, turning to hide under the blanket. "The alcohol made my head swim, and my gag reflex kicked in, but he wouldn't stop until he finished, and then I ran away. I've hated him ever since, although... I think I hate myself more for letting it happen."

Fuck. The edges of his vision bled red with fury, but all that mattered right now was Ivory. Making sure this didn't drag her down. "Sweetheart, you were drunk. Even if you remember saying yes, you couldn't have consented. I should cut his dick off and shove it down his own throat."

"You should," she said bitterly, then looked up. "I mean— no, don't actually do that." Some of the fear fell from her eyes as she saw his expression. Nothing felt better than the pride of having his girl know he'd go to any length to protect her.

"I won't do anything without your permission," he promised, rubbing her back. "But if you change your mind, let me know."

"Okay, sure, Mr. Anti-hero," she said with a roll of her eyes that only she could get away with, and more importantly, a small smile back on her face.

He peeled away the blanket enough to tuck her against him. "Thank you for telling me, and I don't mind avoiding any activities that make you uncomfortable. It's not a problem at all."

She sighed into his touch. "Don't worry, I've never felt that way with you." Her thumbs sought out his waistband, hooking over the elastic. He knew her touch wasn't meant to seduce, even though the mere feel of her skin on his did the trick. It was for her to know she had the power to be there. To touch him and not fear how he'd respond. "I don't think it'll be a problem, but..."

"But?"

"I need to rewrite that experience. I don't want what happened to define me. I still want to enjoy this part of sex; I want to submit." She lifted her head and flicked her eyes to his lips before kissing him lightly. "Only to you."

He kissed her back the same way he always did, easing her mouth open and taking control. She wasn't weak or broken, and he'd show her just how good her desires could be when handled by the right man. "I'll take care of you, Iv."

She blushed. "Thank you." Visibly more at ease, she pulled his arms around her waist and leaned back. "Do you have work today?"

"I have the week off," he replied. "What about you? When's your first class?"

"Nine. I'll have to ask Nia if—" She cut herself off. "Unless you could give me a ride?"

He smiled. "Of course I can."

"I should make breakfast first," she said through a yawn. "Do pancakes sound good? And no arguing today. I want to do it."

"Pancakes sound great."

THIRTY-TWO

THE GENTLE PITTER-PATTER OF RAIN TAPPED ON HER DORM window as she lay awake in the dark hours of late evening. A perfect kind of peace blanketed the room, not silent or still, but a swell that steadily coursed through her veins.

Every second away from her black knight had stretched into an eternity, but somehow, the sun still rose as scheduled for the rest of the week. The snow had begun to melt, and as she counted the hours until Friday night rolled into Saturday, her thoughts churned over what tomorrow might bring.

Adrian agreed to pick her up at ten for the surprise. Of course, they'd first have to go over rules and expectations or have a general conversation—however that would go. Honesty, she was excited no matter what form it took. He couldn't say much that would deter her at this point.

For herself, she hoped he didn't mind being her mentor. She'd been too scared to surf the web when it came to kink, and she'd rather learn in person anyway. As for the basic stuff, the stuff regular people did in everyday relationships and not in so-called arrangements, she really only wanted one thing—him.

She wanted to be by his side day and night, to be trusted in and outside the bedroom. They'd come so far, from strangers to friends and now this, and she didn't want to lose any of that progress because they got more involved. If she was Adrian's woman, then whatever other label came with that would be okay with her. No secrets and no pretense. Just her black knight, exactly the way he was.

If he could agree to that, then she'd be happier than she ever thought possible.

In the morning, she went over everything again while eating breakfast in the cafeteria and couldn't stop smiling as she walked back to her room. The halls were quiet as usual on the weekends. Most students slept in or went home, and the shuffle of her fuzzy slippers was the only sound as she padded toward her dorm. She hadn't picked out what to wear yet and purposely left herself nearly an hour to tear apart her closet.

"Hey Ivory, can I have a minute?"

She stopped at the open door next to her room, mood shifting in an instant. It had been months since she'd seen Serena at the dorms instead of Beta Rho. Jitters crawled up her spine at the thought of Jace, but he was nowhere in sight.

Out of habit, she put on a polite smile and turned to face Serena. "If it's about what happened with Jace, you should know I don't have anything else to say."

She knew why Adrian had done what he did, but that had nothing to do with Serena or Jewelle. It made her more annoyed that Jace had acted so wounded when she knew Adrian purposely pulled his punches.

Serena's trademark bright expression fell. "Actually, I wanted to ask if you were okay. I felt bad about how Jay treated you. I only wanted to ask about what happened, but he took it too far."

Ivory rubbed her arm over the place he'd grabbed her. A small bruise appeared after a day, but it hardly hurt anymore and had already faded. "Yeah, he did. Don't take this the wrong way, but I don't want anything to do with him."

She hoped Jace hadn't made good on his threat and told Serena what happened between them, but even if he did, it didn't matter. Nothing would make her bend to his scheming, and he was delusional to think otherwise.

"I understand. He's been...different lately." Serena's brown eyes clouded, but she squared her shoulders and flipped a strand of blonde hair over her shoulder. "Even though Jewelle told me it was a setup, after how you reacted, I realized you might not have been involved. So I'm—" She looked away, then back again. "I'm sorry."

Empathy squeezed Ivory's heart. Serena had trusted the wrong people, but she wasn't a bad person. "It's not your fault. How about you, though? I've hardly seen you around this semester."

"That's cause I moved most of my stuff to Beta Rho." Serena motioned to the inside of her dorm, which looked almost as bare as when they moved in. "But it didn't all fit, and sometimes a girl needs to sleep in her own bed, you know?"

Ivory nodded. "We all need personal space."

"Absolutely," Serena agreed, her energetic nature recovering. "We should hang out more. I'm starting to think you're the only friend I have left."

Ivory returned the smile, but Serena's words struck a dissonant chord. Where were all of her other friends? "Avril started a study group in the library. I can text you the info. It'd be nice to see you there."

"Okay, I'll try to peek in if I can." Serena paused, halfway back inside her dorm. "And for what it's worth, I don't hold anything against you or Nia."

"That's good to know," Ivory replied, unsure about what had prompted this change in character. Normally, Serena stood by her opinions no matter what. "I don't think Nia heard about what you said, but you could always send her a message."

"Maybe I'll do that." She flashed another smile. "Thanks for the chat." With a final flourish and a wave, she slipped into her room.

Ivory frowned as she walked down the hall and entered her dorm. Earlier, Jace had no reservations about being too rough with her in public...what would he do with Serena behind closed doors?

She wanted to believe Jace wouldn't target a girl who chose to be with him, but something had gotten Serena down. That was another thing she had to bring up with Adrian. Serena might have jumped to conclusions on more than one occasion, but Ivory didn't want to see her get hurt, either.

She leaned against the door as it clicked closed, then sighed. Picking out clothes didn't seem like such a big deal anymore, but she should put something on other than a sweatshirt and leggings.

As much as she'd like to divine the perfect outfit to leave Adrian speechless the moment he saw her, she also didn't want to wear the wrong thing and ruin his surprise. Considering he only traveled by bike, a cute dress might be out of the question. Probably. She peeked through the blinds and saw the rain had lightened to a slow drizzle. If they were going to be outside, then she'd need something warmer. But she didn't want too many layers, just in case...

Better to ask.

She sent off a quick text to Adrian and stripped down to her underwear, digging around her closet for the one thing she'd already planned to wear. Gosh, when had she gotten so many clothes? And how did she manage to cram them all into the dorm's tiny wardrobe?

After tossing out half the contents, the box in question remained out of sight. She collapsed in the pile of clothes on her rug, too exhausted to keep searching. With a defeated groan, she rolled her head to the side, then let out a cry of victory and reached under the bed to grab the pair of shoes she'd ordered months ago.

She wasn't one to splurge, but these had been on sale and actually came in her size. The knee-high boots were too fancy to wear to class and too plain for a party, so she hadn't worn them yet. But they were perfect for today.

Opening the lid, she peeled back the paper wrapping and pulled out two black lace-up boots. The leather still smelled fresh, woodsy and sharp. The soles should be thick enough to keep her feet warm and dry. Hopefully, breaking them in wouldn't be an issue.

Just to be sure, she tried them on. It took a little extra effort to get her heel in, but after tying the laces up, they fit well. She spared a moment to model in front of the mirror. Not too bad paired with her midnight purple panties and black bralette.

Hm...

Adrian might appreciate getting a picture or two before he arrived. She reached for her phone just as it buzzed and scrambled to read his message.

SIR ADRIAN

We'll be outdoors, wear something casual.

Casual. Okay. Stepping around the mess of clothes on the floor, she picked up a soft sweater with lace over the shoulders, then opened her dresser and yanked out a nice pair of jeans. Easy.

Oh no. Looking down, she realized removing the boots would be just as difficult as putting them on. Halfway through undoing the laces, her phone buzzed again.

On my way.

What? Already?

Her eyes flew to the clock, and sure enough, it was a quarter to ten. She'd hardly have time to do anything with her hair or make-up, much less wrestle with these stupid boots. Hopping on one foot, she wiggled out of one before giving up on the other, and then went to her mirror to apply a thin layer of foundation and swipe her eyes with mascara.

The purple ribbon Adrian gave her hung out of her jewelry box, and she grabbed it and tied it in a small bow around her neck. Two birds, one stone.

All she needed was to get her foot out of the other boot and put on—

Her phone rang. She huffed, nearly running into the open drawer to answer the call.

"Hey." Her voice came out breathy and on edge, but she didn't have time to care.

"Still getting ready?" Adrian asked on the other line.

She laughed and sat on her bed. "How'd you know?"

"You don't need to worry about impressing me, Iv, but I figured you would. Mind if I join? I just parked."

"Sure." She didn't want to wait a second longer to see him, even if she wasn't all put together. "But be warned, my room is a mess at the moment. I'm still getting dressed."

He chuckled, and the smooth baritone of his voice washed through her. "I thought telling you to wear something casual would simplify things."

She exhaled. "Is anything simple when it comes to us?"

He paused. "I hope it can be."

"Right." Simple sounded really nice. "I hope so, too."

THIRTY-THREE

IF IVORY WAS GETTING DRESSED, HE'D BE MORE THAN HAPPY TO lend a hand. It was the least he could do as her chivalrous knight.

They'd agreed to meet at ten, and he didn't want to be late by a millisecond. Fidgeting on his porch and fighting the urge to smoke hadn't done him any good. Time with Ivory was too precious to waste. The rest of the day didn't feel like nearly enough, and he secretly hoped she'd agree to stay the night again.

Hanging his helmet on the seat, he set up the first part of her surprise with meticulous care. Presentation would be essential—hopefully she liked it. Once satisfied, he tied his hair in a bun and let out a deep breath.

Only after he heard her final decision would he be able to relax again. She hadn't hinted at any doubts in their conversation last night, but he wanted to give her a proper chance to voice her thoughts. It'd be nearly impossible for her to require something he wasn't willing to give, but regardless, she had to know she'd be equally capable of asking for her desires as he was his. And he did have a few.

He hadn't done this before—started a real relationship. With all his previous arrangements, he'd known they would be temporary and made that abundantly clear. But with Ivory, he couldn't see an end. Moreover, he didn't want to. All he wished for was to keep that sweet smile on her face and be by her side to witness it.

Navigating the sleepy dormitory halls, he found her room number and softly rapped on the door. It opened by a crack, barely enough to see the side of her desk and an open wardrobe. Her voice came from the other side. "Adrian? Is that you?"

"Expecting someone else?"

She laughed. Hell, he'd never get over that sound. "No, but I did say the room was a mess, right? You can come in."

He pushed the door open and stepped into what looked like a page from an object-search puzzle. Almost everything was some shade of purple, clothes and notebooks and pillows scattered around the tiny room. But his witch remained out of sight.

Closing the door, he pivoted until he saw her hidden in the corner...then nearly crumbled on the spot. Sweet and bashful and tempting as ever, she stood practically naked.

When she said she was getting dressed, he hadn't expected this. Her porcelain skin contrasted perfectly with her dark purple hair and plain undergarments—and fuck those legs— one covered up to the knee by one of the sexiest boots he'd ever seen, the other in a simple black stocking. Her hands fidgeted at her side like she remembered too late to be embarrassed. A balance of innocence and seduction only she could pull off.

He swept his gaze back up her body and zeroed in on the ribbon tied around her neck. Like a collar. Like she wanted the world to know she belonged to someone—to him.

"Damn," he whispered, reaching out to brush trembling

fingers along the curve of her shoulder. Her skin felt hot and smooth. This wasn't helping him focus.

"Hi," she whispered, smiling sweetly and biting down on her plump bottom lip.

Fuck it. He tangled his fist in her hair and pulled her to his lips. "You don't know the kind of things I want to do to you right now, sweetheart." A little moan left her lips that went straight to his dick, and he swallowed it with a possessive kiss. "Wicked, filthy things."

She opened her mouth with a whimper, almost fragile in the way it melted on his tongue. But she didn't cave, instead wrapping her arms around his neck and grinding so he could feel the heat of her pussy through their clothes. His hand smoothed down her side, over the flare of her hip, and grabbed her ass.

But now wasn't the time. Not before he was absolutely sure. He broke the kiss, lingering as they caught their breath.

She looked at him through her lashes, and a blush spread over her cheeks. "I, uh, meant to say, how has your morning been?"

"Just got a hell of a lot better." He guided her back to his mouth, unable to resist another kiss. He nipped at her swollen lips, tasting them before leaving a trail of soft and slow kisses along her jaw. "You're turning me into a fucking addict, Iv." He scraped his teeth against her skin and breathed her in. "Can't get enough."

Her lips curved under his into a delicate smile. "Then take me. Take everything."

She delivered the words so earnestly, with a reverent whisper, yet they were powerful enough to crack his heart in two.

He spun and pinned her against the door. Her chest heaved, nipples puckering through her bra. "Please tell me you've thought this through," he panted. "I need to hear what you want, if it's the sex or something more. I need to know that either way, you accept what comes with it."

He knew he sounded desperate, and the bulge in his pants spoke for itself. This time he was the one begging instead of her. He didn't care. All he needed was her answer—would she accept him, as broken as he was?

"I want all of it." She leaned back against the door, letting him take in her flushed cheeks and glittering eyes, the mess he'd made of her carefully brushed hair, and the goosebumps running along her skin. The flicker of her pulse under the ribbon around her neck. "I want you."

Shit. Dammit all to hell.

His eyes flashed, and he grabbed her wrists to raise them above her head. "Do you know what you're saying?" He nudged his knee between her legs. Fuck, she smelled so good. "Do you know what I'll do to you?"

She shook her head. He'd given her every right to be scared, every opportunity to say no, but she looked at him like a mouse who *wanted* to be caught.

He licked his lips. "I'll devour you, Iv. I'll break you a million times over and piece you back together as I please. I'll mark every sigh, take every ounce of your pleasure, covet every drop of your pain." He leaned in and inhaled her breath. "I'll make you mine."

She bit her lip and searched his eyes, then vulnerability overshadowed her arousal. "I'm going to want more than the other girls, Adrian. I want every part of you. Everything they couldn't have."

He groaned. "Sweetheart—"

She cut him off with a kiss.

Fuck waiting.

He needed her. Now.

Not breaking the kiss, he picked her up by the waist. Her legs wrapped around him, and he stumbled across the rug to her bed, laying her down in the mess of pillows and clothes, then crawling over the top. "I can be demanding. Overprotective. Selfish and possessive when it comes to the things I love. I won't care about fitting in or being normal and I won't compromise on giving you anything but the best."

"What's all that mean?" she asked, silky breasts slipping out of her bra. He traced his fingers over her skin, outlining the hem of her panties and the hollow of her stomach. God, she was more than angelic—she was perfect.

"That's what you'll have to deal with." He looked back up at her face. "That's me."

"Well, I'm stubborn," she started, breathless as his hand inched up to her chest. "I care too much, and I try too hard. I'll do anything for the people I love, and I won't ever give up on what I want. I don't need normal or nice or pretty." She gasped as he tugged at the little bow of the ribbon above her collarbone, making sure it fit snug and tight. "And I want you to ruin me more than I've wanted anything else in my entire life."

Her simple admission tore through the fabric of his being. He dipped down and sucked one of her pink nipples into his mouth, rolling the bud before dragging it through his teeth. "That I will," he promised. "You're the most beautiful thing I've ever fucking seen. But I see so much more when I look at you."

True, he saw a woman who could win over any man, who could model in the world's most expensive outfit or nothing at all, but he also saw things that were invisible to the eyes. He felt so many things he couldn't touch, and it made him want her all the more. His desire wasn't just for someone sexy, talented, and kind—she was a person he couldn't live without.

"I see so much more when I look at you, too," she whispered.

He pulled back and ran a hand down the side of her bootless leg, making her squirm. "Tell me, what do you see when you look at me?"

A man who'd lived a broken life? A sinner who refused to alter his course to hell? The cursed soul that would lead to her downfall?

"I see someone who cares just as much as I do. Even though he pretends to be mean and unlovable." Her face broke into a radiant smile. "I see a man who earned my admiration. One who deserves happiness."

THIRTY-FOUR

HE COULD BARELY BREATHE, SO HE KISSED HER INSTEAD. NOT SO
long ago, he would've dismissed her words without a second
thought. But maybe now he could accept them as true. "Do you
want to know what I see when I look at you?"

Her breath hitched. "Yeah."

He kissed her pulse and paused to feel her heartbeat
against his lips, drinking it in. "I see a woman I've been looking
for my whole life. Someone I never had any right to ask for." He
took a deep breath of her sweet scent and looked into yielding
jade eyes. "But I'm asking anyway."

"You know my answer," she whispered.

He reached up and pinned her wrists again, stretching her
out so he could look at every secret crevice, every sacred hollow.
Her angelic form sunk into the cotton sheets, on display like a
precious gem.

"Yes," he breathed. "I do know your answer, and I also know
you're going to be a very good girl, Iv. Just for me."

Her eyes fluttered. "Does that mean—" She cut off as a
blush reddened her face.

"Hm? You don't get to hide from me, sweetheart. Not anymore."

"Do good girls get a reward?" she mumbled, barely audible.

His grip tightened on her wrists, and he slipped a teasing finger around the waistline of her panties. "Yes. They do get a reward."

She squirmed as he dipped his head down to sample her other nipple, then bit into the swell of her breast. Her fingers curled around his while the rest of her relaxed under his touch, submitting to his tenderness and succumbing to his brutality. He traced a line down to the fabric covering her pussy and found her clit, only to give it the slightest stimulation.

The best sound he'd ever heard left her lips, and he savored the tension gathering in her muscles as she arched her back. Kneeling over his sweet witch, he released her wrists and slipped his belt out of its loops.

Her eyes widened with an unspoken question—cheeks flushed, lips a bright strawberry red. Her nipples puckered into pretty perfect points, and he wanted nothing more than to spend the rest of the day exactly like this.

But they had plans. Important plans, so he'd make this quick.

"Legs up," he ordered.

"What about the boot?" she asked, raising her legs anyway. "Won't it get in the way?"

He pressed on her thighs and watched as her pussy unfurled, half-hidden by her dainty undergarments. "No, I like it on you. Besides, I have to remember to keep this short and sweet. If you undress anymore, we'll never leave."

Glancing up at her face, her expression told him she didn't mind that idea at all.

He'd make waiting worth her time. This would just be to take the edge off. An appetizer before the main course.

"Give me your hands." She reached forward, and he

brought her wrists around the back of her knees, then wrapped them in a neat little bundle with the belt. The buckle grazed her skin as he slid it closed, snug but not tight enough to leave marks. "Tight enough?"

"A little more, sir," she squeaked, wavering between need and embarrassment.

By the end of the day, he'd make sure to cure that hesitancy of hers for speaking her mind. He wanted her to feel confident telling him exactly what she needed and how she wanted it.

He tugged on the end of the belt and let the metal bite into her wrist, ensuring she could still wiggle her fingers. "Better?"

She hummed her approval.

No, that wouldn't do. He gave her a warning slap on the ass, and she squeaked again as the sound from his palm filled the room. "Yes, sir."

"Good."

He placed the tail of the leather belt in her palm so she would be able to loosen it at any time or keep it tight. For now, that was a luxury she needed, but it wouldn't always be something he granted.

"Don't let go, or else you'll earn yourself a punishment, and we wouldn't want that, would we?" He met her gaze. "Not when I could so easily take away your reward."

A look of trepidation flashed across her face. His lips curved into a wicked grin. As much as he balanced on the brink of ripping her panties off to taste what was underneath, the thought of denying her—of leaving her wet and needy as he showed her what he'd prepared—made his pulse thunder.

"I'll be good, sir," she affirmed, holding the belt and keeping it taut.

"I'm sure you will be, sweetheart." He caressed her face and dropped his hand to her pussy, hooking one finger around the dark cotton.

She gasped at his touch, legs already beginning to tremble

as he rubbed his knuckle back and forth over her slick, swollen clit. Her heat soaked into him, and the slippery nectar ran onto his rings. Anticipation ripped through the last thread of his patience, and he pulled the thin fabric to the side.

Holy. Fuck.

Despite granting her three orgasms, he'd never *seen* her, and now that he had, the image burned into his brain. Seared into the deepest recess of his fantasies. He could look at her all day.

Even if she tried to cover herself, she wouldn't be able to, all tied up and bound. Completely at his mercy. His fingers gently splayed her open, thumb brushing over her clit and pulling back the hood. He stroked her softly, building up her pleasure at his leisure and absorbing every minute detail.

"God," he whispered. "You are so gorgeous."

She breathed out another whine, and her walls fluttered, greedy and begging to be filled. As if in response, his dick throbbed—but enduring the ache would be well worth it. He couldn't wait to see how much she would endure, how much she could take. What she'd be willing to do for his cock.

The thought acted like heroin, saturating his veins and stealing the breath from his lungs. His beautiful witch accepting his curse, pleading for the cure.

Just how long would she last?

He teased her entrance with his thumb, dipping in up to the first knuckle before pulling out, then going even lower to circle her tight rosebud.

Her little gasp stretched into a groan as his other hand worked her clit at the same time, and he gave her ass another slap, watching as it blushed pink.

"Ah," she groaned, tossing her head on the pillows. "That feels so good."

"Hush." He was about to make her feel a million times better.

Leaning down, he settled between her legs and replaced his

hand with a hot, hungry tongue. She stiffened, then melted as he licked straight up her slit.

"Damn, Iv," he rasped. "I knew you'd be sweeter than syrup, but now I'm gonna need this every day."

She moaned, unable to reply with words. That pleased him even more. He returned to her clit and reveled in her taste, alternating between firm swipes and quick circles with his tongue. Sweet, and so very savory.

Lost in the moment, he forgot about everything but the silk of her pussy. Her feet kicked out and dug into his shoulders, one heel covered by a thick rubber sole, while her toes curled around his jacket on the other side. Next time, he'd have to tie her ankles, too.

"I'm—" She gasped. "I'm so close." Above his head, he could feel her struggling against the restraints, but she hadn't let go of the belt.

Good, because stopping now would be as much a punishment for him as it would be for her. He hummed against her clit and peeled apart her thighs to bury his face into her cunt. She vibrated around him, tipping towards the peak.

He deliberately held back, watching as the pleasure ate her from the inside out, fused into every beautiful part of her. He made her climb higher, let her buckle under the weight of it, cry into the ceiling, and then—finally—he gave her release.

His tongue softened as she came, and he held it to her clit, hands fastened to her hips as she twisted every which way. But there was no escape. There would never be an escape so long as she chose him. Because he would always choose her.

At last, she shuddered out a long breath, and her whole body went limp, eyes drifting closed. The personification of contentment.

Sitting back, he reached down into his boot and pulled out his knife. She still clutched the end of the belt in her hands, and he only had to pull a little to get the same tightness they started with. "Don't move, sweetheart. I don't want to cut you."

Her eyes opened, and she watched through hooded lids as he carved a small nick where the buckle would fit. Then he slipped it off her wrists and massaged the faint red marks that had appeared.

"Feel better?"

"Mhm."

"Good. Hold still." He moved down the bed, wiggled off her boot, and crossed her ankles over each other before wrapping them with the belt. Making a second nick, he slipped it off and fit the belt back into his jean loops. "I'll make better use of that later."

She stared at him, soaking in the meaning of his words. He licked his lips for one more delicious taste and ran a hand over his stubble. Her essence smeared over his chin, and he fully intended to wear it like that all day.

"For now, it's time to get ready for your surprise."

THIRTY-FIVE

Ivory

After *that*, he still had a surprise?

Adrian swept his gaze over her again, dark and commanding and cloaked in his trademark black leather, but he looked more elated than she'd ever seen.

"I might need a minute," she admitted, leaning back on her elbows.

His lips twitched, slick with her juice. "All right. But you're lucky I'm giving you a break."

She laughed. "What a lucky girl I am."

It was supposed to be a joke, but her heart almost burst all over again at realizing what today meant—what this meant.

She could really be his.

She sat up and stretched, noticing the mess in her room, which had become even worse. Half of the pillows on her bed were now scattered along with the heap of clothes on her floor. "It's not usually like this," she explained. "I couldn't find the boots, then you called before I finished getting ready, and—Wow. I can't believe that just happened."

He grinned. "I plan to have it happen a lot more often."

The thought made her weak again, in the best way. "So it's

official? As in, we're..." She trailed off, uncertain of which term to use. Fitting them into a label had never been important, but she wanted to make sure they were on the same page.

"I'd be honored to be your boyfriend." His palm caressed her calf, rings warm and smooth where his skin was hot and rough, and he bent to place a soft kiss on her knee. "Your knight. Your Master. Whatever you want me to be."

She blushed, adoring all three. "Everything. You can be my everything."

"I like that." He grinned, eyes bright and molten gold.

"Are there going to be rules?" she asked.

"A few." He helped her remove the stuck boot and reached for the pair of jeans that had fallen on the floor. "I wanted to show you the surprise regardless of your decision—but now it can be a way to explain my rules."

That piqued her interest. Wiggling into the jeans, she shook off her post-orgasm fatigue and put on her sweater. Adrian kneeled by the bed to lace up her boots.

The simple gesture destroyed her as effectively as all his promising words and indulgent kisses. Not only did he care to take her clothes off, he would get on his knees to help her put them back on. She expected the roles to be reversed—to be the one at his feet, and certainly, there would be a time for that—but she also recognized the action for something deeper. Their exchange of power went both ways. He was willing to give as much as he would take.

She fidgeted, feeling more important than she'd grown accustomed to.

He finished and looked up as she chewed her lip. "Something on your mind?"

She hated to ask. Being vulnerable was much easier when it meant being bound and gagged, but his touch had been both arousing and comforting, and it made her way too honest. "Am

I worth it? Changing your plans and going through all the extra effort to be together?"

Adrian rose to his feet with certainty written in his eyes. "Yes, you are."

Warmth flooded her veins.

He reached out and helped her to her feet beside him. "It'll take time, but you'll get used to knowing your worth. I'll make sure of it."

His unwavering confidence in her had been more than she'd expected, and hearing it spoken so plainly felt like drinking fresh water when she'd been living in a desert. He didn't avoid the topic or reach for reasons to prove her value, either. He accepted her as is, which was more than she'd ever done for herself.

She cast her eyes down, realizing just how much she'd gotten used to belittling herself and accepting the same from others. Some days, she couldn't even tell if her self-perception was her own or a mutated version of someone else's. If her goals and dreams were hers or inherited from her parents.

She looked up, accepting them as true equals. A black knight and his cherished witch. "Thank you."

"My pleasure."

Once dressed and armed with retouched makeup, she made quick work of stuffing the clothes back in her closet and together, they headed out. The earlier rain had reduced to a mist, cold and refreshing against her face, but the clouds remained heavy and clung to the sky as the sun tried to burn its way through.

For weeks, spring had merely been a glimmer on the horizon, but today, its warm tendrils wove into the air. Even the earth beneath her feet seemed more alive, and she imagined seeds germinating as small sprouts rose out of the mud.

As they approached Adrian's bike, a bright splash of purple made her gasp. "Don't tell me," she whispered, spinning to him and bouncing on the balls of her feet. "The extra helmet is for me?"

His smile widened. "Yup. It's all yours, sweetheart."

Dangling from the seat next to his black one hung another helmet with a vibrant violet visor, the rest a matte black. It came with two small, pointed ears laid back on the head like a mythical creature.

She squealed and pounced on him with a bear hug. "Ohmygosh, thankyou-thankyou-thankyou!"

He wrapped his arms around her and returned the embrace, chuckling. "I'm glad you like it, but there's one more thing to go with it."

Electricity hummed in her chest. Nothing could make this day better. Yet there was more.

Adrian stepped up to the bike, unlocked their helmets, and handed hers over. She took it carefully as if it would break at the slightest excess force—even though the helmet would protect her, not the other way around. Inside, she found a pair of deep mauve leather gloves. The soft material stretched slightly around her fingers as she tried them on, forming a perfect barrier against the misty cold.

"These are perfect," she breathed, repeating her thoughts out loud and turning to him. "Thank you so much."

He'd already gotten on the bike, wearing his own helmet for the first time. The crinkles around his eyes showed through his visor as he reached over to help put hers on. "There, now you're all set. Let's go."

Half an hour later, they pulled off on a back road next to what looked like a vacant fenced lot. The large, paved space housed an old warehouse and several smaller sheds with a handful of cars scattered along one end—more than a few of which had cracked windows, patches of rust, and various missing parts. The smell of rain saturated the air, dampening the undertones of rubber and oil.

"Where are we?" she asked as Adrian put out the kickstand and shut off the engine. Little hints of sunlight kept fading in and out from behind the clouds, highlighting the clusters of graffiti on the walls one moment, then plunging them into shadow the next.

He removed his helmet and shook his hair loose. "An old shop-turned-junkyard that's owned by Royal Flush. Raptor gave us permission to use it today, but I'd advise you not to go poking around."

She nodded, glancing over the myriad of graffiti paintings, the largest of which read 'Royal Flush – All or Nothing' around a skeletal hand holding a playing card. Her gaze drifted to other pieces of art as Adrian walked up to the tall chain link fence, unlocking the gate and pushing it open.

When he came back, instead of driving in, he reached over and tugged her hips up to the center of the seat.

"What are you doing?" she giggled, little tingles amplifying his touch.

"Not me," he replied. "*You.*"

Her laughter petered out. "What?"

His eyes still had the little crinkles at the edges, but their golden core looked as serious as ever. He wasn't joking. Her smile dissolved.

"Me...what?"

"You're going to drive the bike."

If the helmet hadn't been strapped under her chin, her jaw would've hit the floor. "Oh, no...no, no, no," she protested. "I'm more than happy to stay in my place *behind* you."

"I'll keep you safe," he assured, not concerned in the least. "You don't have to go fast or drive more than a few feet." He paused, waiting for her to disagree again, but her tongue stuck to the roof of her mouth.

"Bikes are about balance, and so is life," he continued. "There are things within our control and things we can only try to prepare for. It's easy to get thrown off when we come across an obstacle. It's easy to feel like you can't ever get up and trust yourself again, but if we only pay attention to things we can't control, then we start to think we're useless when we aren't. I struggled with that for a long time."

Despite the truth in his words, the mere thought of driving the bike paralyzed her with fear. A pit had quickly sunk in her belly, and she kept her hands firmly locked together in her lap, ignoring the handles now looming within reach. Of everything he could've asked of her, this was the one thing she couldn't do. There was no way.

He gave her a knowing look that did nothing to calm her nerves, then took her gloved hands in his. "If you really don't want to, I won't force it. With me, you'll always get the choice—you can have control or let me take over—but I need you to see you're more capable than you think, Iv. I want you to set yourself free from doubt."

An ache spread from her fingers to her wrist, and she realized her hands had clamped around his, gripping much too tight. The same suffocating feeling resurfaced from when Jace had pressed her to the wall, his fingers digging into her arm. The same feeling she had when her mom told her she wasn't living up to her potential—to the family's expectations. Every time she failed, it felt worse, but here, the consequences would be far more severe.

And disappointing her black knight would hurt most of all.

"I can't," she whispered, unable to lift her voice. "I'll crash. It'll ruin—"

Adrian leaned in and sucked on her neck below the helmet, inching over her sweet spot. His lips cut off her train of thought as her blood pulled to the surface. Everything became fuzzy, her body keen to soak up every ounce of his affection, relishing every sharp tug of pain as it bloomed over her pulse. Her panic twisted into a knife of liquid heat that wound down to her core.

"Say 'I can't' again, and you'll get a mark each time," he warned, tone balancing on that thin line between admonishing and tender.

She took an unsteady breath, the tremble lingering in her voice. "That's supposed to deter me?"

"I could always bite," he murmured, running his teeth over the lace on her shoulder, breath hot against the crisp air.

She shivered.

"I know you can do it," he continued, pulling away enough to look her in the eyes and returning her death grip with a squeeze. "Because you never said you didn't want to, and if it's something you want, I'll make sure you get it."

Desire warred with her unshakable apprehension—the desire to please him but also the desire to prove herself wrong. To prove she was strong enough to handle it.

She nibbled on her lip, relying on the remnants of his touch, the strength of his presence. "Will you ride with me?"

"Of course," he said, then placed her hand on the handlebar. "Let me show you how it works."

He walked her through the basics: what to press and when, how the bike would react, and how it would feel. If she wanted, he told her where to drive once they got past the gate, but she could hardly think about more than that.

Starting the engine seemed like the hardest part, and with his guidance, she memorized each step, repeating the actions as he explained them. Finally, he strapped his helmet on and settled in behind her. The firm plane of abdomen supported her back, his thighs sturdy guardrails and arms a harness that held her in one piece, forcing her to confront the challenge.

She swallowed, hesitant to move a single inch. No matter how much encouragement he offered, the fear wouldn't leave.

"Kickstand first," he reminded.

She nudged the bar, bracing herself as the weight of the bike shifted. Even with both of their feet planted on the ground, it didn't feel stable at all. Knowing the physics that kept the bike moving didn't change the fact that it weighed more than three hundred pounds.

She straightened, refocusing as her mind echoed with a chorus of *I can't. I shouldn't. I'm not built for this.*

"Good, now start the engine." Adrian's voice cut through her thoughts, and she latched onto it.

Tightening her grip, she started the ignition and twisted the throttle. His hand closed in over hers, guiding the engine to a roar that drowned out everything else. All that remained was them and the bike, the pavement and the gate ahead.

Deep breaths. Her torso expanded into his, and she lifted her gaze to look through the small visor.

Adrian had been everything she needed—everything she wanted. He'd been her anthem in the day and her lullaby at night, a man who saw her weakness and turned it into strength. The least she could do was give him this. She could hand over her fear, let him have her insecurity and her trust, and then defy her own self-imposed limits.

"All right," she said, more to herself than to him, and eased the bike forward.

THIRTY-SIX

A DRIAN'S BIKE PURRED, ROLLING AHEAD JUST LIKE SHE ASKED IT to. Her heart shot into her throat, but she kept her hands steady, vibrations coursing through her fingers as she gently brought the beast of metal and speed and power past the front gate. Then she slowed to a stop, and Adrian put his foot down for support.

Exhilaration flooded her system. Against all the odds she stacked against herself, she came out victorious. *She drove the frickin bike.*

"I did it," she breathed, twisting and then repeating louder, "I really did it!"

He squeezed her thighs. "You did."

He didn't need to use words to express his pride. Moreover, her own satisfaction welled up and threatened to burst out of her chest. Such a silly thing to think she couldn't drive fifteen feet past the fence, but she did. She tamed the monster she never thought she could conquer.

"Want to go again?" Adrian asked.

She nodded, not only unafraid but eager to explore this new superpower. "Can I?"

"Try driving in a loop around the warehouse," he suggested. "Take the corners easy and watch out for puddles."

Nodding again, her confidence began to grow. The tires moved nice and smooth over the pavement. At the first turn, she tried to go as slow as possible but soon realized the bike needed more momentum. Sucking in a deep breath, she added more, and it purred a little louder. The wind rushed a little faster. Cold air whisked against her skin and replaced anxiety with something indescribable, a thrilling, pulsing entity in her chest.

Joy.

After finishing her first loop, she went again. And again. She built up the courage to wind around the sheds and warehouses, gaining more speed and even venturing out to the quiet main road where she dared to drive as fast as she would in a regular vehicle.

Elation bubbled through her, and a smile stretched so wide it made her cheeks hurt. The kind of hurt she'd gladly feel every day. One of the rare human experiences that made the world seem large and the gift of living in it even larger. At last, she could breathe easy.

The sun faded, clouds winning their perpetual war, and as the mist thickened to a quiet drizzle, she pulled up to the warehouse and brought them to a stop. Popping out the kickstand and shutting off the engine, she took off her helmet and gazed into the sky.

Her laughter filled the air.

She peeled off the gloves and stretched her hands into the cool, refreshing rain. Flecks of water hit her cheeks, washing away the weight of unfulfilled expectations, the worry and stress of making every right step, calculating every decision, and looking out for everyone else except herself.

Just this once, she had confronted her fear. And even

though it had been at the request of her knight, she knew he'd done it for her.

That fact sent her heart soaring most of all. His wounds had been clear from the beginning. The darkness shrouding his presence, the scars on his hands mirroring the ones on his heart—but she never thought he would see her wounds, and take the time to tend to her as she had for him.

Hanging her helmet on the bike handle, she leaned back as Adrian wrapped his warm arms around her waist and rested his helmet on the opposite handle. Then his lips were in her hair, tickling her ears, kissing the hollow of her neck, and repeating the process on the other side.

Her laughter wouldn't stop, even as Adrian's lips formed a smile against her rain-slick skin.

"Rule number one," he whispered. "Remember to look after yourself." He turned her head so he could speak not only with words but with eyes that shone brighter than the sun. Eyes that couldn't have been any happier or more sincere. "If you aren't sure how, then I'll show you. Every day, I'll teach you how special you are in every way I can think of. It won't always be something you'll like, but know that for me, you come first. No matter what."

She shook her head in awe, heat rising in her cheeks despite the rain until she burned with an emotion that surely hadn't been discovered. Gratitude and happiness, hope and love, admiration and attraction all in one.

"And I'll never let you forget you're my black knight," she replied, voice lowering to a husky whisper as she ran out of breath, lungs starved for air as she drank in the feeling of belonging to such a man. A man more god than human. "My dark, chivalrous, sexy savior."

He hummed as if her words were a sacred prayer. One that pleased him very much. "A little sadistic, too. Don't forget that part." He grinned as he trailed a hand up her thigh while the other wrapped over the ribbon at her neck. His rings pressed into her skin, the metal cold and unforgiving as raindrops rolled down her face.

Her breath hitched, cut off not from the strength of his touch but the gentleness of it, as if he was feeling out every part of her, creating a map that he'd use to uncover her most treasured secrets and hide them away for himself.

Her clothes were damp, and the heat of Adrian's touch seeped into her skin like wildfire. A searing blaze that she wanted to consume her, to devour her alive until all she felt was flame and fire and flesh. Nothing could quench her desire to burn for him and for him alone. She arched back, floating and drowning and burning all at once. Surely she'd perish if not for him holding her so close.

"Are there other rules?" she asked breathlessly, moaning as he pressed his hips into her from behind, the thick length of his erection hard and swollen along his thigh, nudging against her ass.

"*Dammit*," he hissed as if to scold himself. "Yes, there are." His fingers tightened around her throat like he couldn't bear to let her speak, much less move.

"Rule number two," he murmured. "You tell me everything, and I'll do the same for you. No secrets. There's not a single thing you could think or feel that I won't care about. Tell me if you're angry or if you're scared. Tell me if you want to be held, or pet, or fed. Tell me when your pussy is wet and needy, if you need to be fucked, and how you'd like me to do it."

The hand on her thigh inched up to the place where the seam of her pants met, where she was indeed *very* wet and needy, and it had nothing to do with the strands of hair sticking to her face or the droplets running over her chest and down her stomach. She trembled, pushing her hips into his hand.

"Yes," she moan-whispered, not entirely sure what question she was replying to, but knowing the answer was undoubtably yes. "I want you to fill me. I've wanted—"

His fingers tightened again, cutting her off as a guttural growl left the back of his throat. "Last rule," he grit out. "My orders are absolute. I can and will establish additional rules when and where I see fit, and you will follow them. You'll get a safe word, which will either pause or stop what we're doing altogether. It's important you know I will never punish you for using it or for voicing your concerns, but I expect obedience to the best of your ability."

She nodded.

"That's *yes, sir*."

"Yes, sir," she hummed, torn between the ache between her legs and the fullness in her heart.

"Do you have a safe word in mind?"

In all her prior thoughts about this very moment, she hadn't settled on the right word. "I haven't thought of one yet."

"Then you will use 'violet' for now. Is that all right?"

"Yes, sir," she purred, already in love. It fit her too well, and even better, it had been bestowed. A gift. A divine blessing. "I like it a lot."

"Good," he murmured in her ear. "Don't forget it." He relaxed his hand around her throat and coaxed her to lean on his shoulder, letting her eyes peer up at his, which had turned into black orbs surrounded by a ring of gold. "And for me?" His fingers fluttered over her skin with slow, delicious strokes from her neck down to her collarbone. "Do you have any rules or requests?"

She smiled, astounded once again. Of course, he'd think of her when all she could think about was him. "Only one."

The next words caught in her chest, their significance saturated with feeling. This wasn't just about being good, or part of being his submissive. It wasn't something she thought he'd say no to—but it was a desire so potent and so close to her heart that it threatened to rip out her very soul.

"Hm?" he prompted.

"Keep me," she whispered, searching his face. "I don't want anyone else—anything else. I want to be the one you keep and the one who gets to keep you."

He hummed low and dark, then leaned down to brush his lips against hers. "You will always be mine, sweetheart."

He swallowed her mouth with his, parting her lips with insatiable kisses and stroking her tongue the same way he'd stroked her pussy only hours earlier. She moaned, and he ate that, too. "From this point on, I own you. Every sigh, every whisper, every plea. You'll beg for me. Cry for me. You'll come for me and me alone."

His hand dipped down to her breast, easily cupping her in his palm and plucking the hardened nipple through her nearly soaked shirt. Her hips bucked, and her core clenched, flooded with arousal and unbearable need. Her legs kept spread open around the frame of the bike.

She whimpered as he pulled back from her tingling lips. "Now...does my sweet, brave witch think she's earned herself a reward?"

The clouds covered them in soft shadow, rain droplets hanging from his defined eyebrows and long lashes. She sucked in a breath that pushed her chest into his palm. "I hope so, sir."

Staying still was so hard—and so very impossible—but she could do nothing else as her body lay strung out for him, hung over a vast, enticing precipice. The promise in Adrian's words, his touch, and the warm shelter of his hard muscle proved too tempting. Anything he could give her would be a blessing— pain or pleasure, desperation or release.

He pulled his lip between his teeth, then teased his thumb along the seam of her jeans. Her clit pulsed outwardly. "I think you have earned a reward...but I also think you've earned a punishment."

THIRTY-SEVEN

Adrian

His sweet witch shivered in his arms, eyes wide and skin warm even as rain slid over her cheeks and down the slight curve of her neck. Droplets ran under the sweater clinging to her breasts, and he followed their path, rolling the furled tip of her nipple between his fingers.

What a fucking privilege.

Not only did he have the most amazing woman in the world between his legs, she wanted to belong to him—she wanted to call him sir—and he was going to show her just how much that meant.

Watching her wings unfold as she drove his bike, seeing her own it like a personal throne, had left his chest pounding, threatening to tear itself wide open. Maybe he had a heart inside there after all. He wanted nothing more than to see her raised to her rightful place as queen. A person so exalted no one dared think about defiling her.

Except her king, of course.

Except the black knight who would pledge his entire existence to stand at her side. The one person who would protect her at her lowest and worship her at her highest.

"Mm, yes," he affirmed, grinding his hips into her just to feel the friction, the give of her cheeks, and the sigh from her lips as he squeezed her throat. "A reward for being such a good girl and not giving up, even though you wanted to. And a punishment for having such a wonderful smile, for laughing so beautifully it made my dick hard as fucking steel."

She pressed into him as if she had to feel for herself a third time just how true his words were. He twisted her nipple until she let out a squeal and squirmed to no avail. "Teasing me with that sweet ass while you rode my bike like it belonged to you. For that, I should make you ride my cock the same way. *Fuck—*" All the blood in his body surged at the thought. Merely saying the words rendered him speechless.

Taking a deep inhale of the rain-saturated air, he reveled in the smell of earth mixed with the floral scent from her hair, in the rich aroma and taste of her climax lingering in his stubble. He traced the curve of her breast, trailing his hand back down to the front of her jeans. She practically shoved herself into his palm.

He chuckled darkly and took his time fiddling with the button. "Should I open this up and see what's underneath, hm?"

"Yes, sir. Please." She reached her arms up around his neck, stretching her body across the bike to expose every inch to the rain and sky, and to his searing gaze. "I want you to see."

Need hit him like a bullet, white-hot and piercing to the core.

The reward first, then.

"Do I get to play with what I find?" he murmured, releasing her throat to run his hand along her chest and squeeze her other breast. She'd stilled, and that pleased him very much. Already learning so fast. So eager. He popped the button open, toying with the zipper before pulling it down, knick by knick.

She groaned and arched into him, his forearm bracing them together. "Yes, sir."

Two more knicks. He tugged the zipper halfway down.

"Is this pussy mine to please, mine to torture in any way I see fit?" He grinned, knowing every word prolonged her anticipation. Every answer forced her to neglect her own want and focus on his demands.

"Yes, Sir. Please, I can't—"

His teeth sunk into her neck, directly over the hickey he left earlier. "What did I say about that word," he growled against her pulse.

"That I'll—*oh.*" She gasped, unable to continue as he finished pulling down the zipper and rubbed small circles over the thin veil of her panties. They were soaked through as much as the rest of her clothes, but this wetness had nothing to do with the weather. "That I get a mark each time I say it," she managed to finish.

"Good girl." The exposed skin on her stomach pebbled, her legs widening as he rubbed her clit. Then he pulled away the last layer and slipped his fingers between the folds of her pussy. "Now, let me see what I have to work with."

His other hand drew tight circles around her nipple, plucking then teasing again as he spread her labia. She was so soft all over, so pink, her blushing center glossed with her own arousal. So ripe for his picking.

His hunger had grown into an insatiable craving from this morning, his appetite unrivaled for the sweetest fruit of them all. But he maintained an impassive façade, inspecting her like she was merely livestock he'd won in an auction. Testing her quality, ensuring she'd be up to the tasks he wanted her to perform.

Holding her open with his thumb and middle finger, he traced around her entrance, up to the top of her wet seam, and pulled back the hood of her clit. It was exactly as he wanted, swollen and tender and begging. He licked his lips but left it untouched. Rewards were meant to be savored.

Then, his finger traveled down until it pressed against the small ring of muscle behind her entrance. Her back arched, and with all the slick and suddenness of her movement, the tip of his finger breached her tightest hole.

"Shit," he breathed.

She whimpered, immediately trying to settle herself.

Dammit, she was tight. And hot. Wiggling around her rim, he tested her response as she threw back her head and parted her lips.

His cock swelled, some primal caveman instinct telling him to grow even bigger, even harder at the thought of puncturing her most private place. One day, she'd earn that. He had no doubt that one day, she'd earn everything.

For now, though, he had a mission to fulfill.

Easing out gently, he brought his thumb down on her clit and gave it a slow, firm circle. She tensed, the muscles in her stomach clenching in the same way he knew her pussy would, the way it would grip and hold him right where she needed it— and that thought had him stabbing two fingers inside her, pressing down where she pressed back, rubbing that particular rough patch that made her squirm and curl her toes.

"Sir—" She gasped.

Another moan cut her off.

He gave her breast a final tug before gliding over the dainty ribbon at her neck and up her jaw, clamping his hand over her mouth. "Keep moaning, sweetheart. Let me hear all your beautiful cries as I make you come."

Muffled, she did as she was told, her lips pliant under his calloused palm.

"This morning only made you want more, didn't it?" he hummed in her ear, forcing her to take it slow and deep as he curled his fingers and flicked her clit with his thumb, keeping her spread and lubed with her own arousal.

She nodded.

"Good," he murmured. "I'm going to give it to you."

Her thighs trembled as she strangled his bike, just like she'd done to his head earlier. He never knew he'd be so jealous of a hunk of metal.

Twisting his fingers, he pushed them in further until she cried out, then held them there, mirroring the movements he made on her clit. Her tits tightened, straining against the wet fabric—as if there wasn't a single part of her that didn't want his touch as much as he wanted to give it.

She turned her face into his neck, closing her eyes and shaking like a leaf.

"Open your eyes."

She did, and when jade met gold, he pinched her clit. Her pupils dilated, jaw falling unhinged as instinct took over, and her body blushed all over, overcome by pleasure and completeness and every sensation that meant *she belonged to him*.

He didn't stop until she stopped squirming and shuddered with a final release, the flutter and clutch of her pussy melting away. She breathed out a satiated sigh as he uncovered her lips.

"What a very naughty girl." He pulled out his fingers, coated with her nectar to the point that it left a string of evidence between them and fell onto the bike in a shimmering streak. "Leaving a filthy wet mark on my leather seat."

She peered up, a flush in her cheeks and that spark of awakened lust in her eyes. It glowed all the brighter as she registered his words, then saw the gleam that must have shown in his own eyes and the crooked slant of his lips.

"I didn't mean to." She bit her lip, playing along with mock guilt.

No part of her looked guilty or ashamed of what just

happened, and a surge of pride threatened to make him ruin the game and kiss her until they both fell off the bike, then pin her to the ground and make her come until they both passed out. But no, as fun as that would be, what he had in mind was much more tempting.

He raised his hand in front of their faces as if to show off the proof of their sin. The rain misted through a ray of sun in the ever-fickle clouds, and sparkles of moisture glistened along his knuckles, coating his rings like lacquer.

"Taste," he said, offering his incriminating fingers.

She sucked his finger clean, swirling her sweet tongue around him like he'd offered her a piece of candy. He didn't know what turned him on more, the fact that she could enjoy her own pleasure or how she wrapped her lips around him and took him in further.

He groaned. "I believe it's time for your punishment."

She hummed, her teeth scraping his knuckles. How he was starting to love playing games with this woman. The kind that only made her want to play more, to crawl into the dark corners of their hearts and lock out the rest of the world.

"See that smaller shed to the right?" He pointed, and her gaze followed his arm. "It's miscellaneous storage. Old documents and stuff no one looks at anymore."

She gave him a curious glance, so he answered her unspoken inquiry. "Raptor and I used to sneak in when we were younger, looking for things we shouldn't. Never really found anything interesting except for a few old vests with bullet holes."

The other sheds had more interesting contents, but those weren't things he wanted Ivory to know about. Things that once she saw, she'd be held accountable for.

He dropped his voice to the low tone to which she responded so well. "Go inside. You'll find a desk in the center. I want you bent over with your ass ready for me by the time I get back from locking the gate. Wouldn't want anyone interrupting to find out how wet you get from being spanked, now would we?"

THIRTY-EIGHT

THE HINGES ON THE SHED DOOR CREAKED AS SHE PULLED IT OPEN and peeked inside. The scent of damp earth hung in the air from the rain, but the cement floor was bone-dry. A shiver ran down her spine. What if she stumbled into something she shouldn't? This place did belong to a gang of outlaws...

Adrenaline spiked her pulse as she peered further into the small room. A shaft of light from the open doorway illuminated dusty file boxes, various tools, and supplies scattered across industrial metal shelves. As Adrian said, a small desk was positioned in the center of the room. Nothing too inconspicuous. But she wasn't about to go snooping around.

The desk looked old but in good condition—the kind with a cubby under the main surface and a wooden chair welded on. Unlike the rest of the miscellaneous junk, the desk was dust-free, and the floor had been cleared and swept. As if Adrian set it up before they even arrived.

The thought made heat rise to her already flushed cheeks. Between her legs, her pussy blushed in awe, wet and hot under her unbuttoned jeans. He'd planned everything out down to the last detail. Usually, she planned for others, the one who made special treats for birthdays and carried extra supplies in case of emergencies. Today wasn't a holiday, yet Adrian had done so much to let her know she was important.

She traced her fingers over the smooth wood, remembering the first time he bent her over his kitchen counter. The first time he told her to appreciate herself—that he valued not just her but her submission. The first time he brought up punishments and rules. True, she shied away from the thought then, but it hadn't scared her.

He'd made it clear this was her choice. *Her* power, and if she offered that to him, he wouldn't let it go to waste.

Even now, she had the chance to walk back outside. He'd always given her the option to step away, to decide if she really wanted this with him. The answer had already been written in her heart and mind, but this chance to choose him, to choose submission, made it all the more gratifying.

Her heart raced at the opportunity to please him, to bow and relinquish herself to her black knight. To let him hurt her. Punish her. Humiliate her.

He owned her, and in return, she could own him with a single word. Nothing she gave would go unnoticed or unrewarded. He treated her willingness to suffer for his sake as an honor, and he deserved no less.

The front gate squeaked and sliced through her thoughts. She jumped, fumbling to push her jeans and panties down to her thighs. It wouldn't take him long to walk in, and when he did, she wanted to earn his praise.

She spread her legs as much as her pants would allow, then leaned forward and folded her arms over the desk. From this position, everything would be clear as day when he walked in. The swollen, pink cleft between her legs. The rosebud his finger had breached earlier. The dimples around her ass and the plush of her thighs pushed up from the tightness of her jeans.

Worse, she wouldn't be able to see the look on his face. She could only wait, mind and body settling into the space he'd carved out just for her.

The seconds ticked by. She exhaled and rested her head across her arms, strands of wet hair tickling her elbows.

His boots crunched against the gravel outside. Hyper-alert, her pussy throbbed, and her eyes darted to the side in search of his shadow.

Crunch. Crunch.

The footsteps stopped as they reached the doorway.

She was already dripping, at war with the unrelenting urge to squirm or cover herself. Her face blazed with embarrassment, and she closed her eyes with a deep breath.

"Very good."

The dark timbre of his voice soothed over her like an ancient mystical spell. She almost wept with relief.

Adrian stepped into the room and walked behind her, observing quietly until she clenched around nothing but crisp air and heat from his unseen gaze. Then two warm palms smoothed over her ass cheeks, spreading her open until nothing could be hidden. No secret left uncovered.

"What a divine sight," he whispered, bending over and leaving a tender kiss on one cheek. His lips were warm and soft, nothing short of a precious gift. "You've made me an incredibly lucky man, Ivory."

The leather jacket rustled as he straightened and moved to the front of the desk to face her. His smile dazzled her as she opened her eyes. A bolt of electricity shot straight through her heart. "Undo my belt, sweetheart."

Wait. Was he really going to use that?

She bit her lip, deciding not to give in so easily. She'd asked him to break her, after all, and she trusted he knew how to put back the pieces.

Rising to her elbows, she concentrated on tugging out the

tail end of the belt from the loops. Her fingers lingered over the nick he'd made for her wrists and again on the second for her ankles. The leather didn't have any other marks or scratches— meaning it'd been forever altered, forever marked as a tool designed for her. Metal clinked as she tugged on the clasp, and his shameless bulge pressed against the zipper like an impatient, ravenous beast.

"Thank you," he murmured when she was done, and put her hands back on the desk.

His gratitude didn't do much to ease her flare of disappointment, but she responded as she should. "You're welcome, sir."

After slipping the belt out of the rest of the loops, Adrian sat in the chair. The seat looked much too small, but he made it work. Her mind conjured a younger version of him, a boy who sat in the back of the class and, despite keeping to himself, always ended up in detention. The kind who would beat up the bullies and show no remorse. The kind her mom had always warned her about.

He reached down and pulled a pocketknife from his boot, snapping it open and capturing her attention. Curved at the tip and serrated at the base, the blade was black as night with gold embellishments on the handle. The sharp edge shone silver in the light.

"Move back a bit so I won't slip and cut you," he said, placing the belt flat on the desk.

She shimmied away, now propped up on the edge of the desk and forced to hold her own weight. Her feet shuffled, body yearning for more attention while her mind honed in on his movements. Carefully, Adrian started to carve little holes where the nicks had been.

"Sir?"

He glanced up, eyes leveled with hers as he paused his task.

"Have you always carried that?"

"Yes." After ensuring her face held no trace of concern, went back to work, then set the knife down and picked out pieces of cut-off leather.

She chewed her lip. "And at the Halloween party? When Jace's friends pulled the knife on us?"

"Mhm."

Then, none of Jace's threats had meant anything because Adrian had been as prepared as the frat boys were. He probably hadn't pulled out the knife when Jace was beating him up, either.

"Have you ever used it?" she asked.

"Once. I was walking alone late at night, and someone had been following me for a few blocks, so I took it out and started playing around. They turned back." He set the knife down and held the belt up to the light coming in from the doorway. "But I will use it if I have to."

Curious, she picked up the handle and tested its weight in her hand. The metal felt cold and solid but not heavy. Her fingertip brushed over the flat of the blade, and she imagined what it would feel like pressed to her skin. What it would be like held against her throat as Adrian fucked her from behind—

She gasped as her clit pulsed, and the point of the knife sliced into her flesh.

THIRTY-NINE

Ivory

"Ouch," she whispered, unable to look at Adrian as blood welled over her fingerprint.

"Are you okay?" He took her hand to inspect it.

"Yes. I'm sorry, sir." Her skin burned more out of shame than pain. Even while half-naked and bent over a desk, she'd managed to mess up.

He sighed. Picking up the knife, he put it back in her palm and closed both their hands around the handle. She lifted her gaze to his, relieved not to find anger or disappointment, although his expression remained firm and commanding.

"I use my fists as a warning," he said. "And I'll use them as much and as often as I need to. But when I use a weapon, I do it once—to solve the problem permanently."

She nodded. This wasn't a toy.

He brought his other hand in front of the blade. "I have no problem with you picking up the knife, but when you hold a weapon, you do so with the intent to use it."

Moving the knife in her hand along with his, he pressed the tip into his finger and made a mirror of her wound. He didn't flinch, watching her face instead as blood pooled in the shallow cut.

She winced for him. It was all fun and games until real harm came into play.

Even when he toyed with things like pain and punishment, there were real consequences that he had to hold himself accountable for, and she ought to do the same. Tentatively, she raised her finger to his and pressed them together.

He closed his thumb over their fingers and pinched them in place. "Your blood is as good as mine, Iv," he whispered. "If you hurt, I hurt."

"I know." Her weakness had become his. If she wasn't more cautious, she could get them both in trouble. Not just with their games either, but in a world where innocent kids got shot in a park and entitled frat boys took advantage of whoever they wanted.

He released their fingers and wiped them off with the inside of his shirt. "I will do everything to protect both of us, but try to keep yourself safe." She nodded and offered a small smile as he folded the knife and slipped it back into his boot. The sober expression on his face softened. "I'll clean the cut for you when we get back."

Something flickered in his eyes as he pressed her finger to his lips, making the gold flecks more distinct and the emotion clearer. Here she was, supposed to be turned on by presenting herself, by waiting to please him, but instead, it was his concern that flooded her sex all over again.

He let go and walked behind the desk, cutting himself off from her line of sight. Goosebumps rose over her skin, and static danced in the air, separating and connecting them with an almost tangible energy.

"Do you remember your safe word?"

"Yes, sir."

"Say it for me."

"Violet."

He hummed in approval. A tug came at her ankle and brought her foot against the leg of the desk. It forced her stance to widen as the smooth leather of the belt locked her in place. "No matter what, you'll use it if you feel the need?"

"Yes, sir."

"Good." He straightened and gathered her hair, placing it over to one side. His lips ghosted across her shoulder, and then his teeth pulled at the ribbon around her neck. It unraveled, her pulse pounding in its absence.

"I've never done this before," she blurted, breaths quickening. Even if she used the safe word, she'd be stuck. Tied to a desk in the middle of a warehouse owned by criminals.

A reassuring hand smoothed up the back of her thigh and spread her legs further apart. Her knees bent from the strain of the position, back arching to push out her hips. Her forehead dropped down to the desk.

"You please me very much, Iv," Adrian murmured, crouching down. "That's all you need to remember." He secured her other foot, though it wasn't as tight as the first, and stood. "One ankle is tied with the belt, the other with your hair ribbon. If the ribbon breaks or gets untied, you'll get double the number of spankings we left off at, understood?"

Double...that meant if he only planned to spank her ten times, and she broke on the tenth, he'd give her twenty more. She couldn't move as is, but if she tried, it would only make things worse.

"Yes, sir." Her voice wavered, hands gripping the edge of the desk.

"I've always had a certain requirement," Adrian began to muse, but she could hardly focus as she braced herself, watching the toe of his boots disappear and reappear in her line of sight. "When I started with my arrangements, I decided everything would be earned—rewards, punishments, even the chance to be fucked."

"What?" she breathed.

"You'll have to earn my cock," he clarified. "Inch by inch."

She sucked in a breath. What would that take to earn it all? It didn't matter. She'd do it.

"You've earned two inches so far," he said. "One as part of the reward for driving the bike, and another for being exactly how I asked when I walked in." His hand traced over her spine, then ran down her flank. Her pussy practically begged for more, but she knew relief would come only after the punishment. "Are you ready to earn another?"

"Yes, sir." As soon as the whispered words left her mouth, his palm cracked down on her ass. She tensed, body rejecting the pain as it bloomed over her skin.

Then his mouth pressed hot kisses over her vulva, sampling her before pulling back. She moaned and bucked at the loss of contact.

"This is where you say *thank you*."

"Thank you, sir," she repeated. As the sting from the first strike receded, he struck with another. The heat seeped lower, curling into her core and making her gasp.

She thanked him again, gritting her teeth.

"Too much?" he asked.

She shook her head. "No, sir."

The next two hits came in quick succession, harder than the first and with an undeniable sting that bit without shame. Her face contorted. She had to hold her breath as she thanked him.

"Hard enough?" he asked.

"I don't think I could handle much more—*ahh*." She squirmed, barely able to stay still as his tongue swept up her slit, circling her clit and then her asshole. The restraints pulled at her ankles as she became torn between chasing pleasure and running from pain, craving every touch he offered but unable to do anything but take what he dolled out. She refused to move an inch—and it was the most difficult thing she'd ever done.

Two more hits, both unforgiving and with enough of a pause between each for a thank you.

His hands were rough as they gripped her, squeezing, smoothing, and kneading as he saw fit. The metal of his rings pressed into the hot sting. "My handprints look so good on your ass," he murmured. "You have no idea, sweetheart." He exhaled, still rubbing her sore skin. "Does it hurt?"

"Yes," she answered honestly.

A hit cracked down harder than the rest. She yelped, hinging on the point of impact. "Yes, sir. Thank you, sir."

"Do you feel good?"

Her core clenched, aroused, and not aroused enough. Her thoughts wandered no further than the experience of being in her own body, of surrendering it to him. All she wanted was more, for this infinity to stretch on into the next.

"Yes, sir," she answered, as honestly as she did first response.

"Good girl," he replied. The tear of a foil package sounded from behind.

"Don't—" She pleaded, sweat beading on her forehead. "If it's okay...I don't want you to use a condom. I haven't slept with anyone in months, and I'm on birth control." She'd never ached like this. Never felt like she would perish if she didn't get to feel him, skin on skin.

For a moment, he left her hanging. Then admitted, "I've never fucked raw before."

Her face sunk into the desk, no longer able to keep her composure. This man. This glorious god of a man, who had reddened her ass and soaked her pussy, now wrecked her spirit.

What she wouldn't give to be his first. To take his seed and have it spill out of her, to earn every inch and then swallow him whole. She didn't need to answer, her pussy fluttering and legs quaking, chest aching, and lungs straining for air as she hoped he'd take her offer.

To claim her body as a willing sacrifice.

"Please," she whispered.

"Hush," he commanded, tone strong yet with a clear rasp. Then he spread her with his hands, and his bare cock nudged her opening.

She moaned, clenching her fists.

"Fuck," he hissed. "Dammit, you're so hot."

Whether he meant literally or figuratively, she couldn't find the strength to care. In the next moment, the flare of his cockhead dipped into her sex, and she squeezed her eyes shut, dying and reviving over and over as she held herself in place. Even with two inches, he felt thick, stretching her walls and nudging a place inside that could easily send her over the edge.

A smack came down on her ass, and her legs involuntarily tugged against the belt. Oh no. She was losing it. She didn't know how many spankings she'd taken but knew she couldn't take much more.

A harder hit struck over the other. The sting hooked in deep, counteracted by the clench of her pussy on Adrian's dick and followed by a rush of pleasure.

"What do you say?" he snarled.

"Thank you, sir," she squeaked.

He pulled out, then pushed back in. They gasped in unison.

Two more hits. Two more thrusts. Two more thank yous.

She was going to break. There was no choice. Her orgasm built from deep inside, as unavoidable as the descent of a falling star or the unrelenting pull of gravity. Then it hit.

And it hit hard.

FORTY

Adrian

Fuck. Fuck. *Fuck.* He wasn't going to last like this.

Ivory's climax flashed as bright as a bolt of lightning, then rolled through them both like a clap of thunder. With one hand palming the bright prints blooming across her porcelain skin, he forced himself to take long, measured breaths.

But her pussy was hell-bent on coaxing him in, mercilessly gripping his dick as she came. He was going to explode any minute now.

Shit. He pulled out and yanked on his balls with a shuddered exhale. As much as he needed to come, he didn't have anything to clean her up with. The ride back would be uncomfortable enough with a sore ass, and he already felt bad about the cut on her finger. After today, she deserved a whole night of aftercare, and he was determined to give it to her.

Being inside her felt like heaven. Pure, unfettered bliss. It was as good as any joyride—no, better.

Not to mention how unequivocally captivating she was, that heart-shaped ass framed by the gentle arch of her back, a hint of her soft breasts showing through her sweater as they pushed up against the desk. Her legs were another story, plump enough to give him something to grab onto, slender enough to be made of sexy curves that ran from her hips down to her calves.

Still quaking from the orgasm, her clipped gasps filled the room, then concluded with a final, breathless groan that made his dick twitch in agony.

"You're fucking gorgeous," he whispered as she relaxed. He bent to kiss her reddened cheek and removed her restraints. She hadn't broken through the ribbon, but the bow had gotten dangerously close to slipping out.

Still, she'd taken every hit and thanked him for it. If things kept going like this, he'd have to get more creative with the punishments because she was too good at not breaking the rules.

Gliding his hands up her sides, he smiled as she shivered at his touch. Her clothes were still damp from the rain, but her skin was warm, and her hair had dried into long veins of amethyst.

"Come here," he muttered, pulling her up and turning her in his arms.

She sighed and leaned into his shoulder, resting her parted lips against his neck.

"Was I good?" she whispered. Her voice sounded airy like she was still floating on cloud nine. He couldn't be prouder.

"So good," he replied. "So very, very good." He threaded his hand through her hair and brought her hips to his, indulging in a feather-light kiss, savoring her skin and the plump of her lip.

Then he froze. Her hand had found his dick, still pulsing with need and nudging into her belly.

"Don't worry, sweetheart," he choked out and pushed it down.

"I want to," she said softly, leaning back to search his face.

As much as he wanted to control himself and be the knight she praised him as, he was sure her effects on him were more than clear. Even he could feel the tick in his jaw, the grimace pulling at the corner of his mouth. The tightness of his skin under her warm palm.

"For me?" she added. Her jade eyes drifted to the open doorway and the light that spilled in. "Today has been wonderful, so new and different in so many ways. Refreshing. Being with you helped me overwrite so many negative thoughts, so many heavy feelings." She closed her eyes and took a deep breath. "There's just one more thing I need to do. If you'll let me."

He knew. He knew the last thing she needed to overcome, the thing she feared. He hadn't intended to bring it up today and would gladly have given her as much space as she needed or asked for, but as she reopened her eyes, he saw she was ready.

Her history with Jacc held no power over her. Nothing that poor excuse of a lifeform had done could hold her down, and fuck if he would ever let himself get in the way of her healing.

She was royalty, and he'd make sure she was treated as such.

"You can do whatever you want, sweetheart."

A deep blush accompanied her smile as she let go and gingerly pulled her pants over her hips. He couldn't help the way his gaze dropped to linger for one final glance before her panties concealed her pussy.

Her stifled laughter filled the room. "I think I'm a little sore, but I'd love seconds later."

He raked his eyes up her body, not trusting what words might come out next. "Be careful what you ask for."

No doubt she'd be sore all day, but if she thought that would save her, she guessed wrong. He held no reservations about turning her black and blue, then eating her out to soothe the pain until her soul left her body.

She cleared her throat. "So, um..."

Now it was her eyes that lingered, looking at his fully erect penis like a foreign dish at an expensive restaurant. He shrugged off his jacket, folded it in two, and let it fall to his feet between them. The cement would still be harsh, but that would provide enough buffer to let her take her time. His brave queen had asked for what she wanted, and it was time for him to deliver.

"Kneel."

The command smoothed out the worry lines between her eyebrows, relaxing her as she sank to the ground. She got herself settled, then looked up, those wide, attentive eyes filled with trust and longing. Such an eager student. Though with this, he'd give her all the control.

Precum leaked from his slit, his veins large and swollen. He shifted his legs shoulder width apart and shoved his pants down, having zero regrets about going commando this morning. Nothing remained between them save his hard cock, desperate for the smallest drop of her affection. She regarded him with a determined expression and nervously nibbled on her lip.

"Worship me," he ordered in a reverent whisper.

Her eyes flicked up to his. Hell, if an enchantress could look at him like that, he must've been looking at someone else in the mirror this whole time.

Confirming she had permission, she reached out and began to explore, each gentle touch and hesitant caress amplifying his anguish. It was the sweetest torture, the most exquisite form of pain. All she had to do was ask, and he'd let her punish him like this every day for the rest of his life.

His eyelids grew heavy with lust as he watched her investigate, smearing his precum and the remnants of her orgasm around his head. Her finger traced under the ridge of his corona from front to back. Then she raised his heavy cock up to cup his even heavier balls. Leaning forward, she touched her nose to his thigh and breathed in deep.

"Fuck," he hissed. He was going to shoot all over her face if she wasn't careful. "Use that sweet mouth of yours to make me come."

He couldn't live without it, but he wasn't prepared for it either when her tongue swiped out and licked his perineum. She trailed open-mouth kisses down his length and sucked his balls into her mouth. The groan that ripped from the back of his throat sounded so loud he swore it shook the whole room. It certainly shook all of him.

Desperate to maintain his grip on sanity, he focused out a slow breath and closed his eyes, but damn, it was a sight to behold. His self-control wouldn't last long. He watched as she slid her hot lips over his dick, lapping and trying new angles, swallowing more and more each time.

At last, she seemed satisfied and pulled away to look up at him. "I want you to choke me."

The obscene words hung in the air, directly in contrast to her polite tone, eliciting a strangled inhale from his lips.

She trusted him that much—to ask for the exact thing that had hurt her in the first place. It wouldn't take much more for him to spiral over the edge of no return, but he would fulfill her request no matter the cost.

"All right," he said. "If you need me to stop, three taps on my leg. Let me see you do it."

She tapped three times on his thigh, and he nodded. "Hands behind your back."

She did as she was told, holding her wrists, and stared at him expectantly.

"Shit, look at you." He groaned at the sight of her obedience, so meek after asking to be used. "Stay just like that." Grabbing the roots of her hair, he forced her head back farther. "Whenever I tighten my grip, you relax. Understood?"

"Yes, sir."

He practiced gripping harder, and she exhaled, shoulders falling.

"Good girl. Breathe through your nose." As she did, he pulled her head towards his cock and slid himself over her tongue. Her cheeks hollowed as she sucked, and a piercing ache spurred deep in his groin. He yanked himself out. "That's going to make me come, sweetheart."

She smiled, and he all but growled.

After taking another deep breath, he slid in deeper, but not yet at the back of her throat. This was something he needed her to want to do again—fuck, he'd die if she didn't—so he had to check in every step of the way.

He fisted her hair, and she relaxed her jaw, inhaling through her nose. Good. Pulling out, he paused before thrusting in deeper, relishing the scrape of her teeth and the tightness of her tongue. He held himself there while her throat worked to adjust. Tears sprang to her eyes, and he tightened his fist. She forced in a breath through her nose and then relaxed.

One more—he could only give her one more before it would take a literal miracle for him to hold back.

He gave her as much of a smile as he could muster in this state, pulled out slowly, then impaled her again. This time, he had to force his way in, blocking out her source of air and still pushing in farther, nestling her nose into the dark hair at his base.

Panic flashed in her eyes as her body reflexively fought the intrusion, but her hands stayed fixed behind her back. Even as a tear streamed down her cheek, she relaxed her tongue around the underside of his shaft.

"Sweetheart," he croaked but didn't get to finish the sentence as his dick gave one last, profound throb, and he spilled onto her tongue in thick, heavy spurts. She kept her mouth open as he painted those pink strawberry lips and fluttering tongue with his seed.

As he finished, she swallowed, licking her lips and gazing up at him with a satiated expression. And helplessly, he fell apart in her eyes.

"Fuck," he cursed.

She was too good to be true, but if this was a dream, he prayed he'd never wake up.

FORTY-ONE

Adrian

By the time they pulled up to the dorms, the afternoon
had grown colder, and clouds billowed dark and shadowy
across the sky. Ivory sighed and leaned into him, her arms
wrapped snug around his waist. She was still all soft and
cuddly, and he wanted nothing more than to keep his sweet
witch all to himself for as long as he could.

He'd offered to take her out for lunch, but she said she'd
rather stay in, and he had no protests. Once she picked up a
change of clothes and her schoolwork, they would head back to
his apartment, where he could look after her for the rest of the
night.

They rolled to a stop by the back entrance and he shifted
gears, placing his foot on the curb.

"Are you *sure* I can't convince you to let me do my
homework tomorrow?" she asked, taking off her helmet and
nuzzling the nape of his neck.

He clicked his tongue and removed his helmet, too,
allowing her more room to try and convince him. Even though
it wouldn't work. "What kind of chivalrous knight would I be if
I enabled you to procrastinate?"

He turned to tuck his finger under her chin and looked her in the eyes. Dark brown eyelashes swept over her cheekbones, makeup gone, and nothing left but natural beauty to take his breath away. "Plus, I want you all to myself tomorrow," he added. "If you're good and finish your work early, then maybe we can play more later."

She bit her lip and pouted.

"Don't make me punish you again."

"All right, fine." She held back an eye roll just in time and, much to his chagrin, winced as she slid off the bike. "I'll go grab my bag—textbooks included. Be out in five." Her attention flicked down to the seat, and her face paled. "Also, I'm sorry about...you know..." She motioned to the leather. "I'll clean your bike later."

It took him a moment to register what she meant—the mess she'd made at the warehouse. Or, more accurately, the mess his fingers had coaxed out of her.

He grinned and hooked his hand in her jeans to pull her close. "Sweetheart, don't apologize. This seat is never going to get washed again."

Her jaw dropped, and she stumbled over her words. "I'm sure that's not necessary." Darting her gaze away, she blushed. "But if you'd like, we can always...do it again after it's washed."

He laughed. What a dirty girl. Fuck, he loved her for it.

"I'll take you up on that." Leaning over, he whispered in her ear, "Next time, I'll have you come on my boot and make you clean it off with your tongue."

Face scarlet red and eyes wide, her expression was all he needed to verify it turned her on more than she'd admit. He let her go, and she dashed into the dorms.

As he watched her disappear, a nearly forgotten ache panged in his chest. Not so many months ago, he'd watched the same scene but assumed he'd never see her again. That Halloween had been fittingly dark, chilled with winter on its wings and a curse drifting in the air. So much had changed for him since then.

Even though the warmth of summer lingered, new growth budded all around, and a seedling of hope had been planted in his heart, not all their problems were solved. He'd sworn not to act on it, but he still wanted to dig into the circumstances behind his father's murder. He wanted to know who that ring belonged to five years ago and who pulled the trigger. If he couldn't find a way to bring down justice himself, then he wanted that man behind bars.

Just as his hand reached for a pack of cigarettes that wasn't there, the building's door swung open, and Ivory bounded out, practically skipping down the sidewalk with a purple backpack strapped on her shoulders.

"All set," she declared, settling back on the bike and taking her helmet.

"Good. Let's head home." The bike purred as he revved the engine, but the ring of those words echoed louder in his ears.

Home.

Once they got to his apartment, the first order of business was tending to her finger. And tending to his after she insisted on it with the same cute stubbornness that had become his ultimate weakness. He took a quiet moment to brush her hair until it fell in silky tresses, then watched her drink a glass of water before letting her claim the kitchen.

While Ivory happily made sandwiches, he cleared off his desk to give her enough space to work. The clutter was easily sorted, mostly paid bills and junk mail that needed to be filed or thrown in the trash. Except for the printed copy of the police records. He shoved them unceremoniously in the back of the drawer without a second glance.

That bitter taste crept into his mouth again. Maybe he should tell Raptor about the ring and Jace's admittance that it symbolized the Yu family. If nothing else, Raptor had to know something about who could've passed it down.

But that would have to wait until after the weekend because wasting his time with Ivory would be a crime in itself.

Ceramic plates clanked against the wood kitchen table as he walked into the main room, shrugging off his persisting dark thoughts. Barefoot and with purple hair spilling over her shoulders, Ivory had her back turned, ass poking out as she picked through the fridge. He watched with hungry eyes, noticing the two immaculate sandwiches that sat across from one another on the dining table.

"What do you want to drink?" she asked. "Beer? Juice? Water?"

"Juice sounds great." Good thing he stocked up on groceries for this weekend. He'd even managed to find those canned margaritas she liked so much. "Feel free to take whatever you like."

"I'll have juice, too," she said. "Although I did notice my favorite treats on the shelf." Her lips curved into a smile as she turned and closed the fridge with her hip, holding a carton of orange juice. "Better to not get too distracted from my *studies*."

"Good call." He walked over and took the juice from her. One of his hands automatically gripped her hip, slowly sliding down to squeeze her ass through her pair of sweatpants. "Feeling better already, are we?"

Her eyes sparkled as he pressed her into the counter. "Still a bit sore," she admitted, her voice breathless and sweet.

Despite the lingering soreness, she curved towards his touch, arching her back and giving him no choice but to lick the bite mark on her neck. She'd removed the ribbon, and as much as he loved to see it on her, she tasted even better without it. He kissed up her jaw and settled over her mouth. "I like this meal," he rumbled.

She giggled. "But I'm not—"

He cut her off with a nip on her bottom lip, then reached behind her to pull out two glasses from the cupboard. "Sass me one more time, and you'll see who's eating what."

Her hair still smelled faintly of rain, skin warm and fragrant with her natural aromatic scent and hints of sex. He'd never been into candles, but he'd put one in every room if they could replicate her.

A much sweeter scent wafted from the oven, and he backed up to peek inside. Raising his eyebrows, he shot a questioning look over to Ivory.

"I like to munch when I study," she explained with a shrug, face painted with a half-guilty expression as she sat at the table. "I just used what you had on hand. Although I found it odd you've never opened your vanilla extract. Hope you don't mind oatmeal cookies."

"No raisins?" he asked, knowing he'd end up eating them regardless.

"Nope," she said, popping the 'p.' "Just plain oatmeal with extra butter."

"Sounds perfect." He took a seat across from her, disgruntled that the table created too much space between them. "Pretty sure the vanilla extract was part of the supply package my mom and sister brought for the kitchen when I first moved in. I'm glad you found a use for it."

He lingered before taking a bite, pouring his juice as Ivory picked up her sandwich. His father had always insisted on waiting until their mom started eating, and the habit still stuck with him. "If you ever need extra stuff to cook with, let me know," he offered. "I'll try anything you make."

She nodded around a mouthful of food. Satisfied she was happy, he started on his own plate. Sandwiches were a daily item on his menu, which was why he had the ingredients in the first place, but damn, Ivory made this taste better than the deli. He narrowed his eyes at the stack of bread, cheese, and meat.

"How did you make this taste so good?" He was almost afraid to ask.

Her smile radiated from across the table, and he was pleased she'd become better at accepting compliments. "Most people forget sandwiches can be seasoned, too," she replied, sipping her juice like a true connoisseur. "Adding a little of the right herbs goes a long way."

"Mm," he hummed after swallowing another bite. "My sister is going to love you. Her spice selection is as big as the grocery store. Maybe bigger."

"What's she like?" Ivory asked. "She's married to Raptor, right?"

"Yeah," he replied. "Riri is..." He frowned. "Even more stubborn than you are. Hot-headed. Incredibly irritating and irrational. But I'm sure she'd beg to differ." No doubt she'd say the same things about him if asked. Or even if she wasn't.

Ivory laughed. "Is Riley a member of Royal Flush too? How did she meet Raptor?"

He shook his head. "She's not officially sworn in, but with her habit of sticking her nose into things she shouldn't, and now that Raptor has the VP patch, she's well informed, to say the least." He sighed. "As far as their story...it's a long one. After our dad died, we were both a wreck and in a way, Raptor came through for both of us. Of course, a little more so when it comes to her."

Ivory set down her sandwich and ran a finger around the rim of her plate. "If Royal Flush is a motorcycle club...and you obviously have a passion for riding, why didn't you join? Seems like a no-brainer when you have family involved."

He finished his bite, chewing long enough for a pause. "It is. And it isn't."

After another bite, he leaned back and met her gaze. "You know that's what it was all about, right? The shooting? It's Yu and Cortez fighting for power. They tried to keep it quiet, but now I have proof."

Empathy warmed her mossy eyes. "Then why doesn't Cortez want to help? If it's his family, and Royal Flush has the resources..."

"It's never that simple." He exhaled. "It's business for them. Make one wrong move, and it sets off a string of bad events. More people die, and it never ends." He pushed away his plate. "That's why I have to handle this on my own."

He hated to admit it, but Cortez could've known more than he let on this whole time. He didn't want to think that Raptor— and Riley, by extension—knew all these years who had been behind it and stayed silent while he suffered. Of course, abiding by club rules would tie their hands...but even after he'd offered evidence, Royal Flush wasn't willing to do anything. It was too convenient to let him take the fall so they could keep the club looking clean.

"No one else has to die." Ivory reached over and placed her hand over his, a bandage wrapped around her pointer finger— because of the cut from *his* knife. "And if they do, you don't have to bear that burden alone."

Hell, if only life worked that way. If only she didn't need to think about sharing the weight he'd dragged around for so long. He'd chop off his own limbs to keep her the way she was, unburdened and full of life and love.

He opened her hand and traced the lines in her palm. "I had this dream when I was a kid," he murmured. "That one day I'd have a family. One day, I'd be able to protect them and love them and watch them grow up like my dad had wanted to do with us." Her skin felt so soft, so pliable, as he ran his fingertips over hers. "Raptor has his reasons for accepting what Royal

Flush is. I suppose Riri does, too. But that's not what I want my story to be like."

Looking up, he saw her face—not the same four walls of the apartment he'd paced for years, and not the lost girl who'd followed him at the Halloween party—but a woman who took his darkness and turned it into light. A supernova at the center of the universe, burning so bright that she could thrive where he hadn't been able to see, much less function.

And he knew.

He knew the future he'd wanted all along had been her.

FORTY-TWO

Working at a desk had never been her forte. It didn't take long before she ended up in the living room on Adrian's lap, both happily squished in the recliner.

She balanced a textbook over one knee, a notebook and highlighters on the other. Behind her, Adrian read a new fantasy book his mom gifted him for Christmas. It should have been more apparent he liked to read since his bookshelves were well stocked and maintained, but she half expected him to watch TV or play video games like her brother.

He traced soothing patterns through the hair at the nape of her neck, and instead of the background noise she'd grown accustomed to, comfortable silence blanketed the room. She'd been more productive in the past few hours than a whole day at the dorms. Even so, it left her feeling just as worn out. She tapped her pen on the paper, clicked it shut, and let out a sigh. Looking up from her work, she noticed the windows had darkened as night descended.

"How's it going?" Adrian set his book aside and wrapped his arms around her waist. "You've been at it for a while."

"Almost done. I only have a few questions left." Not that

those last few would be easy, as she'd marked the hard ones and saved them for last. But any parts she couldn't figure out would have to be summed down to an educated guess and brought to the professor for help later.

"Almost done with this assignment, or done with everything due on Monday?" Adrian clarified.

She rolled her eyes, knowing he couldn't see. Her black knight had turned into a full-time drill sergeant. "I finished everything due on Monday *and* Tuesday if you must know. I still don't get some parts, but can ask for help after class."

"Good." He gave her a kiss on her shoulder. "Is ten minutes enough to finish your last few questions?"

"Yep, I think so. Staring at the book any longer certainly isn't going to help. If studying by osmosis worked, I'd sleep on the darn class notes."

He chuckled. "I've heard having something to look forward to after work helps with motivation, so I thought a bath would be a good way to start our evening."

"Ooh, a bath?" The way he'd said *start* instead of *finish* had her body stirring to life, especially after taking a backseat during her studies.

He grinned. "Mind letting me up?"

She shifted her books so he could move without disturbing their precarious balance, and he untangled himself from the chair. A sly grin formed on his lips as he disappeared into the bathroom. Butterflies flitted around in her stomach.

He'd been right—getting all the school stuff out of the way had been a wise decision. Something told her she'd never be able to focus after what he had planned.

Or maybe *because* he had something planned.

Rushing water echoed from the bathroom. She changed positions, looked over her homework, scribbled a half-hearted answer, and shut the book.

Restless without Adrian, she picked up her phone and

scrolled through social media to see what everyone else was up to. A post from her mom popped up, showing one of her brother's senior photos and another of an acceptance letter. She straightened.

Brey got into a school? That was great! Which one?

Adrian's cell rang on the kitchen table. She glanced up as he answered and walked out onto the porch. Then, she returned her attention to the post and finished scanning what her mom had written.

Her smile faded, finger frozen on the screen.

Why did reading this get her insides all twisted up? Her mom seemed happy, and Brey must be too, even though he'd only be attending the community college closest to their home. He'd get to work towards his degree and have access to all his gaming equipment at the same time. Maybe even find a way to intersect the two.

She read through the text again. Her mom sounded so proud.

That was it.

She'd never gotten encouragement her senior year. There had been no congratulatory post. No praise for her graduation or acceptance into college. In fact, she'd heard more about how her ex went to Harvard than her own plans.

Not that it should matter. But as she thought about it, accepting her feelings instead of invalidating them, the grip they had began to lift. If someone was going to be proud of her, she wanted it to be for who she was, not for where she attended school or what she did for a living. Even if it hurt that the person she loved didn't see those things in her, it didn't mean they weren't there.

I need you to see you're more capable than you think, Iv. I want you to set yourself free from doubt.

Adrian's words from earlier resurfaced in her mind and the tightness in her chest all but disappeared.. There was no reason to doubt herself or to question her worth. She knew the internet hardly reflected reality—at home, Brey wouldn't be off the hook. He'd put in a lot of effort for this, so she posted a happy comment with lots of emojis.

Looking for her black knight, she found him behind the closed glass door on the porch, shuffling around in the dark. One hand held the phone to his ear while the other clenched into a fist. A frown etched deeper and deeper into his face, and muffled bits of the conversations began to rise in volume.

Her brows furrowed to mirror his. Something must've happened, and she was willing to bet it was a lot more serious than a disheartening social media post. He ran a hand over his stubble, muscles tense, veins standing out along his forearm. That wasn't a good sign.

She stood and debated whether to join him or check on the bath, but before reaching a conclusion, he ended the call and slid open the door.

"What's wrong?" she asked.

Tension snapped through his shoulders and chest as he flexed his fingers. "Raptor called." His eyes softened as he looked at her, but old shadows resurfaced from their depths. "I have to go to The Club. Some asshole punched Riri while she was bartending."

"What?" she whispered. "Is she okay? Who did it—Jace?"

"She's all right." Adrian forced a crooked grin that broke into a scowl. "It's not her first scuffle, by a long shot. Raptor said he had it covered, but—" He swallowed, his Adam's apple bobbing. "It was Jun, Jace's older brother. I don't know if Jace was involved, but either way, it's a warning."

Her heart plummeted into her stomach. They hadn't done so much as plan their next move, but the situation had already gotten worse. At this rate, they couldn't afford to wait for things to die down. The more cautious they tried to be, the more people got hurt in the process.

"I'm going, too," she declared. Like it or not, she wouldn't let Adrian deal with this alone. The last time he got this angry, Jace had threatened her at the Halloween party. She'd let it happen that night. Watched in slow motion as the world spun in different directions. Not tonight.

As she spun to go change in the bedroom, he blew out a long exhale and followed. "I'd much rather you stay. Take a bath and relax. I'll try not to be long."

She shook her head while pulling off her shirt. "I won't be able to do any of that while not knowing what's going on. I want to be there. By your side." The warm touch of his hands stilled her, gliding from her shoulders down her arms. She turned to face him and pulled his hands into hers. "That's where I belong, right?"

Her heart hammered in her chest.

"Yes, but—" He hesitated, lips pursed and pulse ticking on his forehead.

"That's part of this, our agreement," she continued. "Being there when things get hard. You taught me so much today...let me be your balance, too."

Closing his eyes, he took a deep breath and pressed their foreheads together. After another minute, he spoke. "Okay. You can come." Then he added in a whisper, "I just can't let anyone else I love get hurt."

Her breath caught.

He loved her.

Before either of them could say more, she kissed him. Their hands tightened. He froze as if he was afraid to move. Afraid to let his control slip even for a moment.

She didn't care if it did.

His love and his hurt, his anger and his pain, and everything beyond it belonged to her just as much as she belonged to him. Withholding them would feel like tearing apart her own soul, denying what she'd already pledged to give.

She could heal him the same way he healed her. Pressing herself to his chest, she offered all she had in their kiss.

At last, he came back to life, holding her as if fate itself might try to rip her away. He kissed her until they were both out of breath but desperate for more.

She started to form the words to mumble it back, but he kissed her again and stole the phrase before it left her lips. "Not now," he whispered, then pulled away and spoke sternly. "If you come with me, I need to be next to you at all times. Don't leave me for a single minute, understand?"

She nodded. "Okay."

"Good." He squared his shoulders, walked over to his dresser, opened a drawer, and pulled out a gun. Her gaze locked onto the sleek metal, never having seen one in real life. Never been presented with the real threat of death. She didn't have to ask if he was willing to use it.

Noticing her gaze, he tucked it away behind his back. "Just in case. Don't be scared."

"I'm not."

She hurried to finish changing, thankful she'd packed a black dress in case they decided to go out tomorrow.

By the time she remembered to shut off the water in the bathroom, it had almost begun to overflow. Ripples dispersed under her fingertips, hot to the touch as she skimmed the surface. No doubt it'd be ice cold by the time they returned.

FORTY-THREE

Adrian

He needed a damn cigarette.

Still slick from rain, asphalt gave way to lopsided puddles along the curb. The murky water reflected neon lights from downtown's entertainment district, and groups of pedestrians huddled together on the sidewalk to ward off the chill in the air.

A bright blue sign flashed across the front of the most prominent building on the block, a symbol of the club suit of cards. He didn't know who named the place, but always thought *The Club* wasn't very original.

At least it was easy enough to remember, and the place had rapidly grown in popularity since Royal Flush bought it years ago. When Riley decided to go straight into bartending after graduating high school, he hadn't been thrilled, but at least he knew she'd be well-guarded working here.

Or so he thought. They must've let a prospect manage the entrance tonight. Who the fuck let one of the Dragons onto the property, much less a Yu? That shit could've ended with a lot more spilled blood—or worse.

He should've been there.

Normally, he made it a habit to check in every few weeks but hadn't stopped by in a while. If he'd been around, then maybe he could've stopped Jun from waltzing in and attacking her. How many more people would he fail to protect?

His fingers tightened around Ivory's, but her gentle squeeze brought him back. Her hand became his only comfort, warm despite the chilly air and too perfect of a fit for him to admit. Ironically, it was the first time he held hands with a girl other than family. Yet their situation couldn't be less romantic, and the bandage around her finger was a subtle reminder of what could happen if they weren't careful.

Ivory deserved better. She deserved a real date, not some fucked up family drama. A real reason to have put on that pretty black dress and done her hair up with the ribbon.

And yet, she'd almost said—

He didn't dare think about the words that slipped out in his room. Didn't want her to say them back just because he had. It wouldn't be right to ask or expect so much of her, especially when tonight could change her perception about everything.

Still, he stood by what he'd said. It was the truth.

He'd been in love with her for a while now. When that happened didn't matter, nor did he know the exact moment his desire to protect her turned into a need to possess her. But it had, and nothing would change that.

Instead of dwelling on the soft spot Ivory carved out of his granite heart, he focused on the old memories brought back by entering the club's double glass doors. The first time he brought Caspian here during their freshman year. The late nights he spent out with Raptor all the years before that. They'd been young and too careless for their own good, getting into more trouble than they'd bargained for, but determined to earn their respect.

Now, they were all grown, and the only thing that changed was who they had to prove themselves to.

His arm circled Ivory's waist as they walked into the foyer. Behind the entryway, black walls framed a view of the dancefloor, guarded by the bouncer behind a sleek glass countertop. Loud dance music rumbled through the walls as the DJ called out to the crowd.

Adrian nodded to the bouncer, a recruit Raptor had introduced him to a few months ago, and with a nod of acknowledgment, both he and Ivory were waved inside. He scanned the mass of bodies bouncing under the strobe lights and along the second-floor railing, half hoping to find Jace or even Jun glaring back. But they wouldn't be dumb enough to stick around on enemy territory, and if they had, Raptor would've gotten to them already.

A familiar face registered in the corner—Jewelle Yu— cousin to Jun and Jace. She didn't have the same standing in the family as the brothers and wasn't an official Red Dragon, but her magnetism for chaos unnerved him, to say the least. Ivory noticed, too, and gave him a wary glance.

Had Jewelle come to watch, or did they have more planned?

Not wanting to draw attention to the fact he'd noticed Jewelle, he kept his gaze straight and moved farther in. He had to get the whole story before making any irrational moves. From Raptor's call, it sounded like Jun left a message along with the imprint of his fist, but Raptor wouldn't say over the phone.

They ducked under a line of tape sectioning off part of the bar. Shards of broken glass lay scattered in a pool of alcohol on the floor, along with splatters of dried blood. He frowned as anxiety crept back in. Extra security guards had been stationed at the exits, too.

He wordlessly led Ivory into the backroom, where the blasting music faded only slightly. Miscellaneous supplies and boxes of liquor crowded the shelves, along with a large meeting table and a steel gun safe. A metallic tang permeated the air.

Riley sat in the corner on a folding chair, eyes closed and pressing an ice pack to her nose. Raptor hovered at her side, his close-cut hair ruffled and jaw squared.

"I'm fine," Riley snapped as they entered, not bothering to look up. Admittedly, his sister looked more pissed than in pain. Her black work uniform was crisp as always, her thick hair braided down to her waist. "What I need is some damn space, not everyone checking in on me as an excuse to get out of work."

"I see you're still in one piece," Adrian replied dryly. Even if she wouldn't let this affect her, guilt tore into him at seeing her injured.

"Oh great, the cavalry's here," she joked in a lighter tone. Raising her head, her scowl faded as she spotted Ivory.

Raptor's shoulders relaxed, and he met Adrian's gaze, but the creases on his forehead deepened as he took note of the plus one. "Looks like I fucked up your night."

Adrian shook his head. "Not your fault."

Raptor towered above them in his leather cut, crossed arms as thick as tree trunks. The man looked intimidating as hell, and it didn't surprise him when Ivory shifted on her feet. He squeezed her closer before dropping his hand to hers again.

"I told Ivory how much of a pain in the ass you both can be, but I'll introduce you properly." He tipped his head at them both, trying to cut through the tense energy in the room. "Ivory, this is Raptor and my dear sister, Riley."

Riley snorted, wincing as she adjusted the ice pack. "*Dear sister*? Maybe I should get punched more often. Or should I credit your girl for you being nice?"

"Well, he did just call you a pain in the ass, so I'm not sure it was a compliment," Ivory replied. Her lips quirked as she glanced at him. His gaze dipped to the trail of bite marks bruising her neck, and the surrounding gloom dispersed the smallest amount. Nothing meant more than seeing her wearing his mark in public.

Fuck, but now wasn't the time to get riled up.

"She knows you too well," Riley replied with a laugh, followed by another wince as she turned to Ivory. "Glad to meet you. Wish my face hadn't been fucked up for it, though."

Ivory's smile faded. "Are you okay? What happened?"

"I'm fine." Riley waved her hand. "You should probably worry more about Jun. I hope he got a damn concussion from the bottle I slammed in the side of his skull."

Ivory's eyes widened, and Adrian groaned. That would explain the broken glass outside. Neither he nor his sister had ever been good at de-escalating a situation. In grade school, his reputation had been second only to hers.

"You're lucky that didn't provoke him further," Raptor muttered.

Riley huffed and placed a hand over her belly but didn't say anything more.

Adrian's brows knitted. Usually, Riley wouldn't let anyone insinuate that she couldn't hold her own in a fight. In fact, multiple scuffles had been started to prove that very point.

"What's going on?" he asked, directing the question to Raptor as Riley avoided looking his way.

Raptor shifted uncomfortably.

"You can see I'm okay, so don't go all panic mode on me, all right?" Riley said, breaking the silence.

He narrowed his eyes. "Is there something for me to panic about?"

"No." She let out a deep breath and lowered the ice pack. "I'm pregnant."

He forgot how to breathe.

"What?" Gasping to try and fill his deflated lungs, Adrian ran a hand through his hair and cursed. That meant it hadn't just been her at risk. She'd been carrying a whole new life inside her.

His sister was pregnant.

Raptor was going to be a dad...shit, and he was about to become an uncle. In the middle of this whole damn mess, at that. "Riri—"

"I don't need a lecture on safety precautions. That's what I got him for." She jabbed a finger at Raptor. "I'm only in the first trimester, and it's perfectly normal to go to work if I want. I'm not about to sit on my ass at home, bored out of mind."

Adrian swallowed. If that had been his kid and his woman... he glanced over at Ivory.

If she'd been hurt while carrying their—dammit, he shouldn't even finish that thought. His chest pounded so hard that the rest of him started to shake.

They needed to get to the bottom of this.

FORTY-FOUR

"Why did Jun come here?" he demanded.

The single question brought them all back to the gravity of the situation. Riley could've held onto her secret a little longer—until she was ready to share the news, happy and round and irritably confined to a rocking chair in a nursery instead of hunched over in the backroom of a bar—but this threat pushed them all out of their comfort zone.

Raptor understood, nodding and squaring his shoulders. "We can talk out back."

"No need." Adrian shook his head. "Here's fine. Ivory already knows everything I do." Glancing over as she squeezed his hand, he added, "We're in this together."

The corner of Raptor's lips twitched, and Riley stared at him like he'd sprouted fluffy ears. Their reaction made him want to roll his eyes. They should've known Ivory was the real deal. But he'd just confirmed it beyond a doubt.

As long as he'd known them, which for Riley meant his entire life, he'd never trusted anyone else. Not when it came to sensitive topics and, especially not regarding the death of their father. When Raptor came along and earned that trust, Adrian hadn't expected him to become family by law, but if nothing else, the universe was determined to bind him to the people he cared for. Maybe because he couldn't have it any other way.

Raptor cleared his throat. "All right. I suspect Jun caught wind of my request for the police records, and that's what sparked his little tantrum. Never should've trusted Kam," he muttered. "Guy's got one too many connections."

"I also beat up Jace," Adrian admitted. The prick had probably tattled to his older brother. If Jun wanted to get at both him and Raptor, then Riley would be the obvious target. But this also meant Jun had gotten antsy—like he had a secret that needed to stay hidden.

Raptor pinched the bridge of his nose and sighed. "Neither of you know how to keep shit quiet, do you?"

Adrian ignored the jab and turned to Riley. "Did he say anything?"

Her scowl returned as she adjusted the ice pack to her nose. "Just to back off, and that we better keep our noses out of his family's business." She looked like she wanted to spill more of his blood than she already had. "Coward," she spat.

"Going after a woman and a pregnant one at that." Adrian cursed under his breath. All this because he couldn't let the past die.

"We're lucky he didn't know," Raptor added. "But this will get him in trouble. Even Red Dragon has rules against harming women and children. His last name won't save him from that mistake."

Adrian grit his teeth, fighting the urge to light up a cigarette and suffocate his foul mood in the bitter smoke. "So *now* you can get Royal Flush involved?"

"I have no other choice." Raptor glared at him. "It happened on their property."

"If the club didn't want to help before, I don't need them interfering now." Adrian fumed. "And I already made it clear that talking to Cortez about my personal business isn't on the agenda. He's fucked with my life enough as is. Even if Jun made this your problem, I'm not going to just hand over what was *my* issue with *my* family to begin with."

"It's too late. Pres is on his way." Raptor's steel gaze locked onto Adrian's, positioning himself squarely behind Riley. They were both family, too, and he knew it. But Cortez had motives that neither of them had control over.

"For fuck's sake," Adrian hissed, pacing a few steps back and clenching his fists. Nothing that man touched came out unscathed. It was his damn DNA that got his son killed. And if Luke's death had anything to do with the Dragons, then it was all the more reason to stay away.

Years ago, he'd made the decision to ditch any future with Royal Flush. Glancing at Ivory, who had taken to chewing her lip, only solidified his determination to keep their worlds separate. The last thing he needed was to owe Cortez any favors, only to be asked to take up the club patch in return. Getting any closer to a life of drugs and violence wasn't going to happen. Period.

He let out a steady breath to curb some of the anger and took Ivory's hand again. "Leave out the part about the dragon tile." He jabbed a finger at Raptor. "As far as the rest goes, I have a personal issue with Jace. That's all Cortez needs to know."

Raptor's eyebrows shot up, but Adrian pursed his lips. Explaining what he found out about the ring would have to wait for another night. However this shit got handled, if he still went for revenge, it had to be separated from the motorcycle clubs. Neither side wanted war, and he only cared about the man who pulled the trigger, not the politics behind it.

"Sure." Raptor reached into his pocket and pulled out a

pack of cigarettes, tipping the box so one slid out halfway. "You look like shit. Take this and get yourself sorted before Cortez gets here."

Adrian snatched the cigarette and marched outside without another word, mindful to keep his grip light on Ivory's hand as he burst through the backdoor.

A rancid odor of trash and stark shadows along the alley walls echoed the growing despair in his thoughts. The blaring music from inside faded to a low rumble as the door shut behind them. Shooting a glare in either direction, he made sure they were alone, then stepped around a stack of old pallets to give them some semblance of privacy.

He needed to calm down and get his head on straight, but this had turned into a fucking nightmare.

His forehead pounded so hard he couldn't focus. Why did shit always have to go wrong? Why did people have to go out of their way to hurt one another for the sake of power and ego? This damn contest to see who could conquer who was getting out of hand.

Closing his eyes, he leaned back into the unforgiving brick wall. Rolling Raptor's cigarette between his fingers brought a familiar comfort—but so did Ivory's hand, her delicate grip smoothing over his knuckles.

"Are you okay?" she whispered after a minute of silence.

Not really. But hearing her voice, the perfect mixture of silken and assuring, reached into his psyche and quieted his turbulent thoughts.

"I can manage." He sighed and pulled her closer. They'd find a way through this. Somehow, he had to untangle himself from the web of lies and crime without letting it touch Ivory. The sweet smell of her hair reminded him how to breathe, and she circled her arms around his waist, the slope of her breasts nestled to his chest and calming his heart.

"Is Cortez really that bad?" she quietly asked.

He exhaled and tucked away a strand of purple hair that escaped from her ribbon. "It's not him, it's his position." Tipping his head back, he forced himself to breathe in the cold, polluted air and looked for stars he knew would be hidden by city lights. "He's the president of Royal Flush. I won't let him or his damn club interfere with my life. Not anymore."

"Oh," Ivory hummed, nodding as if a gang power struggle was just another physics problem. Her gaze drifted to the cigarette clutched in his hand. "Are you going to smoke that?"

"No." He shook his head and tossed the vile thing on the ground.

His mind was a shit show, caught between reliving the same guilt and rage that haunted him day after day and the iron-clad determination that drove him to protect the people he still could. But as much as his body craved it, shouted at him to smoke just one more time, he wouldn't lose all the progress Ivory helped him gain.

"Adrian," she whispered.

He looked down and caught sight of her black dress, teasing along the bevel of her collarbone in contrast to her pale skin. She looked so out of place in this dingy back alley. Lust mingled with the dark fury gathering in his mind.

"Yes?" He cupped her jaw, felt the thrum of her pulse sure and steady under his fingers.

If he focused on her, then maybe he could stay in the present. Maybe he could regain his humanity, even if the world forced him to become a monster.

"It's okay to hurt." She regarded him with a kind smile and dark olive eyes, pools of shadow that swirled with empathy. "We all need someone else sometimes."

Dammit.

He was so close to breaking. The weight of it all pushing him toward the edge of a cliff—but maybe she knew that even better than he did.

"The only person I need is you," he whispered, dragging her in to brush his lips over hers. He drank in the warm breath of her soft, sweet sigh. Then his hand tangled in her hair, fingers digging into her scalp to hold her in place. Any closer and he'd combust out of need, any farther and his heart would shatter out of desperation.

Either way, he was going to lose. Like he always did.

"I'm here for you," she breathed, eyes fluttering open, lashes a laced veil of shadow. "In whatever way you need me."

Need.

Yes, he needed her. How could she be so sweet and so wickedly tempting at the same time? So caring and so heartfelt that there was no way he could ever let her go? He'd gladly spend the rest of his life in servitude in order to return everything she gave.

A part of him yearned to expose the parts of him he'd locked away. To show her every dark thing he'd dragged around for so many years, wanted her to see every neglected crevice of his being and infuse him with her clever mind and enduring compassion.

Fuck, he wanted to snatch her up and keep her locked inside his chest forever. But surely that was asking too much. Surely, this would be going too far, and so soon after she'd agreed to be his.

She pressed her hips forward into his growing erection, and he groaned in the best kind of agony he'd ever felt. "Sweetheart," he warned.

"Please," she begged.

He needed her, yet she took it upon herself to plead for him.

Flipping them around, he pinned her against the wall between his arms. Heat seeped off her skin and spiked his pulse as her body became pliant and bent to his will.

"You remember how to stop me?" he rasped, muscles flexing, coiled tight and hard.

She shivered. "Yes, sir."

Her breaths were short and quick, lips plump and parted as if she needed more air, needed the oxygen to awaken her senses.

Because now he'd become the predator, and she his prey.

FORTY-FIVE

Adrian

THE SMALL AMOUNT OF LIGHT THAT FILTERED INTO THE ALLEY reflected off Ivory's skin and shone like veins of amethyst in the cascade of her hair, casting a mystic aura around his intoxicating witch.

He hesitated, frozen in this moment. They were treading a thin line—caught between allowing her a glimpse of his darkness and falling victim to the depth of his emotion—with anyone else, he wouldn't try to cross it, but he trusted her to use their safe word if needed. He trusted her to be everything he needed.

Even if it meant letting himself break. For her.

"I like you like this," she said under her breath. "All dark and dangerous."

His fingers skimmed down to her thighs, dancing under the hem of her dress in an illusion of tenderness. It wouldn't be long before Cortez arrived, and he was already strung so tight. He couldn't be gentle like last time.

The thing was, he didn't *want* to be gentle.

"Hell," he cursed. "You have no idea what real danger is, sweetheart."

He slapped the inside of her thigh, and she gasped as he slotted himself between her legs. The position forced her against the wall, trapping her between the brick and his hard body. Her submission fueled his desire, ignited a surge of power that overcame the rest of his pain and despair.

"But if you want dark," he continued. "I'll give you pitch black."

If she wanted to tame his demons, he'd let her. If she wanted his darkness to come out unleashed, he'd open the gate.

She believed he was capable, trusted him with her body enough to give him full control. To her, he was more than a black knight. To her, he could play god and the devil, and he'd be damned if he didn't try his best to live up to both.

"Look at you," he growled, low enough for only them to hear, even though they were alone. "Such a pathetic, pretty little thing. Caught in an alley with someone like me."

Someone who fails the people who love him the most.

Her eyes closed as he licked along her pulse, the sweet saltiness of her skin driving him mad and granting him sanity at the same time. A moan resonated from her throat, and he drew his hand up to wrap around her neck, plucking at her nipple as he went.

"I could make you my personal slut," he whispered, stroking her clit through her panties. "Bet you'd like that, hm? Letting me fuck you? Letting me toy with your soul?"

"Yes," she moaned. "Please, sir."

"That's my fucking good girl." He forced a finger through her drenched folds, grinding it hard against the rough patch of her g-spot. She cried out, and he slapped his palm against her clit. "Hush now."

She clamped her mouth shut as he started to tease her again. Her thighs quivered, pinned apart and dripping with arousal.

"Look at that. You're about to come already." He chuckled. "All from just one finger. Can't wait to see the look on your face when you take my entire cock." The strain of his erection spread into his abdomen, tightening his balls and hooking deep in his groin, but he wouldn't have to wait long.

He turned her chin with his thumb and made her look in his eyes. "I love seeing you struggle. Making you squirm. Damn, you're too good for me, but I'm going to destroy you anyway." He had to pause to catch his breath. "Tell me, sweetheart, how many inches have you earned?"

"Three?" she squeaked, uncertain as she struggled to form words.

He hummed, working his finger in and out at a slow, steady pace. She'd already coated him in nectar, her pussy weeping in relief. "Correct. But I'll be nice and give you four because you took me so well in your tight throat today."

Her eyes widened, and a brief flash of pride lifted the corners of her mouth. Then he thrust in another finger with cruel thrusts, just to watch her come apart. Her head fell back with a silent wail, thighs quivering, sex pulsing as she came.

He tightened his grip on her throat, unable and unwilling to let her savor the moment. "Left arm above your head."

He grabbed the gun from his waist and checked the safety, then pressed the side of the barrel to her wrist and pined it with the metal. She let out a breathless moan.

"Now be a good little slut and take out my dick," he rasped.

She reached down and fumbled with his zipper. His witch was so diligent, so careful with her meticulous movements—the very opposite of the crude display of lust that sprung into her hand. His erection grew all the more enraged at her touch, veins full and swollen, the tip flared and shiny as she smeared a pearl of his leaking precum.

Sliding his hand over hers, he caged her palm against his

dick and guided her fingers to grip him where he wanted, leaving four inches at the top. "Just like that," he breathed.

He didn't need to tell her not to let go. She'd do exactly as he asked, which is why he made her do it. All it would take was one push too far, one impulse left unchecked to break their rules. And at the moment, it took all he had not to tear into her cunt and lose every last shred of himself.

To admit he wanted to ask her for more than he had any right to.

Something moved behind her eyes as if she knew what he couldn't say and could see what he couldn't hide. But then it was gone, her pupils blown wide as he parted her folds and ran himself along her slit.

"You're going to take me in that pretty pussy of yours and let me fill it with my cum," he rasped. "I'm going to pump you full of my seed until it's dripping down your thighs, and when we go back inside, you'll be a good girl and let me reach under your dress to stuff it back in."

She couldn't hold back a strangled whine as he pushed into her, satisfying his lust yet barely scratching a deeper, more persistent need. He lifted her thigh and filled her as much as he was allowed.

His fingers dented her skin, rough and demanding against her yielding softness. Sawing in and out, he picked up the pace and matched the beat of his racing heart with every thrust, propelling them toward the finish line. An electric web banded over his nerves, flaring the network of heat that wound from where they merged. Faint light tinged the edges of his vision and infiltrated his mind until he couldn't see—only feel. Only exist in Ivory's body, in her whispered moans and gentle quivers.

"Adrian," she mumbled.

He leaned in and covered her lips with his, wanting to taste her affection, to let it melt on his tongue as he set them both ablaze.

"Adrian," she repeated, the words leaving her mouth to enter his. Her hand gripped his length tighter. "I need—" She cut off as he angled upwards and hit her sweet spot, her stomach pulling taut and walls contracting.

"I know," he whispered. "Come for me, sweetheart." The rasp of his breath filled his ears, chest heaving as his body crowded her in. She was trapped and exposed, flushed with her dress pushed up, her underwear pulled aside to reveal her swollen, glistening clit. Nothing left hidden between them.

"I need to say that I love you," she gasped.

He stopped, dazed. Her admission struck him in the center of his chest—a direct hit to the core of his being that shook him to the bone.

"You needed to know," she said, breathless as she pulsed around him. The throb of her heart overtook his own.

That was it, the truth he denied himself. The words he wanted but refused to accept.

She loved him.

"Dammit," he cursed. "I love you too, Iv." He fused their lips as her folds sucked him in, swallowing him up and letting him take everything he wanted. So he took. He took and took, and she gave everything she had. Despite his failings, she wanted him. All of him. Even the parts no other person would desire.

Somehow, as sweat dripped down his spine and an ache seared through his ribs, his taking became her taking. Her giving became his giving. So he gave and gave until she took everything he had to offer.

Before he could prepare, he was coming—coming so hard it erupted hot and thick in a never-ending purge. He poured himself deep inside her womb, and still, he was coming. Still, there was more.

For a tiny, infinite moment, he saw Ivory with her stomach round and beautiful, full of evidence of their connection. Carrying a life they created.

With a broken groan, the vision faded, and at last, he emptied himself completely. They slumped together into the wall, entwined in a sweaty, sticky mess.

"I love you," Ivory whispered again, capturing his lips in a kiss so delicate it betrayed the kind of sex they'd just had.

"I know," he replied, unable to keep the edge of longing from his voice. "I love you, too."

FORTY-SIX

Ivory

"I LOVE YOU, TOO."

Her broken, beautiful black knight. Whose love was as fierce as he was faithful and so delicious her legs had become too weak to stand.

Adrian cupped her cheek and kissed her, soft and deep and slow. The velvet caress of his tongue brought her racing heart back to a regular pace. "Thank you, Iv."

She leaned against the wall and clung to him, hoping her touch and words could reach inside the armor shielding him from the rest of the world. "I know you didn't want me to say it, but—" The back door opened with a bang, and she jumped a foot in the air. Adrian clamped a hand over her mouth to muffle her shriek.

Raptor's voice echoed in the alley, separated from them only by the cover of night and a stack of wood pallets. "I'm not about to go out there and see whatever it is you're up to. Cortez is here, so get your asses inside."

The door swung shut, and she breathed a sigh of relief. If he'd come out a moment earlier...

She dropped her gaze between them, where her hand was

still wrapped around Adrian's dick, her dress hiked up to her hips as thick cum leaked down her thighs. She had so much more to say, but it looked like they'd already reached their time limit before being thrown back in the lion's den.

"You were perfect," Adrian whispered as he withdrew and gave her one last chaste kiss. "Did I hurt you?"

She shook her head as he rubbed the marks from her wrist and used his boxers to gently wipe her fingers. "No, I'm okay, just a little out of breath." When he finished, she combed through her hair in an attempt to cover their obvious activities. Then she cleared her throat. "Um, what you said about when we go inside…"

She wasn't sure if he'd remember from the heat of the moment, but as he refastened his belt, he let out a cocky hum. "Ah, yes." His shoulders squared, and he stood a little straighter, tucking the gun back under his jacket. A smirk lifted one side of his mouth. "Do you want to be a good girl for me, Iv?"

She bit her lip. Despite everything that happened, her body grew light and warm again at his question. He wouldn't punish her for backing out or using her safe word if she felt uncomfortable, but she also knew he wouldn't do anything to put either of them at risk.

He smoothed his hands down her dress, making a show of arranging it before slipping underneath and verifying the mess he'd left was still there.

No doubt remained about what she wanted. "Yes, sir. I want to be a good girl for you."

Another pleased hum. His hands skated over her sex in approval.

"Then let's go."

With a sure grip, he led them back inside the club.

The backroom looked the same as they'd left it, dingy but clean and far less crowded than the dancefloor, where the boom of bass vibrated through the wall. Riley had abandoned both the ice pack and her chair to stand next to Raptor, both engaged in conversation with a man who could be no less than a giant.

Raptor had been intimidating enough, but Cortez made him look like a pretty boy in comparison. Coarse black hair and a burly beard framed his weathered face, crinkled like the leather hanging from his shoulders. His features were marred by a crooked nose and slanted teeth that flashed as he laughed at something Raptor said. Both men wore the same vest over their clothes, the symbol of Royal Flush sewn into the backs—a skeletal hand holding an ignited jack of spades.

Cortez looked over Raptor's shoulder and made eye contact with Adrian. "Ah, so you're here after all. Was worried I scared you off."

"You've never scared me," Adrian joked and stepped forward to exchange a clap on the back. The top of his head barely reached Cortez's chin. "Not that I planned to be here, either." He returned to Ivory's side and drew her against him. "Ivory, this is President Cortez. Taught Raptor and me almost everything we know about bikes."

Cortez laughed again as she offered a simple, "Nice to meet you."

"Such a polite little thing," he rumbled. "Don't let the title fool ya. I'm just as much a *pendejo* as the rest of 'em." He turned back to Adrian with a wink. "Now I know why I haven't seen ya around. I'm sure she's better company than me."

"I plead the fifth." Adrian deadpanned and wrapped a firm arm around Ivory. "How's business?"

"Not as bad as it has been," Cortez replied. "Never as good as it could be. You lookin' for work?"

"Not in your area of expertise," Adrian shot back, but Cortez didn't seem bothered. "Besides, classes keep me busy enough. Trying to finish this shit before I'm tempted to take a break."

"Good for you." Cortez gave a sober nod.

"The Club's gotten three new members and five new prospects in the past year," Raptor added. "We've got plenty of manpower. I feel more like a manager than a VP these days."

"So that's why you went and stirred up shit?" Cortez arched an eyebrow at him. "Cause I'm not working you hard enough?" A spark of silent communication passed between them before Cortez turned to Riley. "Speaking of manpower, congrats again. You hoping for a boy or girl?"

"A boy," Riley replied, her smile exhausted but bright. "If we get a girl, and she takes after either of us, I'm not sure we'll be able to reel her in."

They all broke out in a laugh.

Adrian's shoulders shook with an ease he rarely wore around others. Seeing them like this felt almost nostalgic, like she was watching an old family video. These people couldn't be as bad as Adrian said they were. Sure, they might be involved in things her parents would balk at, but when Jace had attacked her, there were no men with loud bikes and scary weapons who she could call for backup.

"Again, I feel bad I had to find out like this," Cortez continued, and a solemn tone descended on the room. "I'm sure you were planning to announce the news under different circumstances."

Riley huffed. "It's not like I could celebrate with you guys, anyway. Can't have any drinks for eight more months." She waved a dismissive hand. "But while you're here, tell the boys to have a beer or two and slip some bills in the tip jar while they're at it."

The crows' feet around Cortez's eyes wrinkled. "I'm sure some of 'em have already taken you up on that. They won't pass on a night out, especially when I tell 'em it changed from protection duty to a party." Then he frowned, accentuating the other lines carved into his face. "But on a serious note, what Jun did was out of line, no questions asked. I'm glad you came out of it all right. Though I can't say I'm surprised our girl gave 'em such a hard time."

"Jun picked the wrong one of us to fuck with, that's for sure." Riley's smile grew into a wicked smirk. "Had better chances going up against Raptor." She glanced up at her husband, but instead of offering a rebuttal, Raptor snorted and crossed his arms.

Ivory severely doubted that Jun's chances would've been good with either of them.

"Givin' him a lump on the head was right," Cortez said. "That'll show his hand in the matter when I speak to their Lingxiu. However," —he cleared his throat and looked at Raptor— "punishment should be handled by Red Dragon, according to their rules and bylaws. I understand you have a personal stake in this, as well as you, Adrian, but I can't start up rivalry when the incident happened between a few individuals."

"Appreciate it, Prez." Raptor inclined his head. "But at the risk of overstepping, I can't trust the Dragons to keep the Yu brothers in line. No one wants to start a war, and we respect you doing your best to keep everyone safe—but I'm not the only one who's been having issues."

Adrian's fingers gripped her waist. She leaned into him, her chest tightening at the thought of Jace.

Cortez narrowed his eyes. "What're you saying? Who's been having issues with who?"

"It's not related to the club," Adrian spoke up. "I had a run-in with Jace—"

"It's my issue, actually," Ivory interrupted. She didn't know how Adrian planned to hide his real motivation, but the best cover-up would be the truth. "Jace hasn't left me alone since last semester. He used blackmail and assaulted me last week on campus." Adrian's arm tensed, and he gave her a concerned glance. "After this, I'm worried he got his brother involved to deal with me."

"So we got two fuckers that can't respect women," Cortez muttered, rubbing his forehead. "I see your issue, but what's your solution?"

"We take care of this the old-fashioned way," Raptor said. "Brother to brother, man to man. All we need are the clubs to supervise."

What did that mean?

Cortez seemed to understand, nodding with a contemplative hum. "I can arrange that. If the Dragons agree."

"We'll handle it ourselves. Just want to do it on fair terms," Adrian added. She gave him a questioning glance, and he pulled her close.

Cortez straightened and clapped his hands. "It's settled then. Well, you boys seem to have a lot on your mind. Let's have a drink."

"Can't pass up one round." Raptor rolled his shoulders as if to shake off the tension.

Adrian squeezed her waist. "We can stick around if you want." Then, in a lower tone, he whispered, "I insist you get something light. I have a promise I intend to keep."

A shiver ran up her arms as his stubble brushed her jaw, breath warm on her neck. "Okay." She shot a smile over at Riley, hoping her blush wasn't visible. "Are you staying, too?"

"Course I am." Riley returned the smile with a chuckle. "I still have a shift to work as soon as these old ladies quit yapping."

"Thank the gods for that," Raptor cut in, a loose smile on his lips that fit him much better than the forced ones from earlier. "Beer always tastes better when it's poured by my old lady."

Riley gave him a healthy shove, even though he didn't budge an inch. Hearty laughter filled the room.

"Call me old again, and I'll let Trick serve your beer," Riley snapped.

"That's if he hasn't collapsed from managing a Saturday night all by himself," Cortez replied. "Poor guy probably hates us all by now."

"Even better," Riley retorted. "He'll be more creative that way."

FORTY-SEVEN

Adrian kept her tucked close as the five moved out of the storage room and back into the throb of music and flashing lights. Perfume and sweat crowded the air, the club packed to the brim.

No one else appeared to know—or care—about what went down earlier, but numerous bikers in black vests lingered near the bar and around the room. She caught hints of the skeletal hand of Royal Flush stitched to their jackets. Several bore indicators of their lifestyle, inky tattoos mingled with scars and gruff, rasping voices.

A collective glance from Adrian, Raptor, and Cortez parted the masses, and they slipped in to stand along the counter. While Adrian leaned over to speak with Raptor, Riley jumped into work mode and helped tackle a line trailing the length of the bar. The other bartender was a thin, ragged man who handed out drinks as he conversed with the others. Their rowdy chatter competed with the music, bits and pieces making their way to her ears.

Ivory let it fade into the background and snuggled into Adrian's chest, grateful he hadn't made an effort to join the rest.

As much as she wouldn't mind getting to know them, they'd had enough introductions for one day. She curled into his protective wall of muscle and took shelter in the barricade of his arms.

He turned away from Raptor and pressed a light kiss on her head. Looking up, a wrinkle pushed between her eyebrows as the concern from earlier resurfaced. "Did that go better than you thought? I know what you said, but I'm not sure what it all meant."

"It went the best it could've." He held her tighter until the whole, hard length of him molded to each curve of her backside. She nuzzled her nose into his neck, and his hair tickled her cheek. "It means I'm going to take care of things," he said. "So we can both be safe and happy. That's all I care about now."

His breath warmed the tip of her ear, and she yearned for another kiss but pulled away instead. In the flickering light, his eyes danced between gold and onyx, the same black knight she fell for months ago. As his gaze met hers, the emptiness he once carried became filled with an emotion so large it threatened to burst between them.

"It means I get a new future," he whispered, barely audible above the music. Then he covered her mouth with his.

She savored the delicacy of his lips, gentle and slow yet commanding. He encompassed her world and consumed everything else. The tip of his fingers traced wide circles over her hips before sliding up the curve of her waist, smoothing over her ribs. He took the time to caress every one, noting the rise and dip of the individual bones and then appreciating how she melted in his arms.

He smelled of sweat and sex but tasted like homemade cookies and felt like a heavenly blanket. His arms flexed under her touch, pulling her in until the swell of his erection pressed into her ass.

Someone cleared their throat, and she broke away with a hot blush. Their kiss had been chaste compared to the ones shared in the alleyway, but it left a flutter in her stomach and fueled the spark of desire between her legs. She shifted, trying to contain the surge of new arousal.

"What can I get for the two lovebirds?" Riley asked, sorting out the counter as she wiped the surface with a rag.

"I'll pass this time around." Adrian turned them to face the counter while maintaining his snug hold and dipped his lips to her neck, brushing her hair to the side.

"Um, I'll take cherry cola if you have it," Ivory replied, hoping her voice didn't betray how lightheaded she'd become. "With lime, please."

"Sure thing," Riley hummed, then made a face. "I don't know what you've done, but you must be made outta pure sugar. I've never seen my brother so head over heels." She shook her head and reached down for a glass. "This must be what he felt watching me and Raptor."

Adrian chuckled against the hollow of her throat and left a trail of kisses that shot all the way to her toes. Did he have to do this right now?

She managed a weak laugh and prayed her knees wouldn't give out. "I can't imagine. But that definitely goes both ways— he's not the only one who got stuck by Cupid's arrow."

Riley poured her drink with a smile. "As it should be. You're a saint for putting up with him, I'll tell you that. I know I've never been able to."

She placed the glass on the counter, ice chinking around the fizz from the soda. "This is my official invitation for you both to come over next weekend. Then I can get all the juicy details while we enjoy some good food with our booze." Riley cast another fleeting glance over to where Adrian had descended on the slope of her shoulder. "And maybe then my brother won't be so distracted."

Heat from the blush overtook her face entirely, but before she could reply, Riley turned and stepped over to the group of bikers, already having downed their first mugs and ready for refills. Ivory reached out to take her cola and cool off but froze as Adrian's fingers inched around the back of her thigh. His other arm banded across her waist, and he nudged her forward, using his abdomen to press her against the counter.

"Are you ready, sweetheart?" he whispered into her neck.

His feather-light kisses deepened into sharp nips, the soft caress of his tongue giving way to possessive scrapes of his teeth. He was all but devouring her on the spot, and at this rate, she wouldn't last long, even if he wanted her to.

"You don't know how bad I want to fuck you right here, right now," he growled into her ear. "Spread you out on this countertop and strip off that pretty dress. Watch the lights glow over your skin and listen to your moans drown out the music as I make you come on my tongue."

She cast a quick glance over to Riley and the others. Between Raptor's back and Adrian's body, her lower half wouldn't be visible to anyone else. Her chest heaved with the effort of not giving in, of not grinding back and impaling herself without a second thought.

"Don't worry about anyone looking," Adrian whispered. "I doubt my sister will be eager to watch any more of our affection, and Raptor knows better than to turn around." His tone lowered to a snarl that could only be taken as a threat. "You're my fucking salvation, sweetheart, but I swear if anyone else gets even a glimpse, I'll damn them straight to hell."

He slid his hand further under her dress, and she had to hold in a sharp inhale, palm clutched around her drink as condensation slid down the glass. "Are you still with me?" His fingers continued to trail upwards, reaching the seam of her panties. "I won't give you the chance to speak much longer."

She stifled a whimper. "Yes, I'll be good. Just like I said."

A low groan left his throat as he found her still wet, finger easily sliding in and slick with both of their cum. "Go on. Drink your soda," he murmured, prodding inside her. "That's all you have to focus on."

Taking a single sip would be a lot more difficult than it sounded. Thankful to be pinned in place as her body responded to his touch, she tried to lift the glass to her lips. But Adrian found her sweet spot, tender from earlier, and her hand wavered. Amber liquid splashed over the rim as she barely managed to muffle her moan.

"Can you come quietly?" he rasped with a strained voice as if he was the one about to implode.

Her heart raced in a steady staccato that outpaced the music. But she could do it. "Yes, sir."

With renewed effort, she took a sip and set the glass on the counter. Her head fell into the crook of Adrian's shoulder as the song turned into a disguise, allowing her hips to sway subtly with the beat and her feet to spread apart.

Using the new position, Adrian moved the hand around her waist down to strum her clit and dipped a second finger inside. The addition stretched her open, increasing the pressure and sending a delicious thrill through her limbs. Her breaths came out short and punctured, her vision glossing over as he worked her body like he'd owned it forever. The pounding bass filled her ears, and endorphins sang through her veins.

She reached for the soda again and exhaled a long, measured breath. The cold condensation served as her only distraction, running down the glass and sliding over her palm. Her thighs tightened, core swelling with the strain of Adrian's increasing demands.

He generously dealt out pleasure yet became purposely savage as he quickened the pace and tightened the circles over her clit. She bit her lip to keep from panting, intent not to let a single sound escape. Adrian's chest made a solid wall against her back, sure and steady as he worked her toward climax. His fingers curled deep and unrelenting.

Her knuckles turned white as she brought the glass to her lips to cover her gasp. "I can't—Adrian, sir—"

She tried to correct herself but could no longer speak as he held himself inside. Her pussy contracted around him as he pressed two fingers on either side of her clit. Her vision went black, and her body gave way. If it weren't for his arm holding her waist, she would have collapsed as she bent forward in agonizing silence.

Only after she could breathe again did Adrian pull out, chuckling as he left a nip at her neck. "You look worn out."

She rasped out a defeated sigh. "I wonder why."

"Want me to take you home?"

She started to shake her head, then realized he didn't mean to the dorms. He meant back with him. Back *home*. The thought of curling up together under the sheets was much more appealing than staying in a busy club and pretending to socialize.

"Yes, please," she whispered, barely able to hold herself up.

"Here." He turned her to face him and took out a bandana from his jeans pocket, discreetly using it to clean her and then kissing her on the lips. "All good?"

Something had changed about him tonight. She could sense that he wasn't holding back as much as usual, and it sent a thrill straight into her heart.

The faintest trace of concern glossed over his eyes, and she nodded as a smile pushed up her cheeks. As brutal and unforgiving as he could be when playing her Sir, he was just as tender and watchful when being the knight sworn to her side.

"More than good."

FORTY-EIGHT

Adrian

Salvation might not have been a strong enough word.

He leaned against the bathroom door frame, content to watch in fascination as Ivory shifted through the most mundane tasks—brushing her teeth, combing her hair, inspecting her face as she removed the last traces of makeup. Her dress hung in a dark curtain over her hips, ruffling where it ended mid-thigh. Her calves tightened as she stretched onto her toes, bare feet curled in two graceful arches.

Every inch of her was perfect. Sublime.

Her eyes found the bite marks on her neck, perhaps noticing them for the first time—but instead of being upset, a small smile lifted the corner of her lips. Damn. This woman must have been made just for him. Without meaning to, a low rumble emanated from his chest.

That was when she caught him staring. With a blush, she turned away from the mirror.

"All done?" he asked, only a little disappointed that the show ended so soon.

"Yeah." Her breath caught as he pulled her to him. He

brushed his palm over the side of her neck and tipped her head back for a kiss.

Fresh mint tingled his tongue as he swept it over hers, taking his time and reveling in her returning caress. Her hands curled around his biceps, lips softening as he licked and sucked until they deepened to the strawberry red he loved so much.

She pulled away with a giggle. "It's really too bad we never got to take that bath."

"Never too late." He ran his hand down the curve of her spine. Even as he suggested it, fatigue pulled at his bones. But if his sweet witch asked, he wouldn't decline.

She smiled and blinked up slowly, processing his words. Then she sighed and leaned into his chest like it was her favorite place on Earth. "I think if we tried that now, I'd fall asleep in ten minutes."

He chuckled. "A quick shower?"

Quick being relative, of course. Compromising the hour-long bath he wanted for a five-minute shower wouldn't cut it. But he could try to keep their activities limited to aftercare, ensuring she felt well enough for what he had planned for tomorrow.

"That sounds nice," she replied.

He dropped his hands to the hem of her dress, eager to remind himself of her body all over again. "Arms up."

She obeyed, and he peeled off the fabric that veiled her beauty. It dropped to the floor with an unceremonious woosh.

He held her gaze for a second, peering into her jade eyes as they flickered with the same questions all women had standing naked before their lover. The questions he'd already answered but would reinforce as many times as she wanted.

"Do you remember what I told you the first time you were in my apartment?" he asked. "What I said you were worthy of?"

She swallowed and peered at him through her lashes. "You said I was worthy of worship."

Her voice quieted as the word left her lips, fragile in its fleeting existence, yet nothing short of monumental in meaning.

She remembered after all this time. "Very good."

He let his gaze travel down the length of her body. Her chest rose with a tense breath, but he didn't stop. He wanted her to see the lust in his eyes, the awe that wove through his being at merely being in her presence.

Amethyst strands of hair fell over her shoulder, and though her breasts were covered by a black bra, the sight of her skin alone sent heat coursing through his veins. The slope of her sides flared into her hips, giving way to pale stretch marks that wrapped around her thighs—to be granted ownership of such value was no less than the highest honor.

"I will worship you till the day I die, Iv. Inside and out." Looking back up to take in the flush on her cheeks, he lifted his hand and unclasped her bra, then slid her panties down until they fell and pooled at her feet. "Starting tonight. Go ahead and get started in the shower. After I grab us some towels and brush my teeth, we can pick up where we left off."

She nibbled her lip as if she wanted to say something but couldn't find the words. He pried her lip loose, debating whether or not to steal another kiss. But before he could decide, she gave him a coy smile and fluttered her eyelashes. "I'll be waiting."

Then she stepped into the shower and let the curtain conceal her from his view.

He almost ripped the damn thing off.

Faster than humanly possible, he finished his tasks and joined his sweet, seductive witch. Suds trailed from the cloth as he ran it over the arch of her spine, massaging his fingertips into the muscles of her back and moving between her thighs. He crouched down and inspected her sex, taking note of every place that was slightly bruised or sore, although Ivory had insisted she felt fine.

He'd kissed each mark that bloomed over her porcelain skin but yearned to kiss them again. To mark her again. To do it all over again and again and again.

Only after he cataloged her condition did he continue to wash her legs, working the cloth around the inside of her knees and down to her ankles. He slipped a finger between each toe until she giggled and squealed. Crystal-clear rivets of water rolled down her body, clinging to the tight points of her nipples and pouring over her ribs.

"Okay, my turn," she said as he stood up and reached for the washcloth.

He smiled and handed it over with the soap. "All right, but I still need to wash your hair."

"Oh." She reached over to her shoulder to grab a strand of hair as if she'd forgotten about it. Or as if she was remembering the time he'd washed it before and everything that had led them to this moment.

"Right," she concluded after a pause, then looked up and twirled her finger in motion for him to turn around.

He did, letting her stay under the stream of hot water as she repeated the process of washing. Her hands were gentle and attentive as she reached for his hips, then splayed her palm over the muscles in his buttocks. She slipped between his legs and prodded her fingers towards his secret places, discovering how a man felt from behind instead of the front.

"Is this okay?" she asked as he tensed involuntarily.

"Of course." He'd allow her the same freedom to explore as she gave him. After all, she hadn't seen him fully unclothed before, and although the thought of himself wasn't exciting in the least, she seemed to be enthralled.

"It's just," she continued. "I've never really touched a man before. Not like this."

He resisted the urge to turn around. "Never?"

The sound of the water changed as if she was shaking her head. "No. I didn't...I've never been that intimate with anyone. Sex was more of an in-and-out thing. And everything else...I guess no one ever wanted me the same way I wanted them."

At that, he turned and took her shoulders in his hands. This would be the most important thing he uttered all day. Perhaps in his whole life. "I want you in every way, Iv. All of you."

Her eyes flicked to his, then trailed slowly down his body with a shy smile. Keen to rise to the occasion, his cock swelled and bounced to his stomach.

She laughed. "I know." Then she added reverently, "Thank you."

He leaned in and kissed every part of her his lips could touch. She melted, connecting them along each dip, along all of their curves and planes. Her arms wrapped around his back and ventured lower to grab his ass. She chuckled into his neck. "It feels a lot better when you do it to me."

"I agree." He gladly obliged, kneading her thighs until a shiver went through her body, and she hummed in contentment.

"No more for tonight, though," he chastised. "Let me wash your hair and tuck you into bed."

Sleepily, she nodded and let him arrange her on her knees, his back blocking the water for a moment as he ran his fingers over her scalp and through her hair. Careful to tip her head so it wouldn't run into her eyes, he let the warm water rinse out the shampoo and repeated the process with conditioner, taking extra time to let it work in.

Once they were both washed, he shut off the water and grabbed a towel, draping it over her shoulders. He dried her hair, wove it into a loose braid, and then scooped her into his arms.

"What are you doing?" she giggled, relaxing as she realized he wouldn't let either of them slip.

"Tucking you in, just like I said." He strode out of the bathroom with her in his arms.

A yawn overtook Ivory's reply. She rested her head against him and closed her eyes. "I'll have to tuck you in, too. Can't let you do all the chores."

"It's far from a chore."

Even though his apartment looked the same as it always had, undecorated and cast with the mundane disregard of a college student, it felt different. Complete. His kitchen table was no longer a slab of wood but a place where they'd eaten and shared memories of their families. His couch and recliner a nest where they'd cuddled. And his normally empty bed, where he now brought the only girl to have ever slept in it. He peeled back the covers and set her down.

"But I want to." She curled up under the sheets, pulling them to her nose and looking at him over the top.

"I'll be there soon," he assured.

After drying himself and turning off the bathroom light, he locked all the doors and gave one last glance through the blinds covering the balcony door. The moon lit up the sky in a silver crescent, rising above campus with an iridescent blue halo.

Memories of summer heat and the ring of gunshots no longer filled his ears. Instead, there was peace. Quiet. Even the incessant urge to uncover the truth of the past, to dig it up just to bury it once and for all, stayed dormant. It hadn't been fair from the beginning, and he might never find the whole truth, but at least he could guarantee the Yu family would never hurt his family again. He'd make sure of it.

Rejoining Ivory in bed, he dragged her into his chest and stole the warmth he'd lost outside.

"Oh, you're cold!" She turned to face him, nuzzling into his chest hair and curling her toes. "See, this is why I needed to tuck you in."

He pressed a kiss to her nose. "You're absolutely right."

She pulled back to look in his eyes. "Thank you for today. I enjoyed all of it, even the parts that didn't go as planned."

"Thank *you*." It was her who made the day worth remembering.

Ivory paused. "You're welcome, but for what?"

He stroked her face, drawing his thumb down her temple to the corner of her lips and following the path with his gaze. How could she not know? "For ruining the man I was so I could be rebuilt into the man you deserve."

His heart had been broken for years, but now, a ray of light and warmth seeped out between the cracks. Although he never did anything to truly merit her love, he would live out the rest of his days earning it.

Her mouth parted, and her eyes grew glossy and bright. "I didn't mean to break you," she whispered as if the thought sorrowed her. "I just hope I'm worthy of the man you've become."

"You should never question that," he murmured and brushed a kiss over her forehead.

She lowered her head and pressed her lips to the center of his chest, right over his beating heart. "You've always been the man I wanted. It was always you, and it always will be."

Emotion caught in his throat. And since one kiss wasn't enough for his sweet witch, she blessed him again and again as he faltered, a peppering of kisses that threatened to shake his very soul. He couldn't speak, even though there were a million things he should say. The subtle softness of her bare skin, the love and gratitude that seeped through her simplest touch, her unabashed honesty—it all shattered him from the inside out.

He drew her lips up to his with trembling fingers. As soon as he tasted her, as soon as she kissed him back with a ferocious passion, his heart really did explode, and the shrapnel spread through every part of his body.

"Sweetheart," he choked out, squeezing his eyes shut before opening them to the best sight in the entire world. "I'm just a man." He wrapped her tight in his arms. "But you—you were sent from heaven, and tomorrow, I'm going to make those lips sing praises all day long."

She laughed, breath tickling his nipples as she nestled into a comfortable position. "I don't think what'll come out would be fit for church."

"It'll be more than enough for a sinner like me." He fixed the blanket around her shoulders. The soft whir of her breath filled the room, already succumbing to sleep. "Goodnight, my sweet witch."

He draped his arm over her waist, then let his consciousness fade.

FORTY-NINE

Ivory

Cocooned from head to toe, she let out a blissful sigh. Cozy sheets wrapped around her shoulders as her legs tangled between fuzzy calves and firm thighs. Her pillow moved to the beat of her heart, rich with the scent of spice and clean skin.

The events of last night and the threat of the Dragons felt like a faded memory, something that only required her attention in a distant reality. She stretched, and something tickled her nose. Then she realized her pillow wasn't a pillow at all but the chest of an immaculate, stark-naked man.

With a contented sigh, she nuzzled into Adrian's side. The copper hue of filtered sunlight pressed behind her eyelids, and she decided to stay in bed for as long as possible. She wanted to soak up every second of this. Just him and her, bathed in morning light.

The fine hairs on Adrian's chest tickled her nose again, so she ran her hand up the sleek contour of his abdomen, brushing over his pecs to move the stray hair aside. His skin pebbled under her fingertips, his nipple hardening as she circled the areola.

Cracking open her eyes, she was greeted by the sight of

Adrian sprawled on his back, face turned down so that his eyelashes dusted over his cheekbones. His lips were parted, rosy pink, and relaxed into a natural curve. Unbearably kissable. Auburn hair had come loose from its bun and fanned across the pillow, the pink-tipped strands mingling with her purple ones.

Blinking, she continued to study him, surprised to find him still in bed and even more astonished he hadn't woken from her movement. The last time they'd slept together, he'd gotten up an hour before her usual alarm, but today, he seemed to enjoy sleeping in as much as she did.

Her gaze fell to the hollow of his neck, then to the nipple she'd teased, which was now tight and round. Uninhibited by his usual attire, she let her hand roam down his chest as the sheets fell away.

A burn seared through her lungs. She'd been holding her breath. With a quiet exhale, she continued to follow the line of his hair as it narrowed and cut down his stomach. One of his arms lay across his waist, fingertips brushing her side as if he couldn't bear not touching her, even in sleep.

She traced around his hand, outlined the rings on his knuckles and smoothed over the skin on his wrist. Dipping down to his navel, she spread out her fingers and absorbed more of his body heat.

Tentatively, she explored lower and drew her fingers over the V at his hips. Her pointer finger found the trail of hair again below his waist, and she followed it, her hand slipping under the covers until she circled his girth. Half-erect, he stirred at her touch and filled her palm. She glanced back up at his face. Still no movement.

How many times had she come yesterday? Five? Six? How many orgasms did he have in store for her today?

She bit her lip in anticipation then tested the waters and squeezed his expanding length. He hardened instantaneously, rigid and thick. Noting each reaction, she slowly stroked up and down, then imagined what he would feel like inside her. When she'd finally earned every inch.

The excitement of pleasing him coursed over her skin like a trance, and with measured movements, she slipped under the covers. There, it became darker, hotter. The scent of him washed over her, followed by a heady rush of arousal.

She carefully squeezed between his legs and cupped his balls one at a time, rolling them in her palm. His cock surged, and she held in an elated squeak. Did he know? Or was he dreaming? But she couldn't stop to lift the covers. Not when she had something better in mind.

Leveraging his cock to her lips, she ran the tip of her tongue up the tight skin of his frenulum, then closed her lips around his head. He shifted, widening his thighs with a throaty groan. Her pussy blushed at the sound, flooding with heat. Motivated all the more, she flattened her tongue and swirled around the crown of his shaft before licking down to his base.

He tasted better than she remembered, fresh from the shower and warm from sleep. With one hand, she continued to work his balls while the other combed over his thigh, relishing the flex of his muscles as she licked back up and sucked on his slit.

He tensed, shifting again as she took him down her throat. His skin slid over her tongue, and she went slow enough to feel him throb.

Eagerly, she incremented the pace bit by bit, transitioning all her attention to his subconscious reactions, to breathing him in and savoring the salty nip of precum that leaked onto her tongue. Her mouth watered, wanting to taste more, to feel more, to swallow every drop, and when she was done, she wanted to come up and see the same satiated expression on his face he'd worn yesterday.

Her pace quickened, cheeks hollowed, palms resting flat

over his hips. The strain and pull of his muscles increased until he jerked, then relaxed with a deep groan. She held him in the back of her throat, knowing he'd woken fully and unsure what to do next.

His hand ventured under the sheets. Finding her head, he gave her a gentle caress and murmured something she couldn't make out, then held her down as he thrust upwards. A thick rope of cum shot into her mouth. She swallowed happily, giggling as his dick gave a defeated pulse.

They both stilled, his heavy breaths puffing in the air and her hum of satisfaction vibrating through his semi-hard erection.

"Come here," he mumbled, reaching for her.

She climbed over him, gratified to see him wearing a radiant smile, slanted from sleep and post-orgasm endorphins.

"Morning," she murmured, kissing the faded remnants of the bruise on his ribs.

"I see someone wanted to start the day with dessert," he rasped.

She grinned against his skin.

He pulled her up to his lips, rougher than she anticipated and urgent, as if they had gotten jealous of the rest of his body. His stubble scratched her cheek, but the gentle press of his mouth quickly soothed her.

"Feeling rested?" He feathered kisses along the outline of her smile and up the bridge of her nose. "Sore at all?"

She shook her head, too lost in his affection to speak.

"Good." He bracketed his hands on her hips and hauled her up and over his chest. Before she could process what was happening, his tongue swept through her folds and dipped into her sex.

She moaned, struggling to find balance. He anchored her to his mouth without room for protest. The lazy ease with which she'd woken up shattered instantly, her limbs seizing with shock and pleasure. He parted her folds with indulgent lips and sought out her clit in slow, deliberate strokes.

"You're soaked." His voice dropped low and crisp, the statement not a compliment but an accusation.

It only made her hotter, and another flood of arousal emphasized his point. Unable to squirm, he held her in place as she gasped again.

He licked a long stroke up her sex and hummed in approval. "Did sucking my dick get you wet?"

She nodded, then remembered he couldn't see because his face was buried in her pussy. "Y-yes."

He dug one hand into her ass and moved the other to her breast, his tongue transitioning to short flicks over her clit that made her jaw open in a silent plea. *Crack.* Her nipple stung from the slap, yet it tightened out more, pointing into the cold air. Ravenous tingles washed over her as Adrian continued to lick her.

"Did you like swallowing my cum?"

Thoughts and emotion jumbled in her brain. Her world reduced to the single point of contact between his tongue and her swollen clit. She swallowed and licked her lips, the taste of him lingering. "Mhm."

He slapped her other nipple. Her legs clenched around his head so hard she felt a wave of guilt. But desperation quickly replaced it, chasing her pleasure as he ground her hips into his mouth and let her fuck his face.

"Needy today, aren't you?" he mumbled into her soft flesh.

She sobbed, unable to choke out an answer as heat expanded and blazed inside her. "I'm—going to—"

"No." He pulled her back and held his tongue still against her clit, effectively prolonging the crest of her orgasm while keeping it just out of reach. Her body bucked against his restraint, driven wild with want.

"Please," she whimpered. "I need to come."

His eyebrows raised. "Need or want?" The puff of his breath teased her tender skin, a mockery of the relief he held hostage. "And you've forgotten my title this morning. That's more than enough to earn you a punishment."

Her head hung in defeat, blood pounding in her ears. "Please, sir...I want you to let me come."

"I will, sweetheart." He kissed her clit, then looked up at her with bright, sadistic eyes. "So pretty when you beg. But you don't get to come yet."

"That's not fair," she whined.

"You're right." He licked from her clit all the way down her slit, circling her tight rosebud and reawakening the sharp edge of his denial. "It's not fair that you taste so good. I should wake up to this every morning." She pouted as he gave her ass cheek one last possessive squeeze. "Today, we're going to test your limits."

She still squirmed despite the warning in his eyes, trying one last time to sway his mind. Testing her limits did sound fun, though, if not a bit scary. "What kind of limits?"

He sat up and slid her onto his waist, the contact almost unbearable against her exposed clit. "For starters, not coming when I tell you not to and not teasing me to try and get your way."

She pouted. "Sorry. I haven't been very good today."

He tilted her chin so she looked up. "You've done nothing wrong, Iv. Don't mix up our games with how I view you. You could never disappoint me."

Her worry faded, and she closed her eyes as he sealed his lips over hers. The tang of her taste coated her tongue, and she cupped his face, running her fingers through his sharp stubble. He turned and placed a tender kiss on the inside of her wrist. "That doesn't mean I won't try to challenge you, especially when I know how sweet the reward will be if you're obedient."

Oh, a reward? If it was worth giving up her orgasm now,

then he must have something incredible in mind. "Am I that predictable?" she asked, biting back a grin.

He chuckled, busy inspecting the cut on her finger, which had sealed overnight. Once satisfied that it wasn't bothering her, he pressed it to his lips. "Don't think I took my own reward for granted. Waking up to your mouth wrapped around my dick was a priceless experience, and I plan to repay you more than double."

Her laugh came out twice as breathless as usual, and insecurities washed away quicker than she had time to register them. Then her stomach grumbled. "How about actual breakfast?" she suggested. "I can make pancakes again."

"I would love that." He tucked a strand of hair behind her ear and let his fingertips continue down her neck. His eyes followed as his hand slid over her shoulder to her waist, landing on her hips. They both looked down and stared at the place where she was all pink, throbbing, and thoroughly soaked.

"I want you dressed like this," he declared.

She wiggled back towards his erection. "Naked?"

"Yes." He pulled her forward with a stern look. "You're allowed a shirt while cooking around the stove. No bra." He plucked at one of her nipples, and it hardened at his touch. "I want access to every part of you. All day."

Her body hummed under his gaze, euphoric at the thought of his hands—much less his mouth or any other part of him—attending to her for a whole day.

"Deal!" She scampered off the bed, then paused in front of his dresser. "May I?"

"Top drawer," he said, getting up as well. The covers fell off his thighs and pooled at his knees.

With a blush, she turned to the dresser and opened the drawer. Careful not to disturb the clutter scattered on top, she found a folded stack of clothes and rifled through them until a familiar design caught her attention—the same skull shirt he'd worn at the Halloween party.

The cotton felt soft and worn like it had been washed a hundred times. She slipped it over her head, and it fell just past the bottom curve of her ass. The shirt covered enough of her skin to maintain a decent warmth but exposed everything else for her knight's free use.

She twirled, giving Adrian a little show. "Does it look good?"

Unashamed hunger flashed behind his golden, lust-filled eyes. "You do."

She giggled. "Wearing your clothes makes me feel like a badass. Maybe I should have worn this instead of my witch costume."

"Your ass is very bad, indeed." His lips twitched. "I'll take care of that later."

Oh no. "That's not what I meant," she protested.

He stood and kissed her on the head, dick pressing impatiently against her hip. Her pussy clenched in anticipation. "Tease me all you want, sweetheart. If you want attention, attention is what you'll get."

FIFTY

As she worked in the kitchen, her black knight's eyes grew as dark and foreboding as his nickname, his lips unnervingly softer with every stolen kiss.

The worst, or maybe the best, reaction was his smile—one of a man equal parts amused and assured by a secret he wasn't willing to share. Somehow she knew he wouldn't touch her until after they ate, and teasing him felt a lot like poking a bear with a six-foot pole—enough distance to feel safe but nowhere near enough to get away unscathed. Risky yet appealing, especially since he'd already promised to give her a challenge.

But how bad could it get?

When they sat down to eat, she felt starved for too many things at once. Starved for the meal in front of them and for the man getting ready to eat it. For more lingering glances and for less space to separate them. For time to skip forward to her reward and for it to slow down so the weekend would never end.

She swallowed her second bite and looked up, hoping Adrian appreciated the meal as much as she did. His eyes met hers, and they both smiled.

"Thank you for the pancakes," he said, spearing a fluffy stack. "These taste even better than the last batch."

"This meal does feel more complete," she agreed, and her stomach chimed in with a rumble. Compared to their last breakfast, this one was a million times better. They'd worked out a way to move forward with their relationship. Adrian had made plans to take care of Jace, and neither had a class or job to rush off to.

Furthermore, she could eat with her eyes as well as her mouth. Raising a glass of cranberry juice to her lips, she tried to conceal her stubborn smile. "I can't believe you're eating like that."

"Mm, doesn't sound like a complaint." He slid the pancakes off the fork with his teeth and leaned forward on his elbows with a wicked grin. The muscles in his chest pulled taut, and his knee brushed hers under the table.

He was enjoying this. Enjoyed how he could wear nothing at all and still hold every ounce of power over her. Enjoyed how she hadn't been allowed release yet, her nipples puckered under the shirt. And how he knew that watching him only made the ache grow worse.

She shook her head. "Nope, not a complaint."

Adrian didn't need clothes. Not on a lazy Sunday morning when she could have this instead. When she could admire the body of a man who effortlessly dominated hers.

"Although, before we start having more fun today, I would like to go over some things," he added while picking up a piece of bacon.

"Oh?" She perked up. Conversations had always been easy with him, whether they were about sex, school, or general life. If he asked to talk, the suggestion came without apprehension. She trusted him with her mental vulnerabilities as much as she did her physical ones.

"Have you attempted power exchange before us?" he asked. "Or done any research into it?"

She shook her head again. "My ex was too vanilla to even think about bringing it up...and that time with Jace had been my only other attempt." She looked down, stirring syrup around her plate with a soggy pancake. "After that, I was too ashamed to do any research."

"Hey, you've been excellent so far." He reached across the table and grabbed her empty hand. She managed a weak smile, reassured by his touch. "Never think you're failing as a submissive. It's the Dominant's responsibility to keep the scene in check, and if something needs to be corrected, we'll work through it together."

Her heart skipped a beat. "Thank you. Things have been so different with us. It's freeing."

"I feel the same, Iv. I can't remember the last time I woke up with a smile." His words sent a ripple of butterflies through her chest. Or maybe it was how his hand held hers, firm in a way she knew he wouldn't let go, soft enough to make her crave more.

He continued. "Part of what makes our dynamic rewarding is that I can keep you happy and safe." His thumb rubbed over the back of her hand. "In order to maintain that, we both need to set limits. By the end of the week, I want a list of things you'd like to try and a list of things you don't. But first, we're going to give you more to base your thoughts on. It's a lot different imagining what something will feel like and actually experiencing it."

She hummed in agreement. So far, all of their interactions had been better than her fantasies. Submitting to him had been rewarding, but it'd also been more intimidating than she first assumed. Being restrained in real life felt a lot different from pretending to be tied up in the safety of her own bed.

"I'll only use our bodies this time, no toys or props," he said. "Once we have a better idea of what you want, I'll buy you your own set, and we can test them all out."

She bit her lip. That sounded fun.

Adrian's hand shifted to pick up her finger, then dragged it through the syrup on her plate. She watched thick amber liquid coat her fingertip as he spoke. "Keep in mind small things can become intense, too. Your safe word is valid in any situation."

He lifted her hand to his mouth, inspecting it before looking her straight in the eyes. "Never underestimate what I can—and will do."

His lips closed around her digit. The silken heat of his tongue sucked off the syrup, and her eyes widened at the same time her thighs clamped shut. He smirked, removing her finger with a pop. "Though I'm sure you'll learn before the day's over."

The pulse from her denied orgasm rushed to the surface. Adrian continued without pause. "That being said, are there any specific activities or positions you know you don't want?"

She chewed her lip as he dragged her finger around his own plate to coat it again. Conjuring the number of things he could do with their bodies alone flooded her brain with endorphins. She was more than willing to throw herself into his creative whims, but she also knew he'd been going easy, and that left her both frightened and terribly aroused.

"*All* parts of our bodies?" she squeaked.

"Yes." He brought her finger to her lips and offered the sweet, sticky mess with hooded eyes. She licked it off. "For both pain and pleasure."

He released her hand, and she sucked in a deep breath. "Right, okay." Confronted with the vast realm of her inexperience and barely able to approach the precipice of his bold implications, the only option left was to be honest.

"I can't really say what my pain tolerance is yet, and the pleasure part sounds pretty great..." A blush heated her face. "I've never done anal. But, I could..." Her eyes flicked up to his and back down again. "...*we* could start preparing." She reached for her juice and took a nonchalant sip. Glancing over the rim of the cup, she saw his lips twitch up.

"I'm more than willing to help with that."

Help didn't quite match the expression on his face. She distracted herself by stuffing the last of her pancakes in her mouth. Pain and general discomfort were things she usually avoided, but Adrian had a way of turning them into tools for her pleasure. The thought of toys and ropes and butt stuff made her nervous and excited at the same time.

"Are you done eating?" he asked.

"Yep." She jumped up to take their dishes to the sink. "You too?"

"Let me take care of these." He took the plates from her hands with a measured calm that betrayed the frisson in the air. Then his voice turned crisp and clear, unmistakable in its command. "In five minutes, I want you laid out on this table, face-up and pussy spread open."

The direct order sent a jolt directly to her clit, unsatisfied and eager to be revisited. As tingles raced over her skin, she watched her black knight walk into the kitchen, confident in his stride and abundantly sexy.

The sweep of his hair fell down to his shoulder blades, back bare down to his thighs, where the muscles along his legs and ass were on full display. Even though he wore none of the armor that inspired his nickname, he still had the aura of a knight. Bold and honorable, and most of all, equipped with a very powerful sword.

She could stare at him all day.

Five minutes.

She spun to retreat into the bathroom. He didn't need to give a warning for her to know he was watching the clock, and if today would be a test, then she wanted to get the highest score.

FIFTY-ONE

Ivory

AFTER FRESHENING UP, SHE DISCARDED HER SHIRT AND scrambled onto the now-clear table. The wood felt cold against her bare skin, hard and solid as she lay down. She took a final glance at Adrian; his back turned as he meticulously dried their dishes with a towel.

How many minutes did she have left? Would he make her wait if she got ready early?

Her heart pounded as she bent her knees and spread her legs, barely making them shoulder-width apart, when the nature of the position sent a shiver down her spine. With her head straight, her line of sight became restricted to the ceiling. The plain white left her thoughts to wonder while every cell in her body called out for its master. For his touch. For his praise. His commands.

She closed her eyes and moved her feet apart another few inches. Goosebumps rose along her skin, yet she felt hot— needy—exactly as Adrian said she was this morning. Exactly as he willed her to be.

Breathe.

Her thoughts mirrored the tone he'd use. Each inhale

seeking his scent. Open and exposed, her pussy clenched around nothing but want.

"Very good, Iv."

She sighed at the sound of his voice, which cut through her restlessness and resonated to the bone. His hand caressed her ankle, lips following.

"Beautiful."

He skimmed up to the inside of her knee, and she basked in his praise.

"For coming on my fingers at the club, you earned another inch." The warm trail of his breath moved over her thigh and hovered past the joint of her leg. She hummed in gratitude.

"You have no idea how proud you made me," he murmured. "How hard I get just thinking about it. How wet you were from being fucked outside in the alley. I'm tempted to go back and make you do it again. Strap a vibrator to your cunt and see how long you last without making a sound."

He exhaled with a soft, low groan and ran his teeth along the curve of her hip. Her pussy melted, dripping onto the table as she tried not to squirm. "So sexy. You enrapture me, Iv."

Her hands curled as he moved farther up, away from where she needed him most. He skimmed under her breasts in false kisses, avoiding her nipples as he spoke into her skin. "That makes five inches in one day. At this rate, the game will be over too soon, and we can't have that."

Dread crept up her spine. He moved to her collarbone and spoke against the rapid flutter of her pulse. "Today, you have two rules. Come when I give you permission, and you'll earn an inch. Come without permission, and you'll lose an inch."

To accentuate the point, his finger hooked deep in her pussy. She gasped at the sudden pressure, the harsh friction as he dragged it out then curled it back in. He kissed her lips and devoured her reaction with a satisfied hum.

But his affection came at a price. The pleasure she'd waited so long for had become a double-edged sword. All the progress she'd made could be lost...

"Do you understand?"

Her muscles tensed, and she sucked in a breath. This was a test, and she'd pass. He wouldn't let her fail. "Yes, sir."

"Good." Adrian withdrew his finger, and she moaned in agony. No matter what he did, this was going to be torture. To have his touch and not be able to come was near impossible, but to go without him entirely would be infinitely worse.

"Hands above your head. Hold onto the edge of the table."

She did as instructed, raising her arms and curling her fingers under the lip of the wood. Adrian grabbed her hips and tugged forward, pulling her body straight. His palms smoothed apart her thighs and pressed them down until she spread as wide as possible. Next went her feet, which were placed on two chairs so her thighs rested flat.

Splayed open like a butterfly on display, she trembled in suspense. A whine left her lips.

She already needed him again—could hardly breathe without his touch—and he knew it. He could see what he'd done in a matter of seconds—watched as her body swelled with the effort of pleasing him. He enjoyed seeing how dark and pink she must have gotten with all the blood rushing between her legs, the slick that coated every inch of her folds.

As if summoned, his fingers entered her with slow and deliberate strokes, hitting her weak spot with each excruciating curl. She clutched the table harder, nails digging into the wood.

"Are you close?" he asked.

Unbearably. Unthinkably. Uncontrollably.

"Yes," she breathed, quickly adding, "Sir."

"Hold it."

She grunted, then clamped her jaw shut as his other hand pinched her nipple. He rolled it between his fingers, tugging it this way and that until her clit screamed with envy. Her pussy clenched on his hand, strained with the effort of resisting release.

Her pants echoed into the ceiling, each one heavier, each hammer of her heart pounding a stake through her chest.

In. Out. Tug. Pinch. Roll.

It took everything she had not to cry and plead for release.

Breathe.

Forcing her eyes open, she blinked up at the ceiling. Her vision sharpened, the world vivid and psychedelic, verging on the border of pain. Then his hand finally slid out.

"Good girl."

She almost cried at the warmth in his voice, her eyes welling with tears of near relief.

"Do you want to come now?"

Yes. God, yes. But that much was obvious, and she knew the right answer. "Only if I'm allowed, sir."

"Very good," he hummed, and the smile on his lips took her breath away as he leaned in for a kiss. His mouth soothed away the ache as she calmed down. Once her head became clear again, he pulled away. "You're not allowed to come. Don't let go of the table."

In another reality, she would've broken the scene. Forced him to give her what she was owed and impaled herself to the hilt because if she hadn't earned that by now, then what had this all been for?

The surrender. The need. The game. The reward, waiting on the other side of her obedience. She'd become merely a pawn for him to use, and her body bowed at the thought. He could split her in two from words alone, and she'd let him.

Her hands tightened on the table as he spread her labia apart. Lightly, he pressed on her clit and rubbed lazy circles that felt like tiny electric jolts. Her back arched. He sunk two fingers inside her.

"Name four of Jupiter's moons."

"What?" she sputtered.

"Jupiter has ninety-two moons. Surely you can name four."

She glared at the ceiling. Of all times, now? It took every ounce of her concentration to count her breaths, and he wanted her to name moons?

A second finger crooked inside her. "Don't make me wait."

Oh, he'd really done it now—

The fingers twisted, and a ruefully obscene moan fell from her lips. Fine. Fine! At this rate, the one thread holding her together was fraying. She needed to finish as fast as possible.

"Europa," she panted. That one was the easiest. The others would take more effort to remember—effort currently being used to not succumb to his torment.

Nothing she'd done had ever been this difficult. No academic test could ever hold a candle to his sadism. Her muscles bunched as her pussy sang, toes stretching to escape euphoria for even a second longer.

Adrian continued with relentless precision. "Good. Keep going."

That bastard.

"Io." The word elongated as it left her lips, transforming into another wretched moan as he increased the pressure. Her clit had a heartbeat of its own. Both her body and her brain had reached their limit, but the next moon was on the tip of her tongue...just a little more...she could do it.

His mouth closed around her nipple.

"No, please, no!" The tears of gratitude from earlier turned against her, rolling down her cheeks in a hot stream.

He didn't stop.

With expert touch, he let her tumble into the abyss. Pleasure consumed every rational thought. It burned through her like a wildfire, beautiful and devastating, obliterating everything in its wake. It dragged her under its control and stripped away what dignity she had left.

She sobbed and shook, nearly rolling onto the floor from the impact. But as the orgasm began to fade, a bitter wave of remorse replaced the high. She'd lost. She came without his permission.

She failed her black knight.

FIFTY-TWO

SHE SEALED HER EYES SHUT AGAINST THE THREAT OF MORE TEARS. "I'm sorry. I couldn't—"

"*Shh*," Adrian soothed, tender while keeping command. "Can you name another moon, sweetheart?"

She looked up, expecting to see disapproval written on his face, but the frown she braced for wasn't there. He didn't look upset, not even in the playful way he'd been during their scene yesterday. Instead, he gleamed with pride and reverent awe, as real as any other time she'd impressed him.

"Ga–something?" she whispered.

He smiled. "Yeah, I think that's one. Let me check." He pulled out his phone and tapped the screen. "To be honest, you could have said anything, and I would've believed you. Here it is—Ganymede. Did I pronounce that correctly?"

She managed a weak laugh. "Ga-nuh-meed, and I have no idea what the fourth biggest moon is called. My mind is mush at the moment."

"Callisto."

"Right. I remember now." She sighed and let herself relax against the table. There had been no rational reason to fear his response. He'd always protect her, even from himself—or, in this case, from herself. "You did that on purpose. You wanted me to fail."

He set the phone down and turned towards her, feathering his fingers up her arms and capturing her hands with his. Their bare chests pressed together, his warm skin to her soft breasts. "Pain isn't always physical." His golden eyes searched hers, prodding for any sign of real harm. "But regardless of form, if you feel it, I own it. I own your success and your failure. In the bedroom, I decide which you'll get. And no matter what, you will always please me."

His words found root deep inside her wrung-out psyche, blooming into a rich bouquet more profound than any temporary pleasure. For once, she didn't have to worry about falling short. She didn't need to think about performing better than someone else. Their sex wasn't about that, and neither was their relationship. They didn't measure themselves in terms of win or lose. They had a partnership, and that bond was more permanent than a contract, more sacred than a promise.

"Thank you, sir," she whispered.

"You're welcome," he replied and rubbed their noses together. "You're so damn smart. No one could have done that but you." She giggled. "I love watching you come." His eyes drifted closed, lips ghosting over hers. "I love the shape of your mouth, the sound of your cries. The feel of you breaking for me." He kissed her sweetly, and she responded in kind. "Ready to earn back the inch you lost?"

She returned to the moment, limbs loose and yearning for proper release. "Yes, sir."

"Good." He straightened as his voice sharpened, sure in her obedience. "Turn your head to the right. Can you read the clock on the oven?"

She focused on the digital numbers. "Yes, sir."

"If you last ten minutes, you can come."

At least thirty minutes had passed since they'd had breakfast. Another ten wouldn't be easy, but it would be doable, especially since she'd already come once—

"*Ahhh—*"

Her cry filled the room, thighs snapping closed as he ran his tongue over her clit. Hot and slippery, he sucked up her juices and swallowed with a deep groan. The sound alone could've made her come again. Lasting thirty seconds felt like a monumental challenge. He wasn't going easy on her, and she didn't want it any other way. His confidence became her confidence. His ownership and mastery became her ownership and mastery. What he desired, she could achieve.

Adrian pried her legs open, lathing his tongue over her pussy and sanding her thighs with his stubble. The intensity of both sensations overtook her nerves. It was all she could do to grip the table, hips bucking into his mouth. Another flood of arousal eclipsed the tenderness left from her orgasm. Need spiked into desperation and churned inside like an endless black hole. With every lick, she craved more. With every taste he demanded, she opened wider in offering.

Faithfully, she kept her eyes on the clock, willing the seconds to tick by faster. But if anything, time slowed down.

All sensation came into focus under the magnifying glass of endurance: his soft and searching tongue, their ragged breaths stolen between messy slurps, the strength and authority of his posture. Her gaze wandered to Adrian's shoulders as they pressed apart her legs, powerfully skilled. His strong arms and hands pinned her in place, flexing as he countered her movements.

After several heavenly yet excruciating minutes, he turned to the side and kissed the inside of her thigh. She exhaled in relief at the merciful break and took in slow, deep breaths to steady her pulse.

His hands slid over the back of her calves, raising her legs as he trailed teasing kisses along her thighs and across her ass, mouth wet and warm. Then his finger pushed into her folds, and he opened her to lick and nibble on everything within reach. She shuddered in unbidden pleasure.

It wasn't her need or want that flooded her veins, but his. His need. His want.

His love.

"Who do you come for?" he whispered against her ravished cunt, rubbing her g-spot.

"You, sir." She gasped as he fucked into her pussy with a quick, deep thrust, and she couldn't help but squirm around his fingers. "I come for you."

"Who do you belong to?" His mouth traveled lower to rim her ass, stretching and branding her with his touch.

"You, sir. I belong to you."

"Damn right." He ran his teeth over her folds and followed with a gentle suckle that left her writhing. "*Every* part of you belongs to me." He pulled back the hood of her clit and gave it a long stroke with the flat of his tongue. "Every smile." *Lick.* "Every laugh." *Lick.* "Every fucking moan and every blessed tear you shed." *Lick.* "Is." *Lick.* "Mine."

As he lapped at her, she spun closer and closer to the approaching orgasm. Her pussy contracted, squeezing his fingers as they probed deep inside. A quick glance at the clock revealed she had only a minute left. Sixty seconds.

Crumbling, she counted down in her head. *Forty-four, forty-three, forty—*

He blew cold air across her clit. Her mind shattered.

"Every thought is mine."

She whimpered, eyes glued on the clock. His fingers stilled.

"I'm going to devour every single drop of your pleasure, sweetheart," he warned.

"S-sir," she panted. "Ten—"

The word barely left her mouth when his mouth touched her again and sucked.

The very laws of physics twisted and bent, pleasure shooting up her spine and infusing every cell in her body with a blinding, breathtaking, binding force. Gravity had no hold on them, her soul raised to an immortal plane where all that existed was the reward granted by her Sir.

Ecstasy stretched on and on, quivering and fusing and twisting until she gave one final, exhausted tremor. Adrian hummed with contentment between her legs, his voice muffled by her thighs. That's when she realized she'd trapped him there, her legs frozen in a vice grip on his shoulders and her hands buried in his hair.

Forcing her limbs to let go, she sat up and bit back a satisfied, delirious smile. His molten eyes lifted, face coated in her nectar.

Then, his lips curled into a deadly smirk. She froze. "Did I say you could let go of the table?"

The next breath caught in her throat. "No, sir."

He clicked his tongue, sliding into the dark persona she both loved and feared. A rush of adrenaline fused with the dopamine in her system, and she was wet and squirming all over again.

"Turn around. Bend over the table." His words came out cold and authoritative.

Her body reacted as if he'd doused her in gasoline and held a match between his fingers. She gulped, dropping her feet to the floor and twisting to lower her torso to the hard surface. The wood pressed into her chest, hard and unyielding against her tender breasts. Tension skated across her skin, but he didn't move to touch her.

"Spread your legs."

She whimpered. Even though they both already knew what he'd see, sliding apart her legs revealed just how slick she'd become, how her own cum dripped down her swollen cunt as it ached for more.

"Wider."

She grit her teeth to hold in the embarrassment of being so defenseless and stretched until her knees could no longer bend. He nudged her open with his foot to his satisfaction, making her rely completely on the table for balance.

"You still want to see how far I can push you?"

Her heart hammered like a jackknife. Helpless, exposed, and drenched, she pressed her face into the wood and bit back a moan. She felt drunk on desire, delirious for his domination.

"Yes, please, sir."

His fist tangled in her hair and lifted her face, his erection grinding into her ass. Her scalp burned as her pussy sang. "Then, from this point on, say anything but your safe word, and I won't let you come at all."

FIFTY-THREE

Every molecule of air evaporated from her lungs. Adrian let her head rest back to the table, but he didn't let go, holding his fingers firm against her skull. His hand remained strong yet forgiving, a reminder that though he was in control, she would always be safe.

His other palm came down fast and hard. She squealed, toes curling against the sting on her ass.

"Hush."

The punishing palm cracked down again. And again. Over and over, one hit blended into the next. Hot, ferocious pain bloomed across her ass and thighs as he held her in place. She stifled her cries as she fought with her body to yield.

"Damn," he breathed. "Your ass looks so pretty painted pink." Another smack. "I could do this all day."

Fire seeped under her skin, intensifying each hit as he gradually spaced them further apart. The burn grew as he waited, her anticipation ramping with every inflated pause. Her nails clawed the table, struggling against the instinctual drive to flee.

Adrian paused and took his hand off her head, only to pin

her arms against her lower back. "That's better, isn't it? Now you don't have to struggle."

She groaned. The hard edge of the table bit into her hips as Adrian's hand kept her back arched, pushing out her bottom. He leaned over and kissed her raw ass. A trail of scorching flames followed his mouth as he licked the sore skin, taking his time to nibble and suck as he pleased. His lips trailed lower, so close to where she wanted him to be...but he stopped just short of her pussy.

Her feet kicked out to no avail, and he pressed her thighs down in response. She choked out a sob as he straightened and landed another searing blow. Her body buckled. She couldn't keep this up much longer.

"Be a good girl," he reminded, running a hand over her flank. "You can take it."

Another smack.

Violet hovered on the edge of her consciousness, but she didn't reach for it. Not yet. If she could hang in for a little longer, take a little more, pleasing him would be worth it. Enduring for him. Earning his pleasure by taking his pain.

She exhaled in time with the next smack. There was no choice but to sink into the burn. To surrender. His following hit ignited another explosion of pain. But another sensation glowed underneath. A sweetness she hadn't been paying attention to.

Her hips rose up to meet his palm, and with a smack harder and meaner than all the others combined, pain-pleasure surged through her body. A moan tumbled from her lips. The shock went straight to her heart, slowing its rapid rhythm so she could absorb every sensation.

Adrian snaked a possessive hand around her throat, his rings pressing into her skin as he pulled her up to his chest. "Such a perfect slut for me." He slowly teased her opening with his waiting erection, filling her until she trembled around his thick cockhead. "This is what you need, isn't it?"

Her low wail echoed off the walls, wrenched straight from her core.

"Mm, yeah," he purred in her ear. "Feel how wet you are? How easily I slide in?" To emphasize his point, he pulled out and pushed back in, adding a few inches to what he gave her the first time. "Fuck, and you're so tight."

He was right.

She'd become so slick and swollen that with each thrust, she felt every ridge, every place he penetrated and infused with pleasure. Her ass still stung from the spanking, mixing endorphins in her blood until she forgot how to interpret it all. But she didn't need to. She didn't need to fight or run or think, only feel. And feel she did, her core clenching around his cock as he worked her at a steady pace.

"You're doing so well, sweetheart." He underscored his praise with a tender kiss, brushing his lips up her jaw. "Gripping my dick so hard I know it's gonna bruise."

His words sent a thrill down her spine, striving to please him without a second thought.

"Shit," he groaned, voice broken and filled with grit. His hands tightened on her throat. "Just like that. Show me how much you like taking my punishment. What a good girl you are."

His other hand released her wrists as he gave her nipple a savage twist. This time, she welcomed the pain, a mercy from tipping into pleasure too soon. His nails raked down her stomach and left red lines that burned all the way to her hips. She retreated to the fading sting—every sensation brought to the surface as he fucked and used and pleased her all at the same time.

Tears welled up for a third time, falling down her flushed cheeks like heavy, cleansing rain. They rolled over the pout of her lips, sweet and salty, then dripped onto Adrian's fingers. He loosened his grip and let a rush of blood flood her brain.

"So damn beautiful when you cry for me," he murmured, breath fanning over the sweat gathering on her skin. "So fucking perfect."

He slid his dick out and hooked his thumb into her pussy, pressing against that one place that unleashed a relentless pulse in her clit. She cried out, shaking like a leaf.

"*Shh, shh.* You're okay. I got you." He turned her head and comforted her with a kiss, licking the tears off her lips and letting her taste them on his tongue. He pulled back enough to search her face. Bright golden eyes peered into her soul, thin halos banding around black blown-out pupils. "Does my sweet witch need to come? You can speak now."

She nodded feebly, his hand caressing her throat as she searched for her lost voice. "Yes, sir. Yes, please."

"I'd like to see you come, too." He smiled around a grimace, his steel cock pulsing against her hip. "I'm going to play with that cute little asshole of yours, sweetheart. And when I do, I'll let you come."

She didn't know whether to feel relieved or worried, anticipation winning out as his thumb pulled out of her pussy to circle her tightest hole. Lubricated by a thick coat of her arousal, he pressed down just enough to test her resistance.

It didn't hurt, but she tensed regardless. He'd touched her there before, and it'd been as pleasurable as it was embarrassing, but it had been brief and without intent to go further. Now, he would be inside her, stretching her open so she could take more.

"Breathe," he murmured. Waiting until she relaxed again, he pushed past her ring of muscle.

Before she had time to calculate the new sensation, his dick slid into her pussy, and she clenched down. *Oh.* This was beyond what she'd felt before, expanding deeper than she thought possible. Even she could tell how tight she was. How his one finger filled her to the point of bursting.

He slowly dragged his thumb out, each millimeter wringing out a new kind of pleasure, then slid back in up to the knuckle. Her head tipped to rest on his shoulder.

"You're fucking amazing," Adrian panted, pushing through her defenses and claiming both her holes with calculated thrusts. "Just imagine how my cock will feel. How good it's going to be when I pump your ass full of my cum."

Her pussy throbbed, and she moaned, closing her eyes as a tremor rolled through her core. Pinned between the table and his dick, between his heaving chest and the firm fingers around her throat, she submitted in every sense of the word. Her muscles went slack, accepting the pain and the pleasure, taking it all in greedy quakes and trembles. He could destroy her—he would destroy her—and she yearned for it.

Their groans combined, bodies in sync as she cracked and split under Adrian's commanding force. Under his will to give her exactly what she needed.

"Go on," he rasped. "Let me feel that gorgeous pussy milk my dick. Take what you deserve, sweetheart."

The orgasm loomed in front of her, its gaping jaws eager to devour her whole. With several swift thrusts, Adrian shuddered, then stilled. He pushed in as deep as he was allowed and bit her shoulder.

She felt the moment he broke, heat and semen pouring into her. She'd pleased him. Her submission made him come apart. A string snapped, and her back arched as his pleasure triggered her release. It curled around her skull, lashing out and binding them together. The sensation filled her until nothing was left but a tingling semblance of reality where her soul fused with his.

She slumped, catching her breath as Adrian panted against her neck. Relaxing into the warm, muscled body surrounding her, she breathed in their mingled scent and sighed. Nothing could compare to this. To being open and honest and free. Unashamed and satisfied. To expressing herself without fear.

Adrian gently pulled out and circled her waist with his arms. Turning her, he wiped off the tears on her cheek with the back of his hand. "Are you okay?"

"More than okay." She smiled at him. Then she yawned.

They both broke out in a laugh, and he brushed his lips over hers. "Tired?" he murmured.

"I might need a few minutes." Her eyes drifted closed. She ran her hands up and over his shoulders, clinging to him for support. "Then I'm all good for round two—three, whatever number we're on."

"I'm pleased you're eager for more," he hummed. "I have an idea for our intermission."

"Oh?" His ideas were always the best.

Then she was being scooped up. After a short walk, a soft cloth was pressed between her legs, and Adrian wiped her clean. He paused. "Fantasy? Rom-com? Thriller?"

She cracked open her eyes and was met with a bookshelf lined with books. As he listed the options, she skimmed over the row of spines.

"Take your pick," he said. "I checked out a few from the library a week ago but never got past opening the cover."

She hummed. A black book stood out, the title embellished in gold. She picked it up to inspect the front and opened to the last page.

"You read backwards?" he asked, amused.

"No." She shut the book with satisfaction. "Just making sure I like the end. I choose this one."

He shook his head. "Hold on, grab this, too." He motioned to the blanket on his bed, and once she had it bundled in her arms, he brought them into the living room and sat down in the recliner. "Sometimes the end is better when you read the beginning, you know."

She tucked the blanket around their shoulders and settled into his lap. "And sometimes, knowing the end makes the beginning more exciting."

"Touché."

As he began reading, she rested her head on his chest and, unable to resist, drifted off to the smooth tenor of his voice.

FIFTY-FOUR

Somehow, the Earth spun faster when she was wrapped in Adrian's arms.

By the time she woke Sunday night, it had already gotten late, and after making sure she was fed and otherwise cared for, he brought her back to the dorms. Stars lit up the sky as their magical weekend came to a close.

At first, she'd been upset about wasting what time they had left, but when the grind of classes kicked in, that extra rest made a huge difference. That, and the memories replaying in her mind like a corrupted fairytale.

Unfortunately, between work and school, they didn't get to see each other nearly as often as they had hoped. It would've all felt like a dream if not for their frequent messages and late-night calls. Which, more often than not, ended in her falling asleep, worn out from studying. Sometimes, she kept a video call open as she did homework just to look over and see his handsome face.

If only she could spend every weekend being thoroughly fucked and cuddled by her black knight. Life would be complete.

Maybe it could be. Maybe things could be simple between them, just like Adrian said. After all, the only obstacle in their way was other people.

Other people who still were the reason she looked over her shoulder when walking to and from class.

Adrian seemed sure Jace and Jun would be taken care of, but that in itself worried her more. He never explained what Raptor meant at the club, and she hadn't found the right moment to ask. But the decision was already made, and for once, no one seemed to be on edge. Riley solidified plans for dinner on Friday, and she figured that'd be the best time to get answers. Until then, she had to keep herself together.

Even though apprehension about running into Jace still haunted her behind a veil of hopeful thoughts.

Ivory scanned the sidewalk and crossed through a crowd of students, weaving towards the library. The last piles of snow had melted, and flowers poked out of the fresh grass, but that didn't stop her from feeling a rush of cold every time she passed a set of Beta Rho letters. She'd been careful to stick to the longer route and didn't cut any corners, avoiding the last place Jace saw her.

Adrian would escort her if she asked, but he had classes of his own, plus shifts at the salon. She couldn't monopolize his time, and if she did, she didn't want it to be because of Jace. She tried to tell herself she was overreacting, that surely Jace only lashed out because he'd been provoked.

Surely, he wouldn't try anything again.

Then her mind wandered to Serena and the forlorn look in her eyes the last time they talked. Jace's temperament affected more than one person, and by the looks of it, he wasn't getting any better.

Taking shelter inside the library, she located their study group's usual table and settled in. Right now, she needed to focus on her chemistry test, not people and events outside her control. She took out her textbook and a pack of notecards, then set about making flashcards. Maybe Adrian could quiz her later.

Avril and a few of her friends arrived, chatting as they sat down. Ivory listened as they caught her up on the school's latest sports matches and then launched into plans they'd made to go on a trip over spring break.

"Spring break?" Ivory cut in, pausing to look up and register what that meant. "Is it coming up?"

Avril nodded, excitement in her eyes. "Yeah, it's in two weeks. I can't wait to ditch this place and forget about school. You don't have plans?"

"I usually just go back home." Ivory shrugged. She'd completely lost track of the semester schedule. If spring break was in two weeks, then she'd have to start making travel arrangements. Her house was only an hour away, but she didn't have a car and always had to ask one of her parents to pick her up.

Unless...she asked Adrian to take her. She'd already met his family, and they had plans together this weekend, so why not invite him to stay at her house over break?

Her parents hadn't cared when she brought over boys before. Though she had a sinking feeling her mom wouldn't be impressed by her daughter showing up on a motorcycle. Sooner or later, they would figure out Adrian didn't fit into the prim and proper life her mom had mapped out. Then again, she hadn't fit into it lately, either.

"Hey guys, guess who's here?" a bright voice called from behind her shoulder. Ivory turned as Serena dropped her pink bag on the table and flashed a beaming smile. "Have room for one more?"

"Yeah, of course we do." Avril made quick introductions for the rest of the group.

A rush of joy eclipsed Ivory's thoughts, and she slotted her spring break plans away for later. Serena had decided to show up, after all. Ivory hadn't been sure she'd accept the invite, but she did. It'd been too long since they were all together like this.

"I'm glad you could make it," Ivory said, arranging her maze of notes off to the side to make room on the table. "Feels like old times."

"Damn, you're right. I miss last semester." Serena sighed. "To be honest, I need a study group, bad. Frat boys know how to party, but I don't get much work done at the house."

"How's that going? Didn't you move in with them?" Avril asked. "I thought girls weren't allowed."

Serena flipped a strand of blonde hair away from her face. "They made an exception because I agreed to clean up after parties and other dumb shit." She scoffed and dismissed her statement with a wave. "Anyway, I'm past all that. Back in the dorms and working on a place of my own next year."

"What about Jace?" Ivory asked. It wasn't a topic she'd planned to bring up, but if Serena had moved out, did that mean something had happened between the two of them?

Serena caught her eyes, and for a split second, her guard lowered to reveal a trace of vulnerability, but then she looked across the table at Avril and threw her head back with a laugh. "You haven't heard? Girl, do I have *the* story for you."

Everyone else looked over, including a few students nearby, but that didn't deter Serena in the least. Garnering attention had probably been her plan from the start.

"Jay almost went to jail."

"No way," Avril breathed, neglecting her notebooks to plant an elbow on the table. "What happened? Are you okay?"

"No one got hurt, thank God." Serena paused for effect. "But apparently, drinking as a passenger is illegal. Did you know that? I wasn't even the one driving!"

"I'm pretty sure they covered it in the alcohol safety course during orientation," Ivory chimed in. "But you aren't the legal drinking age, either."

Serena rolled her eyes. "It's not like I was trying to get caught. I'd barely gotten tipsy when Jewelle missed the stop sign, and I was in the backseat, so I thought I could play it cool, and the cops wouldn't see the damn can. Jay didn't notice because he was busy arguing on the phone with his brother about some secret family nonsense—" She cut off and flicked her eyes over to Ivory before launching on. "After that, the cops came and..."

Serena's words got muffled as Ivory's fingertips went numb, the pen falling from her grip. She looked down at her notes, the lines all blending together.

Jace must have been the one who set up Riley. When he found out Jun would face backlash for it, what would happen next?

Her stomach twisted in knots, and she could barely focus on the rest of the conversation.

"—Apparently, the Mercedes is Jun's car, and we all had to go to the station," Serena continued. "Then they found drugs in Jewelle's purse, and she got arrested. Took up the whole damn night. The worst part is Jace blamed it on me, then said we were finished." She crossed her arms and huffed, more irritated at her ruined night than breaking up with Jace.

"Wow. So what's gonna happen?" Avril prompted.

Serena shrugged. "I have to go to a hearing about it. Guess I'll find out then, but they said because I'm so young the judge will probably go easy."

"That's some scary shit," Avril hummed.

Serena nodded. "Yep. Jewelle has it the worst, though. They searched her purse and found a stash of pills. I didn't even know she carried half that shit on her."

"The same drugs used on Caspian?" Ivory whispered, looking up at Serena.

Her eyes widened, shock crossing her face. "Oh, damn… you're probably right. That means Jewelle lied to us about it all along."

Ivory nodded. "Yeah." They were a little late to catch on, but at least it was out in the open. Maybe Caspian could even press charges now.

"Well, fuck her," Avril declared. "I'm glad you're done with them. Sounds like the whole family's twisted."

A lump formed in Ivory's throat. Avril was right—the Yus were bad news—but she had a feeling the drama wasn't over yet. Jewelle may have ended up behind bars, but Jace and Jun were still on the streets, and they wouldn't go down without a fight.

FIFTY-FIVE

Adrian

Ivory bounded towards the curb as he rounded the corner, no doubt having picked up on the purr of his bike. Sunlight glinted off campus buildings and the clean smell of rain hung in the air.

Heaven knew they'd spent too many hours stressing this week.

Between Riley's incident at the club and Ivory calling him about the Yu's run-in with the police, he hadn't gotten nearly enough quality time with his sweet witch. At least the latter incident would only be a setback for the Dragons, and Cortez verified it shouldn't affect their plans. At dinner tonight, he hoped to get an official date from Raptor, then he could spend the rest of their weekend showing Ivory just how much he missed her.

She'd been a diligent student, both in her studies and researching what she wanted from their dynamic. Her lists came via email this morning, and it gave him all the inspiration he needed to make this weekend better than their last.

He rolled the bike to a stop and pulled off his helmet as she jogged over. She'd swept back her hair with the ribbon, revealing the cutest face on the planet. Her helmet rested under one arm, hips hugged by a pair of jeans, and shoulders covered by a lace cardigan.

"Hey," she breathed, only able to get out one word before he pulled her into a kiss.

Painted her favorite wine-tinted purple, her lips tasted like heaven, supple, and more delicious than he'd remembered. She kissed him back and then happily let him take over, breath warm and enticing as he reacquainted himself with every last detail of her mouth. Damn it. He couldn't stop—nor did he care if he should.

Life almost felt this radiant once before. Before the storm came. Before he stopped looking for the sun and started searching for secrets in every shadow. When the road had stretched out in front of him, and it could've led anywhere because he only needed to go forward.

And right now, just like then, the only place he wanted to be was right where he was.

A muffled laugh hummed between them as Ivory playfully pushed away and broke their contact. The world rushed back into focus: a crowd of students passing by on the sidewalk, the rumble of the engine, the loud thud of his heart. The morning clouds had retreated to reveal a deep blue sky, and for a few precious moments, he tricked himself into believing the worst was over.

"Hi," he replied, remembering to greet her with words before snatching the helmet out of her hands and tugging her into his chest. He captured her lower lip between his teeth with a predatory snarl that felt much more suitable.

She moaned, then giggled until his dick started to get hard. Reluctantly, he let her go and fixed her smeared lipstick with his thumb. Ruining it completely would have to wait.

"Do I look all right?" she asked. "I wasn't sure what to wear for dinner."

Considering he wouldn't be able to take his eyes off her all night, he thought she looked more than all right. But that had less to do with her clothes and more with what he'd do to her once they were off.

"You're breathtaking, as always," he answered, hooking his fingers in her waistband. "As long as you're comfortable, I don't think Riri would care if you show up in rags. She's less about appearances and more about spirit, and you've already proven yourself in that regard."

"I have?" she asked, tipping her head and looking oblivious to her own virtues.

"Of course," he chuckled. "How many women would follow their man into a bar, knowing two hostile biker gangs might break out in a fight any minute?"

She rolled her eyes. "You wouldn't have let me come if it could get that bad. And I would follow you anywhere."

He arched a brow. "Nice try, but that statement works a lot better without adding sass. Remember that I'm keeping track of your punishments, sweetheart."

She pouted. "Already? I don't get one free pass?"

"Hm--no." He smirked. "And I'm going to enjoy every bit of leeway you give me." He handed her helmet back. "Any other questions?"

She pursed her lips. "Any other warnings, sir?"

He laughed. "Just be yourself, Iv. There's nothing for you to worry about...with me or with my family." He slid his hand around her cheek, addicted to the feel of her skin and how her lips tipped into a smile despite trying to hide it. "You're my entire world. You know that, don't you?"

The heat of a blush crept up underneath his fingers. "Yeah," she breathed. "And you're stuck as my black knight, whether you like it or not."

✧✧✧

Twenty minutes later, after their first ride without wind or rain, they arrived in front of his sister's house. Ivory stood as he secured both their helmets to the side of the bike, and he slipped his arm behind her as they walked up the driveway.

Not for the first time, and certainly not for the last, he was struck by the impact of such a small gesture. Of walking beside her, yet being her strength and her paladin at the same time. Of protecting her from every angle while she gracefully shielded him from his own dangers. Of breathing in the spring air and feeling an empty space in his pocket where a pack of cigarettes used to be. Of seeing a place people called home and knowing his wouldn't be dark and empty, or that tomorrow had the potential to be even better than today.

The door opened before they rang the bell, and Riley ushered them in while Raptor yelled a greeting from the kitchen.

"Ooh, look at you," his sister said, already fawning over Ivory. "Making that wind-blown biker hair look sexy! Don't worry, I'm serious. There's nothing to fix." Ivory tucked a strand of hair behind her ear while Riley shot him a pointed look, her own glossy hair falling in natural waves to her waist. "Please don't tell me you've been dragging her around on that bike all winter. This is the first good day we've had, and she's already a natural."

He stared back, unamused. Ivory got a compliment and he got an accusation? But he'd expected no less. "Nice to see you too, sis. What else am I supposed to use, a car that I'll never drive?"

"Well, you'd drive it now," she shot back. "Women need to have some creature comforts, unlike men who think the rougher and tougher, the better."

"I heard that," Raptor shouted from the kitchen.

Something sizzled in the background, and mouth-watering spices wafted through the air. It smelled like his mom's recipe.

"You know tougher is better," Raptor added.

Ivory laughed, then spoke with a faint blush. "I really don't mind the bike. I admit I was terrified at first, but it's growing on me. You ride, too, right?"

Riley's grin stretched from ear to ear. She'd heard the magic words. "You bet I do. Wanna see my beauty? And I don't mean just in looks, but those, too. Just wait until it gets dark. I have pink LEDs under the frame."

Ivory glanced over, and he kissed her on the top of the head before Riley could whisk her away. "Go have fun."

His own smile appeared as she gave him an apologetic wave. From the moment they'd been invited over, he knew this would be inevitable. Riley may have been able to whip a room full of bikers into shape all by herself, but the prospect of adding another woman to their ranks had his sister acting like a kid again—she'd always been the first to make new friends and wasted no time showing off whatever she thought was cool at the time.

Ivory would have fun, though. He didn't need to question whether Riley would give her enough space while providing a warm welcome. Some one-on-one time would benefit them both.

He ventured into the kitchen, hoping Raptor had improved at cooking since they were teenagers. "You're in charge of food tonight?"

A laugh filled the room, and Raptor stepped away from the stove to pull Adrian in for a proper greeting. "Wouldn't that be something," he replied. "No, Riley did all the prep work. I'm just following instructions at this point."

"Any word from Cortez?" Adrian asked, taking a seat at the table.

"Two weeks, Friday night." Raptor returned to his post by the steaming pot. "At the abandoned factory out by old town.

The Dragons agreed to all the terms, so looks like it'll be a fair fight."

Adrian breathed out in relief. "Good. Two weeks then."

"Yep," Raptor agreed, pausing for a beat. "Listen, man, I don't need to know why you went after Jace, and I'm not asking...but whatever you got on him and the Dragons, is this gonna solve it?"

Adrian looked down at the table and flexed his hands. Scratches marred the shine on his gold rings, unlike the polished silver ring that connected the Yu's to his father.

Closure was a fickle thing. For so many years, the hole in his life had felt so large, an impossible void that could only be filled with sin of equal magnitude—but then it was eclipsed by something, or someone, even greater. Figuring out who killed his father would only be valuable if it meant he could keep his family from further harm, and that meant not putting them in more danger.

"Yeah," he finally replied, looking up at Raptor as he closed his fist. "I figured out who my enemy is, but that doesn't mean I'll become them. Better to preserve life than take it."

The corner of Raptor's lips turned up as he nodded. "Can't disagree, and you gotta a helluva lot that's worth preservin'."

"Sure do," Adrian agreed.

They fell into a short silence, his stomach grumbling as the food continued to simmer.

"She ready for all this?" Raptor asked. "Ya know your girl's gonna want to be there, right?"

Adrian felt himself tense before he registered his reaction. The thought of Ivory anywhere near a gang fight put him on edge, but Raptor was right. She'd want to be there, and he had no right to stop her.

"You letting Riley come?" he asked instead of answering.

Raptor sighed. "I'd never let Riley come under the circumstances. But if she listens to me, that'll be a first. All I can do is make sure my guys stay close enough to get her the hell out if shit blows up."

Before they could continue, both women barged back inside through the garage door. Riley had the same wicked grin plastered on her face, and Ivory trailed close behind, holding a purple bandana and looking much more relaxed than when she first arrived.

"I swear, if you don't keep this one, I'm adopting her," Riley announced as she took a seat across the table.

"No offense, but I'm not fond of sharing." He claimed Ivory's hand and guided her into his lap before she could take a seat of her own.

Ivory laughed and wrapped her arm around his shoulders, looking down through her lashes. "Who's keeping who? I don't think I'm giving you a choice."

He tightened his grip on her waist and shook his head, leaning in close to whisper, "That's two."

She shivered but straightened and asked, "Oh, by the way, do you have plans tomorrow morning?"

"Tomorrow?" He glanced over at Riley and narrowed his eyes. He'd been serious about not sharing. "No, but I work from nine to two."

"Perfect." Riley swiveled towards the stove with a spoon in hand. "Then I call dibs on taking her to the shooting range."

His eyebrows shot up, and he looked back at Ivory, who had sprouted a mischievous grin. "Sounds like you two are getting into more trouble than I anticipated," he muttered.

FIFTY-SIX

"Wow, that felt…"

"Scary? Good? Scary-good?" Riley suggested.

Ivory shook her head as she slid into the passenger seat. "Fun," she concluded with a grin. Next time they went shooting, she wanted to bring Nia and the guys, too. Maybe they could call it a triple date.

Sunrays beamed through the windshield of Riley's Sedan and heated the leather interior until it almost burned, contradicting the cool breeze outside. Luckily, neither of them minded rolling all the windows down, and fresh air poured inside as the engine started.

"I'm going to need a lot more practice, though," Ivory added.

"Hey, you did better than you give yourself credit for." Riley adjusted her braid and pulled out of the shooting range's parking lot. "Enough to prove you've got talent."

Ivory laughed. "I couldn't even hit the target on the first two rounds." Shooting a gun felt a lot different than anything she'd done before. Collecting knowledge and mapping out the sky didn't come close to handling raw, physical force.

"On your first two, sure," Riley said. "But after that? You hit the mark more often than half the guys I know."

"You're kidding…" She glanced over, and Riley pursed her lips. If that were the case, she'd hate to rely on those guys in a real shootout. Riley, on the other hand, looked like a natural with a rifle or a handgun. "Maybe we women have higher standards," Ivory muttered.

Riley's smile widened. "Or you're a perfectionist. Either way, I'm game to take you again. Although something tells me Adrian will call dibs on your next visit."

"Mm, I think you're right about that." Ivory grinned and bit her lip. Something about the image of Adrian hitting the target dead center made her blood rush. Even though it'd only been a few hours since they saw each other, a pang of absence spread through her chest at the thought. "Oh, shoot!" she exclaimed as they turned onto the main road. "Completely forgot to put on my seatbelt."

"Looks like you've gotten more used to two wheels than four," Riley teased.

Ivory shook her head and clicked the buckle in place. More like she was used to holding onto Adrian as they drove. It didn't feel right without him in front of her. Or beside her, for that matter.

Glancing at her phone, she sent him a quick text that they were finished. By now, he would be getting home from his shift, and all she wanted was to be back in his arms. To let him tell her everything would be all right, in a way only he could.

He'd explained the details of the fight he and Raptor planned, and though it answered most of her questions, a pit of unease still formed in her gut. Both men were putting their safety on the line —and she didn't put it past Jace or Jun to pull a dirty trick that would get one of them killed. Her learning to shoot hadn't been necessary, but the more ways she could protect herself, the better.

"Hey, this thing with the Dragons..." she started, unsure how to word her question. Of all people, Riley would be the best to ask. "I know the guys are gonna be fine, but I feel like it'll only make Adrian worry if I'm there. I don't know how to support him without being a distraction." He could handle himself, and Raptor would be fighting by his side, but there had to be something else she could do.

Riley glanced over with a sympathetic smile. "Oh honey, he's gonna worry just the same as you worry about him. Being there or not won't change that, but somehow worrying together is a lot better than worrying alone."

Ivory nodded and looked down at her hands.

Riley sighed as she switched lanes. "You're good for him, you know. Most people will see you two and think you're the one who needs protecting, but I know my brother, and he needs what you give him just as much."

"Thanks," Ivory mumbled. "I want to be there for him the same way he's been for me. In fact, you've all been so kind and welcoming." She glanced out the window at passing traffic. "But I—"

She chewed her lip. There had been something else on her mind, and it was about time she admitted it. "I don't think my family will be so accepting. Since meeting him, I've been so much more of who I want to be—confident, secure, and happy, but I don't think my parents will see that. Some days, I don't think they even see me. They only see what they want me to become. Adrian doesn't fit into that."

Riley hummed, nodding as if this wasn't unexpected. "You know, I'm shit at advice. I'd rather duke it out than talk about feelings. Just ask Raptor." She chuckled, then sobered before continuing. "However, I do know a weapon more powerful than a firearm, and that's self-respect. It can be hard to stand up for yourself, especially to the people you love, but it's worth it.

Show them the value of your choices, even if it takes time. That's what counts in the end."

"Mm," Ivory agreed. "It might be a rough road, but there's always a chance it'll get better. I'm not going to give up."

"That's the spirit." They waited at a red light, and Riley drummed her fingers on the steering wheel, the tattooed band of her wedding ring a permanent thread of black around her finger. "Listen, Adrian's a good man—and by that, I mean there are men who have good hearts, and there are men who use those hearts to do good things. Raptor has a good heart, but sometimes I need to kick him in the ass to use it. My brother..." She exhaled, stepping on the gas as the light turned green. "He taught me what a good heart is and how to use it. I see those same traits in you. If any two people can overcome the odds, it's you two."

Ivory felt her smile return. "I'd like to think so, too. Sometimes, I feel a little too invincible next to him. I hope he feels the same around me."

Riley snorted. "Girl, Adrian's been fightin' the world since the day he was born. With you, he's finally winning."

Ivory turned away to hide her blush. "That he is."

For the rest of the drive, she found herself counting the minutes until they reached the apartment complex. Adrian's bike sat parked in its usual spot, and as they pulled up to the entrance, her heart did a little flip. "Thanks again," she told Riley. "I couldn't have asked for a better instructor."

"Course," Riley replied with warm amber eyes. "If you need anything, I got your back. And when the time comes, I might take you up on that offer for babysitting." She placed a tender hand over her stomach.

Ivory's insides began to tingle. Who would she be to that baby? A babysitter? A friend?

Family?

Would she and Adrian ever have kids of their own? Gosh, it

was way too early for those kinds of thoughts. But the idea did sound nice.

Riley had given her something today she didn't know she needed: a second family and a friend. Someone who would stick around even when they had no college parties to attend or homework to study for. Someone who truly cared.

Waving goodbye, she walked into the building and navigated the halls until she reached Adrian's door. Each time she stood here, it felt unreal. Like something she'd only get to experience in her best dreams. Adrian had given her a key just in case he wasn't back in time, but she rang the bell anyway. Her gaze dropped as she shuffled her feet, trying not to appear overly excited.

The door opened to reveal a pair of black socks and the worn hem of Adrian's jeans. But before she could look further, Adrian captured her in an embrace. Strong arms held her right where she wanted to be, and she let out a happy sigh.

"Welcome back, my sweet witch," he whispered into her hair.

She smiled and turned to take in his handsome profile, his sharp jaw and beveled cheekbones, the straight line of his nose. Gold flecks gleamed in his eyes, and he looked at her like he'd never seen such an extraordinary sight in his entire life.

"I missed you," she whispered back. Her lips brushed over his skin, and she purposely skated around his lips, teasing him until he cupped the back of her head to claim her mouth with his.

Her knees went weak. Adrian stepped back without breaking the kiss and pulled them both inside, locking the door. "I hope you've had enough adventures today," he breathed as he kissed down her neck, hands exploring under her shirt and squeezing the bend of her waist. "Because for the rest of the weekend, you're not allowed to leave."

She laughed, more than willing to comply. "Oh, but I'm a dangerous woman now, you know."

"I'm aware." His hand found hers, then brought it to his nose and inhaled. "I can smell gunpowder on your fingers."

"I washed them for like five minutes." She tried to pull away and check for herself, but he tightened his grip and kissed the back of each knuckle.

"It's sexy as hell," he murmured, holding her hand to his lips. As he spoke, he pressed her into the door, and she moaned. The feel of his arousal both deepened her need and offered the promise of relief.

"Don't forget I can be a dangerous man too, sweetheart," he warned.

That was exactly what she'd been counting on.

"Show me, sir."

FIFTY-SEVEN

Ivory

FRESH FROM A QUICK SHOWER, IVORY SWUNG HER LEGS AND wiggled atop the stool, waiting as directed. Adrian hadn't told her what he planned. Only that he was taking charge, and she held no reservations.

Her heart settled into a steady rhythm. She'd normally feel small like this, left naked and alone, but a peaceful ease stilled her wandering thoughts. Adrian deserved her patience as well as her time.

Here, he could take whatever he asked for. In this space, his will was final, allowing all her worries to melt away. Spring break and the Dragons faded from her mind as goosebumps rippled over her arms. Whips of air chased shivers up her thighs, and she flexed her toes. Exposed, her nipples puckered into tight, rosy points. Her eyes turned to the bedroom door.

The apartment was quiet. Too quiet. Endorphins thrummed through her veins as their last weekend replayed in her mind. Now that she'd sent him her list of limits, both what she redlined and what she wanted, he knew her darkest desires.

She had nothing left to hide.

Despite being cut off from each other while he prepared,

she could sense his longing as clearly as her own. How his body and mind yearned for her as much as she did for him. How she could please him simply by existing and how he protected her merely by keeping her heart.

The doorknob turned, and her black knight pinned her with a dark look that sent a jolt straight to her clit. His lips curled in a knowing smirk. "Trying to figure out what I have planned for you?" He tsked and closed the door before she could catch a glimpse of anything beyond. "That won't do."

She flushed as his eyes roamed over her body, assessing with cool authority. With unquestioning ownership.

Braving a look of her own, she took in the cascade of his sleek, auburn hair, falling over broad shoulders and the exposed, hard planes of his pecs. He'd left his jeans on, outlining a growing bulge between his legs. No one else would notice the extra holes carved in his belt, but to her, they stood out like two deep puncture wounds. Like bite marks left by a fanged beast.

The full weight of his attention bore down as he stalked forward with the grace and prowess of a wild panther. She felt small. Powerless.

Adrian stepped between her thighs and eased them apart, calloused palms deliberate in their steady command. Her glistening pussy was on full display, tits poked out like a lewd offering, but his focus lifted to her face.

"You are a masterpiece," he breathed.

The praise coiled low in her belly and heated her from the inside out. Unable to speak, she inhaled his scent—spicy and warm, intimately arousing.

His lips twitched up in a smile that was half in awe and half condescending. He rubbed circles into the inside of her thighs as he continued, "Mine to bend and break. Mine to please and cherish."

His voice held a rough, possessive edge, and she bit back a grin.

Light and shadow glittered in the gold of his eyes as he reached up and brushed a strand of hair behind her ear. The slight graze of his fingertips made her heart race, and her eyelids fluttered.

"Stand up and turn around, sweetheart," he murmured. "Let me braid your hair. We wouldn't want it to get in the way."

Wordlessly, she obeyed and slid off the stool. His calculated gentleness both soothed and sowed seeds of apprehension. The calm before the storm.

After all, they both knew what she'd asked for.

Back turned, Adrian gathered her hair and expertly wove it into a snug braid. Electricity ran up and down her spine in delicious currents. His fingers feathered across her neck as he worked, ghosting caresses here and there. Her ass brushed against the button of his pants, but she resisted the urge to push back. A punishment wouldn't be nearly as exciting as whatever he already planned.

Her eyes drifted closed, and she honed in on his steady breaths, on the heat radiating from his body, and the assurance of being in his presence. As long as she remembered this feeling, she could find peace anywhere. Have the courage to face any trial.

"Feel good?" He gave her hair a light tug.

She smiled. "Yes, sir."

"One last thing." He stepped away, and the bedroom door opened again. When his footsteps returned, something smooth slipped over her eyes. He tied it tight behind her head, and it held her eyelids shut. Her other senses tingled with awareness as her sight vanished.

The ribbon.

"Today, I'll let you earn the last two inches." His words came out crisp, giving away nothing as to what that might entail.

These were the last, and two at a time—it wouldn't be easy. But she was determined to earn each one. "Do you trust me?"

"I trust you with my life, sir," she purred. In every sense.

A pleased hum resonated from the back of his throat as another ripple of arousal flooded her thighs.

"Then it's your life I will play with." Her breath caught as something cold and pointed ran over her shoulder blade. It traveled down her spine and wound over her hip, leaving behind a faint sting. A blade?

She groaned. When she'd put his knife on her list, she hadn't been sure how Adrian would take it, but clearly, he had no objections.

"I won't be holding back, sweetheart," he murmured. "I intend to carve out your soul and claim it for myself."

Her next inhale came out shallow and uneven. She'd wanted pain with pleasure. Poison with the sweet. Icy bitterness mixed with the hot demand of dominance. But knowing it would come didn't dull its effect. "It's yours," she whispered. "I'm yours, sir."

"You are," he promised in a dark, silken hum. His fingers wrapped around her shoulder and guided her to face him, though she couldn't appreciate the sight with the ribbon tied over her eyes. "I'm going to show you exactly what that means."

The knife swirled over her stomach. Her muscles retracted at its sharp touch, blood pulling to the surface. Then it was gone.

Soft, wet lips closed around her nipple. She groaned and arched into the touch. Pleasure consumed her fear of the blade. He kissed over to her other breast, licking and sucking the hard bud before skating up to her jaw. Her body melted, coalescing without hesitation.

Hot puffs of breath warmed her skin as he tasted her for his pleasure. Teasing as she'd done earlier. His lips were slow to meet hers, instead lingering where he saw fit and savoring the spots he found particularly sweet—the hinge of her jaw, the blunt tip of her chin, the pout of her bottom lip.

Finally, his tongue flickered into her mouth, and the world spun sideways. She reached up to grab onto something, anything to keep her from tumbling over. What she found was his waist, the firm furrows of his abdomen, and the soft cotton of his shirt. Her fingers moved on their own accord, dipping under his clothes to admire his tight skin and the muscled chest that hardened under her fingertips.

His mouth grew greedier. Ravenous. Gripping her face, his fingers pushed into the hollow of her cheeks and forced her mouth open wide. He held her still as he sought out every crevice and secret as if to prove each belonged to him.

She raked her nails through the tufts of coarse hair on his chest and pressed her palm to his heart. Passion sparked in the small gap separating their bodies, filling her with hunger. Fueling her fire until it roared.

"Enough," he rasped, breaking their contact with a shudder. He circled her wrists and pulled them out of his shirt, placing them at her side.

She panted to catch her breath, then perked up at the clink of metal and a quick slide of leather. His belt had been freed.

Its cool length snaked around her neck, and Adrian pulled it taut until the cold buckle nestled against her pulse.

"Come," he ordered with a tug.

Stepping forward, she followed his voice and the patient pull of the leash. They'd been no more than a handful of steps from the bedroom, but he led her to the left instead, twisting and turning until she lost track of where they might be. Had the apartment always been this big and spacious? Her steps became wary, oriented only by his movements and the magnetism of their connection.

A door closed behind her, and she startled with a jump. How had they ended up in his room?

Adrian dropped the end of the belt and let the end fall on her chest. "Take a step back to reach the door," he instructed. "Lean against it."

Anticipation diluted her jumbled reality. She shuffled, then felt straps dangling between her skin and the hardwood door. The air began to buzz, swirling around her as she focused all her energy on her black knight. Her world reduced to him alone, body filled only by the sensations he granted.

"I bought us something new for today," he continued. "Could hardly wait to get you all tied up." He picked up her wrists and slipped them into a strap one at a time, tightening the loop until her hands could turn but wouldn't easily fall out. Her fingers curled around the thick woven fabric and found it secured to the door above her head.

"I'm going to pick you up and secure your legs," he warned. His hands slipped under her thighs, biceps bunching as he lifted and set her into a padded strap. Once he helped her get balanced, he fit a bigger loop under her leg above the knee and ensured it was snug.

The strap pulled her thigh over to the bedroom door, and after he repeated the process on the other side, she found herself spread wide, hanging from strings like a puppet. The belt still hung loose around her neck, and it all effectively gave him control over every part of her, able to move or restrain her limbs at a whim.

He hummed, voice deliciously low. An appreciative growl. "You're so pretty like this." His hand smoothed between her pert breasts, moving down her stomach and settling over her womb. "All pink and wet for me."

She didn't need to see it for herself, her pulse echoing between her legs.

He spread her wide with his fingers, and she held her breath. The swell of her clit must be visible, her need more than pathetic—a display of desperation for her Sir, a surrender to his mercy—yet she still wanted to beg for his touch.

The knife trailed up her inner thigh. All the air left her lungs, abdomen tensing at its cold, cruel edge. It traced an unpredictable pattern to her hip, then snaked down and stopped just short of her pubic hair.

A short tap came down on her clit. Shock tore through her like a bullet of acetic relief, but the backside of the blade vanished as quickly as it came.

She groaned and let her head fall against the door. The belt tugged at her throat. Her desire bent in two, instinct demanding she hide and protect herself from the threat while the rest of her thrummed with arousal. Pleasure from being at the receiving end of a weapon, of a tool used to inflict pain and suffering.

"That's my good girl," Adrian praised. "Doesn't it feel good to be my little doll? A plaything for my personal use?"

The knife tapped her left nipple, achingly hard and erect.

"Yes," she whispered as molten heat spread through her veins. "Thank you, sir."

A tap to her right nipple.

Her hips slanted forward as much as the restraints would allow, succumbing to the sensation and her growing desire. "Please, sir," she whimpered.

"Aw, already begging so pretty for me." The blade lay flat against her clit, its throbbing an unbearable rhythm that drowned out every other thought. He held her spread open as her body warmed the metal, then he tipped the sharp edge away and slid the knife over her bundle of nerves. "Say my name when you come."

The knife lifted, then tapped her again and again, relentless as she squirmed and panted. His attacks were direct and steady, unyielding and swift.

"Adrian, sir. Please—" Her tongue twisted around his name

as the orgasm rippled down to her bones. A chorus of bright, shimmering fireworks lit up her cells and flared brilliant light throughout her core. She slumped, grateful for the straps to keep her in place.

The knife vanished, and her knight leaned in to bite her lip. His bulge pressed against her sensitive flesh, and he licked along the inside of her mouth as if he could taste his name tangled up her pleasure. Then he replaced his mouth with metal—warm and slick, coated in her cum.

"Open." He pressed the flat of the blade to her mouth. She parted her lips, high on dopamine and serotonin. "Good girl. Now lick. Show me your tongue."

She traced the blunt end of the knife, tasting herself and the metallic tang of the blade. The saccharine flavor of sin. Adrian's thumb covered the sharp edge, and she indulged in tasting him, too, flicking the rough skin of his finger as she hummed in satisfaction.

"Greedy girl," he scolded without pulling away, steel cock twitching inside his jeans. "Nibbling on my hand with that sweet mouth. If you needed more, you should've asked." He pulled away and slipped a thick finger in her pussy, pushing into the slick, swollen channel and curing against the spot that made her see stars. He groaned as she squirmed. "Fuck. It's like you're trying to swallow me up."

She would if he wanted.

His finger continued to rock inside, coaxing her out of bliss and back into the realm of want and deprivation.

"Damn, this cunt needs to be stretched, doesn't it?" he breathed. "Needs to be molded just how I like." Her pussy gave a flutter of acquiescence. "Yeah, that's what I thought. But I have to save my cock for later, so we're going to use something else to fill you up."

FIFTY-EIGHT

Ivory

THE HAND AT HER MOUTH FELL AWAY ALONG WITH THE KNIFE, then something else nestled between her thighs. It pressed against his finger at her opening, too big to slip in easily but hard and round enough that she knew it would fit. The tip wasn't shaped like a dildo, and her mind reeled as she tried to figure out what it was.

"Do you want to be fucked with my gun, sweetheart?"

A moan left her lips, utterly depraved even to her ears. Those words, combined with the grit in Adrian's voice—the low, commanding tone he could use to get whatever he wanted —nearly sent her over the edge for a second time.

He chuckled. "I'll take that as a yes. But I want to hear you say it. Ask nicely."

"Please fuck me," she whimpered, half delirious.

"Mm, very tempting." A heavy sigh left his lips as he brushed his mouth over hers. "How could I ever resist you? Did you think I'd forget how you said those words?" He let them share a delicate kiss, soft and tender and sensual. "You won me over from day one, from the moment you wanted to be mine."

Amid her scattered thoughts, she searched for a reply, but

with a tongue heavy from his taste and lips tingling in the aftermath of their kiss, no words could match the glow deep in her chest. Fortunately, Adrian didn't seem to need one. His finger slid out and pulled her attention back to the gun. Though the ribbon still wrapped tight around her eyes, she could tell he was using her juices as lube, spreading her arousal up the barrel in preparation to penetrate.

When it pressed against her again, it wedged in the slightest amount, stretching her just like he said it would. The hardness of the steel made it difficult to adjust, the thickness of the barrel more than what she was used to. A nonsensical plea left her lips, *yes* and *more* and *thank you* all jumbled into one.

"That's it." He slid the gun back and forth, warming her up with gentle strokes over her clit, down to her puckered hole to elicit a gasp, and then sunk it inside again. She squirmed with needy impatience, pressure building up within like a corked bottle.

"So perfect," he mused. "I love making you feel good, rubbing my gun against that hard clit and watching you try to fuck yourself on it. Earning my cock like you want it more than anything else in the whole world." He tilted to get a better angle and pushed it in gradually, slow enough for her to accommodate the intrusion. The handle brushed her thighs as the barrel seated as deep as it could go. "You make me so proud."

Her heart fractured at his admiration. With one long stroke, he pumped the gun in and out. She clenched down, accepting its fullness and trembling with an ache so deep it split her psyche. Perhaps this wasn't the gun's intended use, but it proved just as deadly.

The trembles grew as he picked up the pace. They seized her legs and belly and shoulders, blood rushing in her ears, friction winding through in her core. Her body expanded and contracted as he forced her to take it, to crave it, and she was so close, almost there—

"Don't come." The knife pressed to her neck, right above the leather belt. Adrian's voice sounded as strained as she felt, harsh and rough. "Hold it."

His thrusts didn't stop or slow, and she had to force herself to suck in a deep breath. The blade stung against her neck while the gun punished her pussy. She was dripping, whining, caught in the snare of forbidden release. But she didn't come.

"Good girl. Well done." He pulled out the gun but left the knife, and she breathed a sigh of relief. "I think you're ready. You've earned another inch, and now there's only one left."

A cap clicked. Cold lube spread over her already-soaked ass. Then his finger dipped into her virgin hole, and she shivered. Forced into stillness by the knife at her throat, the tightness inside squeezed, the flames of his touch licking every hidden angle. Her jaw hung open as another finger pressed inside, the two of them twisting and stretching and filling.

Only fingers, yet it was so much, so big and demanding. Embarrassingly good.

The knife left her neck, then Adrian pulled on the belt. It constricted around her throat and drew a long whimper from her lips.

"So generous," he praised, "letting me take both of your holes. So filthy." With the rushed pull of a zipper, his dick plunged into her pussy. She gasped, impaled and quivering and defenseless. Filled in both places, it was almost impossible to move, to even breathe. He was everywhere, plugging her ass and her cunt, with his hand at her throat.

The leather jacket brushed against her breasts as he leaned in and whispered against her cheek, "Your asshole is the prettiest thing I've ever seen. Ready to be fucked. Have I earned it, sweetheart? Will you let me give you the last inch?"

She moaned again, trying to nod through the belt and the pleasure. "Yes. Yes, sir."

He hissed as he drew himself out and left her empty, hovering for a moment as if it took all his strength not to finish then and there. "Feel what you do to me," he rasped, teasing her pleated hole with his fat tip. "Feel how much my body wants to please you."

How *much* was accurate. There was so much, too much. Even coated in her nectar and lube, his dick had to shove against her to try and fit. It had to punish as it pleased, to take more than she thought she was able to give.

A chorus of helpless moans spilled from her lips. Then he slipped in. The flare of his hood notched inside, and her muscles held him in place.

He kept the belt taut and stroked her jaw, feeding himself into her ass. "There we go," he murmured, voice strained and breathless. "Just a little more. You're doing so well, Iv. My perfect little witch. You feel amazing, magical. *Shit*—" His hips flexed, and she felt him bottom out.

"All eight inches," he breathed. "Everything you've earned, sweetheart. Does that make you happy?"

"Yes, sir," she hummed. The words sounded far away like they were floating above her. "I'm so happy and full. I want you to fuck me. Please."

"As you wish." Then he began to move for real.

Each drag of his cock felt a million times more electric, the sensation hooking so deep it felt like he could reach all the way to her heart. She relaxed around him as the pressure from earlier climbed higher. Her hands clung to the straps, body strung together only by the thread of desire between them.

"Mm," he groaned. "Can you take more, sweetheart?"

More? She bit her lip. "If you want me to, sir."

He cursed and held himself still as he reached to the side. "That's right, you're going to take whatever I give you. You're going to come with my gun in your pussy and my cock in your ass." As he spoke, the words became her destiny, unavoidable and prophetic.

The gun's barrel slipped between her folds. He tried to hold her open and make it easier to take, but even with the promise of pleasure, it wasn't easy. If the stretch had been obvious before, now it bordered on unbearable. Adrian worked the gun in gently, holding her and whispering praises all the while. How incredible she felt, how tight and hot, and how good she'd feel being stuffed full.

Keeping himself buried to the root, he eased the gun in and out until she moaned and ground herself against it. Then he started to move, and she lost all sanity.

Searing sparks of pleasure tore through her veins. They sizzled in her abdomen and sunk down to her toes. The only things left were pleasure and pain, a harmony of the two that wasn't one or the other but a fusion, a transformation that surged through every cell and imprinted his name on each one. Wound his being with hers.

Just like he'd promised, he'd carved his way into her soul and filled it to the point of bursting. He destroyed her, then pieced her together with his mark. With his claim. His permanence.

His thrusts grew steadier, sure and potent as his thighs kissed hers and drove her into the door. Their pants echoed off the walls. He released the belt to cup her face, and it was the sweet tenderness of his touch that broke the thin surface of her reserves.

Everything imploded at once, fierce and shattering. The climax poured out of her in endless wet waves, one crashing down after the other in a formidable storm.

"So fucking beautiful." The gun clattered to the floor. Then his lips dominated hers as he shoved in one last time and pumped her full of his semen. He kissed her as he came, his hair tickling her skin and heat blossoming low in her belly.

"I love you," she whispered, soothing him with her lips as he shuttered and stroked her face.

"I love you, too, Ivory." Together, they descended from the high, kissing and gasping and murmuring disjointed words that made her heart remember how to beat. At last, he took the belt from her neck and slipped her hands out of the straps. "How do you feel?"

"Amazing," she mumbled. "Exhausted."

The ribbon fell from her eyes, and she blinked as the room came into focus. Her black knight stood there as handsome as ever, rubbing her skin and making sure the marks would fade, letting her senses return. She looked down, and it took a moment for her to register what she saw. First, a towel utterly *soaked*. Second, a gun she didn't recognize, made of brightly colored plastic.

"Wait," she whispered. "What's all that?"

He smiled, then bent to pick up the gun. "It was quite the sight. A world wonder, actually." He let her hold the foreign gun—a plastic toy. "All thanks to my new squirt gun. Accurately named in this case."

"I didn't," she breathed, eyes wide.

"You did," he confirmed. "And I'll make you do it again the next chance I get."

If she wasn't so worn out, she'd have more energy to feel some type of way about that. But as it was, she could only jump to the next thought. "If this was a toy, was the knife fake, too?"

"This?" He held up a metal ruler. Holding her arm, he dragged the edge along her skin. The point of the corner bit into her the same way as the perceived blade. "I wouldn't risk you getting cut. But I will let you believe it in the moment."

She managed a weak laugh and shook her head. "You're more dangerous than I thought."

He hummed absently, though his eyes showed more than a healthy streak of pride. "Can you stand?"

Doubtful. She gripped his shoulders as he undid the rest of the straps, then tested her shaky legs. "I think I can. But I'd prefer if you held me."

Without complaint, he swooped her into his arms. "I'd prefer if I held you, too." Grabbing the blanket off his bed, he bent to kiss her forehead. "I have a movie set up in the living room."

"That sounds perfect," she murmured.

FIFTY-NINE

Adrian

THE FOLLOWING WEEK PASSED IN A BLUR. SHIFTS AT THE SALON transitioned to classwork and late-night video calls with his sweet witch, accompanied by an ache when he couldn't touch her the way he craved. A lurking, resolute grit edged him closer and closer to the fated events of spring break, and when Friday finally came, so did Ivory—several times—as he stripped her bare and fused their agitated spirits. Bodies and hearts entwined, peace returned for a hallowed night.

The next morning, they drove off campus with the midday sun beating on their backs. Normally, a break from school meant more work hours and helping Raptor with a side project, but not this time. Rather than winding through back roads, he traversed a congested highway, rumbling alongside cars and minivans before breaking for speed bumps in a residential village.

Cookie-cutter houses presented a manicured image of modern stone siding and green lawns, complete with black mailboxes dotted along sidewalks colored by children's chalk drawings. Anyone who passed by could tell he didn't belong here, but that wasn't important. Seeing Ivory's world meant as much to him as keeping her safe from his.

She took off her helmet and stretched, no doubt feeling the effects of their trip.

"You all right?" he asked as he shut off the bike and shook out his hair. After such a long ride, he expected her to be wary, but Ivory looked like she'd rather hop back on than go inside.

"Yeah, I'll survive." Her sweet smile came back as she focused on him, the dappled shade from a nearby tree dancing across her face. She let out a nervous laugh. "I told my mom I'd be bringing my boyfriend, but I don't think she expects a biker with pink hair."

"To be fair, I don't think anyone expects a biker with pink hair." He took her helmet and secured it with his to the side of the bike. "Besides, I'd rather have to prove myself than be accepted for appearance or credentials. Part of a knight's duty is to fight for his honor, after all."

Her laugh turned genuine as she leaned into him. "True."

As much as he wanted to tell her everything would work out, he couldn't guarantee that. But he would be clear about his intentions and hope to earn her family's trust.

"Do you always have to be so perfect?" she sighed against his side.

He held her tighter and kissed her forehead, glad to feel some of the apprehension leave her body. "For you, yes."

They locked his bike to the nearest streetlamp, then his hand found hers and he let her guide them up to the front steps. Her parent's house looked no different than the rest, but he studied it with extra attention. This was her home. It held all the precious memories that had made her into who she was and all the people she loved most.

He squeezed her hand, then rested his arm around her waist as she rang the doorbell. They waited for a moment, Ivory fidgeting with the straps on her backpack, then movement passed behind the beveled glass window. The door opened to reveal a woman dressed in a chic blouse and loose white pants, brown hair tumbling over her shoulders. She froze as her gaze passed over them.

"Hi, Mom." Ivory forced a smile and turned to introduce him. "This is my boyfriend, Adrian. The one I said I wanted you to meet."

He nodded, keeping his arm firm as he felt her waiver. "Thank you for having me, Mrs. Monroe."

For a measured second, no one spoke, then her mother's smile revived. "Oh yes, it's my pleasure. I almost didn't recognize you with that purple hair, honey. I'm glad you made it safe." She stepped aside. "Come in. I'm just cleaning up a bit."

She reminded him of Ivory in many ways, her petite form and polite speech. But Ivory wasn't nearly as adept at concealing her emotions.

As they entered, he cast a quick look around the open living room. Cream carpet complimented a cocoa leather sofa and family photos hung on each wall. One set in particular caught his eye, all with the same studio background, but a different version of Ivory as she matured from a girl to a young woman.

He'd never felt the absence of photos in his own home, but these he wanted to copy and hang for himself. An entire museum of pictures would hardly scratch the surface of how often he wanted to look at his girl.

"Your father is out running errands," Mrs. Monroe continued, avoiding looking his way as she picked up a jacket from the sofa arm. "He'll be back by dinner. Until then, I'm sure you want some time to show..."

"Adrian," Ivory politely offered.

"Yes. You'll want to show him around. I know you said he could stay in your room, but" —she cast a fleeting glance in his direction, not quite making eye contact— "I prepared the guest room just in case." She handed Ivory the jacket. "Would you bring this to Brey while you're at it? Tell him the next time I have to pick it up, I'm donating it to charity."

Ivory sighed and tucked the jacket under her arm. "Sure, but I don't think that will deter him."

"It should," Mrs. Monroe reproved and picked up a cloth to dust the shelves in the entertainment center. "Or else he'll be going to college without clothes. I doubt he'd survive if he had to live on his own. No wonder he didn't try for a better school."

"I thought you were glad he got into the community college?" Ivory's eyebrows pulled into a knot he reflexively wanted to smooth. Instead, he took off his boots and placed them in line with her sneakers.

"For Brey, yes, it's certainly an accomplishment." Mrs. Monroe paused and turned to acknowledge him for the first time since they walked in. "Ivory's always been our brightest. I still remember when she won first place in the sixth-grade science fair, and now she's all grown up and off to college. She's destined to make a difference in the world."

"I couldn't agree more." He picked his words carefully, choosing to ignore her insinuated comparison and the piercing scrutiny in her eyes. "I've seen Ivory work harder than most people I know, in school and in every other part of her life."

"All right, guys, enough about me." Ivory turned red and tugged him towards the hall. "Let's go meet my brother."

Introductions with Brey went much smoother, and they spent almost twenty minutes talking about online games and ways to turn streaming into a part-time job. Adrian knew a few people who had done it while taking classes, and he gave Brey a list of websites to check out.

Then he noticed the series of manga books that had been his favorite pastime as a kid.

"Hey, Iv. You ever read these?" he asked, picking up the first volume.

"Finally, someone who appreciates greatness," Brey gloated.

Ivory groaned. "Don't get him started. I've heard enough to know there's no way I'm reading all twenty-seven volumes."

"We could watch the animated version," he suggested. "You'd like it."

She scrunched her nose, the side of her face lit with blue LEDs. "You sure?"

"I guarantee it."

"Come on, sis," Brey chimed in with a smug look. "After all these years, you gotta give it a chance."

"Fine," she huffed. "I'll try the first few episodes. Everyone happy now?"

Brey pumped his fist in the air, spinning in his chair. "Victory at last!"

"This isn't fair," Ivory mumbled. "You're already teaming up against me."

"It's for your own good," Adrian chuckled and pulled her under his arm. "When do I get to see your room?" She'd relaxed since their interaction with her mom, but her energy still felt lower than usual, so he wanted to check in. And steal a few kisses while he was at it.

"Oh, right. It's upstairs." She pivoted towards the door and said goodbye to Brey. "Guess we'll see you at dinner. Do me a favor and try not to bug Mom before then, okay?"

"Yeah, yeah," Brey replied while reaching for his headphones. "I'm holding you to this, though. It's finally time *you* owed *me* a movie night."

Ivory rolled her eyes, and as they stepped into the hall, Adrian pinched her side. She jumped out of the doorway with a squeal. "Hey!"

Her pout only reinforced his smile. "You know I'd never

turn down a movie marathon when it means I get to cuddle you all night."

She bit her lip and guided him to the staircase. "You make a tough argument, sir."

He shook his head. The tough part would be making sure that cuddling was all they did.

SIXTY

ALONG THE WAY TO HER BEDROOM, IVORY POINTED OUT THE LESS important doors: office, closet, bathroom, upstairs bathroom, her parents' room. The house felt spacious, with modern decor and minimal furniture. Nothing had been left out of place. Compared to where he'd grown up, it felt like a mansion.

They reached the last door, and Ivory pushed it open to reveal purple walls covered in movie posters. A desk sat in the corner under a small window, while in the back, a row of shelves were lined with cute stuffed animals. Entering her childhood room somehow made him nostalgic, though he had no memories here. Ivory's life was woven into every detail—from the blankets on her bed to the stars on the ceiling—and he wanted to experience every part of it.

Ivory discarded her backpack on the desk next to a pile of books and opened the curtains. Then collapsed on her bed. "Well, we survived so far," she mumbled, grabbing a pillow with a deep sigh.

He closed the door and laid down next to her, tucking her against his side. It'd only been half a day, but he already missed her body curled with his. "We haven't even gotten to the baby photos yet," he teased.

She groaned and hid her face, then propped herself up on her elbows. "Wait. I do have all my old yearbooks. It'll be a little less painful if you see my awkward middle school photos without everyone else around."

"Sounds fun," he agreed. "Although..." He pulled her towards him and nuzzled her neck. "I'm a little busy at the moment." A strangled sound escaped her lips as he found her sweet spot and pressed her into the sheets, which smelled like fabric softener and her shampoo.

"It would be rude to interrupt," she mumbled.

Satisfied only when the last traces of tension left her muscles, and she transformed into a gooey mess of smiles and sweet giggles, he leaned back and tucked a pillow under his head. "All right, I'm ready."

Several yearbooks and a few hours later, they headed downstairs for dinner. A colorful salad sat on the table, and a hot skillet crackled on the stove. Mrs. Monroe bustled about the kitchen with her hair tied in a messy bun.

She reminded him so much of Ivory for a moment that he couldn't suppress a small smile. Maybe one day, they'd have a home like this. Minus the part about their kids dating. His daughter would have to be at least fifty years old before she got a boyfriend.

"I made fajitas," Mrs. Monroe announced, looking over at Ivory. "Since they're your favorite."

"Aw, thanks," Ivory replied as her eyes lit up. She went to the first row of cupboards and retrieved some glasses, so he followed behind to help.

"When do I get my favorite meal?" Brey grumbled, emerging from his room.

Adrian reached over for a glass, but Ivory swatted away his hand. "You're the guest, silly."

He opened his mouth in protest, but then another door opened, and a deep voice called out from down the hall, "I hear my favorite daughter is back."

Ivory grinned as she turned around. "I'm your only daughter, Dad."

Immediately, Adrian recognized the man's green eyes and oval face—a harder, older version of Ivory. He wore jeans and a loose button-up, average-looking but replicating Ivory's signature kindness as she turned into his outstretched arms.

When they finished, he turned to Adrian. "Nice to meet you. I'm glad Ivory decided to introduce us."

His tone held none of the poorly concealed judgment that Ivory's mother had implied, and Adrian accepted his hearty handshake. "The pleasure is mine."

"All right, food's hot and ready," Mrs. Monroe announced. "Let's eat."

They all took seats around the table, him and Ivory on one side, with her parents on the other and Brey at one end. The food tasted delicious, a high compliment considering he'd grown used to his sister's cooking. Once the conversation turned to him, he could only get a bite in every so often as he answered the usual questions.

"Psychology...do you plan to get your doctorate?" Mrs. Monroe inquired.

He laughed and set down his fajita. "Right now, I'm just trying to get through my bachelor's."

She frowned. "A bachelor's in psychology can only go so far. Ivory's high school sweetheart is going to Harvard, you know."

He froze, biting back the remark that comment deserved.

"Mom," Ivory scolded with a mortified expression. "He's my ex! And I couldn't care less about him being at Harvard."

"I just don't see how you can go from someone like that to someone like this," Mrs. Monroe replied.

Adrian bristled. Her parents had no right to dismiss him or

push their daughter onto someone she didn't want, but he held his tongue. It wasn't the time to interfere just yet. Whatever Mrs. Monroe thought of him needed to come out eventually. Nothing good would happen if it didn't get addressed.

Ivory's fork clattered to her plate. "Someone like what? Someone who I chose to be with instead of someone you pre-approved?"

"Someone who's a distraction," Mrs. Monroe replied, picking at her salad and keeping her tone level as if she'd said nothing wrong. "I didn't send you to school to go party and fall for some wannabe biker who won't be able to support you."

Ivory's jaw dropped. Adrian straightened, preparing to intervene.

"Let it go, Mom," Brey sighed. "No one cares about that stuff but you." He took his plate to the sink and left the table, then retreated into his room.

Stony silence fell over the group as Ivory stared down at her food. Her parents shared a subtle look, and Adrian cleared his throat. "Mrs. Monroe, I'll be the first to admit Ivory deserves the world. Let me make it clear that I wouldn't be here if I wasn't willing to support her in every way." He met her eyes. "Maybe you should do the same."

She met his gaze as he continued, "I also know for a fact she's as smart as you say she is, and Ivory is more than capable of deciding how and with whom to spend her time. She's done nothing but her best. You, of all people, should recognize that."

Ivory's knee bumped his under the table, and when he looked over, a blush had crept over her face. She shouldn't look so surprised. There were a thousand more things he could say, a thousand reasons to prove exactly how amazing she was.

Mrs. Monroe opened her mouth, then closed it as Ivory's father placed a hand on her shoulder and spoke in her place. "I think enough has been said. Why don't we let the topic cool off for now? Ivory isn't a little girl anymore, and we've barely gotten to know Adrian. Give it some time." He said something about taking care of the dishes, and Mrs. Monroe excused herself to check on the laundry.

"I'm sorry," Ivory mumbled after they were alone, deflated.

He reached over and grabbed her hand, hating how dejected she looked as he rubbed slow circles on her skin with the pad of his thumb. "Better sooner than later."

"She'll come around." Mr. Monroe sighed as he returned to the dining room. "Once the stubbornness fades, she's not all that bad." He sat back down and grabbed a second serving. "And I'll talk to her."

"It's fine, Dad." Ivory picked up her food and slowly finished eating.

"For the record, I never did like that fella you dated in high school," Mr. Monroe added.

"Really?" Ivory asked, looking up.

"Could tell he wasn't all there. Didn't take you seriously enough. Adrian, however"—Mr. Monroe nodded towards him — "stood up instead of caving. That's not easy to do around your mother. And you seem to be a lot more comfortable around him. Already better in my book."

"I appreciate that," Adrian replied, returning the nod and looking at Ivory, who had begun to look more relieved. The knot in his stomach started to uncoil. "I meant every word—I'm here for Ivory in any way she needs."

Her blush returned, and he reached over to squeeze her thigh.

"Oh, I'm not giving her over just yet." Mr. Monroe crossed his arms, leaning back. "If you plan to steal her away, we need to negotiate my cookie deliveries, or it ain't gonna work." One side of his lips quirked up to reveal a hidden smile.

"So now my baking is all that matters?" Ivory scoffed, the frown on her face fighting to stay in place.

"Cookie deliveries..." Adrian mused. "How many batches for you to walk her down the aisle to me?"

Ivory's blush turned bright red. "Um...that's..."

Mr. Monroe laughed. "We'll have to work out the details on that one."

SIXTY-ONE

Ivory

"Just one mor—" A yawn took over her last syllable, muffled by the pillow on Adrian's lap. Credits and character drawings played over the screen as the ending song filled the living room.

Adrian tucked the blanket around her shoulders. "You'd have to keep your eyes open for that."

His body heat radiated through their clothes, and she snuggled further into his embrace. "I can tell what's happening by the sound effects. You just have to tell me who's winning the fight."

"Or, we continue tomorrow." He hooked an arm under her knees and lifted her off the couch before she could protest.

After watching a few episodes on their first night, the rest of spring break turned into an anime marathon. Brey joined them every now and then, and between making baked goods and replenishing their supplies of popcorn and pizza, they'd camped out in the living room almost all day and night. Her mom hadn't voiced any further disapproval, but her interactions were lukewarm at best.

They needed to have a more in-depth conversation at some

point, but for now, Ivory didn't mind giving the issue space as her dad suggested. For the first time, she felt confident in where she stood, even if it meant going against the grain.

Not once had Adrian put her down or made her feel less than good enough, and she'd started to believe in herself the same way. Her well-being came before living up to anyone else's expectations and staying true to what she wanted filled a hole she didn't know she had.

"All right," she relented, leaning into Adrian as he climbed the stairs. "I guess we have one more day to finish the season." His hard chest felt more comfortable than the softest pillow, and cradled in his arms like a princess, she couldn't help but feel like a little girl again.

They had one more day before her black knight was called to duty—before the fight with Jace and Jun—and right now, she could almost pretend their domestic hiatus would last forever. Every minute of it had to be cherished.

Adrian reached her room and gingerly dumped her on the bed, then locked the door and closed the curtains. The plastic stars she'd stuck on the ceiling lit up with a faint glow, and the darkness in the room receded under streaks of pale moonlight seeping through the edge of the windows. It looked like a magic fantasy world and reminded her of something she'd been meaning to bring up when they were alone.

She blinked over at him, no longer as tired without his body next to hers. When he returned to her side, she caught his hand and wove their fingers together, the smooth metal of his rings pressing into her skin. "Were you serious about what you said?" she whispered. "About what you told my dad the other night?"

He sat next to her, a silhouette of shadow and glittering gold eyes. Bringing her hand to his lips, he held it there and watched her quietly, then left a lingering kiss on her ring finger. "I'm more serious than I've ever been. I'll do whatever it takes to pledge my devotion to you. Even if it means giving up everything I have, I'd do it in a heartbeat to take your hand in marriage. To make you my wife."

Time slowed to a standstill. She stared at their entwined fingers, unable to form a coherent sentence. Could this be her reality? Could *he* be her reality—for the rest of her life?

"Have I ever told you what my rings mean?" he asked.

She shook her head.

Extending both hands, he curled down each finger with a ring as he spoke, three on his right and one on his left. "Mum, Dad, Riri, and me." His left thumb rubbed over the empty space on his left ring finger. "I've wanted to get one for you for a while now, but when I thought about it, there's only one kind of ring I'd want from you." His eyes lifted to hers. "And that's a wedding ring."

Her breath caught, chest threatening to burst. Such a permanent thing seemed impossible when they didn't know what tomorrow would bring. But her heart knew what it wanted the moment he said it.

"I'd want that, too." She looked up from his hands, mesmerized with every contour of his face, with the sweep of hair that had fallen out of its bun and the strong column of his neck. With his firm jaw and soft inviting lips, a mixture of benevolence and fortitude that personified the man she'd swear her soul to over and over again. "I want to marry you more than anything."

A dream-like smile broke out on her face because this had to be a dream. It was too good not to be.

She turned to stare up at the ceiling, breathless for no other reason than pure elation. "I can't count how many nights I laid here wishing for the same thing. Wishing for you. For a man who would hold my hand and teach me new things, who would be there to support me when I stumbled and wipe away my tears when I cried. A man who would be my best friend and my family and—"

She cut herself off as heat flared in her cheeks.

Adrian leaned over, becoming a part of her handcrafted night sky. "A man who would be what?"

"That part's embarrassing." She hid her face, forgetting that it was too dark to see her blush.

A noise left the back of his throat, and he pulled her hands to the side of her head, pinning her wrists with a gentle caress over her veins. "If I get to be your *husband...*" He paused at that word, emphasizing it almost like a threat. Or a promise. "I want to be everything you need. I want to know all of you, especially the parts no one else gets to see. So tell me, sweetheart, what kind of man did you wish for?"

His lips ghosted over her temple, and she sighed. She couldn't actually admit to this. Wanting it now was different from wanting it back then. Those thoughts had been locked away for good reason. Reserved for the one who, she'd hoped, would fulfill them.

"I wanted a man who would teach me about sex," she whispered, every inch of her body aflame with desire. With the obscenities her younger self had dared to conjure in false innocence. "Someone who would show me what making love felt like, but who would also show me what it felt like to be used. To be kissed and to be bitten. To be adored, and at the same time, to be nothing more than an object for their gratification. Someone older and bigger and stronger who would use those things to toy with me. I wanted to be their fantasy as much as they were mine."

Her hands clutched the blanket until her knuckles hurt, holding it to her chest as if it would be a sufficient barrier. But there were no barriers between her and Adrian, exactly as she'd always wanted. He knew all too well how wet she'd gotten under her pajamas, and he'd used it to his advantage. Just like she wanted him to.

An intrigued rumble emanated from his chest as he settled

down beside her. The stretch of his body against hers felt larger than usual, with her thoughts stripped naked and her heart left to race in frenzied anticipation.

"I fantasized, too," he murmured, teeth nipping at her ear. "About having a wife like you. Having a woman of my own to fuck any way I pleased." His hand crept under the waistband of her pants. "To teach her about my body and about hers, which would also be mine."

She shivered as his fingers found her wet center. "What would you teach her?"

He spread her open, finger grazing over her clit. "Whatever she wanted to know."

Instead of giving it the steady pressure that would tip her over the edge, he traced around her folds as if he'd memorized each one. Her hips lifted to meet his hand, legs spreading as he explored deeper. "I want to know you," she whispered. "Tell me about your fantasies."

His other hand brushed through her hair, and she turned into waiting lips. He captured her in a kiss that pulled taut every invisible string inside her, loosening her muscles until she became a boneless pile of want.

"I don't need fantasies anymore," he mumbled against her mouth. "I have you, and you are all of them."

He pulled on the waistline of her pants, and after sliding them off, she sat up on her elbows so he could lift off her shirt. His hand unhooked her bra with ease, tossing it aside. She watched him watching her, dropping his gaze as her underwear came off next. He squeezed the plump of her thighs and then traced back up to pinch her butt, holding her still as she squirmed.

"My sweet Ivory. My future wife."

Sitting back on his knees, he observed her from the shadows. One hand pressed down her stomach while the other worked off his sweatpants. "For every night until I get to say my vows in public, I will brand them onto your skin in private. I'll punish you for every second you consume my thoughts and praise you for every moment you're in my arms until that's the only thing I know how to do."

She bit her lip to keep from moaning. Everyone else was asleep, but she couldn't guarantee she'd be able to control her sound. Her nipples pulled into taut points, legs bent at the knees and spread so Adrian could use her any way he wanted.

Unable to not touch him, she reached for his shirt, and then that, too, landed across the room. Her hands slid down his sides as his arms caged her in.

"I'm going to fill you with my poison," he murmured as he brought his lips back to hers. "Show you things only a man like me can make you feel." He dropped his pants to the mattress and kicked them off the bed, flicking his eyes to hers. "A man who belongs only to you."

Her heart thudded in its cage. His touch was a balm, his words an incantation.

She laid back as he arranged her underneath him. Feet hooked over his shoulders, he eased into her with a hiss. "Damn, you have such a tight pussy, with those pretty little lips that were made to swallow me over and over again. Made to please me for the rest of my life."

"Forever," she breathed. "I want to be yours forever."

He bit into her neck and pressed their hips together, flush until she could feel him at the base of her spine. "There is no till death do us part, sweetheart," he rasped. "You'll always be mine."

His hips pumped in and out, slow and hard enough to feel every ridge, every place where his body echoed his words. "One day, I'm going to put a baby in your belly. I'll breed you every night until you grow nice and full and round for me. We'll have our home and our family and our whole future. Just for us."

She arched her back as her mouth hung open in a silent

moan. He grabbed her hips and pulled her against him, lifting and impaling her cunt with sharp thrusts. She burst beneath him, undulating in wave after wave of rapture, visions of their life flashing through her mind.

He came with a growl, emptying himself and marking her as completely as a man was meant to mark his woman.

"Ours," she whispered, fingers trembling as she brushed hair from his face and pulled him down beside her.

"Ours," he echoed.

SIXTY-TWO

ADRIAN'S PALM WARMED HERS, HIS GRIP SURE AND STEADY. IT WAS the only certainty she had left. Between the rift her mom had created and Adrian's fated clash with the Dragons, everything she loved felt like it teetered in precarious balance. But as they stepped out of her home, she welcomed whatever awaited down the road. After all, she couldn't lose with her black knight at her side.

She took a deep breath as a cool breeze wisped around her neck and caught a few stray hairs that had escaped her braid. Rays from the late afternoon sun painted the pavement in copper hues, its slanted light cutting through new leaves on the trees and glinting off the handlebars of Adrian's bike.

They'd already said goodbye to Brey before he went to school, and her father had wished them a safe trip as he headed to work. She'd been more than embarrassed when he made Adrian promise to take care of her, but after giving them both a parting hug, she appreciated her father's concern. At least one of her parents would welcome Adrian back.

"Are you sure you don't want to stay the weekend?" her mom asked, tugging a shawl around her shoulders to keep off the chill as she stood in the open doorway. "It felt like you were only here for a few days."

Ivory gave her a half-hearted smile. Things had calmed down between them, though not in the way she'd hoped. Her mom learned to stop ignoring Adrian after getting called out and even let him talk without adding snide remarks, but Ivory didn't know if they'd ever come to an understanding.

"Thanks," she replied. "Adrian has work in the morning, so we have to get back to campus." Of course, they had a different reason to leave, but that was close enough to the truth.

"Oh, all right then." Her mom paused and shifted on her feet. "Before you go, I owe you both an apology."

Ivory tensed. Her mother rarely offered that kind of thing, and the ones she did had never been this direct.

To her surprise, her mom turned to face Adrian. "I admit it was wrong to impose my opinions on Ivory. I've given you plenty of reasons to dislike me, and I know if you left, Ivory would have left with you." She paused, and her eyes softened. "But you didn't—I know that wasn't for my sake. It's clear that you care for her, and despite my reservations, perhaps it's time I trust Ivory to make her own choices. Will you forgive my first impressions?"

"Of course," Adrian hummed, more courteous than Ivory anticipated. "I'd appreciate getting a fair chance."

"Thank you." Mrs. Monroe smiled and looked back at Ivory. "Honey, you've always had such bright potential. But your father pointed out that by trying to push you forward, I failed to mention the most important part—you deserve the best. And only you can decide what that means to you. You've made it clear that no one can bring you down, including me." Her expression warmed. "I'm proud, and I love you."

Ivory's heart came to a stuttering halt. Out of everything that could've been said, she least expected to hear that.

Astonishment cut through all of the responses she had prepared.

"Mom," she choked out, then stepped forward and gave her mom one last hug. Even if they'd steadily been growing apart the last few years, there was still hope. "Thanks," she whispered. "I love you, too."

Warmth from their embrace filled her chest, and as she and Adrian walked down the steps and waved goodbye, a glow of satisfaction emanated through her spirit. Maybe everything would work out after all. They just had to get through tonight.

The ride back to campus felt shorter than she remembered. After dropping off her backpack and fixing dinner, Adrian gave her a stern lecture about tonight, including not leaving Riley's side under any circumstances, and they set out for the abandoned factory.

The sun dipped toward the horizon as the wind picked up, weaving a chill into the air. Modern houses thinned into a silent forest with forgotten buildings hiding in the trees. Long shadows crept onto the roads, thin, intangible fingers reaching under their tires. She clung to Adrian, hyperaware of the gun wedged between them and the premise of his impending fight.

This wouldn't be an academic negotiation or a match with a fair referee. This was gang life, and the winner would earn his place with sweat and blood.

Adrian would get hurt.

Though she hated to think about it, she knew it was the only way. Jace never respected anything less, and Jun could only be worse. This was as much to ward them off as it was to protect herself and Adrian from any of the Dragons, to show the Yu's that their sins hadn't been forgotten—much less forgiven.

The closer they got, the more bikes joined them. Engines roared as they entered the lonely ghost town, their riders marked by leather jackets as black as night itself and stitched with an ignited ace of spades held in a skeletal hand.

She spotted the factory before they turned down a hidden sideroad, broken pieces of a neglected industrial giant. Its rusted corpse loomed in the middle of an overgrown clearing, and gravel crunched under their tires as Adrian parked at the end of a long line of Harleys.

The stars shone clearer out here, nested within a dark, moonless sky that looked down on the crumbling structure. Concrete pillars held up a metal frame, and splintered glass windows gave way to vine-covered walls stained with several layers of graffiti.

In the center of the ruins, under a section without a roof, a couple dozen men gathered in groups. They'd pushed away the rubble to make a small arena, and several trash cans bordered the circle, ablaze with fire that illuminated their faces in sharp angles and flickering shadows. A restless energy wound through their ranks. So far, it looked like only half the party had shown up, shaved heads and dragon tattoos nowhere to be seen.

She looked away as Adrian cut the engine and took off his helmet, winding his hair into a tight bun. A primal sense of dread gripped her heart, its urgency almost instinctual. Closing her eyes, she inhaled the scent of pine and burnt wood.

Unlike the day she'd tamed Adrian's bike, tonight, the knot in her stomach was made of real fear. This wasn't a place for her to be, and it wasn't hard to tell she stood out. If anything went wrong, what could she do? Would she only get in the way?

Adrian plucked the helmet from her hands and hung it on the handlebar. Head down, she clenched her fingers into fists to stop them from trembling.

"Hey." He covered her hand with one of his and cupped her jaw. "Look at me."

The steadiness in his voice calmed her nerves the same way it always did. She exhaled and raised her gaze to a set of familiar gold eyes.

"As long as you're with me, I can't lose," he murmured.

A smile cracked through her wall of worry. "I know."

He leaned in and pressed a kiss to her forehead, then trailed his lips down her nose and sealed his mouth over hers. "Tonight, we earn our freedom," he whispered.

She nodded, entangling their fingers and squeezing his hand.

He helped her off the bike and then led her to where Raptor stood, one arm slung over Riley's shoulders while the other rested inside the pocket of Riley's hoodie, discreetly over her stomach. The pair looked like nothing in the world could touch them, not even the lick of scorching flames. But she could tell they were on edge, their eyes in constant surveillance over the gathering crowd.

"All set?" Adrian asked. Embers popped in the metal barrel, and smoke swirled thick in the air.

Riley nodded.

"Couldn't be better." Raptor flashed a grin that showed off his canines. "Feels like a great night to knock the sense into a couple of baby lizards."

Adrian chuckled and cracked his knuckles, then wrapped an arm around Ivory's waist to hold her close. "Hell yeah, it does."

A menacing roar ripped through the sky, and a flash of headlights rounded the corner. Turning, she watched as a pack of bikes poured into the clearing. They rode two abreast, with one in the lead of both rows. Their knuckles flashed with silver and red jewels, revving their engines. Dark tattoos curled along their skulls like black ink on ancient scrolls.

"Red Dragon," she whispered under her breath.

"Yeah," Adrian replied, pulling her close.

Raptor stepped in front of them and Riley came up on her other side. Grateful for the barrier, Ivory lifted her chin and hardened her gaze. She wasn't the same lost soul Jace took advantage of anymore. He could taunt her all he wanted, but they all knew who would lose in the end.

Jace wasn't hard to find, riding at the head of the second line next to a biker who shared a keen, almost familial, resemblance. That could only be his brother, Jun. His expression looked much more frightening, a jagged red scar cut into the side of his forehead and his lips slanted in a permanent scowl. The leader at their head, the man she assumed to be Jace and Jun's father, wore a wrinkled face with black eyes devoid of all emotion.

The group swung their bikes around, kicking up clouds of dust and parking in formation across from Royal Flush. As the air cleared, Cortez walked into the middle of the clearing. The rest of the men—excluding Raptor, who only moved a few feet in front of Riley—formed a semi-circle behind the barrels.

"The Lingxiu," Cortez called. "Yu."

Yu, the Dragon's leader, stepped off his bike and walked over to shake hands with Cortez. "My friend," he spoke as the corner of his mouth twitched. "And dear rival. I see you've come prepared." Yu tipped his chin over Cortez's shoulder.

"As have you." Cortez rubbed his beard and spit on the ground next to their feet. "Fair fight's all we want. But if shit gets messy, we know how to clean it up."

Yu chuckled. "If I wanted a mess, you'd have it by now."

Their gazes leveled, sparking like two steel weapons. Even the wind ceased as a tense stalemate fell across the ruins.

"Let's get this shit over with." Cortez rolled his jaw and curled a finger towards Raptor and Adrian. "Send your boys over so we can check 'em. And if anything happens to my men outside the ring, you'll have more than a mess on your hands."

Ivory sucked in a sharp breath. This was it.

In two steps, Raptor came to Riley's side and pulled her in for a kiss that made Ivory blush. "For good luck," he whispered to his wife.

Ivory turned to her own knight, who removed the knife from his boot and held it out to her, along with his gun. She took them delicately, slipping the knife into her pocket and keeping the gun in her dominant hand.

"Good luck," she whispered and chewed the inside of her cheek.

A cocky grin spread over Adrian's lips. The tension from earlier had vanished. A true black knight stood before her, all poise and muscle, shoulders set and chest as strong as a plate of armor.

"Save your kisses, sweetheart." He put two fingers to his lips, then pressed them to hers as an unspoken vow. "I'll take one for my victory instead."

The warm, soft touch of his fingertips made her shiver, and she smiled as he turned away. But an ache still pounded through her chest as the two men walked off, their strides in sync as they stepped into no man's land.

A handful of members from the Red Dragon came over to pat down Adrian and Raptor while Jace and Jun endured the same treatment from Royal Flush. Once both parties had been cleared, the others stepped back behind the barrels. Cortez and Yu stood off to the side, their aura a dark, menacing authority that commanded everyone's attention.

"No weapons." Cortez raised his voice and looked over both sides. "That goes for everyone."

Yu continued, "The fight is over when one party surrenders or both men from one side are knocked unconscious. If anyone interferes, I'll remove them myself." His hand came to rest on the pistol at his hip.

A chill crawled up her spine. She adjusted her grip on Adrian's gun. Even though she knew how to use it, the metal felt heavy in her hand, cold and smooth as her finger slid over the barrel beside the trigger.

Both leaders turned to the men standing center stage, shooting each other glares of animosity, then they shared a silent nod.

The match had begun.

SIXTY-THREE

HE ROLLED HIS SHOULDERS, CRACKING HIS NECK AS JACE SNEERED at him a few paces away.

"Just can't get enough of me, can you?" Jace smirked as if his taunt actually carried weight. Last time, he'd been *allowed* the upper hand. He was mistaken if he thought that'd ever happen again.

Adrian's smile widened.

No one touched his family and got away with it. Especially not his sweet witch.

His lips twitched at the memory of her holding onto his weapons, ethereal and devastatingly exquisite, his guiding starlight cloaked in darkness. The best sight in the whole fucking world. For her sake, he'd fight the devil himself.

Speaking of which, Jun turned with a sneer. "Fucking pricks. I'll make damn sure to get it through your thick skulls to stay in your lane."

Adrian readied his fists and shifted onto the balls of his feet.

"Hey, got the wrong opponent, fucker." Raptor followed with a lightning-fast swing that hit Jun square in the jaw. The crowd erupted as Jun spat out blood. Raptor's face darkened. "That one's for Riley. The rest are for me."

Then all hell broke loose.

Jace launched forward, aiming for Adrian's head, but he swerved just in time and then lunged back in full force. Blocking the next hit, he fired off a jab to Jace's side and landed an uppercut in quick succession. Their arms and fists collided with brutal force, and they exchanged blow after blow.

Breaking away, he sucked in a deep breath and circled Jace.

By the grunts and groans coming from the left, it seemed Jun had his hands full. Raptor bested almost anyone in bulk, but Adrian knew Jun would be lighter and faster. Both VPs had the honor and pride of their MC on the line, unwilling to face a loss in front of their men. Their match wouldn't end anytime soon.

Jace wouldn't be so lucky.

Panting, Adrian wiped the sweat from his brow. Adrenaline surged through his system, and blood trickled from his knuckles, slick and sticky between his fingers. His ribs burned, stinging from a sharp inhale as he side-stepped a hit aimed at his ribs. Time to end this.

He ducked and spun on his heel, then grabbed Jace's collar and slammed a fist into his nose. A satisfying *crack* preceded a hot rush of blood. With a hiss, Jace jabbed his elbow into Adrian's chest, and they broke apart.

A wave of murmurs echoed throughout the crowd, some cheering while others cursed. It all faded into the background, pointless noise as he prowled around Jace.

Facing each other head-on, Adrian drew a painful breath as Jace licked blood off his lips. The silver rings on Jace's hand flashed in the firelight, mirroring those on his brother's hand. The sight made Adrian's vision burn white hot.

"How's that privilege feeling now?" Adrian taunted. "Still think like you can get away with anything you want?" He sprung forward and landed a hard blow to Jace's stomach, digging into his liver. Jace grunted and contorted his face in pain. "Still think you can get away with murder, and no one would care?"

Doubled over, Jace snarled at him through a row of bloody teeth. "I said no one would care about *you*, asshole."

Adrian unleashed a solid kick that knocked Jace to the ground. Red Dragon shouted while Royal Flush roared. Then he got what he'd been looking for.

That pathetic look in Jace's dull eyes. Not one of a murderer.

Fear.

Adrian locked an arm around Jace's neck and held him from behind. "If you were capable of killing, I'd be dead by now," he rasped. "You didn't have to walk away that night. You could've come after me anytime, but instead, you targeted Ivory. You're the weak one, and you know it."

Jace struggled to reply, fingers clawing at Adrian's arm, but it was no use. His body had its limits, and without oxygen, he slumped into unconsciousness on the cold cement.

"Get up!"

"On your feet, Jace!"

The Dragons' encouragements were of no use. Maybe now they'd see how pathetic Jace was. Adrian tossed his body to the side and stood up, eyes narrowing over toward Jun and Raptor.

Before the match began, he saw something he couldn't forget. Jun carried a Glock-19. The same weapon that fired the bullets found at the crime scene. Bullets that ended his father's life. Was he supposed to chalk it all up as coincidence? One person who had motive, opportunity, *and* the murder weapon?

It was past time he found out the truth, even if he had to beat both brothers to a pulp.

For a split second, Jun caught Adrian's deathly stare. That was all Raptor needed. His fist sailed through the air and connected an uppercut to the side of Jun's head. Bracing himself, Jun retaliated with a swift kick to the inside of Raptor's knee and followed with a harsh jab to his throat.

"Always getting in my fucking way," Jun muttered as Raptor shuffled back with a grunt. He turned to glare at Adrian. "Like father, like son."

"What the fuck did you say about my father?" Adrian growled. The corner of his vision grew dark.

Raptor paused, eyeing them as Jun sneered and took a step closer. A quiet stillness fell over the crowd as the men waited to see what would happen next.

"Do you think winning tonight means it's over?" Jun popped his jaw. "It's over when I fucking say it's over. When my gun puts a bullet through your thick skull."

Adrian's blood ran cold. Those were the words of a killer. "You shot him."

Even he could hear the twist of hatred in his voice, the undercurrent of rage ready to crush everyone in its depths.

Jun's face transformed into wicked triumph, gleeful that he'd hit where it hurt most. "Yeah. That's right. I killed your old man on the same night I took out that asshole's son." He cocked his head toward Cortez. Bloodlust tainted his features, eyes absorbing all traces of light, and his lips curled in a wide, awful grin. Crimson liquid dripped down his face and stained his clothes. "Should've seen the look on his face when he died. Oh, wait—you did, didn't you?"

That fucking *bastard*.

Adrian lunged at the same time Jun reached for a brick that had been pushed into the ring. Shouts signified a wave of chaos on the sidelines, then a gunshot rang through the air.

"Enough," Cortez yelled, silencing the crowd in an instant.

Raptor yanked Adrian back and tackled Jun to the ground, knocking away the brick. Several Dragons rushed over to pull a dazed but conscious Jace to the sidelines.

Yu frowned at his sons, then focused on Jun. "Stand up," he ordered.

Jun threw Raptor off, and they both got to their feet, returning to opposite sides of the arena.

Cortez lowered his gun and cocked his head. "Thought I heard something interesting just now." He took a few measured strides toward Jun. "Care to repeat yourself?"

No one spoke. Jun bristled, but he wasn't enough of a fool to incriminate himself more than once.

Too damn bad that it was too late.

Adrian raised his voice and cut through the silence. "If he doesn't want to talk, I will."

He stepped over to the sidelines, where Riley held up a square box for everyone to see. Next to her, Ivory looked between them with questioning apprehension.

Like hell he'd leave tonight without a guarantee of her safety. The recording device had been a backup, one that would pick up conversation from long distances in order to catch Jace if he made any threats, but now they had something better. Adrenaline buzzed through his veins.

Taking the device from Riley, he showed Cortez. "Got it all right here." Adrian turned his eyes toward Yu. "After all these years."

He clicked the replay button and sped forward. Static from the fire and shuffling bodies muddled the background, but then the sounds of the fight grew quiet, and Jun's words came out unmistakably clear.

"I killed your old man on the same night I took out that asshole's son."

Fury tore across Cortez's face, and without hesitation, he pointed his gun at Jun. Half a second later, every member of Red Dragon drew their weapons, aiming at the other end of the clearing where Royal Flush stared down the barrel of their own guns.

"Stop."

Yu's voice froze the countless trigger-happy fingers; the men willing to die despite being locked in a futile stalemate. "This was outside of my knowledge, but I'll be the one to deal with it." He held up his hand, and with a nod from Cortez, both sides lowered their guns.

Yu turned to Jun. "You are the Laoda. My eldest son. You could have ruled half of my empire, but instead, you tore it down by going around my back to feed your own ego. Then again by leaving the job unfinished. I taught you better than that."

Yu scowled and raised his weapon at Adrian's chest, intending to destroy the evidence and the one who held it.

"Don't!" someone shrieked.

Fuck. No. Not that voice.

Not her.

Adrian turned, oblivious to the gun aimed at his heart or to the fact that he was about to die by the same people who had murdered his father.

Ivory pointed his gun at Yu. Risking her life for his. Shedding her innocence in order to preserve his own tarnished, corrupt existence.

The gentle features he'd grown accustomed to were replaced with hardened determination, arms unwavering and locked in position. She leveled her gaze on her target, but he knew her muscles were tuned into his slightest movement.

His heart tore a frantic cadence into his chest, and every moment they'd ever shared flashed before his eyes. He'd die a thousand deaths before he'd sacrifice hers.

You could tell so much about a person from the way you looked at them.

And now, he looked at her as if she were his very soul. Because that was the truth. The only truth that mattered.

There were no options left. He tossed the recording aside

and stepped between Ivory and Yu, who regarded him with hard eyes.

Adrian set his jaw. He wouldn't back down. Not before, and not now.

"You should know," Yu muttered under his breath. "A father's honor rests on his son. Yours would be proud."

Bang.

SIXTY-FOUR

HE SUCKED IN ONE FINAL BREATH BEFORE THE END. BUT THE PAIN didn't come. Digging his fingers into the fabric over his chest, he found it untorn.

To his left, Jun's body crumpled to the ground. A shocked expression was frozen over his face, but his eyes went dull and lifeless.

A petrified hush spread through the ruins. Even the wildlife seemed to take pause, crickets and whispers of wind through the trees halting to witness the moment. A cloud passed over the stars and plunged them into a darkness lit only by the crackling, ceaseless fires. Greedy flames consumed the oxygen no one else dared to breathe.

"Let us all rest in peace. Blood for blood." Yu lowered his gun—the same one that just killed his son. It must've hurt like hell to rip his own family apart, but he gave no sign of distress, his grim acceptance unflinching. Even so, a heavy sorrow emanated from his rigid stature. "One life to spare us from another war and set the record straight."

As head of Red Dragon, a sacrifice had been the most logical option, but that didn't make it any less astonishing. Yu chose to end the life of one instead of many, to take out his own pawn instead of giving it to the enemy.

After Jun's confession, Cortez wouldn't have let the Dragons leave without starting a war, and both sides would've taken heavy casualties. Adrian knew his death would've faded amongst the rest, but as long as Ivory could make it out alive, he had accepted it. Riley would've taken care of her and helped her grieve.

He couldn't have spared himself only to lose what made his heart beat in the first place. But for some reason, fate had other plans.

Cortez shared a long, tense stare with Yu. Both of their expressions gave nothing away. Without further discussion, Cortez turned his back to Yu and joined the rest of Royal Flush.

The men erupted with cheers. Their howls deafened him, their meaning even harder to grasp.

Was it finally over?

Vengeance had been served—he'd found the man who murdered his father, and now that man was dead. A life for a life. But the gratification he'd been expecting didn't come. Not until he heard that voice again, breaking through the chorus of gruff shouts and hollers.

"Adrian!"

His heart kicked into high gear, remembering only now what it meant to be alive. She was still here. And so was he.

For the first time tonight, he could smell the scent of smoke in the air, taste the tang of blood that coated his tongue. He saw Ivory through the corner of his eye and turned to capture her in his arms. Then he gave her the kiss she'd been promised. The kiss he'd wanted to give her ever since Halloween night.

A kiss that meant he truly belonged to her.

She kissed him with equal fervor, claiming him as entirely as he'd claimed her. Perhaps it was her magic that had kept him safe all along. Her love had sealed him away from the gaping gates of hell. Her lips were the very essence of heaven, his saving grace and an eternal balm that cured his deepest wounds.

There were no more chains to bind him. No more foes to defeat. Only her to hold, to cherish, to keep.

Forever.

"I love you so much," he mumbled into her mouth, seeking out the warmth from each drop of blood flowing through her veins, from the thrum of her heart, and the squeeze of her hands against his chest.

"You did it," she breathed into his neck, then pulled back to look at him with unshed tears in her eyes. He wiped off the few that escaped and traced around her trembling lips.

"You were so brave, Iv," he praised. Her eyes flicked to the side, darting over the spot where Jun had fallen. He pulled her closer. "Are you okay?"

"Yeah," she mumbled, snuggling into his side. "I'm glad he's gone."

Raptor came up and clapped him on the shoulder. "Congrats."

Adrian winced, the effects of the fight finally sinking into his weary bones. A fight that lasted much longer than one night. "Same to you, R."

None of this would have gone to plan without the support of his family, even if they weren't all bound by blood. Raptor had stood with him and helped to keep everyone safe, all without batting an eye.

Extending a hand, Raptor held out the recording device. A few scratches marred the edges, but it was still intact. "Found this for ya. Keep it safe, although you shouldn't need it for now."

Adrian took it with a nod. If Jace became a problem down the road, a few key pieces of that recording would be enough reason for the police to launch an investigation into the Red Dragon.

"Damn, our girl's got balls." Riley strode over with a proud grin. In greeting, she punched his arm, thankfully holding back enough to only appear like it hurt. He grunted as she turned to Ivory. "We might have to make you an honorary club member so you can teach these boys what it takes to be a man."

Ivory laughed, still tucked safe inside his embrace. "That was a one-time thing." She glanced up and no doubt caught the dark warning flash in his eyes.

"If she ever tries that again, I swear I'll lock her up in the highest tower and personally see to it she never escapes." Despite his very real, very serious threat, everyone laughed.

"Looks like you found your own kind of crazy." Raptor smirked at the two of them. "Suits you, little bro."

Adrian leaned in and gave Ivory another kiss, already missing the feel of her lips. "That it does."

They watched the Dragons lift Jun's body into the bed of a truck, Royal Flush standing guard to ensure everyone left without further confrontation. The last of the bikes began to peel away.

"I guess we're all heading back." Riley leaned against Raptor, fatigue slipping into her features.

"Us too," Adrian agreed, eager to leave this place behind. "Stay safe."

"Thank you for everything," Ivory added, to which Raptor and Riley both smiled. They left with a wave, following Royal Flush out of the clearing and into the abyss of the night.

As soon as they disappeared, Ivory smacked him on the chest. He wheezed. "You didn't tell me about the recording device. I could've helped, you know."

He tucked her against him as she pouted, trapping her arms from causing further damage. She could do whatever she wanted with him once they got home, but he still had to be in one piece to drive them there.

"We didn't know if it would work or if there would be anything worth recording in the first place. I only wanted it there as a precaution." He brought his lips to her hair, then kissed down the side of her face. She broke, giving into the emotion, and he licked tears off the pout of her lips. "I didn't need you to be worried about anything else."

At that, a few more tears rolled down her cheeks. "I was so worried." She gasped with a small sob and buried her face in his neck. "You could've—he almost—"

"*Shh.*" He ran his palm down the back of her head and over the ripples of her braid, clutching her as tight as he could. Strain and exhaustion pulled at his muscles as he willed their souls to unite.

Her tears continued to dampen his skin, breaths warm and wispy against his pulse. There had been a day when he vowed never to make her cry, and most of all, to never bring her unwanted pain. He'd protect her with everything he had—that would never change. But out of everything he'd been through, one truth rang out clear: life and pain were synonymous. As long as he held a right to existence, he held a right to the suffering that came with it.

Pain was a privilege. One that made the good things—the important things—all the more precious.

Life wouldn't be complete without sorrow or anger, without pleasure and joy. And his love for Ivory wouldn't be as meaningful if they didn't endure through it all. If his devotion to her didn't outmatch even the stars in their brilliance, shining on for lightyears in vast darkness and traveling to the farthest reaches of the universe.

No, their love had no expiration.

Ivory pulled back and wiped her eyes, smiling radiantly despite her tears. "We should probably go."

"We should," he agreed. "After I kiss you one more time."

Not that one more time would ever be enough. *Enough* wasn't in his vocabulary when it came to her, but she indulged him, and the taste of his blood on her lips brought everything back into sharp focus.

"I need to get you home and clean myself up," he noted, taking her hand. She hummed in agreement and let him lead them to the bike.

"So what happens now?" she asked, turning her eyes to his as she picked up her helmet. "What are you going to do when it's all over?"

"We do whatever we want, sweetheart." He swung a leg over the seat, then pulled her in for a second kiss. "Come on."

EPILOGUE

THEY SAY TIME IS LINEAR, BUT IT NEVER FEELS LIKE A STRAIGHT course. Years can bleed together, one after the other, until an event occurs that becomes the most pivotal moment of your life. A singularity that changes you forever.

And sometimes, that same thing happens at the same time in another person's life, and the two events connect. A bridge connects the gaps in what feels like an otherwise inconsequential existence, and two people fuse into one.

That's what happened between him and Ivory. Maybe it wasn't as scientific—less of a wormhole and more of a miracle —but it felt just as profound.

Over the past few months, their life had become more of an impossible dream-turned-reality. One where laughter came too easy, and his chest burst with feelings he never imagined he'd be capable of. It felt as if Ivory had knit herself into every fiber of his being, like she'd altered his very DNA. Even his apartment had more life in it—not to mention a lot more purple.

Sometimes, all of it made him afraid to blink. But today, that feeling arose with renewed potency.

"Almost ready?" he called from the bedroom, shrugging on a freshly dry-cleaned suit jacket. Formal attire wasn't his forte, and he'd avoided formal events since his father's funeral, but he had to admit the tailored black cotton fit perfectly. Without Ivory, he'd be lost.

She'd gone above and beyond to make the most out of tonight, and he was more than proud of all her hard work. Few words could express how he felt about being her date—the one who got to stand at her side and call her his, to show her off and take her home after it was over.

"Um...yes," his sweet witch answered from the bathroom.

He knew that tone. She wasn't almost ready.

He grabbed the black tie off his dresser and slipped it around his neck, then went to check on her. Fumbling with the sleeve, he paused in the bathroom doorway. Dammit, why were these cuffs so hard to button?

Ivory set her make-up brush on the counter and turned with an amused smile. "Need help?"

Her eyes took a long sweep over his form in appreciation of her handiwork, lingering on his chest, where he'd left the top buttons undone, and a few dark hairs curled into sight.

To her credit, her outfit captivated him just as much. Modest, but at the same time, begging to be torn off. A pale pink dress flowed around her like loose petals while her hair fell in ombre hues of brown, pastel pink, and purple—his one contribution to her style—and a small string of pearls adorned her neck.

He extended his arm to offer the uncooperative cuff, and Ivory's face softened into an expression he recognized all too well. "From the look in your eyes, you'd rather I be helping you," he murmured.

A guilty hum left her lips, painted lashes fanning over a rosy pink blush on her cheekbones. He had to call on every ounce of his self-restraint to stop from mauling her then and there.

"If you do that, we'll never get to the wedding on time," she replied after a pause as if it hadn't been the first response that came to mind.

He held no qualms about taking a detour. Caspian and Nia would understand. "We can be fashionably late, as they say."

Ivory rolled her eyes and popped the button in place. She reached for his other sleeve, but he grabbed the back of her neck and brought his lips to her ear. "If I didn't know better, I'd think you're turning into a little brat."

A shiver passed through her and went straight into him. She melted at his words, betraying the lingering fatigue despite all her excitement. Her head tilted to expose more of her neck, and she sighed as she reluctantly stated the obvious. "I'm the coordinator. And the Maid of Honor. I can't be late."

He brushed his lips over her freshly showered skin, basking in the sweet warmth of her natural scent. "Then don't tempt me," he whispered. "I'd more than enjoy smearing all that pretty make-up you put on and turning you into a beautiful mess for me to devour."

She let out a faint groan but forced herself to pull away and fixed his undone cuff. "The make-up will have to come off sometime...you could always help?" Her lips pressed into a presumptuous smile, and she gazed up at him with a scandalous shine in her green eyes.

"What a generous offer," he hummed. It might not be their wedding night—yet—but that didn't mean he couldn't enjoy his bride-to-be as soon as they got back home. Besides, he'd have much more fun if he spent the evening imagining ways to ruin her as soon as it was over.

After she finished with the buttons and knotted his tie, he slid his hand up her arm and gingerly took her wrist. Time froze, as it always did when they took a moment to be quiet and still, and he didn't have to watch her face to know they were looking at the same thing, their thoughts all but synonymous.

Lifting her hand to his lips, he pressed a kiss to the golden engagement band around her finger. One that matched the shiny new ring on his.

Eight months, three weeks, and a handful of days passed since she'd approached him on Halloween night. Almost four months since Jun died. And he'd counted every second that his sweet witch could be in his arms, safe and happy and cherished. He spent years trying to spite fate for taking away his family, and finally, it gave him someone in return.

He sighed and let go of her hand. "I came to help, but I think I ended up being more of a distraction."

Ivory rewarded him with a loving grin. "That's okay. I enjoy you being a distraction." Her tease earned a glare, which only made her giggle. "I really am almost done. Is everything else ready?"

He leaned forward and pressed a kiss to her forehead. "I'll go double-check."

At first, he hadn't understood why Ivory wanted to wait to put on their own wedding. Making babies was one thing, and as much as he wanted to inflate her belly and let their mini-mes run around wild, he knew it would be better for everyone if that happened after graduation. But making her his wife felt too important. Too monumental to set aside.

Tonight gave him a new perspective.

Between helping everyone get to where they needed to be and ensuring everything happened when it needed to happen, he'd barely seen Ivory outside of taking the wedding party photos.

Like hell he'd let her out of his sight at their own wedding.

He didn't care about decorations or food or if anyone else came at all—but Ivory did. She'd want her special day to be flawless, and she deserved no less. Rushing things would only add unnecessary stress, so their big event could take as long as she needed. Until then, he'd celebrate her every day on his own. After all, she'd always be his.

The wedding venue's ballroom glowed with the soft white light of hanging orbs, a romantic ballad playing through the speakers as the two newlyweds spun in slow motion on the dancefloor.

Caspian had stepped up and wore a fashionable tux while Nia donned a simple, elegant white gown. The epitome of a happily ever after. For the first time tonight, they both looked at ease, able to enjoy each other's company without splitting their attention between the other guests.

He'd watched them struggle to grow together, but against the odds, they did it. Maybe their strength is what had inspired him. Maybe helping Caspian had afforded him some good karma. Either way, seeing his friends happy was a priceless gift. Finding his happiness alongside them was a blessing he never anticipated.

They'd gotten a bigger turnout than he expected. He'd seen Avril helping Ivory for most of the evening, and was surprised to hear Serena got an invite, too. Of course, it turned out she couldn't make it. Both Nia and Caspian's families had come, and outside of him and Caspian not-so-politely convincing Nia's stepfather to leave before the bar opened, everyone had been supportive. Ivory clearly enjoyed shining a spotlight on her friends—some things about her would never change, and those lucky enough to get a piece of her heart knew just how fiercely and persistently she loved.

Waiting for Ivory to finish whatever task she'd gone off to now, he rubbed the petal of a flower he didn't know the name of between his thumb and finger, wishing it was Ivory's skin instead. She felt softer. Warmer. Better in every way imaginable. Nia had purposely thrown her bridal bouquet to Ivory, yet he ended up guarding it while she faithfully returned to her duties.

"Hey."

He glanced up as Ivory's voice filtered through the crowd, more subdued than usual as she emerged to stand by his side. Instinctively, he discarded the flower and reached for her hand. "How's it going?"

Her fading smile said more than her words, giving away her exhaustion, happiness, and pride all wrapped in one. "I think I got everything taken care of."

That's exactly what he needed to hear. He offered his thigh and pulled her close. "Sit."

In her state, she didn't need to be told twice. She followed his gentle tug and folded herself into his lap, then deflated against his chest. He banded an arm around her waist while keeping their fingers entwined. "Have you had any cake yet?"

"A little." She stifled a yawn and laid her head on his shoulder.

Of course, Ivory offered to bake for the event, but Nia wisely insisted she was already doing too much. From the looks of it, if Ivory tried to work herself any harder, she'd collapse on the spot.

He reached over to his plate and pinched off a bite-sized piece of the slice he'd been saving. "Want some?"

Her face lit up, and she parted her lips, humming as she licked icing off his fingers. "Mm, it's so good."

He grinned as her enthusiasm returned, and he quietly fed her more, piece by piece, until she came back to life. The slow melody over the speakers shifted into a new song, and he leaned in to whisper against the shell of her ear, "Do you want to dance? Or are you too tired?"

She turned to grace him with a tender kiss, sugary and

sensual. He pulled her against him, making her ass press into his hardening erection. His hand tangled in the hair at the nape of her neck, and she broke into a smile. He licked her lips, craving a taste of her happiness.

"Nothing a foot rub when we get home won't fix," she murmured, then stood and pulled him along with her. Her expression looked as radiant as it was seductive.

But before they reached the dancefloor, he pivoted and led her to the open exit door.

"Wait, where are we going?" She bit her lip, drawing his attention to the shine their kiss had left, her bottom lip swollen and strawberry red.

Instead of answering, he continued to walk them out to the gardens. The music filtered out in subdued tones, the air cool and refreshing as dim light from a row of lamps lit their path. He stopped in front of a small iron bench, then kneeled alongside the rose bushes to slip off her shoes.

"You don't need these." His hands glided along her ankles, rubbing the marks her straps had left on her skin. Why she insisted on wearing heels, he didn't know.

Memories flooded back from their first ride together. How stubborn she'd been and how the need to protect her overrode his every thought. He should've known from the moment he'd been concerned about her *feet* that she'd be his wife. Not that he had a particular thing for feet—he had a thing for every part of her—but it certainly hadn't been an attraction he felt with anyone else.

Ivory wiggled her toes in the grass, giggling as he left delicate kisses around her knees until she shifted to open her thighs. The scent of her arousal bloomed sweeter than any rose, and his cock swelled with need. Before he lost all logic, he stood back up.

"That's much better," she sighed. Her eyes fluttered open, and she gazed at him like he'd just rescued her from a tall, dark tower. But they both knew the truth. If he were a knight, his armor would be black. If he'd saved her, it was only to keep her captive in a much taller, darker tower. All to himself.

"Good," he murmured.

"The moon's so bright," she noted as he walked them out onto the lawn. "It was darker, then. The night we met."

He hummed in affirmation and placed his hands on her hips, the fabric of her dress glossy and smooth under his palm. "Not dark enough to hide your blush, though."

She hid her face in his neck and grinned against his skin. "Yet you still turned me down."

He tucked his fingers under her chin and brought her face back to his. "I wanted to protect you."

"From yourself?" She shook her head and reached her arms around his neck. "Silly boy. Clearly, you're the one who needed protection." Her lips hovered over his in a brazen tease. "Now I get to keep you all to myself."

A possessive sound came from the back of his throat, something that could only be described as a growl, and he sunk his teeth into her lip. Her words ignited a fire in his chest, and her kiss fanned the flames. She molded her body to his, pressing his erection into the dip between her hip and the plush mound of her sex.

He groaned into her mouth and tipped her head back to reclaim what belonged to him. His tongue smoothed over hers, their bodies dancing to much more than the music. He trailed hot bites over her jaw and sucked on the pulse fluttering in her neck.

"What if I'd said yes?" she whispered, breathless. "When you offered to play that game?"

His words all those months ago echoed in his mind. *Then are you looking for a game? To let me play with you until I've had my fill? Because that's what I offer.*

He'd been rude on purpose. To make sure she said no, because if she hadn't...

He pulled away. "That's a dangerous question, sweetheart."

"What?" She gave him a look that said that's exactly what she'd hoped to hear.

He splayed his hand between her shoulder blades and brought his lips to the hinge of her jaw, tickling her skin with barely-there kisses to remind her what *danger* really meant. That he could control her with the slightest touch. That he owned her as effectively with tenderness as he did with unyielding demands. "Your sexy witch costume filled my head with more ideas than you want to know."

She shivered.

He gripped her hair hard enough to elicit a moan from her lips and looked down at her face. She wore the same expression she had that night, like she wanted to see how far he could push her. Like she knew it was forbidden and wanted it anyway.

Damn, there'd be no end to the things he wanted to do to her.

"I couldn't wait to sink my teeth into your pretty plum lips," he said, bringing his hands back down to her waist. "If you said yes, I'd make sure you ended the night screaming my name. But you'd have to work for it. You'd have to convince me to give it to you."

"How would I do that?" Her voice became breathless and wispy, saturated with need.

He ran his nose down along her shoulder to her chest. Her skin felt hot, her heart hammering out a strong, lustful rhythm. "Don't think I didn't notice the way you looked into the woods. Like you were drawn to the darkness. Like you wanted to find something there...or wanted something to find you."

Her breath caught. He coaxed their bodies to start dancing again, moving in casual, slow circles. "If I had it my way, I'd dress you in boots and that same cute cloak. Nothing else. Then your sweet tits would be on display, that pussy ready to take me whenever I wanted."

Fuck, the mental image alone was enough to make pre-cum leak from his cock. He nudged it against her core, and the friction from their clothes nearly squeezed until he burst.

"I'd make you run," he whispered. "Follow you until you forget where you went. Until you questioned if I'd left you alone or if some starving wolf might find you unaware. You'd be so on edge. Your thighs wet, your pussy swollen from waiting and wanting, your nipples cold and needing my mouth."

Her lips parted as leaves rustled in the trees.

"Then I'd take you."

She met his eyes, overflowing with lust and longing, and turned her gaze toward the forest on the edge of the property.

But someone else was already there.

Caspian carried Nia in both arms, her dress hiked up to her hips, and they escaped from their own party behind the first line of trees.

"Oh my," Ivory whispered and turned into him. "I have to pretend I didn't see that."

He chuckled. "Close your eyes, sweetheart. Let me distract you. I'll tell you what happens when good girls want to misbehave."

Don't forget to leave a review, share with a friend, and stick around for more heart—and panty—melting romance!

SERENA'S SUMMER PLANS JUST GOT A LOT MORE COMPLICATED.

Hot summer days, sleepless nights, and a cowboy who refuses to play by the rules.

The moment his new coworker steps onto Hollow Oak Ranch, all Grant sees is trouble. But her glossy exterior isn't the only thing that fades under the country sun. Serena reminds him of a time before the accident, before his dreams were swapped for a shattered heart, and soon their fun and games begin to spiral out of control. They're two broken halves of the same whole and it'll take an act of grace to piece them back together...or love, if they're willing to brave the fall.

ACKNOWLEDGMENTS

This book is a small tribute to those who feel trapped in their personal darkness. You are not alone.

There is too much suffering, betrayal, and heartbreak in this world—not enough healing, accountability, and compassion. The negative effects of abuse or neglect can be impossible to cure. However, that pain does not need to define us. It's our privilege to define ourselves, and I hope we can each embrace the pain and struggles *and* joy inherent in life.

I have no words to express the depth of my gratitude to my husband, for finding purpose in each other and for teaching me what love truly means.

Thank you to all the beta readers, to the authors who gave me some of their time, and to my ARC and street team. Thank you to everyone who reads this and supports my books, whether online or in person. I couldn't keep publishing without you.

Marissa and Lindsey—your talent is spot-on. You're always there to support me when needed and motivate me to get my next project ready to share. Keep being awesome.

Kristen—collaborating on character art is really too fun. Each scene you bring to life inspires me to write it even better than I planned.

Adrian and Ivory—thank you for letting me write your story. I hope you don't mind that I shared it with the world.

And God—you know how much I stumble, but I'll keep trying.

On to the next page,

Siberia

ABOUT THE AUTHOR

Siberia writes sinful romance for the soul, featuring characters who are as unapologetically smutty as they are sentimental. She's a true romantic and can often be found trying new foods, making blanket forts, and taking long walks on the beach with her husband.

Join her email list to keep up with new updates, giveaways, ARC opportunities, and more!

Author website: beacons.ai/siberia
Reader Group: facebook.com/groups/sweetsinners
Instagram: @siberiathewriter